Murder MERRY
most

32 CHRISTMAS CRIME STORIES FROM THE WORLD'S BEST MYSTERY WRITERS

Edited by
Abigail Browning

GRAMERCY BOOKS
New York

This 2002 edition published by Gramercy Books, an imprint of Random House Value Publishing, Inc., 280 Park Avenue, New York, NY 10017, by arrangement with Dell Magazines, 475 Park Avenue South, New York, NY 10016.

Gramercy is a registered trademark and the colophon is a trademark of Random House, Inc.

Printed in the United States of America.

Random House
New York • Toronto • London • Sydney • Auckland
www.randomhouse.com

A catalog record for this title is available from the Library of Congress.

ISBN: 0-517-22119-5

9 8 7 6 5 4 3 2 1

CONTENTS

CONTENTS

CONTENTS

ACKNOWLEDGMENTS

"A Matter of Life and Death" by Georges Simenon, copyright © 1952 by Georges Simenon, reprinted by permission of the Author's Estate; "A Winter's Tale" by Ann Cleeves, copyright © 1994 by Ann Cleeves, reprinted by permission of Murray Pollinger Literary Agency; "As Dark as Christmas Gets" by Lawrence Block, copyright © 1997 by Lawrence Block, used by permission of the author; "Believing in Santa" by Ron Goulart, copyright © 1994 by Ron Goulart, reprinted by permission of the author; "Christmas Cop" by Thomas Adcock, copyright © 1986 by Davis Publications, Inc., reprinted by permission of the author; "Christmas Party" by Martin Werner, copyright © 1991 by Davis Publications, Inc., reprinted by permission of the author; "Dead on Christmas Street" by John D. MacDonald, copyright © Dorothy P. MacDonald Trust, reprinted by permission of Diskant Associates; "Grist for the Mills of Christmas" by James Powell, copyright © 1994 by James Powell, reprinted by permission of the author; "I Saw Mommy Killing Santa Claus" by George Baxt, copyright © 1990 by Davis Publications, Inc., reprinted by permission of the author; "Miss Crindle and Father Christmas" by Malcom Gray, copyright © 1990 by Davis Publications, Inc., reprinted by permission of Curtis Brown, Ltd.; "Murder Under the Mistletoe" by Margery Allingham, copyright © 1962 by Margery Allingham, © renewed, reprinted by permission of P. & M. Youngman Carter, Ltd.; "Mystery for Christmas" by Anthony Boucher, copyright © 1942 by Anthony Boucher, reprinted by permission of Curtis Brown, Ltd.; "On Christmas Day in the Morning" by Margery Allingham, copyright © 1952 by P. & M. Youngman Carter, Ltd., reprinted by permission of the Estate; "Pass the Parcel" by Peter Lovesey, copyright © 1994 by Peter Lovesey, reprinted by permission of Gelfman Schneider Literary Agents; "Rumpole and the Chambers Party" by John Mortimer, copyright © 1988 by Advanpress, Ltd., reprinted by permission of Sterling

INTRODUCTION

The Yuletide season has proven irresistible ground for mystery writers, and *Murder Most Merry* is a collection of the best in Christmas crimes. These 32 stories from *Ellery Queen's Mystery Magazine* and *Alfred Hitchcock's Mystery Magazine* span from hard-boiled police procedurals to cozy mysteries to fantasy adventures. With mysteries embracing sentiments ranging from world-weary cynicism to uplifting joy, this collection provides a holiday feast for mystery fans.

On his "Santa Claus Beat," Rex Stout's Art Hipple pines for a Christmas Eve murder truly befitting the season. In John D. MacDonald's story, a young woman ends up "Dead on Christmas Street," and the cops corner the desperate murderer using unconventional resources. Robert Turner offers a "Christmas Gift" anyone would be pleased to receive, and solving mysteries means more than just finding criminals when we go along with "Inspector Tierce and the Christmas Visits," by Jeffry Scott.

Professional thief Nick Velvet welcomes the holiday spirit when he attempts "The Theft of the Christmas Stocking," by Edward D. Hoch, while Thomas Larry Adcock's "Christmas Cop" stumbles across a gang of criminals who understand that it is better to give than to receive.

In a trio of tales featuring the bespectacled Mr. Albert Campion, Margery Allingham explores the darker side of the human spirit and lifts it into the light. "On Christmas Day in the Morning," an elderly woman embraces the enduring love and promise of Christmas in the face of life's tragedies. When there's "Murder Under the Mistletoe," an old acquaintance of Campion's draws on his expertise to solve an impossible crime. And, "The Case is Altered" on holiday in the country, when Campion explores a series of peculiar events.

From the first perplexing and then intriguing "Supper With Miss Shivers," by Peter Lovesey, to the "Christmas Party" with a twist by Martin Werner, to "The Adventure of the Blue Carbuncle" classic by Sir Arthur Conan Doyle, here are Christmas crimes every mystery reader will love to unwrap, one clue at a time.

Abigail Browning
April 2002

Ann Cleeves

A WINTER'S TALE

In the hills there had been snow for five days, the first real snow of the winter. In town it had turned to rain, bitter and unrelenting, and in Otterbridge it had seemed to be dark all day. As Ramsay drove out of the coastal plain and began the climb up Cheviot the clouds broke and there was a shaft of sunshine which reflected blindingly on the snow. For days he had been depressed by the weather and the gaudy festivities of the season, but as the cloud lifted he felt suddenly more optimistic.

Hunter, sitting hunched beside him, remained gloomy. It was the Saturday before Christmas and he had better things to do. He always left his shopping until the last minute—he enjoyed being part of the crowd in Newcastle. Christmas meant getting pissed in the heaving pubs on the Big Market, sharing drinks with tipsy secretaries who seemed to spend the last week of work in a continuous office party, It meant wandering up Northumberland Street where children queued to peer in at the magic of Fenwick's window and listening to the Sally Army band playing carols at the entrance to Eldon Square. It had nothing to do with all this space and the bloody cold. Like a Roman stationed on Hadrian's Wall, Hunter thought the wilderness was barbaric.

Ramsay said nothing. The road had been cleared of snow but was slippery, and driving took concentration. Hunter was itching to get at the wheel—he had been invited to a party in a club in Blyth and it took him as long as a teenage girl to get ready for a special evening out.

Ramsay turned carefully off the road, across a cattle grid, and onto a track.

"Bloody hell!" Hunter said. "Are we going to get up there?"

"The farmer said it was passable. He's been down with a tractor."

"I'd better get the map," Hunter said miserably. "I suppose we've got a grid reference. I don't fancy getting lost out here."

"I don't think that'll be necessary," Ramsay said. "I've been to the house before."

Hunter did not ask about Ramsay's previous visit to Blackstoneburn. The inspector rarely volunteered information about his social life or friends. And apart from an occasional salacious curiosity about Ramsay's troubled marriage and divorce, Hunter did not care. Nothing about the inspector would have surprised him.

The track no longer climbed but crossed a high and empty moor. The horizon was broken by a dry stone wall and a derelict barn, but otherwise there was no sign of habitation. Hunter felt increasingly uneasy. Six geese flew from a small reservoir to circle overhead and settle back once the car had passed.

"Greylags," Ramsay said. "Wouldn't you say?"

"I don't bloody know." Hunter had not been able to identify them even as geese. And I don't bloody care, he thought.

The sun was low in the sky ahead of them. Soon it would be dark. They must have driven over an imperceptible ridge because suddenly, caught in the orange sunlight, there was a house, grey, small-windowed, a fortress of a place surrounded by byres and outbuildings.

"That's it, is it?" Hunter said, relieved. It hadn't, after all, taken so long. The party wouldn't warm up until the pubs shut. He would make it in time.

"No," Ramsay said. "That's the farm. It's another couple of miles yet."

He was surprised by the pleasure he took in Hunter's discomfort, and a little ashamed. He thought his relationship with his sergeant was improving. Yet it wouldn't do Hunter any harm, he thought, to feel anxious and out of place. On his home ground he was intolerably confident.

The track dipped to a ford. The path through the water was rocky and the burn was frozen at the edges. Ramsay accelerated carefully up the bank and as the back wheels spun he remembered his previous visit to Blackstoneburn. It had been high summer, the moor scorched with drought, the burn dried up almost to a trickle. He had thought he would never come to the house again.

As they climbed away from the ford they saw the Black Stone, surrounded by open moor. It was eight feet high, truly black with the setting sun behind it, throwing a shadow onto the snow.

Hunter stared and whistled under his breath but said nothing. He would not give his boss the satisfaction of asking for information. The information came anyway. Hunter thought Ramsay could have been one of those guides in bobble hats and walking boots who worked at weekends for the National Park.

"It's a part of a circle of prehistoric stones," the inspector said. "Even if there weren't any snow you wouldn't see the others at this distance. The bracken's grown over them." He seemed lost for a moment in memory. "The house was named after the stone, of course. There's been a dwelling on this site since the fourteenth century."

"A bloody daft place to put a house," Hunter muttered. "If you ask me. . . ."

They looked down into a valley onto an L-shaped house built around a flagged yard, surrounded by windblown trees and shrubs.

"According to the farmer," Ramsay said, "the dead woman wasn't one of the owner's family. . . ."

"So what the hell was she doing here?" Hunter demanded. The emptiness made him belligerent. "It's not the sort of place you'd stumble on by chance."

"It's a holiday cottage," Ramsay said. "Of sorts. Owned by a family from Otterbridge called Shaftoe. They don't let it out commercially but friends know that they can stay here. . . . The strange thing is that the farmer said there was no car. . . ."

The track continued up the hill and had, Hunter supposed, some obscure agricultural use. Ramsay turned off it down a potholed drive and stopped in the yard, which because of the way the wind had been blowing was almost clear of snow. A dirty green Land Rover was already parked there, and as they approached a tall, bearded man got out and stood impassively, waiting for them to emerge from the warmth of their car. The sun had disappeared and the air was icy.

"Mr. Helms." The inspector held out his hand. "I'm Ramsay. Northumbria Police."

"Aye," the man said. "Well, I'd not have expected it to be anyone else."

"Can we go in?" Hunter demanded. "It's freezing out here."

Without a word the farmer led them to the front of the house. The wall was half covered with ivy and already the leaves were beginning to be tinged with frost. The front door led directly into a living room. In a grate the remains of a fire smouldered, but there was little warmth. The three men stood awkwardly just inside the room.

"Where is she?" Hunter asked.

"In the kitchen," the farmer said. "Out the back."

Hunter stamped his feet impatiently, expecting Ramsay to lead the way. He knew the house. But Ramsay stood, looking around him.

"Had Mr. Shaftoe asked you to keep an eye on the place?" he asked. "Or did something attract your attention?"

"There was someone here last night," Helms said. "I saw a light from the back."

"Was there a car?"

"Don't know. Didn't notice."

"By man, you're a lot of help," Hunter muttered. Helms pretended not to hear.

"But you might have noticed," Ramsay persisted, "fresh tyre tracks on the drive."

"Look," Helms said. "Shaftoe lets me use one of his barns. I'm up and down the track every day. If someone had driven down using my tracks how would I know?"

"Were you surprised to see a light?" Ramsay asked.

"Not really," Helms said. "They don't have to tell me when they're coming up."

"Could they have made it up the track from the road?"

"Shaftoe could. He's got one of those posh Japanese four-wheel-drive jobs."

"Is it usual for him to come up in the winter?"

"Aye." Helms was faintly contemptuous. "They have a big do on Christmas Eve. I'd thought maybe they'd come up to air the house for that. No one's been in the place for months."

"You didn't hear a vehicle go back down the track last night?"

"No. But I wouldn't have done. The father-in-law's stopping with us and he's deaf as a post. He had the telly so loud you can't hear a thing."

"What time did you see the light?"

Helms shrugged. "Seven o'clock maybe. I didn't go out after that."

"But you didn't expect them to be staying?"

"No. Like I said, I expected them to light a fire, check the calor gas, clean up a bit, and then go back."

"So what caught your attention this morning?"

"The gas light was still on," Helms said.

"In the same room?"

Helms nodded. "The kitchen. It was early, still pretty dark outside, and I thought they must have stayed and were getting their breakfasts. It was only later, when the kids got me to bring them over, that I thought it was strange."

"I don't understand," Ramsay said. "Why did your children want to come?"

"Because they're sharp little buggers. It's just before Christmas. They thought Shaftoe would have a present for them. He usually brings them something, Christmas or not."

"So you drove them down in the Land Rover? What time was that?"

"Just before dinner. Twelvish. They'd been out sledging and Chrissie, my wife, said there was more snow on her kitchen floor than out on the fell. I thought I'd earn a few brownie points by getting them out of her hair." He paused and for the first time he smiled. "I thought I'd get a drink for my trouble. Shaftoe always kept a supply of malt whisky in the place, and he was never mean with it."

"Did you park in the yard?"

"Aye. Like I always do."

"That's when you noticed the light was still on?"

Helms nodded.

"What did you do then?"

"Walked round here to the front."

"Had it been snowing?" Ramsay asked.

"There were a couple of inches in the night but it was clear by dawn."

"What about footprints on the path? You would have noticed if the snow had been disturbed."

"Aye," Helms said. "I might have done if I'd got the chance. But I let the dog and the bairns out of the Land Rover first and they chased round to the front before me."

"But your children might have noticed," Ramsay insisted.

"Aye," Helms said without much hope. "They might."

"Did they go into the house before you?"

"No. They were still on the front lawn throwing snowballs about when I joined them. That's when I saw the door was open and I started to think something was up. I told the kids to wait outside and came in on my own. I stood in here feeling a bit daft and shouted out the back to Shaftoe. When there was no reply I went on through."

"What state was the fire in?" Ramsay asked.

"Not much different from what it's like now. If you bank it up it stays like that for hours."

There was a pause. "Come on then," Ramsay said. "We'd best go through and look at her."

The kitchen was lit by two gas lamps mounted on one wall. The room was small and functional. There was a small window covered on the outside by bacterial-shaped whirls of ice, a stainless-steel sink, and a row of units. The woman, lying with one cheek against the red tiles, took up most of the available floor space. Ramsay, looking down, recognised her immediately.

"Joyce," he said. "Rebecca Joyce." He looked at Helms. "She was a friend of the Shaftoe family. You don't recognise her?"

The farmer shook his head.

Ramsay had met Rebecca Joyce at Blackstoneburn. Diana had invited him to the house when their marriage was in its final throes and he had gone out of desperation, thinking that on her own ground, surrounded by her family and friends, she might be calmer. Diana was related to the Shaftoes by marriage. Her younger sister Isobel had married one of the Shaftoe sons and at that summer house party they were all there: old man Shaftoe, who had made his money out of scrap, Isobel, and her husband Stuart, a grey, thin-lipped man who had brought the family respectability by proposing to the daughter of one of the most established landowners in Northumberland.

Rebecca had been invited as a friend, solely, it seemed, to provide entertainment. She had been at school with Diana and Isobel and had been outrageous, apparently, even then. Looking down at the body on the cold kitchen floor, Ramsay thought that despite the battered skull he still saw a trace of the old spirit.

"I'll be off then. . . ." Helms interrupted his daydream. "If there's nothing else."

"No," Ramsay said. "I'll know where to find you."

"Aye. Well." He sloped off, relieved. They heard the Land Rover drive away up the track and then it was very quiet.

"The murder weapon was a poker," Hunter said. "Hardly original."

"Effective though." It still lay on the kitchen floor, the ornate brass knob covered with blood.

"What now?" Hunter demanded. Time was moving on. It was already six o'clock. In another hour his friends would be gathering in the pubs of Otterbridge preparing for the party.

"Nothing," Ramsay said, "until the pathologist and the scene-of-crime team arrive." He knew that Hunter wanted to be away. He could have sent him off in the car, arranged a lift for himself with the colleagues who would arrive later, earned for a while some gratitude and peace, but a perverseness kept him quiet and they sat in the freezing living room, waiting.

When Ramsay met Rebecca Joyce it had been hot, astoundingly hot for the Northumberland hills, and they had taken their drinks outside onto the lawn. Someone had slung a hammock between two Scotch pines and Diana had lain there moodily, not speaking, refusing to acknowledge his presence. They had argued in the car on the way to Blackstoneburn and he was forced to introduce himself to Tom Shaftoe, a small, squat man with silver sideburns. Priggish Isobel and anonymous Stuart he had met before. The row had been his fault. Diana had not come home the night before, and he had asked quietly, restraining his jealousy, where she had been. She had lashed out in a fury, condemning him for his Methodist morals, his dullness.

"You're just like your mother," she had said. The final insult. "All hypocrisy and thrift."

Then she had fallen stubbornly and guiltily silent and had said nothing more to him all evening.

Was it because of her taunts that he had gone with Rebecca to look at the Black Stone? Rebecca wore a red Lycra tube which left her shoulders bare and scarcely covered her buttocks. She had glossy red lipstick and black curls pinned back with combs. She had been flirting shamelessly with Stuart all evening and then suddenly to Ramsay she said:

"Have you ever seen the stone circle?"

He shook his head, surprised, confused by her sudden interest.

"Come on then," she had said. "I'll show you."

In the freezing room at Blackstoneburn, Hunter looked at his boss and thought he was a mean bastard, a kill-joy. There was no need for them both to be there. He nodded towards the kitchen door, bored by the silence, irritated because Ramsay would not share information about the dead woman.

"What did she do then?" he asked. "For a living."

Ramsay took a long time to reply and Hunter wondered if he was ill, if he was losing his grip completely.

"She would say," the inspector answered at last, "that she lived off her wits."

He had assumed that because she had been to school with Diana and Isobel her family were wealthy, but discovered later that her father had been a hopeless and irresponsible businessman. A wild scheme to develop a Roman theme park on some land close to Hadrian's Wall had led to bankruptcy, and Rebecca had left school early because the fees could not be paid. It was said that the teachers were glad of an excuse to be rid of her.

"By man," said Hunter, "what does that mean?"

"She had a few jobs," Ramsay said. "She managed a small hotel for a while, ran the office of the agricultural supply place in Otterbridge. But she couldn't stick any of them. I suppose it means she lived off men."

"She was a whore?"

"I suppose," Ramsay said, "it was something like that."

"You seem to know a lot about her. Did you know her well, like?"

The insolence was intended. Ramsay ignored it.

"No," he said. "I only met her once."

But I was interested, he thought, interested enough to find out more about her, attracted not so much by the body in the red Lycra dress, but by her kindness. It was the show, the decadent image, which put me off. If I had been braver I would have ignored it.

Her attempt to seduce him on that hot summer night had been a kindness, an offer of comfort. Away from the house she had taken his hand and they had crossed the burn by stepping stones, like children. She had shown him the round black stones hidden by bracken and then put his hand on her round, Lycra-covered breast.

He had hesitated, held back by his Methodist morals and the thought of sad Diana lying in the hammock on the lawn. Rebecca had been kind again, unoffended.

"Don't worry," she said, laughing, kissing him lightly on the cheek. "Not now. If you need me you'll be able to find out where I am."

And she had run away back to the others, leaving him to follow slowly, giving him time to compose himself.

Ramsay was so engrossed in the memory of his encounter with Rebecca Joyce that he did not hear the vehicles outside or the sound of voices. He was jolted back to the present by Hunter shouting: "There they are. About bloody time, too." And by the scene-of-crime team at the door bending to change their shoes, complaining cheerfully about the cold.

"Right then," Hunter said. "We can leave it to the reinforcements." He looked at his watch. Seven o'clock. The timing would be tight but not impossible. "I suppose someone should see the Shaftoes tonight," he said. "They're the most likely suspects. I'd volunteer for the overtime myself but I'm all tied up this evening."

"I'll talk to the Shaftoes," Ramsay said. It was the least he could do.

Outside in the dark it was colder than ever. Ramsay's car would not start immediately and Hunter swore under his breath. At last it pulled away slowly, the heater began to work, and Hunter began to relax.

"I want to call at the farm," Ramsay said. "Just to clear up a few things."

"Bloody hell!" Hunter said, convinced that Ramsay was prolonging the journey just to spite him. "What's the matter now?"

"This is a murder enquiry," Ramsay said sharply. "Not just an interruption to your social life."

"You'll not get anything from that Helms," Hunter said. "What could he know, living up there? It's enough to drive anyone crazy."

Ramsay said nothing. He thought that Helms was unhappy, not mad.

"Rebecca always goes for lonely men," Diana had said cruelly on the drive back from Blackstoneburn that summer. "It's the only way she can justify screwing around."

"What's your justification?" he could have said, but Diana was unhappy too, and there had seemed little point.

They parked in the farm yard. In a shed cattle moved and made gentle noises. A small woman with fine pale hair tied back in an untidy ponytail let them into the kitchen where Helms was sitting in a high-backed chair, his stockinged feet stretched ahead of him. He was not surprised to see them. The room was warm despite the flagstone floor. A clothes horse, held together with binder twine, was propped in front of the range and children's jeans and jerseys steamed gently. The uncurtained window was misted with condensation. Against one wall was a large square table covered by a patterned oilcloth, with a pile of drawing books and a scattering of felt-tipped pens. From another room came the sound of a television and the occasional shriek of a small child.

Chrissie Helms sat by the table. She had big hands, red and chapped, which she clasped around her knees.

"I need to know," Ramsay said gently, "exactly what happened."

Hunter looked at the fat clock ticking on the mantelpiece and thought his boss was mad. Ramsay turned to the farmer.

"You were lying," he said. "It's so far-fetched, you see. Contrived. A strange and beautiful woman found miles from anywhere in the snow. Like a film. It must be simpler than that. You would have seen tracks when you took the tractor up to the road to clear a path for us. It's lonely out here. If you'd seen a light in Blackstoneburn last night you'd have gone in. Glad of the company and old

Shaftoe's whisky."

Helms shook his head helplessly.

"Did he pay you to keep quiet?" Hunter demanded. Suddenly, with a reluctant witness to bully he was in his element. "Or did he threaten you?"

"No," Helms said, "it were nothing like that."

"But she was there with some man?" Hunter was jubilant.

"Oh," Helms's wife said quietly, shocking them with her interruption, "she was there with some man."

Ramsay turned to the farmer. "She was your mistress?" he said, and Hunter realised he had known all along.

Helms said nothing.

"You must have met her at the agricultural suppliers in Otterbridge. Perhaps when you went to pay your bill. Perhaps she recognised you. She often came to Blackstoneburn."

"I recognised her," Helms said.

"You'd hardly miss her," the woman said. "The way she flaunted herself."

"No." The farmer shook his head. "No, it wasn't like that."

He paused.

"You felt sorry for her . . . ?" Ramsay prompted.

"Aye!" Helms looked up, relieved to be understood at last.

"Why did you bring her here?" Ramsay asked.

"I didn't. Not here."

"But to Blackstoneburn. You had a key? Or Rebecca did?"

Helms nodded. "She was lonely," he said. "In town. Everyone thinking of Christmas. You know."

"So you brought her up to Blackstoneburn," Hunter said unpleasantly. "For a dirty weekend. Thinking you'd sneak over to spend some time with her. Thinking your wife wouldn't notice."

Helms said nothing.

"What went wrong?" Hunter demanded. "Did she get greedy? Want more money? Blackmail? Is that why you killed her?"

"You fool!" It was almost a scream, and as she spoke the woman stood up with her huge red hands laid flat on the table. "He wouldn't have harmed her. He didn't kill her. I did."

"You must tell me," Ramsay said again, "exactly what happened."

But she needed no prompting. She was desperate for their understanding. "You don't know what it's like here," she said. "Especially in the winter. Dark all day. Every year it drives me mad. . . ." She stopped, realising she was making little sense, and continued more rationally. "I knew he had a woman, guessed. Then I saw them in town and I recognised her too. She was wearing black stockings and high heels, a dress that cost a fortune. How could I compete with that?" She looked down at her shapeless jersey and jumble-sale trousers. "I thought he'd grow out of it, that if I ignored it, he'd stop. I never thought he'd bring her here." She paused.

"How did you find out?" Ramsay asked.

"Yesterday afternoon I went out for a walk. I left the boys with my dad. I'd been in the house all day and just needed to get away from them all. It was half-past three, starting to get dark. I saw the light in Blackstoneburn and Joe's Land Rover parked outside. Like you said, we're desperate here for company, so I went around to the front and knocked at the door. I thought Tom Shaftoe was giving him a drink."

"There was no car," Ramsay said.

"No," she said. "But Tom parks it sometimes in one of the sheds. I didn't suspect a thing."

"Did you go in?"

"Not then," she said calmly. "When there was no reply I looked through the window. They were lying together in front of the fire. Then I went in. . . ." She paused again. "When she saw me she got up and straightened her clothes. She laughed. I suppose she was embarrassed. She said it was an awkward situation and why didn't we all discuss it over a cup of tea. Then she turned her back on me and walked through to the kitchen." Chrissie Helms caught her breath in a sob. "She shouldn't have turned her back," she said. "I deserved more than that. . . ."

"So you hit her," Ramsay said.

"I lost control," Chrissie said. "I picked up the poker from the grate and I hit her."

"Did you mean to kill her?"

"I wasn't thinking clearly enough to mean something."

"But you didn't stop to help her?"

"No," she said. "I came home. I left it to Joe to sort out. He owed me that. He did his best, but I knew we'd not be able to carry it through." She looked at her husband. "I'll miss you and the boys," she said. "But I'll not miss this place. Prison'll not be much different from this."

Hunter walked to the window to wait for the police Land Rover. He rubbed a space in the condensation and saw that it was snowing again, heavily. He thought that he agreed with her.

James Powell

GRIST FOR THE MILLS OF CHRISTMAS

The tabloid press dubbed the corner of southern Ontario bounded by Windsor, Sarnia, and St. Thomas "The Christmas Triangle" after holiday travelers began vanishing there in substantial numbers. When the disappearances reached twenty-seven, Wayne Sorley, editor-at-large of *The Traveling Gourmet* magazine, ever on the alert for offbeat articles, penciled in a story on "Bed-and-Breakfasting Through the Triangle of Death" for an upcoming Christmas number, intending to combine seasonal decorations and homey breakfast recipes (including a side article on "Muffins from Hell") with whatever details of the mysterious triangle came his way.

So when the middle of December rolled around, Sorley flew to Detroit, rented a car, and drove across the border into snow, wind, and falling temperatures.

He quickly discovered the bed-and-breakfast people weren't really crazy about the Christmas Triangle slant. Some thought it was bad for business. Few took the disappearances as lightly as Sorley did. To make matters worse, his reputation had preceded him. The current issue of *The Traveling Gourmet* contained his "Haunted Inns of the Coast of Maine" and his side article "Cod Cakes from Hell," marking him as a dangerous guest to have around. Some places on Sorley's itinerary received him grudgingly. Others claimed no record of his reservations and threatened to loose the dog on him if he didn't go away.

On the evening of the twenty-third of December, and well behind schedule, Sorley arrived at the last bed-and-breakfast on his prearranged itinerary to find a handwritten notice on the door. "Closed by the Board of Health." Shaking his fist at the dark windows, Sorley decided then and there to throw in the towel. To hell with the damn Christmas Triangle! So he found a motel for the night, resolving to get back across the border and catch the first available flight for New York City. But he awoke late to find a fresh fall of snow and a dead car battery.

It was midafternoon before Sorley, determined as ever, was on the road again. By six o'clock the snow was coming down heavily and aslant and he was still far from his destination. He drove on wearily. What he really needed now, he told himself, was a couple of weeks in Hawaii. How about an article on "The Twelve Luaus of Christmas"? This late they'd have to fake it. But what the hell, in Hawaii they have to fake the holidays anyway.

Finally Sorley couldn't take the driving anymore and turned off the highway to find a place for the night. That's when he saw the "Double Kay B & B" sign with the shingle hanging under it that said "Vacancy." On the front lawn beside the sign stood a fine old pickle-dish sleigh decorated with Christmas tree lights. Plastic reindeer lit electrically from within stood in the traces. Sorley pulled into the driveway and a moment later was up on the porch ringing the bell.

Mrs. Kay was a short, stoutish, white-haired woman with a pleasant face which, except for an old scar from a sharp-edged instrument across the left cheekbone, seemed untouched by care. She ushered Sorley inside and down a carpeted hallway and up the stairs. The house was small, tidy, bright, and comfortably arranged. Sorley couldn't quite find the word to describe it until Mrs. Kay showed him the available bedroom. The framed naval charts on the walls, the boat in a bottle, and the scrimshawed narwhal tusk on the mantel gave him the word he was looking for. The house was ship-shape.

Sorley took the room. But when he asked Mrs. Kay to recommend a place to eat nearby she insisted he share their dinner. "After all, it's Christmas Eve," she said. "You just freshen up, then, and come downstairs." Sorley smiled his thanks. The kitchen smells when she led him through the house had been delicious.

Sorley went back out to his car for his suitcase. The wind had ratcheted up its howl by several notches and was chasing streamers of snow down the road and across the drifts. But that was all right. He wasn't going anywhere. As he started back up the walk someone inside the house switched off the light on the bed-and-breakfast sign.

Sorley came out of his room pleased with his luck. Here he was settled in for the night with a roof over his head and a hot meal and a warm bed in the bargain. Suddenly Sorley felt eyes watching him, a sensation as strong as a torch on the nape of his neck. But when he looked back over his shoulder the hall was empty. Or had something tiny just disappeared behind the lowboy against the wall? Frowning, he turned his head around. As he did he caught the glimpse of a scurry, not the thing itself, but the turbulence of air left in the wake of some small creature vanishing down the stairs ahead of him. A mouse, perhaps. Or, if they were seagoing people, maybe the Kays kept rats. Sorley made a face. Then, shaking his head at his overheated imagination, he went downstairs.

Mrs. Kay fed him at a dining room table of polished wood with a single place setting. "I've already eaten," she explained. "I like my supper early. And Father, Mr. Kay, never takes anything before he goes to work. He'll just heat his up in the microwave when he gets home." The meal was baked finnan haddie. Creamed smoked haddock was a favorite Sorley had not seen for a long time. She served it with a half bottle of Alsatian Gewurtztraminer. There was Stilton cheese and a fresh pear for dessert. "Father hopes you'll join him later in the study for an after-dinner drink," said Mrs. Kay.

The study was a book-lined room decorated once again with relics and artifacts of the sea. The light came from a small lamp on the desk by the door and the fire burning in the grate. A painting of a brigantine under sail in a gray sea hung above the mantel. Mr. Kay, a tall, thin man with a long, sallow, clean-shaven face, heavy white eyebrows, and patches of white hair around his ears, rose from one of two wing-backed chairs facing the fire. As he shook his guest's hand he examined him and seemed pleased with what he saw. "Welcome, Mr. Sorley." Here was a voice that might once have boomed in the teeth of a gale. "Come sit by the fire."

Before sitting, Sorley paused to admire a grouping of three small statues on the mantel. They were realistic representations of pirates, each with a tarred pigtail and a brace of pistols, all three as ugly as sin and none more than six inches tall. A peglegged pirate. Another with a hook for a hand. The third wore a black eye patch. Seeing his interest, Mr. Kay took peg leg down and displayed it in his palm. "Nicely done, are they not? I'm something of a collector in the buccaneer line. Most people's family trees are hung about with horse thieves. Pirates swing from mine." He set the statue back on the mantel. "And I'm not ashamed of it. With all this what-do-you-call-it going round, this historical revisionism, who knows what's next? Take Christopher Columbus, eh? He started out a saint. Today he's worse than a pirate. Some call him a devil. And Geronimo has gone from devil incarnate to the noble leader of his people. But here, Mr. Sorley. Forgive my running on. Sit down and join me in a hot grog."

Sorley's host poured several fingers of a thick dark rum from a heavy green bottle by his foot, added water from the electric teakettle steaming on the hearth, urging as he passed him the glass, "Wrap yourself around that."

The drink was strong. It warmed Sorley's body like the sun on a cold spring day. "Thank you," he said. "And thanks for the excellent meal."

"Oh, we keep a good table, Mother and I. We live well. Not from the bed-and-breakfast business, I can tell you that. After all, we only open one night a year and accept only a single guest."

When Sorley expressed his surprise, Mr. Kay explained, "Call it a tradition. I mean, we certainly don't need the money. I deal in gold coins—you know, doubloons, moidore—obtained when the price was right. A steal, you might say. So, yes, we live well." He looked at his guest. "And what do you do for a living, Mr. Sorley?"

Sorley wasn't listening. For a moment he thought he'd noticed something small move behind Mr. Kay, back there in the corner where two eight-foot-long bamboo poles were leaning, and was watching to catch sight of it again. When Mr. Kay repeated his question Sorley told him what he did and briefly related his adventures connected with the aborted article.

Mr. Kay laughed like thunder, slapped his knees, and said, "Then we are indeed well met. If you like, I'll tell you the whole story about the Christmas Triangle. What an evening we have ahead of us, Mr. Sorley. Outside a storm howls and butts against the windows. And here we sit snug by the fire with hot drinks in our fists, a willing taleteller and . . ."

". . . an eager listener," said Sorley, congratulating himself once again on how well things had worked out. He might get his article yet.

Mr. Kay toasted his guest silently, thought for a moment, and then began. "Now years ago, when piracy was in flower, a gangly young Canadian boy named Scattergood Crandal who had run off to join the pirate trade in the Caribbean finally earned his master-pirate papers and set out on a life's journey in buccaneering. But no pantywaist, warm-water pirating for him, no rummy palm-tree days under blue skies. Young Crandal dreamed of home, of cool gray summers plundering the shipping lanes of the Great Lakes, of frosty winter raiding parties skating up frozen rivers with mufflers around their necks and cutlasses in their teeth, surprising sleeping townspeople under their eiderdowns.

"So with his wife's dowry Crandal bought a ship, the *Olson Nickelhouse*, and sailed north with his bride, arriving in the Thousand Islands just as winter was closing the St. Lawrence. The captain and his wife and crew spent a desperate four months caught in the ice. Crandal gave the men daily skating lessons. But they were slow learners and there were to be no raiding parties that winter. By the end of February, with supplies running low, the men ate the captain's parrot. And once having eaten talkative flesh, it was a small step to utter cannibalism. One snowy day Crandal came upon them dividing up the carcasses of three ice fishermen. He warned them, 'Don't do it, you fellows. Eating human flesh'll stunt your growth and curl your toes!' But it was too late. Those men were already slaves to that vile dish whose name no menu dares speak."

As Mr. Kay elaborated on the hardships of that first year he took his guest's glass, busied himself with the rum and hot water, and made them both fresh drinks. For his part, Sorley was distracted by bits of movement on the edges of his vision. But when he turned to look, there was never anything there. He decided it was only the jitters brought on by fatigue from his long drive in bad weather. That and the play of light from the fire.

"Now Crandal knew terror was half the pirate game," continued Mr. Kay. "So the loss of the parrot hit him hard. You see, Mr. Sorley, this Canadian lad had never mastered the strong language expected from pirate captains and counted on the parrot to hold up that end of things. The blue jay he later trained to stride his shoulder hadn't quite the same effect and was incredibly messy. Still, pirates know to go with the best they have. So he had these fly-ers printed up announcing that Captain Crandal, his wife (for Mrs. Crandal was no slouch with the cutlass on boarding parties), and his cannibal crew, pirates late of the Caribbean, were now operating locally, vowing Death and Destruction to all offering resistance. At the bottom he included a drawing of his flag, a skeleton with a cutlass in one bony hand and in the other a frying pan to underscore the cannibal reference.

"Well, the flyer and flag made Crandal the hit of the season when things started up again on the Lakes that spring. In fact, the frying pan and Crandal's pale, beanpole appearance and his outfit of pirate black earned him the nick-name Death-Warmed-Over. And as Death-Warmed-Over the Pirate he so ter-rorized the shipping lanes that soon the cold booty was just rolling in, cargoes of mittens and headcheese, sensible swag of potatoes and shoes, and vast plunder in the hardware line, anvils, door hinges, and barrels of three-penny nails which Crandal sold for gold in the colorful and clamorous thieves' bazaars of Rochester and Detroit."

"How about Niagara Falls?" asked Sorley, to show he knew how to play along with a tall tale. He was amused to detect a slur in his voice from the rum.

"What indeed?" smiled Mr. Kay, happy with the question. He rose and lifted the painting down from its nail above the mantel and rested it across Sorley's knees. "See those iron rings along the water line? We fitted long poles through them, hoisted the *Olson Nickelhouse* out of the water, and made heavy portage of her around the falls."

As Mr. Kay replaced the painting Sorley noticed that the group of three pirates on the mantel had rearranged themselves. Or was the strong drink and the heat from the fire affecting his concentration?

"Well," said Mr. Kay, "as cream rises, soon Crandal was Pirate King with a pirate fleet at his back. And there was no manjack on land or sea that didn't tremble at the mention of Death-Warmed-Over. Or any city either. Except for one.

"One city on the Canadian side sat smugly behind the islands in its bay and resisted Crandal's assaults. Its long Indian name with a broadside of o's in

15

it translated out as 'Gathering Place for Virtuous Moccasins.' But Crandal called it 'Goody Two-Shoes City' because of its reek of self-righteousness. Oh, he hated the world as a pirate must and wished to do creation all the harm he could. But Goody Two-Shoes City he hated with a special passion. Early on he even tried a Sunday attack to catch the city by surprise. But the inhabitants came boiling out of the churches and up onto the battlements to pepper him with cannonballs with such a will that, if their elected officials hadn't decided they were enjoying themselves too much on the Sabbath and ordered a cease-fire, they might have blown the *Olson Nickelhouse* out of the water."

Here Mr. Kay broke off his narrative to poke the fire and then to stare into the flames. As he did, Sorley once again had the distinct impression he was being watched. He turned and was startled to find another grouping of lit-tle pirate statues he hadn't noticed before on a shelf right at the level of his eye in the bookcase beside the fireplace. They held drawn dirks and cutlasses in their earnest little hands and had pistols stuck in their belts. And, oh, what ugly little specimens they were!

"Then, early one December," Mr. Kay continued, "Crandal captured a cargo of novelty items from the toy mines of Bavaria. Of course, in those days toys were quite unknown. Parents gave their children sensible gifts like socks or celluloid collars or pencil boxes at Christmas. Suddenly Crandal broke into a happy hornpipe on the frosty deck, for it had come to him how he could harm Goody Two-Shoes City and make it curse his name forever. But he would need a disguise to get by the guards at the city gate who had strict orders to keep a sharp eye out for Death-Warmed-Over. So he changed his black outfit for a red one with a pillow for fatness, rouge for his gray cheeks, a white beard to make him look older, and a jolly laugh to cover his pirate gloom. Then, on Christmas Eve, he put the *Olson Nickelhouse* in close to shore and sneaked into Goody Two-Shoes City with a wagonload of toys crated up like hymnals. That night he crept across the rooftops and down chimneys and by morning every boy and girl had a real toy under the Christmas tree.

"Well, of course, the parents knew right away who'd done the deed and what Crandal was up to. Next Christmas, they knew, they'd have to go and buy a toy in case Crandal didn't show up again or risk a disappointed child. But suppose he came next year, too? Well, that would mean that the following year the parents would have to buy two toys. Then three. And on and on until children no longer knew the meaning of the word 'enough.'

" 'Curse Crandal and the visit from the *Olson Nickelhouse*,' the parents muttered through clenched teeth. But their eavesdropping children misheard and thought they said 'Kris Kringle' and something about a visit from 'Old Saint Nicholas.' As if a saint would give a boy a toy drum or saxophone to drive his father mad with, as if a saint would give a girl a Little Dolly Clotheshorse doll and set her dreaming over fashion magazines when she should be helping her mother in the kitchen." Mr. Kay laughed until the tears came to his eyes. "Well, the Pirate King knew he'd hit upon a better game than making fat landlubbers walk an icy gangplank over cold gray water. And since the Crandals had salted away a fortune in gold coins they settled down here and started a reindeer farm so Crandal could Kringle full-time with the missus as Mrs. Kringle and the crew as his little helpers." Mr. Kay looked up. "Isn't that right, Mother?"

Mrs. Kay had appeared in the doorway with a red costume and a white beard over her arm and a pair of boots in her hand. "That's right, Father. But it's time to get ready. I've loaded the sleigh and harnessed the reindeer."

Mr. Kay got to his feet. "And here's the wonderfully strange and miraculous thing, Mr. Sorley. As the years passed we didn't age. Not one bit. What did you call it, Mother?"

"The Tinker Bell Effect," said Mrs. Kay, putting down the boots and holding up the heavily padded red jumpsuit trimmed with white for Mr. Kay to step into.

"If children believe in you," explained Mr. Kay, as he did up the Velcro fasteners, "why then you're eternal and evergreen. Plus you can fly through the air and so can your damn livestock!"

Mrs. Kay laughed a fine contralto laugh. "And somewhere along the line children must have started believing in Santa's little helpers, too," she said. "Because our pirate crew didn't age either. They just got shorter."

Mr. Kay nodded. "Which fitted in real well with their end of the operation."

"The toy workshop?" asked Sorley.

Mr. Kay smiled and shook his head. "No, that's only a myth. We buy our toys, you see. Not that Mother and I were going to spend our own hard-earned money for the damn stuff. No, the crew's little fingers make the counterfeit plates to print what cash we need to buy the toys. Electronic ones, mostly. Wonderful for stunting the brain, cramping the soul, and making ugly noises that just won't quit."

"Hold it." Sorley wagged a disbelieving finger. "You're telling me you started out as Death-Warmed-Over the Pirate and now you're Santa Claus?"

"Mr. Sorley, I'm as surprised as you how things worked out. Talk about revisionism, eh? Yesterday's yo-ho-ho is today's ho-ho-ho." Mr. Kay stood back and let his wife attach his white beard with its built-in red plastic cheeks.

"But where does the Christmas Triangle business fit in?" demanded Sorley. "We've got twenty-seven people who disappeared around here last year alone."

"Copycats," insisted Mr. Kay. "As I said, Mother and I only take one a year, what we call our Gift from the Night. But of course, when the media got

17

onto it the copycats weren't far behind. Little Mary Housewife can't think of a present for Tommy Tiresome who has everything, so she gives him a slug from a thirty-eight between the eyes and buries him in the basement, telling the neighbors he went to visit his mother in Sarnia. Little Billy Bank Manager with a shortage in the books and a yen for high living in warmer climes vanishes into the Christmas Triangle with a suitcase of money from the vault and reemerges under another name in Rio. And so on and so on. Copycats."

"Father's right. We only take one," said Mrs. Kay. "That's what our agreement calls for."

Mr. Kay nodded. "Last year it was an arrogant young bastard from the SPCA investigating reports on mistreated reindeer. Tell me my business, would he?" Mr. Kay's chest swelled and his eyes flashed. "Well, Mother and I harnessed him to the sleigh right between Dancer and Prancer. And his sluggard backside got more than its share of the lash that Christmas Eve, let me tell you. He was blubbering like a baby by the time I turned him over to my scurvy crew."

"I don't understand," said Sorley. But he was beginning to. He stood up slowly, utterly clearheaded and sober. "You mean your cannibal crew ate him?" he demanded in a horrified voice.

"Consider the fool from the SPCA part of our employee benefits package," shrugged Mr. Kay. "Oh, all right," he conceded when he saw Sorley's outrage, "so my little shipmates are evil. Evil. They've got wolfish little teeth and pointed carnivore ears. And don't think those missing legs and arms were honestly come by in pirate combat. Not a bit of it. There's this game they play. Like strip poker but without the clothes. They're terrible, there's no denying it. But you know, few of us get to pick the people we work with. Besides, I don't give a damn about naughty or nice."

Sorley's voice was shrill and outraged. "But this is hideous. Hideous. I'll go to the police."

"Go, then," said Mr. Kay. "Be our guest. Mother and I won't stand in your way."

"You'd better not try!" warned Sorley defiantly, intending to storm from the room. But when he tried he found his shoelaces were tied together. He fell forward like a dead weight and struck his head, blacking out for a moment. When he regained consciousness he was lying on his stomach with his thumbs lashed together behind his back. Before Sorley's head cleared he felt something being shoved up the back of his pant legs, over his buttocks, and up under his belt. When they emerged out beyond the back of his shirt collar he saw they were the bamboo poles that had been leaning in the corner.

Before Sorley could try to struggle free, a little pirate appeared close to his face, a grizzled thing with a hook for an arm, little curly-toed shoes and a bandanna pulled down over the pointed tops of its ears. With a cruel smile it placed the point of its cutlass a menacing fraction of an inch from Sorley's left eyeball and in language no less vile because of the tiny voice that uttered it, the creature warned him not to move.

Mrs. Kay was smiling down at him. "Now don't trouble yourself over your car, Mr. Sorley. I'll drive into the city later tonight and park it where the car strippers can't miss it. Father'll pick me up in the sleigh on his way back."

Mr. Kay had been stamping his boots to get them on properly. Now he said, "Give us a kiss, Mother. I'm on my way." Then the toes of the boots hove into view on the edge of Sorley's vision. "Good-bye, Mr. Sorley," said his host. "Thanks for coming. Consider yourself grist for the mills of Christmas."

As soon as Mr. Kay left the room, Sorley heard little feet scramble around him and more little pirates rushed to man the ends of the bamboo poles in front of him. At a tiny command the crew put the cutlasses in their teeth and, holding their arms over their heads, hoisted Sorley up off the floor. He hung there helplessly, suspended front and back.

The little pirates lugged Sorley out into the hall and headed down the carpet toward the front door. He didn't know where they were taking him. But their progress was funereally slow, and, swaying there, Sorley conceived a frantic plan of escape. He knew his captors were tiring under their load. If they had to set him down to rest, he would dig in with his toes and, somehow, work his way to his knees. At least there he'd stand a chance.

Sorley heard sleigh bells. He raised his chin. Through the pane of beveled glass in the front door he saw the sleigh on the lawn rise steeply into the night, Christmas tree lights and all, and he heard Mr. Kay's booming "Yo-ho-ho-ho."

Suddenly Sorley's caravan stopped. He got ready, waiting for them to put him down. But they were only adjusting their grips. The little pirates turned him sideways and Sorley saw the open door and the top of the cellar steps and smelled the darkness as musty as a tomb. Then he felt the beginning of their big heave-ho. It was too damn late to escape now. Grist for the mills of Christmas? Hell, he was meat for the stew pots of elfdom.

Lawrence Block

AS DARK AS CHRISTMAS GETS

It was 9:45 in the morning when I got to the little bookshop on West Fifty-sixth Street. Before I went to work for Leo Haig I probably wouldn't have bothered to look at my watch, if I was even wearing one in the first place, and the best I'd have been able to say was it was around ten o'clock. But Haig wanted me to be his legs and eyes, and sometimes his ear, nose, and throat, and if he was going to play in Nero Wolfe's league, that meant I had to turn into Archie Goodwin, for Pete's sake, noticing everything and getting the details right and reporting conversations verbatim.

Well, forget that last part. My memory's getting better—Haig's right about that part—but what follows won't be word for word, because all I am is a human being. If you want a tape recorder, buy one.

There was a lot of fake snow in the window, and a Santa Claus doll in handcuffs, and some toy guns and knives, and a lot of mysteries with a Christmas theme, including the one by Fredric Brown where the murderer dresses up as a department store Santa. (Someone pulled that a year ago, put on a red suit and a white beard and shot a man at the corner of Broadway and Thirty-seventh, and I told Haig how ingenious I thought it was. He gave me a look, left the room, and came back with a book. I read it—that's what I do when Haig hands me a book—and found out Brown had had the idea fifty years earlier. Which doesn't mean that's where the killer got the idea. The book's long out of print—the one I read was a paperback, and falling apart, not like the handsome hardcover copy in the window. And how many killers get their ideas out of old books?)

Now if you're a detective yourself you'll have figured out two things by now—the bookshop specialized in mysteries, and it was the Christmas season. And if you'd noticed the sign in the window you'd have made one more deduction: i.e., that they were closed.

I went down the half flight of steps and poked the buzzer. When nothing happened I poked it again, and eventually the door was opened by a little man with white hair and a white beard—all he needed was padding and a red suit, and someone to teach him to be jolly. "I'm terribly sorry," he said, "but I'm afraid we're closed. It's Christmas morning, and it's not even ten o'clock."

"You called us," I said, "and it wasn't even nine o'clock."

He took a good look at me, and light dawned. "You're Harrison," he said. "And I know your first name, but I can't—"

"Chip," I supplied.

"Of course. But where's Haig? I know he thinks he's Nero Wolfe, but he's not gone housebound, has he? He's been here often enough in the past."

"Haig gets out and about," I agreed, "but Wolfe went all the way to Montana once, as far as that goes. What Wolfe refused to do was leave the house on business, and Haig's with him on that one. Besides, he just spawned some unspawnable cichlids from Lake Chad, and you'd think the aquarium was a television set and they were showing *Midnight Blue*."

"Fish." He sounded more reflective than contemptuous. "Well, at least you're here. That's something." He locked the door and led me up a spiral staircase to a room full of books, full as well with the residue of a party. There were empty glasses here and there, hors d'oeuvres trays that held nothing but crumbs, and a cut-glass dish with a sole remaining cashew.

"Christmas," he said, and shuddered. "I had a houseful of people here last night. All of them eating, all of them drinking, and many of them actually singing." He made a face. "I didn't sing," he said, "but I certainly ate and drank. And eventually they all went home and I went upstairs to bed. I must have, because that's where I was when I woke up two hours ago."

"But you don't remember."

"Well, no," he said, "but then, what would there be to remember? The guests leave and you're alone with vague feelings of sadness." His gaze turned inward. "If she'd stayed," he said, "I'd have remembered."

"She?"

"Never mind. I awoke this morning, alone in my own bed. I swallowed some aspirin and came downstairs. I went into the library."

"You mean this room?"

"This is the salesroom. These books are for sale."

"Well, I figured. I mean, this is a bookshop."

"You've never seen the library?" He didn't wait for an answer but turned to open a door and lead me down a hallway to another room twice the size of the first. It was lined with floor-to-ceiling hardwood shelves, and the shelves were filled with double rows of hardcover books. It was hard to identify the books, though, because all but one section was wrapped in plastic sheeting.

"This is my collection," he announced. "These books are not for sale. I'll only part with one if I've replaced it with a finer copy. Your employer doesn't collect, does he?"

21

"Haig? He's got thousands of books."

"Yes, and he's bought some of them from me. But he doesn't give a damn about first editions. He doesn't care what kind of shape a book is in, or even if it's got a dust jacket. He'd as soon have a Grosset reprint or a book-club edition or even a paperback."

"He just wants to read them."

"It takes all kinds, doesn't it?" He shook his head in wonder. "Last night's party filled this room as well as the salesroom. I put up plastic to keep the books from getting handled and possibly damaged. Or—how shall I put this?"

Any way you want, I thought. You're the client.

"Some of these books are extremely valuable," he said. "And my guests were all extremely reputable people, but many of them are good customers, and that means they're collectors. Ardent, even rabid collectors."

"And you didn't want them stealing the books."

"You're very direct," he said. "I suppose that's a useful quality in your line of work. But no, I didn't want to tempt anyone, especially when alcoholic indulgence might make temptation particularly difficult to resist."

"So you hung up plastic sheets."

"And came downstairs this morning to remove the plastic, and pick up some dirty glasses and clear some of the debris. I puttered around. I took down the plastic from this one section, as you can see. I did a bit of tidying. And then I saw it."

"Saw what?"

He pointed to a set of glassed-in shelves, on top of which stood a three-foot row of leather-bound volumes. "There," he said. "What do you see?"

"Leather-bound books, but—"

"Boxes," he corrected. "Wrapped in leather and stamped in gold, and each one holding a manuscript. They're fashioned to look like finely bound books, but they're original manuscripts."

"Very nice," I said. "I suppose they must be very rare."

"They're unique."

"That too."

He made a face. "One of a kind. The author's original manuscript, with corrections in his own hand. Most are typed, but the Elmore Leonard is handwritten. The Westlake, of course, is typed on that famous Smith-Corona manual portable of his. The Paul Kavanagh is the author's first novel. He only wrote three, you know."

I didn't, but Haig would.

"They're very nice," I said politely. "And I don't suppose they're for sale."

"Of course not. They're in the library. They're part of the collection."

"Right," I said, and paused for him to continue. When he didn't I said, "Uh,

I was thinking. Maybe you could tell me . . ."

"Why I summoned you here." He sighed. "Look at the boxed manuscript between the Westlake and the Kavanagh."

"Between them?"

"Yes."

"The Kavanagh is *Such Men Are Dangerous*," I said, "and the Westlake is *Drowned Hopes*. But there's nothing at all between them but a three-inch gap."

"Exactly," he said.

"*As Dark as It Gets,*" I said. "By Cornell Woolrich."

Haig frowned. "I don't know the book," he said. "Not under that title, not with Woolrich's name on it, nor William Irish or George Hopley. Those were his pen names."

"I know," I said. "You don't know the book because it was never published. The manuscript was found among Woolrich's effects after his death."

"There was a posthumous book, Chip."

"*Into the Night,*" I said. "Another writer completed it, writing replacement scenes for some that had gone missing in the original. It wound up being publishable."

"It wound up being published," Haig said. "That's not necessarily the same thing. But this manuscript, *As Dark—*"

"*—As It Gets.* It wasn't publishable, according to our client. Woolrich evidently worked on it over the years, and what survived him incorporated unresolved portions of several drafts. There are characters who die early on and then reappear with no explanation. There's supposed to be some great writing and plenty of Woolrich's trademark paranoid suspense, but it doesn't add up to a book, or even something that could be edited into a book. But to a collector—"

"Collectors," Haig said heavily.

"Yes, sir. I asked what the manuscript was worth. He said, 'Well, I paid five thousand dollars for it.' That's verbatim, but don't ask me if the thing's worth more or less than that, because I don't know if he was bragging that he was a big spender or a slick trader."

"It doesn't matter," Haig said. "The money's the least of it. He added it to his collection and he wants it back."

"And the person who stole it," I said, "is either a friend or a customer or both."

"And so he called us and not the police. The manuscript was there when the party started?"

"Yes."

"And gone this morning?"

"Yes."

"And there were how many in attendance?"

"Forty or fifty," I said, "including the caterer and her staff."

"If the party was catered," he mused, "why was the room a mess when you saw it? Wouldn't the catering staff have cleaned up at the party's end?"

"I asked him that question myself. The party lasted longer than the caterer had signed on for. She hung around herself for a while after her employees packed it in, but she stopped working and became a guest. Our client was hoping she would stay."

"But you just said she did."

"After everybody else went home. He lives upstairs from the bookshop, and he was hoping for a chance to show her his living quarters."

Haig shrugged. He's not quite the misogynist his idol is, but he hasn't been at it as long. Give him time. He said, "Chip, it's hopeless. Fifty suspects?"

"Six."

"How so?"

"By two o'clock," I said, "just about everybody had called it a night. The ones remaining got a reward."

"And what was that?"

"Some fifty-year-old Armagnac, served in Waterford pony glasses. We counted the glasses, and there were seven of them. Six guests and the host."

"And the manuscript?"

"Was still there at the time, and still sheathed in plastic. See, he'd covered all the boxed manuscripts, same as the books on the shelves. But the cut-glass ship's decanter was serving as a sort of bookend to the manuscript section, and he took off the plastic to get at it. And while he was at it he took out one of the manuscripts and showed it off to his guests."

"Not the Woolrich, I don't suppose."

"No, it was a Peter Straub novel, elegantly handwritten in a leatherbound journal. Straub collects Chandler, and our client had traded a couple of Chandler firsts for the manuscript, and he was proud of himself."

"I shouldn't wonder."

"But the Woolrich was present and accounted for when he took off the plastic wrap, and it may have been there when he put the Straub back. He didn't notice."

"And this morning it was gone."

"Yes."

"Six suspects," he said. "Name them."

I took out my notebook. "Jon and Jayne Corn-Wallace," I said. "He's a retired stockbroker, she's an actress in a daytime drama. That's a soap opera."

"Piffle."

"Yes, sir. They've been friends of our client for years, and customers for

24

about as long. They're mystery fans, and he got them started on first editions."

"Including Woolrich?"

"He's a favorite of Jayne's. I gather Jon can take him or leave him."

"I wonder which he did last night. Do the Corn-Wallaces collect manuscripts?"

"Just books. First editions, though they're starting to get interested in fancy bindings and limited editions. The one with a special interest in manuscripts is Zoltan Mihalyi."

"The violinist?"

Trust Haig to know that. I'd never heard of him myself. "A big mystery fan," I said. "I guess reading passes the time on those long concert tours."

"I don't suppose a man can spend all his free hours with other men's wives," Haig said. "And who's to say that all the stories are true? He collects manuscripts, does he?"

"He was begging for a chance to buy the Straub, but our friend wouldn't sell."

"Which would make him a likely suspect. Who else?"

"Philip Perigord."

"The writer?"

"Right, and I didn't even know he was still alive. He hasn't written anything in years."

"Almost twenty years. *More Than Murder* was published in nineteen eighty."

Trust him to know that, too. "Anyway," I said, "he didn't die. He didn't even stop writing. He just quit writing books. He went to Hollywood and became a screenwriter."

"That's the same as stopping writing," Haig reflected. "It's very nearly the same as being dead. Does he collect books?"

"No."

"Manuscripts?"

"No."

"Perhaps he wanted the manuscripts for scrap paper," Haig said. "He could turn the pages over and write on their backs. Who else was present?"

"Edward Everett Stokes."

"The small-press publisher. Bought out his partner, Geoffrey Poges, to became sole owner of Stokes-Poges Press."

"They do limited editions, according to our client. Leather bindings, small runs, special tip-in sheets."

"All well and good," he said, "but what's useful about Stokes-Poges is that they issue a reasonably priced trade edition of each title as well, and publish works otherwise unavailable, including collections of short fiction from otherwise uncollected writers."

"Do they publish Woolrich?"

"All his work has been published by mainstream publishers, and all his stories collected. Is Stokes a collector himself?"

"Our client didn't say."

"No matter. How many is that? The Corn-Wallaces, Zoltan Mihalyi, Philip Perigord, E. E. Stokes. And the sixth is—"

"Harriet Quinlan."

He looked puzzled, then nodded in recognition. "The literary agent."

"She represents Perigord," I said, "or at least she would, if he ever went back to novel-writing. She's placed books with Stokes-Poges. And she may have left the party with Zoltan Mihalyi."

"I don't suppose her client list includes the Woolrich estate. Or that she's a rabid collector of books and manuscripts."

"He didn't say."

"No matter. You said six suspects, Chip. I count seven."

I ticked them off. "Jon Corn-Wallace. Jayne Corn-Wallace. Zoltan Mihalyi. Philip Perigord. Edward Everett Stokes. Harriet Quinlan. Isn't that six? Or do you want to include our client, the little man with the palindromic first name? That seems farfetched to me, but—"

"The caterer, Chip."

"Oh. Well, he says she was just there to do a job. No interest in books, no interest in manuscripts, no real interest in the world of mysteries. Certainly no interest in Cornell Woolrich."

"And she stayed when her staff went home."

"To have a drink and be sociable. He had hopes she'd spend the night, but it didn't happen. I suppose technically she's a suspect, but—"

"At the very least she's a witness," he said. "Bring her."

"Bring her?"

He nodded. "Bring them all."

It's a shame this is a short story. If it were a novel, now would be the time for me to give you a full description of the off-street carriage house on West Twentieth Street, which Leo Haig owns and where he occupies the top two floors, having rented out the lower two stories to Madam Juana and her All-Girl Enterprise. You'd hear how Haig had lived for years in two rooms in the Bronx, breeding tropical fish and reading detective stories, until a modest inheritance allowed him to set up shop as a poor man's Nero Wolfe.

He's quirky, God knows, and I could fill a few pleasant pages recounting his quirks, including his having hired me as much for my writing ability as for my potential value as a detective. I'm expected to write up his cases the same way

Archie Goodwin writes up Wolfe's, and this case was a slam-dunk, really, and he says it wouldn't stretch into a novel, but that it should work nicely as a short story.

So all I'll say is this: Haig's best quirk is his unshakable belief that Nero Wolfe exists. Under another name, of course, to protect his inviolable privacy. And the legendary brownstone, with all its different fictitious street numbers, isn't on West Thirty-fifth Street at all but in another part of town entirely.

And someday, if Leo Haig performs with sufficient brilliance as a private investigator, he hopes to get the ultimate reward—an invitation to dinner at Nero Wolfe's table.

Well, that gives you an idea. If you want more in the way of background, I can only refer you to my previous writings on the subject. There have been two novels so far, *Make Out With Murder* and *The Topless Tulip Caper*, and they're full of inside stuff about Leo Haig. (There were two earlier books from before I met Haig, *No Score* and *Chip Harrison Scores Again*, but they're not mysteries and Haig's not in them. All they do, really, is tell you more than you'd probably care to know about me.)

Well, end of commercial. Haig said I should put it in, and I generally do what he tells me. After all, the man pays my salary.

And, in his own quiet way, he's a genius. As you'll see.

"They'll never come here," I told him. "Not today. I know it will always live in your memory as The Day the Cichlids Spawned, but to everybody else it's Christmas, and they'll want to spend it in the bosoms of their families, and—"

"Not everyone has a family," he pointed out, "and not every family has a bosom."

"The Corn-Wallaces have a family. Zoltan Mihalyi doesn't, but he's probably got somebody with a bosom lined up to spend the day with. I don't know about the others, but—"

"Bring them," he said, "but not here. I want them all assembled at five o'clock this afternoon at the scene of the crime."

"The bookshop? You're willing to leave the house?"

"It's not entirely business," he said. "Our client is more than a client. He's a friend, and an important source of books. The reading copies he so disdains have enriched our own library immeasurably. And you know how important that is."

If there's anything you need to know, you can find it in the pages of a detective novel. That's Haig's personal conviction, and I'm beginning to believe he's right.

"I'll pay him a visit," he went on. "I'll arrive at four-thirty or so, and perhaps I'll come across a book or two that I'll want for our library. You'll arrange that they all arrive around five, and we'll clear up this little business." He frowned in thought. "I'll tell Wong we'll want Christmas dinner at eight tonight. That should give us more than enough time."

Again, if this were a novel, I'd spend a full chapter telling you what I went through getting them all present and accounted for. It was hard enough finding them, and then I had to sell them on coming. I pitched the event as a second stage of last night's party—their host had arranged, for their entertainment and edification, that they should be present while a real-life private detective solved an actual crime before their very eyes.

According to Haig, all we'd need to spin this yarn into a full-length book would be a dead body, although two would be better. If, say, our client had wandered into his library that morning to find a corpse seated in his favorite chair, *and* the Woolrich manuscript gone, then I could easily stretch all this to sixty thousand words. If the dead man had been wearing a deerstalker cap and holding a violin, we'd be especially well off; when the book came out, all the Sherlockian completists would be compelled to buy it.

Sorry. No murders, no Baker Street Irregulars, no dogs barking or not barking. I had to get them all there, and I did, but don't ask me how. I can't take the time to tell you.

"Now," Zoltan Mihalyi said. "We are all here. So can someone please tell me why we are all here?" There was a twinkle in his dark eyes as he spoke, and the trace of a knowing smile on his lips. He wanted an answer, but he was going to remain charming while he got it. I could believe he swept a lot of women off their feet.

"First of all," Jeanne Botleigh said, "I think we should each have a glass of eggnog. It's festive, and it will help put us all in the spirit of the day."

She was the caterer, and she was some cupcake, all right. Close-cut brown hair framed her small oval face and set off a pair of China-blue eyes. She had an English accent, roughed up some by ten years in New York, and she was short and slender and curvy, and I could see why our client had hoped she would stick around.

And now she'd whipped up a batch of eggnog, and ladled out cups for each of us. I waited until someone else tasted it—after all the mystery novels Haig's forced on me, I've developed an imagination—but once the Corn-Wallaces had tossed off theirs with no apparent effect, I took a sip. It was smooth and delicious, and it had a kick like a mule. I looked over at Haig, who's not much of a drinker, and he was smacking his lips over it.

"Why are we here?" he said, echoing the violinist's question. "Well, sir, I shall tell you. We are here as friends and customers of our host, whom we may be able to assist in the solution of a puzzle. Last night all of us, with the exception of course of myself and my young assistant, were present in this room. Also present was the original manuscript of an unpublished novel by Cornell Woolrich. This morning we were all gone, and so was the manuscript. Now we have returned. The manuscript, alas, has not."

"Wait a minute," Jon Corn-Wallace said. "You're saying one of us took it?"

"I say only that it has gone, sir. It is possible that someone within this room was involved in its disappearance, but there are diverse other possibilities as well. What impels me, what has prompted me to summon you here, is the likelihood that one or more of you knows something that will shed light on the incident."

"But the only person who would know anything would be the person who took it," Harriet Quinlan said. She was what they call a woman of a certain age, which generally means a woman of an uncertain age. Her figure was a few pounds beyond girlish, and I had a hunch she dyed her hair and might have had her face lifted somewhere along the way, but whatever she'd done had paid off. She was probably old enough to be my mother's older sister, but that didn't keep me from having the sort of ideas a nephew's not supposed to have.

Haig told her anyone could have observed something, and not just the guilty party, and Philip Perigord started to ask a question, and Haig held up a hand and cut him off in mid-sentence. Most people probably would have finished what they were saying, but I guess Perigord was used to studio executives shutting him up at pitch meetings. He bit off his word in the middle of a syllable and stayed mute.

"It is a holiday," Haig said, "and we all have other things to do, so we'd best avoid distraction. Hence, I will ask the questions and you will answer them. Mr. Corn-Wallace. You are a book collector. Have you given a thought to collecting manuscripts?"

"I've thought about it," Jon Corn-Wallace said. He was the best-dressed man in the room, looking remarkably comfortable in a dark blue suit and a striped tie. He wore bull-and-bear cufflinks and one of those watches that's worth five thousand dollars if it's real or twenty-five if you bought it from a Nigerian street vendor. "He tried to get me interested," he said, with a nod toward our client. "But I was always the kind of trader who stuck to listed stocks."

"Meaning?"

"Meaning it's impossible to pinpoint the market value of a one-of-a-kind item like a manuscript. There's too much guesswork involved. I'm not buying books with an eye to selling them, that's something my heirs will have to worry about, but I do like to know what my collection is worth and whether or not it's been a good investment. It's part of the pleasure of collecting, as far as I'm concerned. So I've stayed away from manuscripts. They're too iffy."

"And had you had a look at *As Dark as It Gets?*"

"No. I'm not interested in manuscripts, and I don't care at all for Woolrich."

"Jon likes hardboiled fiction," his wife put in, "but Woolrich is a little weird for his taste. I think he was a genius myself. Quirky and tormented, maybe, but what genius isn't?"

Haig, I thought. You couldn't call him tormented, but maybe he made up for it by exceeding the usual quota of quirkiness.

"Anyway," Jayne Corn-Wallace said, "I'm the Woolrich fan in the family. Though I agree with Jon as far as manuscripts are concerned. The value is pure speculation. And who wants to buy something and then have to get a box made for it? It's like buying an unframed canvas and having to get it framed."

"The Woolrich manuscript was already boxed," Haig pointed out.

"I mean generally, as an area for collecting. As a collector, I wasn't interested in *As Dark as It Gets*. If someone fixed it up and completed it, and if someone published it, I'd have been glad to buy it. I'd have bought two copies."

"Two copies, madam?"

She nodded. "One to read and one to own."

Haig's face darkened, and I thought he might offer his opinion of people who were afraid to damage their books by reading them. But he kept it to himself, and I was just as glad. Jayne Corn-Wallace was a tall, handsome woman, radiating self-confidence, and I sensed she'd give as good as she got in an exchange with Haig.

"You might have wanted to read the manuscript," Haig suggested.

She shook her head. "I like Woolrich," she said, "but as a stylist he was choppy enough *after* editing and polishing. I wouldn't want to try him in manuscript, let alone an unfinished manuscript like that one."

"Mr. Mihalyi," Haig said. "You collect manuscripts, don't you?"

"I do."

"And do you care for Woolrich?"

The violinist smiled. "If I had the chance to buy the original manuscript of *The Bride Wore Black*," he said, "I would leap at it. If it were close at hand, and if strong drink had undermined my moral fiber, I might even slip it under my coat and walk off with it." A wink showed us he was kidding. "Or at least I'd have been tempted. The work in question, however, tempted me not a whit."

"And why is that, sir?"

Mihalyi frowned. "There are people," he said, "who attend open rehearsals and make surreptitious recordings of the music. They treasure them and even bootleg them to other like-minded fans. I despise such people."

"Why?"

"They violate the artist's privacy," he said. "A rehearsal is a time when one refines one's approach to a piece of music. One takes chances, one uses the occasion as the equivalent of an artist's sketch pad. The person who records it is in essence spraying a rough sketch with fixative and hanging it on the wall of his personal museum. I find it unsettling enough that listeners record concert performances, making permanent what was supposed to be a transitory experience. But to record a rehearsal is an atrocity."

"And a manuscript?"

"A manuscript is the writer's completed work. It provides a record of how he arranged and revised his ideas, and how they were in turn adjusted for better or worse by an editor. But it is finished work. An unfinished manuscript . . ."

"Is a rehearsal?"

"That or something worse. I ask myself, what would Woolrich have wanted?"

"Another drink," Edward Everett Stokes said, and leaned forward to help himself to more eggnog. "I take your point, Mihalyi. And Woolrich might well have preferred to have his unfinished work destroyed upon his death, but he left no instructions to that effect, so how can we presume to guess his wishes? Perhaps, for all we know, there is a single scene in the book that meant as much to him as anything he'd written. Or less than a scene—a bit of dialogue, a paragraph of description, perhaps no more than a single sentence. Who are we to say it should not survive?"

"Perigord," Mihalyi said. "You are a writer. Would you care to have your unfinished work published after your death? Would you not recoil at that, or at having it completed by others?"

Philip Perigord cocked an eyebrow. "I'm the wrong person to ask," he said. "I've spent twenty years in Hollywood. Forget unfinished work. My *finished* work doesn't get published, or 'produced,' as they so revealingly term it. I get paid, and the work winds up on a shelf. And, when it comes to having one's work completed by others, in Hollywood you don't have to wait until you're dead. It happens during your lifetime, and you learn to live with it."

"We don't know the author's wishes," Harriet Quinlan put in, "and I wonder how relevant they are."

"But it's his work," Mihalyi pointed out.

"Is it, Zoltan? Or does it belong to the ages? Finished or not, the author has left it to us. Schubert did not finish one of his greatest symphonies. Would you have laid its two completed movements in the casket with him?"

"It has been argued that the work was complete, that he intended it to be but two movements long."

"That begs the question, Zoltan."

"It does, dear lady," he said with a wink. "I'd rather beg the question than be undone by it. Of course I'd keep the *Unfinished Symphony* in the repertoire. On the other hand, I'd hate to see some fool attempt to finish it."

"No one has, have they?"

"Not to my knowledge. But several writers have had the effrontery to finish *The Mystery of Edwin Drood*, and I do think Dickens would have been better served if the manuscript had gone in the box with his bones. And as for sequels, like those for *Pride and Prejudice* and *The Big Sleep*, or that young fellow who had the colossal gall to tread in Rex Stout's immortal footsteps . . . "

Now we were getting onto sensitive ground. As far as Leo Haig was concerned, Archie Goodwin had always written up Wolfe's cases, using the transparent pseudonym of Rex Stout. (Rex Stout = fat king, an allusion to Wolfe's own regal corpulence.) Robert Goldsborough, credited with the books written since the "death" of Stout, was, as Haig saw it, a ghostwriter employed by Goodwin, who was no longer up to the chore of hammering out the books. He'd relate them to Goldsborough, who transcribed them and polished them up. While they might not have all the narrative verve of Goodwin's own work, still they provided an important and accurate account of Wolfe's more recent cases.

See, Haig feels the great man's still alive and still raising orchids and nailing killers. Maybe somewhere on the Upper East Side. Maybe in Murray Hill, or just off Gramercy Park . . .

The discussion about Goldsborough, and about sequels in general, roused Haig from a torpor that Wolfe himself might have envied. "Enough," he said with authority. "There's no time for meandering literary conversations, nor would Chip have room for them in a short-story-length report. So let us get to it. One of you took the manuscript, box and all, from its place on the shelf. Mr. Mihalyi, you have the air of one who protests too much. You profess no interest in the manuscripts of unpublished novels, and I can accept that you did not yearn to possess *As Dark as It Gets*, but you wanted a look at it, didn't you?"

"I don't own a Woolrich manuscript," he said, "and of course I was interested in seeing what one looked like. How he typed, how he entered corrections . . . "

"So you took the manuscript from the shelf."

"Yes," the violinist agreed. "I went into the other room with it, opened the box, and flipped through the pages. You can taste the flavor of the man's work in the visual appearance of his manuscript pages. The words and phrases x'd out, the pencil notations, the crossovers, even the typographical errors. The computer age puts paid to all that, doesn't it? Imagine Chandler running Spel-Chek, or Hammett with justified margins." He sighed. "A few minutes with the script made me long to own one of Woolrich's. But not this one, for reasons I've already explained."

"You spent how long with the book?"

"Fifteen minutes at the most. Probably more like ten."

"And returned to this room?"

"Yes."

"And brought the manuscript with you?"

"Yes. I intended to return it to the shelf, but someone was standing in the way. It may have been you, Jon. It was someone tall, and you're the tallest person here." He turned to our client. "It wasn't you. But I think you may have been talking with Jon. Someone was, at any rate, and I'd have had to step between the two of you to put the box back, and that might have led to questions as to why I'd picked it up in the first place. So I put it down."

"Where?"

"On a table. That one, I think."

"It's not there now," Jon Corn-Wallace said.

"It's not," Haig agreed. "One of you took it from that table. I could, through an exhausting process of cross-questioning, establish who that person is. But it would save us all time if the person would simply recount what happened next."

There was a silence while they all looked at each other. "Well, I guess this is where I come in," Jayne Corn-Wallace said. "I was sitting in the red chair, where Phil Perigord is sitting now. And whoever I'd been talking to went to get another drink, and I looked around, and there it was on the table."

"The manuscript, madam?"

"Yes, but I didn't know that was what it was, not at first. I thought it was a finely bound limited edition. Because the manuscripts are all kept on that shelf, you know, and this one wasn't. And it hadn't been on the table a few minutes earlier, either. I knew that much. So I assumed it was a book someone had been leafing through, and I saw it was by Cornell Woolrich, and I didn't recognize the title, so I thought I'd try leafing through it myself."

"And you found it was a manuscript."

"Well, that didn't take too keen an eye, did it? I suppose I glanced at the first twenty pages, just riffled through them while the party went on around me. I stopped after a chapter or so. That was plenty."

"You didn't like what you read?"

"There were corrections," she said disdainfully. "Words and whole sentences crossed out, new words penciled in. I realize writers have to work that way, but when I read a book I like to believe it emerged from the writer's mind fully formed."

"Like Athena from the brow of What's-his-name," her husband said.

"Zeus. I don't want to know there was a writer at work, making decisions, putting words down and then changing them. I want to forget about the writer entirely and lose myself in the story."

"Everybody wants to forget about the writer," Philip Perigord said, helping himself to more eggnog. "At the Oscars each year some ninny intones, 'In the beginning was the Word,' before he hands out the screenwriting awards. And you hear the usual crap about how they owe it all to chaps like me who put words in their mouths. They say it, but nobody believes it. Jack Warner called us

33

schmucks with Underwoods. Well, we've come a long way. Now we're schmucks with Power Macs."

"Indeed," Haig said. "You looked at the manuscript, didn't you, Mr. Perigord?"

"I never read unpublished work. Can't risk leaving myself open to a plagiarism charge."

"Oh? But didn't you have a special interest in Woolrich? Didn't you once adapt a story of his?"

"How did you know about that? I was one of several who made a living off that particular piece of crap. It was never produced."

"And you looked at this manuscript in the hope that you might adapt it?"

The writer shook his head. "I'm through wasting myself out there."

"They're through with you," Harriet Quinlan said. "Nothing personal, Phil, but it's a town that uses up writers and throws them away. You couldn't get arrested out there. So you've come back East to write books."

"And you'll be representing him, madam?"

"I may, if he brings me something I can sell. I saw him paging through a manuscript and figured he was looking for something he could steal. Oh, don't look so outraged, Phil. Why not steal from Woolrich, for God's sake? He's not going to sue. He left everything to Columbia University, and you could knock off anything of his, published or unpublished, and they'd never know the difference. Ever since I saw you reading, I've been wondering. Did you come across anything worth stealing?"

"I don't steal," Perigord said. "Still, perfectly legitimate inspiration can result from a glance at another man's work—"

"I'll say it can. And did it?"

He shook his head. "If there was a strong idea anywhere in that manuscript, I couldn't find it in the few minutes I spent looking. What about you, Harriet? I know you had a look at it, because I saw you."

"I just wanted to see what it was you'd been so caught up in. And I wondered if the manuscript might be salvageable. One of my writers might be able to pull it off, and do a better job than the hack who finished *Into the Night*."

"Ah," Haig said. "And what did you determine, madam?"

"I didn't read enough to form a judgment. Anyway, *Into the Night* was no great commercial success, so why tag along in its wake?"

"So you put the manuscript . . . "

"Back in its box, and left it on the table where I'd found it."

Our client shook his head in wonder. *"Murder on the Orient Express,"* he said. "Or in the Calais coach, depending on whether you're English or American. It's beginning to look as though everyone read that manuscript. And I never noticed a thing!"

"Well, you were hitting the sauce pretty good," Jon Corn-Wallace reminded him. "And you were, uh, concentrating all your social energy in one direction."

"How's that?"

Corn-Wallace nodded toward Jeanne Botleigh, who was refilling someone's cup. "As far as you were concerned, our lovely caterer was the only person in the room."

There was an awkward silence, with our host coloring and his caterer lowering her eyes demurely. Haig broke it. "To continue," he said abruptly. "Miss Quinlan returned the manuscript to its box and to its place upon the table. Then—"

"But she didn't," Perigord said. "Harriet, I wanted another look at Woolrich. Maybe I'd missed something. But first I saw you reading it, and when I looked a second time it was gone. You weren't reading it and it wasn't on the table, either."

"I put it back," the agent said.

"But not where you found it," said Edward Everett Stokes. "You set it down not on the table but on that revolving bookcase."

"Did I? I suppose it's possible. But how did you know that?"

"Because I saw you," said the small-press publisher. "And because I wanted a look at the manuscript myself. I knew about it, including the fact that it was not restorable in the fashion of *Into the Night*. That made it valueless to a commercial publisher, but the idea of a Woolrich novel going unpublished ate away at me. I mean, we're talking about Cornell Woolrich."

"And you thought—"

"I thought, why not publish it as is, warts and all? I could do it, in an edition of two or three hundred copies, for collectors who'd happily accept inconsistencies and omissions for the sake of having something otherwise unobtainable. I wanted a few minutes' peace and quiet with the book, so I took it into the lavatory."

"And?"

"And I read it, or at least paged through it. I must have spent half an hour in there, or close to it."

"I remember you were gone awhile," Jon Corn-Wallace said. "I thought you'd headed on home."

"I thought he was in the other room," Jayne said, "cavorting on the pile of coats with Harriet here. But I guess that must have been someone else."

"It was Zoltan," the agent said, "and we were hardly cavorting."

"Kanoodling, then, but—"

"He was teaching me a yogic breathing technique, not that it's any of your business. Stokes, you took the manuscript into the john. I trust you brought it back?"

"Well, no."

"You took it home? You're the person responsible for its disappearance?"

"Certainly not. I didn't take it home, and I hope I'm not responsible for its disappearance. I left it in the lavatory."

"You just left it there?"

"In its box, on the shelf over the vanity. I set it down there while I washed my hands, and I'm afraid I forgot it. And no, it's not there now. I went and looked as soon as I realized what all this was about, and I'm afraid some other hands than mine must have moved it. I'll tell you this—when it does turn up, I definitely want to publish it."

"If it turns up," our client said darkly. "Once E. E. left it in the bathroom, anyone could have slipped it under his coat without being seen. And I'll probably never see it again."

"But that means one of us is a thief," somebody said.

"I know, and that's out of the question. You're all my friends. But we were all drinking last night, and drink can confuse a person. Suppose one of you did take it from the bathroom and carried it home as a joke, the kind of joke that can seem funny after a few drinks. If you could contrive to return it, perhaps in such a way that no one could know your identity . . . Haig, you ought to be able to work that out."

"I could," Haig agreed. "If that were how it happened. But it didn't."

"It didn't?"

"You forget the least obvious suspect."

"Me? Dammit, Haig, are you saying I stole my own manuscript?"

"I'm saying the butler did it," Haig said, "or the closest thing we have to a butler. Miss Botleigh, your upper lip has been trembling almost since we all sat down. You've been on the point of an admission throughout and haven't said a word. Have you in fact read the manuscript of *As Dark as It Gets*?"

"Yes."

The client gasped. "You have? When?"

"Last night."

"But—"

"I had to use the lavatory," she said, "and the book was there, although I could see it wasn't an ordinary bound book but pages in a box. I didn't think I would hurt it by looking at it. So I sat there and read the first two chapters."

"What did you think?" Haig asked her.

"It was very powerful. Parts of it were hard to follow, but the scenes were strong, and I got caught up in them."

"That's Woolrich," Jayne Corn-Wallace said. "He can grab you, all right."

"And then you took it with you when you went home," our client said. "You were so involved you couldn't bear to leave it unfinished, so you, uh, borrowed it." He reached to pat her hand. "Perfectly understandable," he said, "and perfectly innocent. You were going to bring it back once you'd finished it. So all this fuss has been over nothing."

"That's not what happened."

"It's not?"

"I read two chapters," she said, "and I thought I'd ask to borrow it some other time, or maybe not. But I put the pages back in the box and left them there."

"In the bathroom?"

"Yes."

"So you never did finish the book," our client said. "Well, if it ever turns up I'll be more than happy to lend it to you, but until then—"

"But perhaps Miss Botleigh has already finished the book," Haig suggested.

"How could she? She just told you she left it in the bathroom."

Haig said, "Miss Botleigh?"

"I finished the book," she said. "When everybody else went home, I stayed."

"My word," Zoltan Mihalyi said. "Woolrich never had a more devoted fan, or one half so beautiful."

"Not to finish the manuscript," she said, and turned to our host. "You asked me to stay," she said.

"I *wanted* you to stay," he agreed. "I wanted to *ask* you to stay. But I don't remember . . . "

"I guess you'd had quite a bit to drink," she said, "although you didn't show it. But you asked me to stay, and I'd been hoping you would ask me, because I wanted to stay."

"You must have had rather a lot to drink yourself," Harriet Quinlan murmured.

"Not that much," said the caterer. "I wanted to stay because he's a very attractive man."

Our client positively glowed, then turned red with embarrassment. "I knew I had a hole in my memory," he said, "but I didn't think anything significant could have fallen through it. So you actually stayed? God. What, uh, happened?"

"We went upstairs," Jeanne Botleigh said. "And we went to the bedroom, and we went to bed."

"Indeed," said Haig.

"And it was . . . "

"Quite wonderful," she said.

"And I don't remember. I think I'm going to kill myself."

"Not on Christmas Day," E. E. Stokes said. "And not with a mystery still

37

unsolved. Haig, what became of the bloody manuscript?"

"Miss Botleigh?"

She looked at our host, then lowered her eyes. "You went to sleep afterward," she said, "and I felt entirely energized, and knew I couldn't sleep, and I thought I'd read for a while. And I remembered the manuscript, so I came down here and fetched it."

"And read it?"

"In bed. I thought you might wake up, in fact I was hoping you would. But you didn't."

"Damn it," our client said, with feeling.

"So I finished the manuscript and still didn't feel sleepy. And I got dressed and let myself out and went home."

There was a silence, broken at length by Zoltan Mihalyi, offering our client congratulations on his triumph and sympathy for the memory loss. "When you write your memoirs," he said, "you'll have to leave that chapter blank."

"Or have someone ghost it for you," Philip Perigord offered.

"The manuscript," Stokes said. "What became of it?"

"I don't know," the caterer said. "I finished it—"

"Which is more than Woolrich could say," Jayne Corn-Wallace said.

"—and I left it there."

"There?"

"In its box. On the bedside table, where you'd be sure to find it first thing in the morning. But I guess you didn't."

"The manuscript? Haig, you're telling me you want the *manuscript?*"

"You find my fee excessive?"

"But it wasn't even lost. No one took it. It was next to my bed. I'd have found it sooner or later."

"But you didn't," Haig said. "Not until you'd cost me and my young associate the better part of our holiday. You've been reading mysteries all your life. Now you got to see one solved in front of you, and in your own magnificent library."

He brightened. "It is a nice room, isn't it?"

"It's first-rate."

"Thanks. But Haig, listen to reason. You did solve the puzzle and recover the manuscript, but now you're demanding what you recovered as compensation. That's like rescuing a kidnap victim and insisting on adopting the child yourself."

"Nonsense. It's nothing like that."

"All right, then it's like recovering stolen jewels and demanding the jewels themselves as reward. It's just plain disproportionate. I hired you because I wanted the manuscript in my collection, and now you expect to wind up with it in your collection."

It did sound a little weird to me, but I kept my mouth shut. Haig had the ball, and I wanted to see where he'd go with it.

He put his fingertips together. "In *Black Orchids,*" he said, "Wolfe's client was his friend Lewis Hewitt. As recompense for his work, Wolfe insisted on all of the black orchid plants Hewitt had bred. Not one. All of them."

"That always seemed greedy to me."

"If we were speaking of fish," Haig went on, "I might be similarly inclined. But books are of use to me only as reading material. I want to read that book, sir, and I want to have it close to hand if I need to refer to it." He shrugged. "But I don't need the original that you prize so highly. Make me a copy."

"A copy?"

"Indeed. Have the manuscript photocopied."

"You'd be content with a . . . a copy?"

"And a credit," I said quickly, before Haig could give away the store. We'd put in a full day, and he ought to get more than a few hours' reading out of it. "A two-thousand-dollar store credit," I added, "which Mr. Haig can use up as he sees fit."

"Buying paperbacks and book-club editions," our client said. "It should last you for years." He heaved a sigh. "A photocopy and a store credit. Well, if that makes you happy . . . "

And that pretty much wrapped it up. I ran straight home and sat down at the typewriter, and if the story seems a little hurried it's because I was in a rush when I wrote it. See, our client tried for a second date with Jeanne Botleigh, to refresh his memory, I suppose, but a woman tends to feel less than flattered when you forget having gone to bed with her, and she wasn't having any.

So I called her the minute I got home, and we talked about this and that, and we've got a date in an hour and a half. I'll tell you this much, if I get lucky, I'll remember. So wish me luck, huh?

And, by the way . . .

Merry Christmas!

John Mortimer

RUMPOLE AND THE SPIRIT OF CHRISTMAS

I realized that Christmas was upon us when I saw a sprig of holly over the list of prisoners hung on the wall of the cells under the Old Bailey.

I pulled out a new box of small cigars and found its opening obstructed by a tinseled band on which a scarlet-faced Santa was seen hurrying a sleigh full of carcinoma-packed goodies to the Rejoicing World. I lit one as the lethargic screw, with a complexion the color of faded Bronco, regretfully left his doorstep sandwich and mug of sweet tea to unlock the gate.

"Good morning, Mr. Rumpole. Come to visit a customer?"

"Happy Christmas, officer," I said as cheerfully as possible. "Is Mr. Timson at home?"

"Well, I don't believe he's slipped down to his little place in the country."

Such were the pleasantries that were exchanged between us legal hacks and discontented screws; jokes that no doubt have changed little since the turnkeys unlocked the door at Newgate to let in a pessimistic advocate, or the cells under the Coliseum were opened to admit the unwelcome news of the Imperial thumbs-down.

"My mum wants me home for Christmas."

Which Christmas? It would have been an unreasonable remark and I refrained from it. Instead, I said, "All things are possible."

As I sat in the interviewing room, an Old Bailey hack of some considerable experience, looking through my brief and inadvertently using my waistcoat as an ashtray, I hoped I wasn't on another loser. I had had a run of bad luck during that autumn season, and young Edward Timson was part of that huge south London family whose criminal activities provided such welcome grist to the Rumpole mill. The charge in the seventeen-year-old Eddie's case was nothing less than wilful murder.

"We're in with a chance, though, Mr. Rumpole, ain't we?"

Like all his family, young Timson was a confirmed optimist. And yet, of course, the merest outsider in the Grand National, the hundred-to-one shot, is in with a chance, and nothing is more like going round the course at Aintree than living through a murder trial. In this particular case, a fanatical prosecutor named Wrigglesworth, known to me as the Mad Monk, was to represent Beechers, and Mr. Justice Vosper, a bright but wintry-hearted judge who always felt it his duty to lead for the prosecution, was to play the part of a particularly menacing fence at the Canal Turn.

"A chance. Well, yes, of course you've got a chance, if they can't establish common purpose, and no one knows which of you bright lads had the weapon."

No doubt the time had come for a brief glance at the prosecution case, not an entirely cheering prospect. Eddie, also known as "Turpin" Timson, lived in a kind of decaying barracks, a sort of highrise Lubianka, known as Keir Hardie Court, somewhere in south London, together with his parents, his various brothers, and his thirteen-year-old sister, Noreen. This particular branch of the Timson family lived on the thirteenth floor. Below them, on the twelfth, lived the large clan of the O'Dowds. The war between the Timsons and the O'Dowds began, it seems, with the casting of the Nativity play at the local comprehensive school.

Christmas comes earlier each year and the school show was planned about September. When Bridget O'Dowd was chosen to play the lead in the face of strong competition from Noreen Timson, an incident occurred comparable in historical importance to the assassination of an obscure Austrian archduke at Sarejevo. Noreen Timson announced in the playground that Bridget O'Dowd was a spotty little tart unsuited to play any role of which the most notable characteristic was virginity.

Hearing this, Bridget O'Dowd kicked Noreen Timson behind the anthracite bunkers. Within a few days, war was declared between the Timson and O'Dowd children, and a present of lit fireworks was posted through the O'Dowd front door. On what is known as the "night in question," reinforcements of O'Dowds and Timsons arrived in old bangers from a number of south London addresses and battle was joined on the stone staircase, a bleak terrain of peeling walls scrawled with graffiti, blowing empty Coca-cola tins and torn newspapers. The weapons seemed to have been articles in general domestic use, such as bread knives, carving knives, broom handles, and a heavy screwdriver. At the end of the day it appeared that the upstairs flat had repelled the invaders, and Kevin O'Dowd lay on the stairs. Having been stabbed with a slender and pointed blade, he was in a condition to become known as "the deceased" in the case of the Queen against Edward Timson. I made an application for bail for my client which was refused, but a speedy trial was ordered.

So even as Bridget O'Dowd was giving her Virgin Mary at the comprehensive, the rest of the family was waiting to give evidence against Eddie Timson in that home of British drama, Number One Court at the Old Bailey.

"I never had no cutter, Mr. Rumpole. Straight up, I never had one," the defendant told me in the cells. He was an appealing-looking lad with soft brown eyes, who had already won the heart of the highly susceptible lady who wrote his social inquiry report. ("Although the charge is a serious one, this is a young man who might respond well to a period of probation." I could imagine the steely contempt in Mr. Justice Vosper's eye when he read that.)

"Well, tell me, Edward. Who had?"

"I never seen no cutters on no one, honest I didn't. We wasn't none of us tooled up, Mr. Rumpole."

"Come on, Eddie. Someone must have been. They say even young Noreen was brandishing a potato peeler."

"Not me, honest."

"What about your sword?"

There was one part of the prosecution evidence that I found particularly distasteful. It was agreed that on the previous Sunday morning, Eddie "Turpin" Timson had appeared on the stairs of Keir Hardie Court and flourished what appeared to be an antique cavalry saber at the assembled O'Dowds, who were just popping out to Mass.

"Me sword I bought up the Portobello? I didn't have that there, honest."

"The prosecution can't introduce evidence about the sword. It was an entirely different occasion." Mr. Barnard, my instructing solicitor who fancied himself as an infallible lawyer, spoke with a confidence which I couldn't feel. He, after all, wouldn't have to stand up on his hind legs and argue the legal toss with Mr. Justice Vosper.

"It rather depends on who's prosecuting us. I mean, if it's some fairly reasonable fellow—"

"I think," Mr. Barnard reminded me, shattering my faint optimism and ensuring that we were all in for a very rough Christmas indeed, "I think it's Mr. Wrigglesworth. Will he try to introduce the sword?"

I looked at "Turpin" Timson with a kind of pity. "If it is the Mad Monk, he undoubtedly will."

When I went into Court, Basil Wrigglesworth was standing with his shoulders hunched up round his large, red ears, his gown dropped to his elbows, his bony wrists protruding from the sleeves of his frayed jacket, his wig pushed back, and his huge hands joined on his lectern in what seemed to be an attitude of devoted prayer. A lump of cotton wool clung to his chin where he had cut himself shaving. Although well into his sixties, he preserved a look of boyish clumsiness. He appeared, as he always did when about to prosecute on a charge carrying a major punishment, radiantly happy.

"Ah, Rumpole," he said, lifting his eyes from the police verbals as though they were his breviary. "Are you defending *as usual?*"

"Yes, Wrigglesworth. And you're prosecuting *as usual?*" It wasn't much of a riposte but it was all I could think of at the time.

"Of course, I don't defend. One doesn't like to call witnesses who may not be telling the truth."

"You must have a few unhappy moments then, calling certain members of the Constabulary."

"I can honestly tell you, Rumpole—" his curiously innocent blue eyes looked at me with a sort of pain, as though I had questioned the doctrine of the immaculate conception "—I have never called a dishonest policeman."

"Yours must be a singularly simple faith, Wrigglesworth."

"As for the Detective Inspector in this case," counsel for the prosecution went on, "I've known Wainwright for years. In fact, this is his last trial before he retires. He could no more invent a verbal against a defendant than fly."

Any more on that tack, I thought, and we should soon be debating how many angels could dance on the point of a pin.

"Look here, Wrigglesworth. That evidence about my client having a sword: it's quite irrelevant. I'm sure you'd agree."

"Why is it irrelevant?" Wrigglesworth frowned.

"Because the murder clearly wasn't done with an antique cavalry saber. It was done with a small, thin blade."

"If he's a man who carries weapons, why isn't that relevant?"

"A man? Why do you call him a man? He's a child. A boy of seventeen!"

"Man enough to commit a serious crime."

"*If* he did."

"If he didn't, he'd hardly be in the dock."

"That's the difference between us, Wrigglesworth," I told him. "I believe in the presumption of innocence. You believe in original sin. Look here, old darling." I tried to give the Mad Monk a smile of friendship and became conscious of the fact that it looked, no doubt, like an ingratiating sneer. "Give us a chance. You won't introduce the evidence of the sword, will you?"

"Why ever not?"

"Well," I told him, "the Timsons are an industrious family of criminals. They work hard, they never go on strike. If it weren't for people like the Timsons, you and I would be out of a job."

"They sound in great need of prosecution and punishment. Why shouldn't I tell the jury about your client's sword? Can you give me one good reason?"

"Yes," I said, as convincingly as possible.

"What is it?" He peered at me, I thought, unfairly.

"Well, after all," I said, doing my best, "it is Christmas."

It would be idle to pretend that the first day in Court went well, although Wrigglesworth restrained himself from mentioning the sword in his opening speech, and told me that he was considering whether or not to call evidence about it the next day. I cross-examined a few members of the clan O'Dowd on the presence of lethal articles in the hands of the attacking force. The evidence about this varied, and weapons came and went in the hands of the inhabitants of Number Twelve as the witnesses were blown hither and thither in the winds of Rumpole's cross-examination. An interested observer from one of the other flats spoke of having seen a machete.

"Could that terrible weapon have been in the hands of Mr. Kevin O'Dowd, the deceased in this case?"

"I don't think so."

"But can you rule out the possibility?"

"No, I can't rule it out," the witness admitted, to my temporary delight.

"You can never rule out the possibility of anything in this world, Mr. Rumpole. But he doesn't think so. You have your answer."

Mr. Justice Vosper, in a voice like a splintering iceberg, gave me this unwelcome Christmas present. The case wasn't going well, but at least, by the end of the first day, the Mad Monk had kept out all mention of the sword. The next day he was to call young Bridget O'Dowd, fresh from her triumph in the Nativity play.

"I say, Rumpole, I'd be *so* grateful for a little help."

I was in Pommeroy's Wine Bar, drowning the sorrows of the day in my usual bottle of the cheapest Chateau Fleet Street (made from grapes which, judging from the bouquet, might have been not so much trodden as kicked to death by sturdy peasants in gum boots) when I looked up to see Wrigglesworth, dressed in an old mackintosh, doing business with Jack Pommeroy at the sales counter. When I crossed to him, he was not buying the jumbo-sized bottle of ginger beer which I imagined might be his celebratory Christmas tipple, but a tempting and respectably aged bottle of Chateau Pichon Longueville.

"What can I do for you, Wrigglesworth?"

"Well, as you know, Rumpole, I live in Croydon."

"Happiness is given to few of us on this earth," I said piously.

"And the Anglican Sisters of St. Agnes, Croydon, are anxious to buy a present for their Bishop," Wrigglesworth explained. "A dozen bottles for Christmas. They've asked my advice, Rumpole. I know so little about wine. You wouldn't care to try this for me? I mean, if you're not especially busy."

"I should be hurrying home to dinner." My wife, Hilda (She Who Must Be Obeyed), was laying on rissoles and frozen peas, washed down by my last bottle of Pommeroy's extremely ordinary. "However, as it's Christmas, I don't mind helping you out, Wrigglesworth."

The Mad Monk was clearly quite unused to wine. As we sampled the claret together, I saw the chance of getting him to commit himself on the vital question of the evidence of the sword, as well as absorbing an unusually decent bottle. After the Pichon Longueville I was kind enough to help him by sampling a Boyd-Cantenac and then I said, "Excellent, this. But of course the Bishop might be a burgundy man. The nuns might care to invest in a decent Macon."

"Shall we try a bottle?" Wrigglesworth suggested. "I'd be grateful for your advice."

"I'll do my best to help you, my old darling. And while we're on the subject, that ridiculous bit of evidence about young Timson and the sword—"

"I remember you saying I shouldn't bring that out because it's Christmas."

"Exactly." Jack Pommeroy had uncorked the Macon and it was mingling with the claret to produce a feeling of peace and goodwill towards men. Wrigglesworth frowned, as though trying to absorb an obscure point of theology.

"I don't quite see the relevance of Christmas to the question of your man Timson threatening his neighbors with a sword."

"Surely, Wrigglesworth—" I knew my prosecutor well "—you're of a religious disposition?" The Mad Monk was the product of some bleak northern Catholic boarding school. He lived alone, and no doubt wore a hair shirt under his black waistcoat and was vowed to celibacy. The fact that he had his nose deep into a glass of burgundy at the moment was due to the benign influence of Rumpole.

"I'm a Christian, yes."

"Then practice a little Christian tolerance."

"Tolerance towards evil?"

"Evil?" I asked. "What do you mean, evil?"

"Couldn't that be your trouble, Rumpole? That you really don't recognize evil when you see it."

"I suppose," I said, "evil might be locking up a seventeen-year-old during Her Majesty's pleasure, when Her Majesty may very probably forget all about him, banging him up with a couple of hard and violent cases and their own chamber-pots for twenty-two hours a day, so he won't come out till he's a real, genuine, middle-aged murderer."

"I did hear the Reverend Mother say—" Wrigglesworth was gazing vacantly at the empty Macon bottle "—that the Bishop likes his glass of port."

"Then in the spirit of Christmas tolerance I'll help you to sample some of Pommeroy's Light and Tawny."

A little later, Wrigglesworth held up his port glass in a reverent sort of fashion.

"You're suggesting, are you, that I should make some special concession in this case because it's Christmastime?"

"Look here, old darling." I absorbed half my glass, relishing the gentle fruitiness and the slight tang of wood. "If you spent your whole life in that highrise hell-hole called Keir Hardie Court, if you had no fat prosecutions to occupy your attention and no prospect of any job at all, if you had no sort of occupation except war with the O'Dowds—"

"My own flat isn't particularly comfortable. I don't know a great deal about *your* home life, Rumpole, but you don't seem to be in a tearing hurry to experience it."

"Touché, Wrigglesworth, my old darling." I ordered us a couple of refills of Pommeroy's port to further postpone the encounter with She Who Must Be Obeyed and her rissoles.

"But we don't have to fight to the death on the staircase," Wrigglesworth pointed out.

"We don't have to fight at all, Wrigglesworth."

"As your client did. "

"As my client *may* have done. Remember the presumption of innocence."

"This is rather funny, this is." The prosecutor pulled back his lips to reveal strong, yellowish teeth and laughed appreciatively. "You know why your man Timson is called 'Turpin' ?"

"No." I drank port uneasily, fearing an unwelcome revelation.

"Because he's always fighting with that sword of his. He's called after Dick Turpin, you see, who's always dueling on television. Do you watch television, Rumpole?"

"Hardly at all."

"I watch a great deal of television, as I'm alone rather a lot." Wrigglesworth referred to the box as though it were a sort of penance, like fasting or flagellation. "Detective Inspector Wainwright told me about your client. Rather amusing, I thought it was. He's retiring this Christmas."

"My client?"

"No. D.I. Wainwright. Do you think we should settle on this port for the

Bishop? Or would you like to try a glass of something else?"

"Christmas," I told Wrigglesworth severely as we sampled the Cockburn, "is not just a material, pagan celebration. It's not just an occasion for absorbing superior vintages, old darling. It must be a time when you try to do good, spiritual good to our enemies."

"To your client, you mean?"

"And to me."

"To you, Rumpole?"

"For God's sake, Wrigglesworth!" I was conscious of the fact that my appeal was growing desperate. "I've had six losers in a row down the Old Bailey. Can't I be included in any Christmas spirit that's going around?"

"You mean, at Christmas especially it is more blessed to give than to receive?"

"I mean exactly that." I was glad that he seemed, at last, to be following my drift.

"And you think I might give this case to someone, like a Christmas present?"

"If you care to put it that way, yes."

"I do not care to put it in *exactly* that way." He turned his pale-blue eyes on me with what I thought was genuine sympathy. "But I shall try and do the case of R. *v*. Timson in the way most appropriate to the greatest feast of the Christian year. It is a time, I quite agree, for the giving of presents."

When they finally threw us out of Pommeroy's, and after we had considered the possibility of buying the Bishop brandy in the Cock Tavern, and even beer in the Devereux, I let my instinct, like an aged horse, carry me on to the Underground and home to Gloucester Road, and there discovered the rissoles, like some traces of a vanished civilization, fossilized in the oven. She Who Must Be Obeyed was already in bed, feigning sleep. When I climbed in beside her, she opened a hostile eye.

"You're drunk, Rumpole!" she said. "What on earth have you been doing?"

"I've been having a legal discussion," I told her, "on the subject of the admissibility of certain evidence. Vital, from my client's point of view. And, just for a change, Hilda, I think I've won."

"Well, you'd better try and get some sleep." And she added with a sort of satisfaction, "I'm sure you'll be feeling quite terrible in the morning."

As with all the grimmer predictions of She Who Must Be Obeyed, this one turned out to be true. I sat in the Court the next day with the wig feeling like a lead weight on the brain and the stiff collar sawing the neck like a blunt execution. My mouth tasted of matured birdcage and from a long way off I heard Wrigglesworth say to Bridget O'Dowd, who stood looking particularly saintly and virginal in the witness box, "About a week before this, did you see the defendant, Edward Timson, on your staircase flourishing any sort of weapon?"

It is no exaggeration to say that I felt deeply shocked and considerably betrayed. After his promise to me, Wrigglesworth had turned his back on the spirit of the great Christmas festival. He came not to bring peace but a sword.

I clambered with some difficulty to my feet. After my forensic efforts of the evening before, I was scarcely in the mood for a legal argument. Mr. Justice Vosper looked up in surprise and greeted me in his usual chilly fashion.

"Yes, Mr. Rumpole. Do you object to this evidence?"

Of course I object, I wanted to say. It's inhuman, unnecessary, unmerciful, and likely to lead to my losing another case. Also, it's clearly contrary to a solemn and binding contract entered into after a number of glasses of the Bishop's putative port. All I seemed to manage was a strangled, "Yes."

"I suppose Mr. Wrigglesworth would say—" Vosper, J., was, as ever, anxious to supply any argument that might not yet have occurred to the prosecution "—that it is evidence of 'system.' "

"System?" I heard my voice faintly and from a long way off. "It may be, I suppose. But the Court has a discretion to omit evidence which may be irrelevant and purely prejudicial."

"I feel sure Mr. Wrigglesworth has considered the matter most carefully and that he would not lead this evidence unless he considered it entirely relevant."

I looked at the Mad Monk on the seat beside me. He was smiling at me with a mixture of hearty cheerfulness and supreme pity, as though I were sinking rapidly and he had come to administer extreme unction. I made a few ill-chosen remarks to the Court, but I was in no condition, that morning, to enter into a complicated legal argument on the admissibility of evidence.

It wasn't long before Bridget O'Dowd had told a deeply disapproving jury all about Eddie "Turpin" Timson's sword. "A man," the judge said later in his summing up about young Edward, "clearly prepared to attack with cold steel whenever it suited him."

When the trial was over, I called in for refreshment at my favorite watering hole and there, to my surprise, was my opponent Wrigglesworth, sharing an expensive-looking bottle with Detective Inspector Wainwright, the officer in charge of the case. I stood at the bar, absorbing a consoling glass of Pommeroy's ordinary, when the D.I. came up to the bar for cigarettes. He gave me a friendly and maddeningly sympathetic smile.

"Sorry about that, sir. Still, win a few, lose a few. Isn't that it?"

"In my case lately, it's been win a few, lose a lot!"

"You couldn't have this one, sir. You see, Mr. Wrigglesworth had promised it to me."

"He had *what?*"

"Well, I'm retiring, as you know. And Mr. Wrigglesworth promised me faithfully that my last case would be a win. He promised me that, in a manner of speaking, as a Christmas present. Great man is our Mr. Wrigglesworth, sir, for the spirit of Christmas."

I looked across at the Mad Monk and a terrible suspicion entered my head. What was all that about a present for the Bishop? I searched my memory and I could find no trace of our having, in fact, bought wine for any sort of cleric. And was Wrigglesworth as inexperienced as he would have had me believe in the art of selecting claret?

As I watched him pour and sniff a glass from his superior bottle and hold it critically to the light, a horrible suspicion crossed my mind. Had the whole evening's events been nothing but a deception, a sinister attempt to nobble Rumpole, to present him with such a stupendous hangover that he would stumble in his legal argument? Was it all in aid of D.I. Wainwright's Christmas present?

I looked at Wrigglesworth, and it would be no exaggeration to say the mind boggled. He was, of course, perfectly right about me. I just didn't recognize evil when I saw it.

John D. MacDonald

DEAD ON
CHRISTMAS STREET

The police in the first prowl car on the scene got out a tarpaulin. A traffic policeman threw it over the body and herded the crowd back. They moved uneasily in the gray slush. Some of them looked up from time to time.

In the newspaper picture the window would be marked with a bold X. A dotted line would descend from the X to the spot where the covered body now lay. Some of the spectators, laden with tinsel- and evergreen-decorated packages, turned away, suppressing a nameless guilt.

But the curious stayed on. Across the street, in the window of a department store, a vast mechanical Santa rocked back and forth, slapping a mechanical hand against a padded thigh, roaring forever, "Whaw haw ho ho ho. Whaw haw ho ho ho." The slapping hand had worn the red plush from the padded thigh.

The ambulance arrived, with a brisk intern to make out the DOA. Sawdust was shoveled onto the sidewalk, then pushed off into the sewer drain. Wet snow fell into the city. And there was nothing else to see. The corner Santa, a leathery man with a pinched, blue nose, began to ring his hand bell again.

Daniel Fowler, one of the young Assistant District Attorneys, was at his desk when the call came through from Lieutenant Shinn of the Detective Squad. "Dan? This is Gil. You heard about the Garrity girl yet?"

For a moment the name meant nothing, and then suddenly he remembered: Loreen Garrity was the witness in the Sheridan City Loan Company case. She had made positive identification of two of the three kids who had tried to pull that holdup, and the case was on the calendar for February. Provided the kids didn't confess before it came up, Dan was going to prosecute. He had the Garrity girl's statement, and her promise to appear.

"What about her, Gil?" he asked.

"She took a high dive out of her office window—about an hour ago. Seventeen stories, and right into the Christmas rush. How come she didn't land on somebody, we'll never know. Connie Wyant is handling it. He remembered she figured in the loan-company deal, and he told me. Look, Dan. She was a big girl, and she tried hard not to go out that window. She was shoved. That's how come Connie has it. Nice Christmas present for him."

"Nice Christmas present for the lads who pushed over the loan company, too," Dan said grimly. "Without her there's no case. Tell Connie that. It ought to give him the right line."

Dan Fowler set aside the brief he was working on and walked down the hall. The District Attorney's secretary was at her desk. "Boss busy, Jane?"

She was a small girl with wide, gray eyes, a mass of dark hair, a soft mouth. She raised one eyebrow and looked at him speculatively. "I could be bribed, you know."

He looked around with exaggerated caution, went around her desk on tiptoe, bent and kissed her upraised lips. He smiled down at her. "People are beginning to talk," he whispered, not getting it as light as he meant it to be.

She tilted her head to one side, frowned, and said, "What is it, Dan?"

He sat on the corner of her desk and took her hands in his, and he told her about the big, dark-haired, swaggering woman who had gone out the window. He knew Jane would want to know. He had regretted bringing Jane in on the case, but he had had the unhappy hunch that Garrity might sell out, if the offer was high enough. And so he had enlisted Jane, depending on her intuition. He had taken the two of them to lunch, and had invented an excuse to duck out and leave them alone.

Afterward, Jane had said, "I guess I don't really like her, Dan. She was suspicious of me, of course, and she's a terribly vital sort of person. But I would say that she'll be willing to testify. And I don't think she'll sell out."

Now as he told her about the girl, he saw the sudden tears of sympathy in her gray eyes. "Oh, Dan! How dreadful! You'd better tell the boss right away. That Vince Servius must have hired somebody to do it."

"Easy, lady," he said softly.

He touched her dark hair with his fingertips, smiled at her, and crossed to the door of the inner office, opened it and went in.

Jim Heglon, the District Attorney, was a narrow-faced man with glasses that had heavy frames. He had a professional look, a dry wit, and a driving energy.

"Every time I see you, Dan, I have to conceal my annoyance," Heglon said. "You're going to cart away the best secretary I ever had."

"Maybe I'll keep her working for a while. Keep her out of trouble."

"Excellent! And speaking of trouble—"

"Does it show, Jim?" Dan sat on the arm of a heavy leather chair which faced Heglon's desk. "I do have some. Remember the Sheridan City Loan case?"

"Vaguely. Give me an outline."

"October. Five o'clock one afternoon, just as the loan office was closing. Three punks tried to knock it over. Two of them, Castrella and Kelly, are eighteen. The leader, Johnny Servius, is nineteen. Johnny is Vince Servius's kid brother.

"They went into the loan company wearing masks and waving guns. The manager had more guts than sense. He was loading the safe. He saw them and slammed the door and spun the knob. They beat on him, but he convinced them it was a time lock, which it wasn't. They took fifteen dollars out of his pants, and four dollars from the girl behind the counter and took off.

"Right across the hall is the office of an accountant named Thomas Kistner. He'd already left. His secretary, Loreen Garrity, was closing up the office. She had the door open a crack. She saw the three kids come out of the loan company, taking their masks off. Fortunately, they didn't see her.

"She went to headquarters and looked at the gallery, and picked out Servius and Castrella. They were picked up. Kelly was with them, so they took him in, too. In the lineup the Garrity girl made a positive identification of Servius and Castrella again. The manager thought he could recognize Kelly's voice.

"Bail was set high, because we expected Vince Servius would get them out. Much to everybody's surprise, he's left them in there. The only thing he did was line up George Terrafierro to defend them, which makes it tough from our point of view, but not too tough—if we could put the Garrity girl on the stand. She was the type to make a good witness. Very positive sort of girl."

"Was? Past tense?"

"This afternoon she was pushed out the window of the office where she works. Seventeen stories above the sidewalk. Gil Shinn tells me that Connie Wyant has it definitely tagged as homicide."

"If Connie says it is, then it is. What would conviction have meant to the three lads?"

"Servius had one previous conviction—car theft; Castrella had one conviction for assault with a deadly weapon. Kelly is clean, Jim."

Heglon frowned. "Odd, isn't it? In this state, armed robbery has a mandatory sentence of seven to fifteen years for a first offense in that category. With the weight Vince can swing, his kid brother would do about five years. Murder seems a little extreme as a way of avoiding a five-year sentence."

"Perhaps, Jim, the answer is in the relationship between Vince and the kid. There's quite a difference in ages. Vince must be nearly forty. He was in the big time early enough to give Johnny all the breaks. The kid has been thrown out of three good schools I know of. According to Vince, Johnny can do no wrong. Maybe that's why he left those three in jail awaiting trial—to keep them in the clear on this killing."

"It could be, Dan," Heglon said. "Go ahead with your investigation. And let me know."

Dan Fowler found out at the desk that Lieutenant Connie Wyant and Sergeant Levandowski were in the Interrogation Room. Dan sat down and waited.

After a few moments Connie waddled through the doorway and came over to him. He had bulging blue eyes and a dull expression.

Dan stood up, towering over the squat lieutenant. "Well, what's the picture, Connie?"

"No case against the kids, Gil says. Me, I wish it was just somebody thought it would be nice to jump out a window. But she grabbed the casing so hard, she broke her fingernails down to the quick.

"Marks you can see, in oak as hard as iron. Banged her head on the sill and left black hair on the rough edge of the casing. Lab matched it up. And one shoe up there, under the radiator. The radiator sits right in front of the window. Come listen to Kistner."

Dan followed him back to the Interrogation Room. Thomas Kistner sat at one side of the long table. A cigar lay dead on the glass ashtray near his elbow. As they opened the door, he glanced up quickly. He was a big, bloated man with an unhealthy grayish complexion and an important manner.

He said, "I was just telling the sergeant the tribulations of an accountant."

"We all got troubles," Connie said. "This is Mr. Fowler from the D.A.'s office, Kistner."

Mr. Kistner got up laboriously. "Happy to meet you, sir," he said. "Sorry that it has to be such an unpleasant occasion, however."

Connie sat down heavily. "Kistner, I want you to go through your story again. If it makes it easier, tell it to Mr. Fowler instead of me. He hasn't heard it before."

"I'll do anything in my power to help, Lieutenant," Kistner said firmly. He turned toward Dan. "I am out of my office a great deal. I do accounting on a contract basis for thirty-three small retail establishments. I visit them frequently.

"When Loreen came in this morning, she seemed nervous. I asked her what the trouble was, and she said that she felt quite sure somebody had been following her for the past week.

"She described him to me. Slim, middle height, pearl-gray felt hat, tan

53

raglan topcoat, swarthy complexion. I told her that because she was the witness in a trial coming up, she should maybe report it to the police and ask for protection. She said she didn't like the idea of yelling for help. She was a very—ah—independent sort of girl."

"I got that impression," Dan said.

"I went out then and didn't think anything more about what she'd said. I spent most of the morning at Finch Pharmacy, on the north side. I had a sandwich there and then drove back to the office, later than usual. Nearly two.

"I came up to the seventeenth floor. Going down the corridor, I pass the Men's Room before I get to my office. I unlocked the door with my key and went in. I was in there maybe three minutes.

"I came out and a man brushes by me in the corridor. He had his collar up, and was pulling down on his hatbrim and walking fast. At the moment, you understand, it meant nothing to me.

"I went into the office. The window was wide open, and the snow was blowing in. No Loreen. I couldn't figure it. I thought she'd gone to the Ladies' Room and had left the window open for some crazy reason. I started to shut it, and then I heard all the screaming down in the street.

"I leaned out. I saw her, right under me, sprawled on the sidewalk. I recognized the cocoa-colored suit. A new suit, I think. I stood in a state of shock, I guess, and then suddenly I remembered about the man following her, and I remembered the man in the hall—he had a gray hat and a tan topcoat, and I had the impression he was swarthy-faced.

"The first thing I did was call the police, naturally. While they were on the way, I called my wife. It just about broke her up. We were both fond of Loreen."

The big man smiled sadly. "And it seems to me I've been telling the story over and over again ever since. Oh, I don't mind, you understand. But it's a dreadful thing. The way I see it, when a person witnesses a crime, they ought to be given police protection until the trial is all over."

"We don't have that many cops," Connie said glumly. "How big was the man you saw in the corridor?"

"Medium size. A little on the thin side."

"How old?"

"I don't know. Twenty-five, forty-five. I couldn't see his face, and you understand I wasn't looking closely."

Connie turned toward Dan. "Nothing from the elevator boys about this guy. He probably took the stairs. The lobby is too busy for anybody to notice him coming through by way of the fire door. Did the Garrity girl ever lock herself in the office, Kistner?"

"I never knew of her doing that, Lieutenant."

Connie said, "Okay, so the guy could breeze in and clip her one. Then, from the way the rug was pulled up, he lugged her across to the window. She came to as he was trying to work her out the window, and she put up a battle. People in the office three stories underneath say she was screaming as she went by."

"How about the offices across the way?" Dan asked.

"It's a wide street, Dan, and they couldn't see through the snow. It started snowing hard about fifteen minutes before she was pushed out the window. I think the killer waited for that snow. It gave him a curtain to hide behind."

"Any chance that she marked the killer, Connie?" Dan asked.

"Doubt it. From the marks of her fingernails, he lifted her up and slid her feet out first, so her back was to him. She grabbed the sill on each side. Her head hit the window sash. All he had to do was hold her shoulders, and bang her in the small of the back with his knee. Once her fanny slid off the sill, she couldn't hold on with her hands any longer. And from the looks of the doorknobs, he wore gloves."

Dan turned to Kistner. "What was her home situation? I tried to question her. She was pretty evasive."

Kistner shrugged. "Big family. She didn't get along with them. Seven girls, I think, and she was next to oldest. She moved out when she got her first job. She lived alone in a one-room apartment on Leeds Avenue, near the bridge."

"You know of any boyfriend?" Connie asked.

"Nobody special. She used to go out a lot, but nobody special."

Connie rapped his knuckles on the edge of the table. "You ever make a pass at her, Kistner?"

The room was silent. Kistner stared at his dead cigar. "I don't want to lie to you, but I don't want any trouble at home, either. I got a boy in the Army, and I got a girl in her last year of high. But you work in a small office alone with a girl like Loreen, and it can get you.

"About six months ago I had to go to the state Capital on a tax thing. I asked her to come along. She did. It was a damn fool thing to do. And it— didn't work out so good. We agreed to forget it ever happened.

"We were awkward around the office for a couple of weeks, and then I guess we sort of forgot. She was a good worker, and I was paying her well, so it was to both our advantages to be practical and not get emotional. I didn't have to tell you men this, but, like I said, I don't see any point in lying to the police. Hell, you might have found out some way, and that might make it look like I killed her or something."

"Thanks for leveling," Connie said expressionlessly. "We'll call you if we need you."

Kistner ceremoniously shook hands all around and left with obvious relief.

As soon as the door shut behind him, Connie said, "I'll buy it. A long time ago I learned you can't jail a guy for being a jerk. Funny how many honest people I meet I don't like at all, and how many thieves make good guys to knock over a beer with. How's your girl?"

Dan looked at his watch. "Dressing for dinner, and I should be, too," he said. "How are the steaks out at the Cat and Fiddle?"

Connie half closed his eyes. After a time he sighed. "Okay. That might be a good way to go at the guy. Phone me and give me the reaction if he does talk. If not, don't bother."

Jane was in holiday mood until Dan told her where they were headed. She said tartly, "I admit freely that I am a working girl. But do I get overtime for this?"

Dan said slowly, carefully, "Darling, you better understand, if you don't already, that there's one part of me I can't change. I can't shut the office door and forget the cases piled up in there. I have a nasty habit of carrying them around with me. So we go someplace else and I try like blazes to be gay, or we go to the Cat and Fiddle and get something off my mind."

She moved closer to him. "Dull old work horse," she said.

"Guilty."

"All right, now I'll confess," Jane said. "I was going to suggest we go out there later. I just got sore when you beat me to the draw."

He laughed, and at the next stop light he kissed her hurriedly.

The Cat and Fiddle was eight miles beyond the city line. At last Dan saw the green-and-blue neon sign, and he turned into the asphalt parking area. There were about forty other cars there.

They went from the check room into the low-ceilinged bar and lounge. The only sign of Christmas was a small silver tree on the bar; a tiny blue spot was focused on it.

They sat at the bar and ordered drinks. Several other couples were at the tables, talking in low voices. A pianist played softly in the dining room.

Dan took out a business card and wrote on it: *Only if you happen to have an opinion.*

He called the nearest bartender over. "Would you please see that Vince gets this?"

The man glanced at the name. "I'll see if Mr. Servius is in." He said something to the other bartender and left through a paneled door at the rear of the bar. He was back in less than a minute, smiling politely.

"Please go up the stair. Mr. Servius is in his office—the second door on the right."

"I'll wait here, Dan," Jane said.

"If you are Miss Raymer, Mr. Servius would like to have you join him, too," the bartender said.

Jane looked at Dan. He nodded and she slid off the stool.

As they went up the stairs, Jane said, "I seem to be known here."

"Notorious female. I suspect he wants a witness."

Vincent Servius was standing at a small corner bar mixing himself a drink when they entered. He turned and smiled. "Fowler, Miss Raymer. Nice of you to stop by. Can I mix you something?"

Dan refused politely, and they sat down.

Vince was a compact man with cropped, prematurely white hair, a sun-lamp tan, and beautifully cut clothes. He had not been directly concerned with violence in many years. In that time he had eliminated most of the traces of the hoodlum.

The overall impression he gave was that of the up-and-coming clubman. Golf lessons, voice lessons, plastic surgery, and a good tailor—these had all helped; but nothing had been able to destroy a certain aura of alertness, ruthlessness. He was a man you would never joke with. He had made his own laws, and he carried the awareness of his own ultimate authority around with him, as unmistakable as a loaded gun.

Vince went over to the fieldstone fireplace, drink in hand, and turned, resting his elbow on the mantel.

"Very clever, Fowler. 'Only if you happen to have an opinion.' I have an opinion. The kid is no good. That's my opinion. He's a cheap punk. I didn't admit that to myself until he tried to put the hook on that loan company. He was working for me at the time. I was trying to break him in here—buying foods.

"But now I'm through, Fowler. You can tell Jim Heglon that for me. Terrafierro will back it up. Ask him what I told him. I said, 'Defend the kid. Get him off if you can, and no hard feelings if you can't. If you get him off, I'm having him run out of town, out of the state. I don't want him around.' I told George that.

"Now there's this Garrity thing. It looks like I went out on a limb for the kid. Going out on limbs was yesterday, Fowler. Not today and not tomorrow. I was a sucker long enough."

He took out a crisp handkerchief and mopped his forehead. "I go right up in the air," he said. "I talk too loud."

"You can see how Heglon is thinking," Dan said quietly. "And the police, too."

"That's the hell of it. I swear I had nothing to do with it." He half smiled. "It would have helped if I'd had a tape recorder up here last month when the Garrity girl came to see what she could sell me."

Dan leaned forward. "She came here?"

"With bells on. Nothing coy about that kid. Pay off, Mr. Servius, and I'll change my identification of your brother."

"What part of last month?"

"Let me think. The tenth it was. Monday the tenth."

Jane said softly, "That's why I got the impression she wouldn't sell out, Dan. I had lunch with her later that same week. She had tried to and couldn't."

Vince took a sip of his drink. "She started with big money and worked her way down. I let her go ahead. Finally, after I'd had my laughs, I told her even one dollar was too much. I told her I wanted the kid sent up.

"She blew her top. For a couple of minutes I thought I might have to clip her to shut her up. But after a couple of drinks she quieted down. That gave me a chance to find out something that had been bothering me. It seemed too pat, kind of."

"What do you mean, Servius?" Dan asked.

"The setup was too neat, the way the door *happened* to be open a crack, and the way she *happened* to be working late, and the way she *happened* to see the kids come out.

"I couldn't get her to admit anything at first, because she was making a little play for me, but when I convinced her I wasn't having any, she let me in on what really happened. She was hanging around waiting for the manager of that loan outfit to quit work.

"They had a system. She'd wait in the accountant's office with the light out, watching his door. Then, when the manager left, she'd wait about five minutes and leave herself. That would give him time to get his car out of the parking lot. He'd pick her up at the corner. She said he was the super-cautious, married type. They just dated once in a while. I wasn't having any of that. Too rough for me, Fowler."

There was a long silence. Dan asked, "How about friends of your brother, Servius, or friends of Kelly and Castrella?"

Vince walked over and sat down, facing them. "One—Johnny didn't have a friend who'd bring a bucket of water if he was on fire. And two—I sent the word out."

"What does that mean?"

"I like things quiet in this end of the state. I didn't want anyone helping those three punks. Everybody got the word. So who would do anything? Now both of you please tell Heglon exactly what I said. Tell him to check with

Terrafierro. Tell him to have the cops check their pigeons. Ask the kid himself. I paid him a little visit. Now, if you don't mind, I've got another appointment."

They had finished their steaks before Dan was able to get any line on Connie Wyant. On the third telephone call he was given a message. Lieutenant Wyant was waiting for Mr. Fowler at 311 Leeds Street, Apartment 6A, and would Mr. Fowler please bring Miss Raymer with him.

They drove back to the city. A department car was parked in front of the building. Sergeant Levandowski was half asleep behind the wheel. "Go right in. Ground floor in the back. 6A."

Connie greeted them gravely and listened without question to Dan's report of the conversation with Vince Servius. After Dan had finished, Connie nodded casually, as though it was of little importance, and said, "Miss Raymer, I'm not so good at this, so I thought maybe you could help. There's the Garrity girl's closet. Go through it and give me an estimate on the cost."

Jane went to the open closet. She began to examine the clothes. "Hey!" she exclaimed.

"What do you think?" Connie asked.

"If this suit cost a nickel under two hundred, I'll eat it. And look at this coat. Four hundred, anyway." She bent over and picked up a shoe. "For ages I've dreamed of owning a pair of these. Thirty-seven fifty, at least."

"Care to make an estimate on the total?" Connie asked her.

"Gosh, thousands. I don't know. There are nine dresses in there that must have cost at least a hundred apiece. Do you have to have it accurate?"

"That's close enough, thanks." He took a small blue bankbook out of his pocket and flipped it to Dan. Dan caught it and looked inside. Loreen Garrity had more than $1100 on hand. There had been large deposits and large withdrawals—nothing small.

Connie said, "I've been to see her family. They're good people. They didn't want to talk mean about the dead, so it took a little time. But I found out our Loreen was one for the angles—a chiseler—no conscience and less morals. A rough, tough cookie to get tied up with.

"From there, I went to see the Kistners. Every time the old lady would try to answer a question, Kistner'd jump in with all four feet. I finally had to have Levandowski take him downtown just to get him out of the way. Then the old lady talked.

"She had a lot to say about how lousy business is. How they're scrimping and scraping along, and how the girl couldn't have a new formal for the Christmas dance tomorrow night at the high school gym.

"Then I called up an accountant friend after I left her. I asked him how Kistner had been doing. He cussed out Kistner and said he'd been doing fine;

in fact, he had stolen some nice retail accounts out from under the other boys in the same racket. So I came over here and it looked like this was where the profit was going. So I waited for you so I could make sure."

"What can you do about it?" Dan demanded, anger in his voice, anger at the big puffy man who hadn't wanted to lie to the police.

"I've been thinking. It's eleven o'clock. He's been sitting down there sweating. I've got to get my Christmas shopping done tomorrow, and the only way I'll ever get around to it is to break him fast."

Jane had been listening, wide-eyed. "They always forget some little thing, don't they?" she asked. "Or there is something they don't know about. Like a clock that is five minutes slow, or something. I mean, in the stories . . ." Her voice trailed off uncertainly.

"Give her a badge, Connie," Dan said with amusement.

Connie rubbed his chin. "I might do that, Dan. I just might do that. Miss Raymer, you got a strong stomach? If so, maybe you get to watch your idea in operation."

It was nearly midnight, and Connie had left Dan and Jane alone in a small office at headquarters for nearly a half hour. He opened the door and stuck his head in. "Come on, people. Just don't say a word."

They went to the Interrogation Room. Kistner jumped up the moment they came in. Levandowski sat at the long table, looking bored.

Kistner said heatedly, " As you know, Lieutenant, I was perfectly willing to cooperate. But you are being high-handed. I demand to know why I was brought down here. I want to know why I can't phone a lawyer. You are exceeding your authority, and I—"

"Siddown!" Connie roared with all the power of his lungs.

Kistner's mouth worked silently. He sat down, shocked by the unexpected roar. A tired young man slouched in, sat at the table, flipped open a notebook, and placed three sharp pencils within easy reach.

Connie motioned Dan and Jane over toward chairs in a shadowed corner of the room. They sat side by side, and Jane held Dan's wrist, her nails sharp against his skin.

"Kistner, tell us again about how you came back to the office," Connie said.

Kistner replied in a tone of excruciating patience, as though talking to children, "I parked my car in my parking space in the lot behind the building. I used the back way into the lobby. I went up—"

"You went to the cigar counter."

"So I did! I had forgotten that. I went to the cigar counter. I bought three cigars and chatted with Barney. Then I took an elevator up."

"And talked to the elevator boy."

"I usually do. Is there a law?"

"No law, Kistner. Go on."

"And then I opened the Men's Room door with my key, and I was in there maybe three minutes. And then when I came out, the man I described brushed by me. I went to the office and found the window open. I was shutting it when I heard—"

"All this was at two o'clock, give or take a couple of minutes?"

"That's right, Lieutenant." Talking had restored Kistner's self-assurance.

Connie nodded to Levandowski. The sergeant got up lazily, walked to the door, and opened it. A burly, diffident young man came in. He wore khaki pants and a leather jacket.

"Sit down," Connie said casually. "What's your name?"

"Paul Hilbert, officer."

The tired young man was taking notes.

"What's your occupation?"

"I'm a plumber, officer. Central Plumbing, Incorporated."

"Did you get a call today from the Associated Bank Building?"

"Well, I didn't get the call, but I was sent out on the job. I talked to the super, and he sent me up to the seventeenth floor. Sink drain clogged in the Men's Room."

"What time did you get there?"

"That's on my report, officer. Quarter after one."

"How long did it take you to finish the job?"

"About three o'clock."

"Did you leave the Men's Room at any time during that period?"

"No, I didn't."

"I suppose people tried to come in there?"

"Three or four. But I had all the water connections turned off, so I told them to go down to sixteen. The super had the door unlocked down there."

"Did you get a look at everybody who came in?"

"Sure, officer."

"You said three or four. Is one of them at this table?"

The shy young man looked around. He shook his head. "No, sir."

"Thanks, Hilbert. Wait outside. We'll want you to sign the statement when it's typed up."

Hilbert's footsteps sounded loud as he walked to the door. Everyone was watching Kistner. His face was still, and he seemed to be looking into a remote and alien future, as cold as the back of the moon.

Kistner said in a husky, barely audible voice. "A bad break. A stupid thing. Ten seconds it would have taken me to look in there. I had to establish the time. I talked to Barney. And to the elevator boy. They'd know when she fell. But I had to be some place else. Not in the office.

"You don't know how it was. She kept wanting more money. She wouldn't have anything to do with me, except when there was money. And I didn't have any more, finally.

"I guess I was crazy. I started to milk the accounts. That wasn't hard; the clients trust me. Take a little here and a little there. She found out. She wanted more and more. And that gave her a new angle. Give me more, or I'll tell.

"I thought it over. I kept thinking about her being a witness. All I had to do was make it look like she was killed to keep her from testifying. I don't care what you do to me. Now it's over, and I feel glad."

He gave Connie a long, wondering look. "Is that crazy? To feel glad it's over? Do other people feel that way?"

Connie asked Dan and Jane to wait in the small office. He came in ten minutes later; he looked tired. The plumber came in with him.

Connie said, "Me, I hate this business. I'm after him, and I bust him, and then I start bleeding for him. What the hell? Anyway, you get your badge, Miss Raymer."

"But wouldn't you have found out about the plumber anyway?" Jane asked.

Connie grinned ruefully at her. He jerked a thumb toward the plumber. "Meet Patrolman Hilbert. Doesn't know a pipe wrench from a faucet. We just took the chance that Kistner was too eager to toss the girl out the window— so eager he didn't make a quick check of the Men's Room. If he had, he could have laughed us under the table. As it is, I can get my Christmas shopping done tomorrow. Or is it today?"

Dan and Jane left headquarters. They walked down the street, arm in arm. There was holly, and a big tree in front of the courthouse, and a car went by with a lot of people in it singing about We Three Kings of Orient Are. Kistner was a stain, fading slowly.

They walked until it was entirely Christmas Eve, and they were entirely alone in the snow that began to fall again, making tiny perfect stars of lace that lingered in her dark hair.

Malcolm Gray

MISS CRINDLE AND FATHER CHRISTMAS

Christmas comes reluctantly to Much Cluning. Huddling in its valley, the village looks even drearier than usual under grey December skies. There is no tree outside the village hall, and the single string of fairy lights along the High Street hardly creates an air of festivity. The housewives complain about the extra work Christmas brings and the men about the expense. They only do it for the kids, they say. All the same, it is doubtful if they really mean it, or if they would want to see the season abolished even if they could, and a fair number go to church or chapel on Christmas morning.

A few days before Christmas last year, Harriet Richards stood in the yard at her brother's farm giving him a piece of her mind. At twenty-two, Harriet was as generous and warm-hearted as she was pretty. "Do you have to be such a Scrooge?" she demanded angrily.

"Go away," Jason told her coldly. He was nine years older than his sister and he had no use for the season of goodwill. The only good thing about it to his mind was the profit he made on his flock of chickens and turkeys. He was damned if he was going to give any of them away to layabouts who weren't prepared to get off their backsides and work. He said as much to Harriet.

"Layabouts!" she exclaimed furiously. "Do you call old Mrs. Randall a layabout?"

"It's her husband's job to provide for her, not mine."

"When he's nearly eighty and crippled with arthritis?"

"Ach!" Jason said, disgusted.

"And she's not the only one," Harriet went on. "There's Josie Gardner with her three kids. And Bert Renwick and Phoebe," she added, forestalling her brother's attempt to interrupt her. "It's not their fault they can't afford anything but the bare necessities."

"They get their pensions," Jason retorted. "And benefits. They wouldn't

63

get those if people like me didn't pay too damned much in taxes."

"Oh," Harriet said, exasperated, "I don't know how Sheila puts up with you!" And, turning, she started toward the house.

"If you think I breed those birds to feed all the lame ducks in the village, you'd better think again!" Jason called after her.

There were times when she could strangle him, Harriet thought furiously. It wasn't as if he couldn't afford three or four turkeys. By local standards, he was well off. But he seemed to feel that people expected him to give them. It put him on the defensive, and he resented it.

Her sister-in-law was in the kitchen. "Have you and Jason been arguing again?" she asked, amused.

"You could say so." Harriet, still boiling with indignation, explained.

"He works hard," Sheila reminded her. "And he's inclined to think other people don't. There's so much to do at this time of year, he gets worn out."

"He could afford to pay another man if he wasn't so mean," Harriet said bitterly. "Anyway, it's not just this time, it's always."

Soon afterward, she left. Sheila watched her go, thinking.

Later that evening Harriet had a very public quarrel with Colin Loates, her boy friend. Nobody who heard it was quite sure what it was about, but Harriet went home in tears.

Miss Crindle met her in the street the next day. Miss Crindle was a large woman with greying hair and a cheerful manner. Until her retirement three years ago, she had taught at Much Cluning Primary School for more than thirty years, and both Harriet and Colin had been among her brightest pupils. So had Jason, who hadn't been as clever as his sister but by hard work had gained a scholarship to Leobury School and gone on to university. Harriet could have gone, too, but she preferred to stay home and work with the horses her father bred for show jumping.

Colin had been the brightest of the three, a cheeky little boy with charm and a talent for mischief. Miss Crindle had never quite forgiven him for leaving school at sixteen to go into his father's grocery shop.

"And how is Colin?" Miss Crindle inquired that morning.

Harriet looked surprised. "Haven't you heard, Miss Crindle? I thought everybody had. We had a row last night and it's all over."

Miss Crindle noticed that Harriet's left eye was twitching and that she looked embarrassed. All the same, she didn't seem too distressed. She had always been a sensible girl, Miss Crindle thought, and things were different nowadays. In her time, if a girl and her boy friend split up she would be upset for days. "I'm sorry," she said.

Harriet shrugged. "I'll get over it," she said ruefully.

Miss Crindle was sure she would. A girl like Harriet, vivacious and attractive, would find no shortage of young men.

That afternoon, Colin, driving back from Leobury, slewed off the road into a ditch two miles from the village. He explained that he had swerved to avoid a pheasant and skidded, but the popular theory was that his mind hadn't been on his driving, he was thinking about Harriet and their row. Whatever the cause, his car was well and truly stuck and he had to walk to the nearest house and phone the garage to come and tow him out.

They were still doing it when Billy Powis, having run all the way home, blurted out breathlessly to his mother that he had just seen Santa Claus. Mary Powis was busy making mince pies. She laughed but didn't pay too much attention. She was used to her son's tales.

"Oh, dear?" she said.

"But I did, Mum," the seven-year-old insisted.

"Had he got his sledge and reindeer?"

Billy hesitated. He was a truthful little boy and he couldn't really remember, he had been too excited. "He'd got something," he mumbled. More certainly he added, "And he had a sack over his shoulder."

"Where was he?"

"I told you, at the edge of Brackett's Wood. He went into the trees."

"You shouldn't make up stories, Billy," Mary told him mildly. "It's telling fibs, and that's naughty."

"I did see him," Billy persisted. He was learning early that it is bad enough to be suspected when one is guilty, but much worse when one is innocent. "He was all in red, with white stuff on his coat, and he had a big red hood and boots. Like he does when he comes to our school party."

Oh, dear, Mary thought. She decided that the best course would be to ignore her son's tale. "Go and wash your hands," she said.

At the same time, Sheila Richards was trying without success to ring her sister-in-law. Harriet's mother told her Harry was out. She didn't know where, but she didn't suppose she would be long. Sheila thanked her and said she would try again later.

Billy Powis wasn't the only inhabitant of Much Cluning to see Father Christmas. Two other people saw him, and they were grownups. The first was George Townley, the owner of the general store-cum-post office. While Billy was running home to tell his mother what he had seen, George was returning from visiting his sister at Little Cluning. As he drove down the hill into the village, he saw a figure in red with a hood and carrying a sack disappear into the trees beside the road. He was unwise enough to mention it to one of his customers, and soon the story was all over the village. George Townley had started seeing things, and he believed in Santa Claus.

It had been getting colder during the day, and about five o'clock it started to snow. By the time most of Much Cluning went to bed, there was a three-inch covering over everything and it was still snowing. It stopped during the night, but the temperature dropped further.

The second adult to see Father Christmas was Miss Crindle. At one o'clock in the morning of December the twenty-third, she had to get out of bed to go to the bathroom. On her way back, she looked out of the window. It was a fine clear night with a moon. There was never much noise in the valley, but now every sound was muffled by the thick layer of snow.

Just across the road, a figure dressed in scarlet and white, its head covered by a hood, was turning the corner round the back of the Renwicks' cottage. It was bowed under the weight of the sack slung over its right shoulder. Miss Crindle blinked. There were no children's parties at that hour, and any devoted father who was inclined to go to the lengths of dressing up to deliver his offsprings' presents would hardly do so two days before Christmas.

Miss Crindle told herself that if it wasn't a fond father, it must be a burglar. She considered calling the police. But she disliked the idea of being thought an overimaginative old fool and, anyway, everybody knew the Renwicks were almost destitute. No burglar would try his luck there. She climbed back into bed, and the next day she kept what she had seen to herself.

She said nothing even when Phoebe Renwick, who was well over seventy and worn out from caring for her invalid husband, told her her news. When she came down that morning and opened the back door, there on the doorstep there had been a parcel wrapped in gift paper. In it there was a small turkey already plucked and drawn and a tiny Christmas pudding.

"I couldn't believe it," Phoebe said. She was close to tears. "We haven't been able to have a turkey for over twenty years. Not since soon after Bert was first ill and had to give up work. We can't keep it, of course, it wouldn't be right, but it was a lovely thought."

"Of course you can keep it," Miss Crindle told her with spirit.

"No. We were brought up not to accept what we hadn't paid for, or to ask for charity, and we never have, neither of us."

"You call a present charity? Anyway," Miss Crindle added reasonably, "who would you give it back to?"

"I hadn't thought of that," Phoebe admitted.

"You keep it and be glad there are people in the village who think of others," Miss Crindle told her. "You can say a prayer for them in chapel on Christmas morning."

The old lady's eyes moistened. "I will tonight, too," she said.

Busy with her thoughts, Miss Crindle went back indoors and resumed the cleaning she had been doing when she heard Mrs. Renwick calling her. Who was the kind soul who had left the parcel on the old couple's step? She had no doubt that it was the person in Santa Claus costume she had seen during the night, but who was he? Or she?

Not that it mattered: if somebody wanted to do the old couple a good turn surreptitiously, good luck to them. Only why the fancy dress? Such ostentation seemed out of keeping with leaving the parcel secretly in the middle of the night. It was like a disguise, and it made her a little uneasy.

The Renwicks weren't the only beneficiaries of Much Cluning's own Santa Claus: the Randalls, Josie Gardner, and an elderly lady named Willings with a crippled son had found similar parcels at their back doors that morning. By evening the story was all over the village.

Miss Crindle heard it, and she wondered still more.

Neither of the Richardses had heard about the parcels. Bracketts Farm was a mile out of Much Cluning and they'd been busy there all day. Thus there was no reason for Sheila to suspect anything when Jason came into the kitchen during the afternoon and asked her, "Has Mrs. Grundy been for her bird?"

Sheila had been right, he was tired. The woman who helped deal with the turkeys was ill with flu and he had been driving himself hard for days. He was also suspicious.

"No," Sheila answered without looking up from what she was doing at the sink. "She said she'd come tomorrow."

Jason swore.

"Why, what's the matter? It doesn't make any difference."

"It's gone."

Sheila looked up then. "What do you mean?"

"What I say," Jason told her angrily. "It's clear enough, isn't it? It's been pinched."

His wife stared at him. "Are you sure?" she asked. But she could see from Jason's face he was. "Have any of the others gone?"

"I don't know. I was only looking for hers."

"Can't she have another one?" Sheila tried to be practical, but she knew it wouldn't assuage Jason's anger.

"Of course she bloody well can't," he retorted. "The others are all sold, you know that. And you know how fussy she is."

Sheila did know. Mrs. Grundy lived at Much Cluning Hall and, although she was pleasant enough, she disliked being thwarted or inconvenienced. Her manner implied that she expected her life to run as smoothly as the Rolls-

Royce her husband drove. Oh, God, Sheila thought, it looked like being a miserable Christmas. Jason would be in a foul mood for days. A terrible thought occurred to her. "Hadn't you better count them?" she asked.

"I'm going to."

Jason strode across the yard to the big shed where the dead birds, plucked and drawn, were laid out in rows along the shelves. Sheila followed and watched while he counted them. There should be ninety, she knew. Christmas turkeys might be profitable, but they were only a sideline to the main business of the farm, the crops and sheep.

"There are four gone!" Jason shouted. "Four! That's the best part of fifty pounds!" He turned furiously. "I'm going to ring the police!"

"Jason, do you think—?" Sheila asked weakly.

But he was in no mood to pay attention, and she followed him uneasily into the house.

It was nearly an hour before P.C. Tom Roberts arrived. He had been at the site of a road accident four miles away and the theft of four turkeys hadn't seemed like the crime of the century, even in Much Cluning. Clearly Jason Richards didn't agree with him.

"They must have got in during the night," he said. Waiting had done nothing to soothe his anger. "You can see their tracks."

He led the way through the churned-up slush in the yard, past the farm buildings to a small meadow bounded on the far side by a low hedge. It was still freezing hard, and the snow, several inches deep, was crisp and unbroken save for a clearly designed set of footprints leading from the yard to the hedge near the point where it met the road. Jason had said "they," Roberts thought, but there was only one set. Smallish prints, too.

"Looks like he came this way," he agreed. "Was the shed locked at night?"

"No." Jason sounded as if he were daring the policeman to criticize him. "The padlock's fastened with a peg. We've never had anything stolen before."

Roberts walked back across the yard.

"Where are you going?" Jason demanded.

"Don't want to disturb the tracks then, do we, sir?" Roberts said. He walked along the road and across to the point where, it seemed, the thief had forced his way through the hedge. There was still just enough light for him to make out the tuft of material caught on a twig. He picked it out carefully and frowned. It was bright-red and thin. Hardly the sort of clothing a man would wear to go stealing turkeys on a freezing-cold night. Not what most men would wear at any time, come to that. He tucked the fragment away between two pages of his notebook and returned to where the farmer was watching.

The turkeys must have been stolen on one of the last two nights, Jason told him. He had counted them two days ago.

Tom Roberts lived in the village. He knew about George Townley's seeing a figure dressed like Santa Claus disappearing into Brackett's Wood and about the mysterious parcels which had appeared on certain doorsteps last night. There had been four of them, each one containing a turkey. And four turkeys had been taken from Jason's shed. Roberts was well aware of the dangers of putting two and two together and making sixteen, but it looked to him very much as if some joker had been playing twin roles, Robin Hood and Santa Claus.

Of all the people in the village, he could think of only one who possessed the sort of mind to think up a ploy like that and the cheek to carry it out: Colin Loates. Colin had never been suspected of dishonesty, but he was— what was the word? —unpredictable. Sometimes his sense of humor ran away with him. After all, everybody knew Jason Richards could well afford the loss of four birds, and the recipients of the parcels were genuinely deserving cases. If it had been up to him personally, Roberts would have felt inclined to say, "Good luck to him," and write the case off as unsolved. But it wasn't, and theft was theft, however good the motive. So he promised Jason he would make inquiries and went to see Colin.

He found him at his father's shop, making up orders for the next day.

When Colin heard why he was there, he laughed. "Serve Jason right," he said.

"You've no idea who might have done it?" Roberts asked him.

"Me? No. I don't know why you should come to me about it. You're the one who's supposed to know about all the crime that goes on here."

"Where were you the last two nights?" Roberts asked him.

"What time?"

"Anytime."

"Home in bed. "

They eyed each other. Colin seemed to think the whole business was a great joke, and that annoyed Roberts a little. He looked down at the other man's feet. They must be size nines, at least. The boots which made the tracks in the snow on Jason Richards' meadow had been no bigger than sevens. All the same, "Have you got any wellingtons?" he asked.

"Course I have," Colin answered.

"Where are they?"

"In the boot of my car. Why?"

"Do you mind if I have a look at them?"

"Not if you want to."

They went out to the yard at the back of the shop where Colin's old Escort was parked. He opened the boot and brought out a pair of worn grey wellingtons. Roberts studied them. They were size ten.

"All right, thanks," he said.

Colin just grinned. "Do you think I took Jason's turkeys?" he asked.

Roberts didn't answer.

Miss Crindle heard about the theft the next morning when she was doing her last-minute Christmas shopping. It seemed to justify her fears, and she decided that she must talk to Tom Roberts.

"You think the turkeys the Renwicks and the others got were the ones somebody stole from Jason Richards' shed, don't you?" she asked him.

"I can't say, Miss Crindle," the policeman replied cautiously.

"Of course you can, everybody else is." Miss Crindle swept his objection aside. "And you suspect you know who it was, don't you?"

Roberts eyed his visitor. Muffled up in what looked like two or three layers of jumpers and cardigans under her coat, she looked bigger than ever. It would have been easy to put her down as a silly busybody, but Roberts knew better. Miss Crindle was an intelligent woman. And if she took a keen interest in what went on in Much Cluning, she was no mischief-maker. "We're pursuing our inquiries," he said.

"So I should hope," she told him briskly. "Although I must confess, my sympathies are rather with the thief." She paused, then continued with obvious embarrassment, "I thought I should tell you, I saw Father Christmas last night."

Roberts gaped at her. For a moment he wondered if she had suddenly gone queer. "I'm sorry?" he stammered.

"Somebody dressed as Santa Claus left the parcels. I happened to look out of my window about one o'clock and I saw them going round behind the Renwicks' house. I didn't say anything about it, there didn't seem any point, and I've no wish to be thought mad, but if the birds were stolen—"

"You've no idea who it was?" Roberts asked, recovering a little.

"None," Miss Crindle answered firmly. "I can't even say if it was a man or a woman. I suppose you know George Townley saw them, too, two or three days ago?"

Roberts nodded. "It looks as if whoever took the turkeys was wearing red," he said grimly. "He left this caught on the hedge where he pushed through." He took out his notebook and showed Miss Crindle the fragment of cloth.

She studied it with interest. "It looks like a piece from a Santa Claus costume," she observed. She gave the policeman a shrewd look. "I suppose you think it was Colin Loates?"

This time Tom Roberts wasn't startled, he knew half the village would be supposing the same thing. "It wasn't him," he said.

"Oh?" Miss Crindle couldn't quite conceal her curiosity.

Roberts was undecided how much he should reveal. He knew the old girl had helped the police when Ralph Johns was murdered and the Chief Inspector had a high regard for her. And he could do with some help now. "The thief left footprints from the hedge across to the shed," he explained. "They were sixes or sevens, and Colin takes tens. I've seen his boots. Besides, when George Townley saw his Santa Claus, they were towing Colin's car out of a ditch along the Leobury road."

Miss Crindle hadn't known that, but she was rather glad. "Have you any idea who it may have been?" she inquired.

"No," Roberts admitted.

Miss Crindle was afraid *she* had, and after Roberts had gone she walked across the road. The Renwicks had few visitors—even the milkman called only every other day—and the footprints in the snow along the side of the cottage were still as clear as when they were made. She studied them thoughtfully, then she went to see Harriet Richards.

She didn't beat about the bush. "What do you know about Father Christmas and Jason's stolen turkeys?" she demanded.

"Me?" The girl looked surprised. "Nothing, Miss Crindle."

"Harriet," Miss Crindle told her sternly, "your eyelid's twitching. That's the second time it's done it in the last four days."

For some unaccountable reason Harriet blushed.

"Theft is a crime," Miss Crindle continued. "It can have very serious consequences. Sometimes for the wrong person. You may disapprove of Jason but, even if you aren't having anything to do with Colin now, you wouldn't want him to get into trouble, would you?"

"No," Harriet said.

Miss Crindle nodded. "Good. What size wellingtons do you take?"

"Sevens."

"And where were you at one o'clock the night before last?"

Harriet smiled, and for the first time that morning there was a hint of her old mischief. "At Leobury," she answered. "I went to see Pat Dellar. It started to freeze hard, there was a lot of slush on the road, and I stayed the night."

Miss Crindle gazed at the girl for quite a long time. Then, "Think about it, my dear," she said.

On her way home, she met Mary Powis and Billy.

"I've seen Father Christmas," the little boy announced triumphantly.

"Billy!" his mother reproved him. "You thought you saw him on Monday, and you know he doesn't come out until Christmas Eve. And only after dark then." She smiled apologetically at Miss Crindle.

But Miss Crindle was interested. "Where did you see him, Billy?" she asked.

"By Brackett's Wood," Billy replied.

"What time was it?"

"I don't know. But it got dark soon."

"You aren't the only person who saw him," Miss Crindle said. "I saw him, too, and so did Mr. Townley." It was too much, she thought.

When she got home, she phoned Pat Dellar, who was one of her old pupils. Pat confirmed that Harriet had spent last night there.

Miss Crindle asked after her parents, they talked for a minute or two longer, and when Miss Crindle put down the phone she sat for some time, thinking. It was clear that Colin hadn't stolen the turkeys. There was only one set of footprints and he couldn't have worn size six or seven boots. Moreover, he hadn't been the Father Christmas Billy Powis and George Townley had seen. Nor could Harriet have played Santa Claus—she had been miles away when the parcels had been delivered the night before last. So who had?

After twenty minutes, Miss Crindle came to a decision. She made two telephone calls, then put on another cardigan and her coat and went to see Sheila Richards.

"It was all a mistake," Jason said, looking uncomfortable.

P.C. Roberts eyed him stolidly. He was quite sure it hadn't been a mistake, but if Jason was going to maintain it had, there wasn't much he could do.

"The turkeys had been put aside," Jason went on. It would have been obvious to the most obtuse listener that his heart wasn't in it. "They hadn't been stolen at all."

"I see, sir," Roberts said. He was tempted to add something about wasting police time being an offense, but decided against it. "So you don't want us to take any further action?"

"No." Jason almost writhed. Further action was what he wanted above almost everything else, but Sheila had made it all too clear that if he didn't drop the whole business she would leave him. She wasn't given to making idle threats, and Jason had believed her. For all his faults, he loved his wife.

It was Miss Crindle who was responsible. He didn't know what she had told Sheila, but whatever it was it had had a marked effect.

In fact, Miss Crindle had said quite simply that she knew who had taken the turkeys and that she hoped Jason's wife would be able to persuade him to drop the whole matter. She looked down at Sheila's feet. Sheila was nearly six feet tall, and her feet were much larger than her sister-in-law's. "It was Colin, wasn't it?" Sheila said.

Miss Crindle smiled enigmatically.

"But—" Sheila looked distraught "—Jason was sure it was Harry. He said she'd talked about the Renwicks and the Randalls and Josie Gardner a few days ago. She said he ought to give them turkeys."

"It was," Miss Crindle said.

"But it can't have been," Sheila protested. "Harry was staying with Pat the night the parcels were left."

"That wasn't her," Miss Crindle agreed.

"Then who?"

"Colin. It was Harriet's idea. She was very angry with Jason and she thought she'd teach him a lesson and help some people to have a better Christmas at the same time. She suggested it to Colin and he jumped at the idea."

"But they'd fallen out," Sheila objected. "She told me they had a terrible row. I still don't see."

"They took it in turns to cover each other," Miss Crindle told her. "First, while Colin was being towed out of that ditch, Harriet was making sure she was seen in her Santa Claus getup at the other end of the village. They wanted people to talk about Santa Claus being about."

"It's the sort of daft idea that would appeal to them," Sheila agreed miserably. "They've never grown up, either of them."

"We can do with a touch of youthful spirits sometimes," Miss Crindle said. "They didn't look on what they were doing as stealing."

"I tried to phone her that afternoon. Mum said she was out."

Miss Crindle nodded. "She knew Jason didn't lock the shed. She went there that night, took the four smallest turkeys, and carried them across the meadow to Colin, who was waiting in his car. She's a strong girl and it wasn't very far. Colin hid them until the next night, then, while Harriet was safe at the Dellars', he delivered them. *He* couldn't have stolen them, because the footprints in the snow were too small, and Harriet couldn't have delivered them because she was miles away. There was only one set of prints in the meadow and only one round the Renwicks'. Nobody was looking for two people working alternately."

Sheila stared at her. "Except you," she said. "Whatever made you think of it?"

"Well—" Miss Crindle hesitated, then she smiled. "First, their quarrel was a little too public. Harriet and Colin may be high-spirited, but they wouldn't want to have a real argument with half the village looking on. It was almost as if it were being staged for other people's benefit. And when I saw Harriet just afterward, she didn't seem upset at all. Then her eyelid started twitching. It did it again when she told me she didn't know anything about the turkeys. I *knew* she was involved then."

"Oh," Sheila said, understanding.

"It's always done that when she's telling fibs, ever since she was a little girl at school," Miss Crindle said. "When you're a teacher as long as I was, you don't forget things like that. Then, the footprints at the Renwicks' aren't the same size as the others—they must be tens, at least. I tackled Harriet just now, and she told me the truth."

"Oh," Sheila said again. Uneasily she added, "I wonder what Jason's going to say."

"I'm sure you can manage him," Miss Crindle told her.

Mrs. Grundy laughed. "Then I'll have to get another one," she said cheerfully. "Really, Mr. Richards, it doesn't matter at all. To be frank, a ten-pound turkey would have been far too big for just my husband and me. I'm sure Mrs. Gardner and her children will enjoy it much more. But I must insist you let me pay you for it."

Jason met her eye, then looked away. "No," he said gruffly. "That's all right, Mrs. Grundy, I've written those four birds off. They're a present from us. After all, it's Christmas. "

Mrs. Grundy nearly fainted.

Anthony Boucher

MYSTERY FOR CHRISTMAS

That was why the Benson jewel robbery was solved—because Aram Melekian was too much for Mr. Quilter's temper.

His almost invisible eyebrows soared, and the scalp of his close-cropped head twitched angrily. "Damme!" said Mr. Quilter, and in that mild and archaic oath there was more compressed fury than in paragraphs of uncensored profanity. "So you, sir, are the untrammeled creative artist, and I am a drudging, hampering hack!"

Aram Melekian tilted his hat a trifle more jauntily. "That's the size of it, brother. And if you hamper this untrammeled opus any more, Metropolis Pictures is going to be suing its youngest genius for breach of contract."

Mr. Quilter rose to his full lean height. "I've seen them come and go," he announced; "and there hasn't been a one of them, sir, who failed to learn something from me. What is so creative about pouring out the full vigor of your young life? The creative task is mine, molding that vigor, shaping it to some end."

"Go play with your blue pencil," Melekian suggested. "I've got a dream coming on."

"Because I have never produced anything myself, you young men jeer at me. You never see that your successful screen plays are more my effort than your inspiration." Mr. Quilter's thin frame was aquiver.

"Then what do you need us for?"

"What—Damme, sir, what indeed? Ha!" said Mr. Quilter loudly. "I'll show you. I'll pick the first man off the street that has life and a story in him. What more do you contribute? And through me he'll turn out a job that will sell. If I do this, sir, then will you consent to the revisions I've asked of you?"

"Go lay an egg," said Aram Melekian. "And I've no doubt you will."

Mr. Quilter stalked out of the studio with high dreams. He saw the horny-handed son of toil out of whom he had coaxed a masterpiece signing a contract with F.X. He saw a discomfited Armenian genius in the background busily devouring his own words. He saw himself freed of his own sense of frustration, proving at last that his was the significant part of writing.

He felt a bumping shock and the squealing of brakes. The next thing he saw was the asphalt paving.

Mr. Quilter rose to his feet undecided whether to curse the driver for knocking him down or bless him for stopping so miraculously short of danger. The young man in the brown suit was so disarmingly concerned that the latter choice was inevitable.

"I'm awfully sorry," the young man blurted. "Are you hurt? It's this bad wing of mine, I guess." His left arm was in a sling.

"Nothing at all, sir. My fault. I was preoccupied . . ."

They stood awkwardly for a moment, each striving for a phrase that was not mere politeness. Then they both spoke at once.

"You came out of that studio," the young man said. "Do you" (his tone was awed) "do you *work* there?"

And Mr. Quilter had spotted a sheaf of eight and a half by eleven paper protruding from the young man's pocket. "Are you a writer, sir? Is that a manuscript?"

The young man shuffled and came near blushing. "Naw. I'm not a writer. I'm a policeman. But I'm going to be a writer. This is a story I was trying to tell about what happened to me— But are you a writer? In *there?*"

Mr. Quilter's eyes were aglow under their invisible brows. "I, sir," he announced proudly, "am what makes writers tick. Are you interested?"

He was also, he might have added, what makes *detectives* tick. But he did not know that yet.

The Christmas trees were lighting up in front yards and in windows as Officer Tom Smith turned his rickety Model A onto the side street where Mr. Quilter lived. Hollywood is full of these quiet streets, where ordinary people live and move and have their being, and are happy or unhappy as chance wills, but both in a normal and unspectacular way. This is really Hollywood— the Hollywood that patronizes the twenty-cent fourth-run houses and crowds the stores on the Boulevard on Dollar Day.

To Mr. Quilter, saturated at the studio with the other Hollywood, this was always a relief. Kids were playing ball in the evening sun, radios were tuning in to Amos and Andy, and from the small houses came either the smell of cooking or the clatter of dish-washing.

And the Christmas trees, he knew, had been decorated not for the benefit of the photographers from the fan magazines, but because the children liked them and they looked warm and friendly from the street.

"Gosh, Mr. Quilter," Tom Smith was saying, "this is sure a swell break for me. You know, I'm a good copper. But to be honest I don't know as I'm very bright. And that's why I want to write, because maybe that way I can train myself to be and then I won't be a plain patrolman all my life. And besides, this writing, it kind of itches-like inside you."

"*Cacoëthes scribendi,*" observed Mr. Quilter, not unkindly. "You see, sir, you have hit, in your fumbling way, on one of the classic expressions for your condition."

"Now that's what I mean. You know what I mean even when I don't say it. Between us, Mr. Quilter . . . "

Mr. Quilter, his long thin legs outdistancing even the policeman's, led the way into his bungalow and on down the hall to a room which at first glance contained nothing but thousands of books. Mr. Quilter waved at them. "Here, sir, is assembled every helpful fact that mortal need know. But I cannot breathe life into these dry bones. Books are not written from books. But I can provide bones, and correctly articulated, for the life which you, sir— But here is a chair. And a reading lamp. Now, sir, let me hear your story."

Tom Smith shifted uncomfortably on the chair. "The trouble is," he confessed, "it hasn't got an ending."

Mr. Quilter beamed. "When I have heard it, I shall demonstrate to you, sir, the one ending it inevitably must have."

"I sure hope you will, because it's got to have and I promised her it would have and— You know Beverly Benson?"

"Why, yes. I entered the industry at the beginning of talkies. She was still somewhat in evidence. But why . . . ?"

"I was only a kid when she made *Sable Sin* and *Orchids at Breakfast* and all the rest, and I thought she was something pretty marvelous. There was a girl in our high school was supposed to look like her, and I used to think, 'Gee, if I could ever see the real Beverly Benson!' And last night I did."

"Hm. And this story, sir, is the result?"

"Yeah. And this too." He smiled wryly and indicated his wounded arm. "But I better read you the story." He cleared his throat loudly. "*The Red and Green Mystery,*" he declaimed. "By Arden Van Arden."

"A pseudonym, sir?"

"Well, I sort of thought . . . Tom Smith—that doesn't sound like a writer."

"Arden Van Arden, sir, doesn't sound like anything. But go on."

And Officer Tom Smith began his narrative:

THE RED AND GREEN MYSTERY

by ARDEN VAN ARDEN

It was a screwy party for the police to bust in on. Not that it was a raid or anything like that. God knows I've run into some bughouse parties that way, but I'm assigned to the jewelry squad now under Lieutenant Michaels, and when this call came in he took three other guys and me and we shot out to the big house in Laurel Canyon.

I wasn't paying much attention to where we were going and I wouldn't have known the place anyway, but I knew *her*, all right. She was standing in the doorway waiting for us. For just a minute it stumped me who she was, but then I knew. It was the eyes mostly. She'd changed a lot since *Sable Sin*, but you still couldn't miss the Beverly Benson eyes. The rest of her had got older (not older exactly either—you might maybe say richer) but the eyes were still the same. She had red hair. They didn't have technicolor when she was in pictures and I hadn't even known what color her hair was. It struck me funny seeing her like that—the way I'd been nuts about her when I was a kid and not even knowing what color her hair was.

She had on a funny dress—a little-girl kind of thing with a short skirt with flounces, I guess you call them. It looked familiar, but I couldn't make it. Not until I saw the mask that was lying in the hall, and then I knew. She was dressed like Minnie Mouse. It turned out later they all were—not like Minnie Mouse, but like all the characters in the cartoons. It was that kind of a party— a Disney Christmas party. There were studio drawings all over the walls, and there were little figures of extinct animals and winged ponies holding the lights on the Christmas tree.

She came right to the point. I could see Michaels liked that; some of these women throw a big act and it's an hour before you know what's been stolen. "It's my emeralds and rubies," she said. "They're gone. There are some other pieces missing too, but I don't so much care about them. The emeralds and the rubies are the important thing. You've got to find them."

"Necklaces?" Michaels asked.

"A necklace."

"Of emeralds *and* rubies?" Michaels knows his jewelry. His old man is in the business and tried to bring him up in it, but he joined the force. He knows a thing or two just the same, and his left eyebrow does tricks when he hears or sees something that isn't kosher. It was doing tricks now.

"I know that may sound strange, Lieutenant, but this is no time for discussing the esthetics of jewelry. It struck me once that it would be exciting to have red and green in one necklace, and I had it made. They're perfectly cut and matched, and it could never be duplicated."

Michaels didn't look happy. "You could drape it on a Christmas tree," he said. But Beverly Benson's Christmas tree was a cold white with the little animals holding blue lights.

78

Those Benson eyes were generally lovely and melting. Now they flashed. "Lieutenant, I summoned you to find my jewelry, not to criticize my taste. If I wanted a cultural opinion, I should hardly consult the police."

"You could do worse," Michaels said. "Now tell us all about it."

She took us into the library. The other men Michaels sent off to guard the exits, even if there wasn't much chance of the thief still sticking around. The Lieutenant told me once, when we were off duty, "Tom," he said, "you're the most useful man in my detail. Some of the others can think, and some of them can act; but there's not a damned one of them can just stand there and look so much like the Law." He's a little guy himself and kind of on the smooth and dapper side; so he keeps me with him to back him up, just standing there.

There wasn't much to what she told us. Just that she was giving this Disney Christmas party, like I said, and it was going along fine. Then late in the evening, when almost everybody had gone home, they got to talking about jewelry. She didn't know who started the talk that way, but there they were. And she told them about the emeralds and rubies.

"Then Fig—Philip Newton, you know—the photographer who does all those marvelous sand dunes and magnolia blossoms and things—" (her voice went all sort of tender when she mentioned him, and I could see Michaels taking it all in) "Fig said he didn't believe it. He felt the same way you do, Lieutenant, and I'm sure I can't see why. 'It's unworthy of you, darling,' he said. So I laughed and tried to tell him they were really beautiful—for they are, you know—and when he went on scoffing I said, 'All right, then, I'll show you.' So I went into the little dressing room where I keep my jewel box, and they weren't there. And that's all I know."

Then Michaels settled down to questions. When had she last seen the necklace? Was the lock forced? Had there been any prowlers around? What else was missing? And suchlike.

Beverly Benson answered impatiently, like she expected us to just go out there like that and grab the thief and say, "Here you are, lady." She had shown the necklace to another guest early in the party—he'd gone home long ago, but she gave us the name and address to check. No, the lock hadn't been forced. They hadn't seen anything suspicious, either. There were some small things missing, too—a couple of diamond rings, a star sapphire pendant, a pair of pearl earrings—but those didn't worry her so much. It was the emerald and ruby necklace that she wanted.

That left eyebrow went to work while Michaels thought about what she'd said. "If the lock wasn't forced, that lets out a chance prowler. It was somebody who knew you, who'd had a chance to lift your key or take an impression of it. Where'd you keep it?"

"The key? In my handbag usually. Tonight it was in a box on my dressing table."

Michaels sort of groaned. "And women wonder why jewels get stolen! Smith, get Ferguson and have him go over the box for prints. In the meantime, Miss Benson, give me a list of all your guests tonight. We'll take up the servants later. I'm warning you now it's a ten-to-one chance you'll ever see your Christmas tree ornament again unless a fence sings; but we'll do what we can. Then I'll deliver my famous little lecture on safes, and we'll pray for the future."

When I'd seen Ferguson, I waited for Michaels in the room where the guests were. There were only five left, and I didn't know who they were yet. They'd all taken off their masks; but they still had on their cartoon costumes. It felt screwy to sit there among them and think: This is serious, this is a felony, and look at those bright funny costumes.

Donald Duck was sitting by himself, with one hand resting on his long-billed mask while the other made steady grabs for the cigarette box beside him. His face looked familiar; I thought maybe I'd seen him in bits.

Three of them sat in a group: Mickey Mouse, Snow White, and Dopey. Snow White looked about fourteen at first, and it took you a while to realize she was a woman and a swell one at that. She was a little brunette, slender and cool-looking—a simple real kind of person that didn't seem to belong in a Hollywood crowd. Mickey Mouse was a hefty blond guy about as tall as I am and built like a tackle that could hold any line; but his face didn't go with his body. It was shrewd-like, and what they call sensitive. Dopey looked just that—a nice guy and not too bright.

Then over in another corner was a Little Pig. I don't know do they have names, but this was the one that wears a sailor suit and plays the fiddle. He had bushy hair sticking out from under the sailor cap and long skillful-looking hands stretched in front of him. The fiddle was beside him, but he didn't touch it. He was passed out—dead to the world, close as I could judge.

He and Donald were silent, but the group of three talked a little.

"I guess it didn't work," Dopey said.

"You couldn't help that, Harvey." Snow White's voice was just like I expected—not like Snow White's in the picture, but deep and smooth, like a stream that's running in the shade with moss on its banks. "Even an agent can't cast people."

"You're a swell guy, Madison," Mickey Mouse said. "You tried, and thanks. But if it's no go, hell, it's just no go. It's up to her."

"Miss Benson is surely more valuable to your career." The running stream was ice cold.

Now maybe I haven't got anything else that'd make me a good detective, but I do have curiosity, and here's where I saw a way to satisfy it. I spoke to all of them and I said, "I'd better take down some information while we're waiting for the Lieutenant." I started on Donald Duck. "Name?"

"Daniel Wappingham." The voice was English. I could tell that much. I don't have such a good ear for stuff like that, but I thought maybe it wasn't the best English.

"Occupation?"

"Actor."

And I took down the address and the rest of it. Then I turned to the drunk and shook him. He woke up part way but he didn't hear what I was saying. He just threw his head back and said loudly, "Waltzes! Ha!" and went under again. His voice was guttural—some kind of German, I guessed. I let it go at that and went over to the three.

Dopey's name was Harvey Madison; occupation, actor's representative—tenpercenter to you. Mickey Mouse was Philip Newton; occupation, photographer. (That was the guy Beverly Benson mentioned, the one she sounded that-away about.) And Snow White was Jane Newton.

"Any relation?" I asked.

"Yes and no," she said, so soft I could hardly hear her.

"Mrs. Newton," Mickey Mouse stated, "was once my wife." And the silence was so strong you could taste it.

I got it then. The two of them sitting there, remembering all the little things of their life together, being close to each other and yet somehow held apart. And on Christmas, too, when you remember things. There was still something between them even if they didn't admit it themselves. But Beverly Benson seemed to have a piece of the man, and where did Dopey fit in?

It sort of worried me. They looked like swell people—people that belonged together. But it was my job to worry about the necklace and not about people's troubles. I was glad Michaels came in just then.

He was being polite at the moment, explaining to Beverly Benson how Ferguson hadn't got anywhere with the prints and how the jewels were probably miles away by now. "But we'll do what we can," he said. "We'll talk to these people and find out what's possible. I doubt, however, if you'll ever see that necklace again. It was insured, of course, Miss Benson?"

"Of course. So were the other things, and with them I don't mind. But this necklace I couldn't conceivably duplicate, Lieutenant."

Just then Michael's eye lit on Donald Duck, and the eyebrow did tricks worth putting in a cartoon. "We'll take you one by one," he said. "You with the tail-feathers, we'll start with you. Come along, Smith."

Donald Duck grabbed a fresh cigarette, thought a minute, then reached out again for a handful. He whistled off key and followed us into the library.

"I gave all the material to your stooge here, Lieutenant," he began. "Name, Wappingham. Occupation, actor. Address—"

Michaels was getting so polite it had me bothered. "You won't mind, sir," he purred, "if I suggest a few corrections in your statement?"

Donald looked worried. "Don't you think I know my own name?"

"Possibly. But would you mind if I altered the statement to read: Name, Alfred Higgins. Occupation, jewel thief—conceivably reformed?"

The Duck wasn't so bad hit as you might have thought. He let out a pretty fair laugh and said, "So the fat's in the fire at last. But I'm glad you concede the possibility of my having reformed."

"The possibility, yes." Michaels underlined the word. "You admit you're Higgins?"

"Why not? You can't blame me for not telling you right off; it wouldn't look good when somebody had just been up to my old tricks. But now that you know— And by the way, Lieutenant, just how do you know?"

"Some bright boy at Scotland Yard spotted you in an American picture. Sent your description and record out to us just in case you ever took up your career again."

"Considerate of him, wasn't it?"

But Michaels wasn't in a mood for bright chatter any longer. We got down to work. We stripped that duck costume off the actor and left him shivering while we went over it inch by inch. He didn't like it much.

At last Michaels let him get dressed again. "You came in your car?"

"Yes."

"You're going home in a taxi. We could hold you on suspicion, but I'd sooner play it this way."

"Now I understand," Donald said, "what they mean by the high-handed American police procedure." And he went back into the other room with us.

All the same that was a smart move of Michaels'. It meant that Wappingham-Higgins-Duck would either have to give up all hope of the jewels (he certainly didn't have them on him) or lead us straight to them, because of course I knew a tail would follow that taxi and camp on his doorstep all next week if need be.

Donald Duck said goodnight to his hostess and nodded to the other guests. Then he picked up his mask.

"Just a minute," Michaels said. "Let's have a look at that."

"At this?" he asked innocent-like and backed toward the French window. Then he was standing there with an automatic in his hand. It was little but damned nasty-looking. I never thought what a good holster that long bill would make.

"Stay where you are, gentlemen," he said calmly. "I'm leaving undisturbed, *if* you don't mind."

The room was frozen still. Beverly Benson and Snow White let out little gasps of terror. The drunk was still dead to the world. The other two men looked at us and did nothing. It was Donald's round.

Or would've been if I hadn't played football in high school. It was a crazy chance, but I took it. I was the closest to him, only his eyes were on Michaels. It was a good flying tackle and it brought him to the ground in a heap consisting mostly of me. The mask smashed as we rolled over on it and I saw bright glitters pouring out.

Ferguson and O'Hara were there by now. One of them picked up his gun and the other snapped on the handcuffs. I got to my feet and turned to Michaels and Beverly Benson. They began to say things both at once about what a swell thing I'd done and then I keeled over.

When I came to I was on a couch in a little dark room. I learned later it was the dressing room where the necklace had been stolen. Somebody was bathing my arm and sobbing.

I sort of half sat up and said, "Where am I?" I always thought it was just in stories people said that, but it was the first thing popped into my mind.

"You're all right," a cool voice told me. "It's only a flesh wound."

"And I didn't feel a thing. . . . You mean he winged me?"

"I guess that's what you call it. When I told the Lieutenant I was a nurse he said I could fix you up and they wouldn't need the ambulance. You're all right now." Her voice was shaky in the dark, but I knew it was Snow White.

"Well, anyways, that broke the case pretty quick."

"But it didn't." And she explained: Donald had been up to his old tricks, all right; but what he had hidden in his bill was the diamonds and the sapphire and the pearl earrings, only no emerald and ruby necklace. Beverly Benson was wild, and Michaels and our men were combing the house from top to bottom to see where he'd stashed it.

"There," she said. She finished the story and the bandaging at the same time. "Can you stand up all right now?"

I was still kind of punchy. Nothing else could excuse me for what I said next. But she was so sweet and tender and good I wanted to say something nice, so like a dumb jerk I up and said, "You'd make some man a grand wife."

That was what got her. She just went to pieces—dissolved, you might say. I'm not used to tears on the shoulder of my uniform, but what could I do? I didn't try to say anything—just patted her back and let her talk. And I learned all about it.

How she'd married Philip Newton back in '29 when he was a promising young architect and she was an heiress just out of finishing school. How the fortune she was heiress to went fooey like all the others and her father took the quick way out. How the architect business went all to hell with no building going on and just when things were worst she had a baby. And then how

83

Philip started drinking, and finally— Well, anyways, there it was.

They'd both pulled themselves together now. She was making enough as a nurse to keep the kid (she was too proud to take alimony), and Philip was doing fine in this arty photographic line he'd taken up. A Newton photograph was The Thing to Have in the smart Hollywood set. But they couldn't come together again, not while he was such a success. If she went to him, he'd think she was begging; if he came to her, she'd think he was being noble. And Beverly Benson had set her cap for him.

Then this agent Harvey Madison (that's Dopey), who had known them both when, decided to try and fix things. He brought Snow White to this party; neither of them knew the other would be here. And it was a party and it was Christmas, and some of their happiest memories were Christmases together. I guess that's pretty much true of everybody. So she felt everything all over again, only—

"You don't know what it's done for me to tell you this. Please don't feel hurt; but in that uniform and everything you don't seem quite like a person. I can talk and feel free. And this has been hurting me all night and I had to say it."

I wanted to take the two of them and knock their heads together; only first off I had to find that emerald and ruby necklace. It isn't my job to heal broken hearts. I was feeling O.K. now, so we went back to the others.

Only they weren't there. There wasn't anybody in the room but only the drunk. I guessed where Mickey and Dopey were: stripped and being searched.

"Who's that?" I asked Snow White.

She looked at the Little Pig. "Poor fellow. He's been going through torture tonight too. That's Bela Strauss."

"Bella's a woman's name."

"He's part Hungarian." (I guess that might explain anything.) "He comes from Vienna. They brought him out here to write music for pictures because his name is Strauss. But he's a very serious composer—you know, like . . ." and she said some tongue twisters that didn't mean anything to me. "They think because his name is Strauss he can write all sorts of pretty dance tunes, and they won't let him write anything else. It's made him all twisted and unhappy, and he drinks too much."

"I can see that." I walked over and shook him. The sailor cap fell off. He stirred and looked up at me. I think it was the uniform that got him. He sat up sharp and said something in I guess German. Then he thought around a while and found some words in English.

"Why are you here? Why the police?" It came out in little one-syllable lumps, like he had to hunt hard for each sound. I told him. I tried to make it simple, but that wasn't easy. Snow White knew a little German, so she helped.

"Ach!" he sighed. "And I through it all slept!"

"That's one word for it," I said.

But this thief of jewels—him I have seen." It was a sweet job to get it out of him, but it boiled down to this: Where he passed out was on that same couch where they took me—right in the dressing-room. He came to once when he heard somebody in there, and he saw the person take something out of a box. Something red and green.

"Who was it?"

"The face, you understand, I do not see it. But the costume, yes. I see that clear. It was Mikki Maus." It sounded funny to hear something as American as Mickey Mouse in an accent like that.

It took Snow White a couple of seconds to realize who wore the Mickey Mouse outfit. Then she said "Philip" and fainted.

Officer Tom Smith laid down his manuscript. "That's all, Mr. Quilter."

"All, sir?"

"When Michaels came in, I told him. He figured Newton must've got away with the necklace and then the English crook made his try later and got the other stuff. They didn't find the necklace anywhere; but he must've pulled a fast one and stashed it away some place. With direct evidence like that, what can you do? They're holding him."

"And you chose, sir, not to end your story on that note of finality?"

"I couldn't, Mr. Quilter. I . . . I like that girl who was Snow White. I want to see the two of them together again and I'd sooner he was innocent. And besides, when we were leaving, Beverly Benson caught me alone. She said, 'I can't talk to your Lieutenant. He is *not* sympathetic. But you . . .'" Tom Smith almost blushed. "So she went on about how certain she was that Newton was innocent and begged me to help her prove it. So I promised."

"Hm," said Mr. Quilter. "Your problem, sir, is simple. You have good human values there in your story. Now we must round them out properly. And the solution is simple. We have two women in love with the hero, one highly sympathetic and the other less so; for the spectacle of a *passée* actress pursuing a new celebrity is not a pleasant one. This less sympathetic woman, to please the audience, must redeem herself with a gesture of self-immolation to secure the hero's happiness with the heroine. Therefore, sir, let her confess to the robbery."

"Confess to the . . . But Mr. Quilter, that makes a different story out of it. I'm trying to write as close as I can to what happened. And I promised—"

"Damme, sir, it's obvious. She did steal the necklace herself. She hasn't worked for years. She must need money. You mentioned insurance. The necklace was probably pawned long ago, and now she is trying to collect."

"But that won't work. It really was stolen. Somebody saw it earlier in the evening, and the search didn't locate it. And believe me, that squad knows how to search."

"Fiddle-faddle, sir." Mr. Quilter's close-cropped scalp was beginning to twitch. "What was seen must have been a paste imitation. She could dissolve that readily in acid and dispose of it down the plumbing. And Wappingham's presence makes her plot doubly sure; she knew him for what he was, and invited him as a scapegoat."

Tom Smith squirmed. "I'd almost think you were right, Mr. Quilter. Only Bela Strauss did see Newton take the necklace."

Mr. Quilter laughed. "If that is all that perturbs you . . ." He rose to his feet. "Come with me, sir. One of my neighbors is a Viennese writer now acting as a reader in German for Metropolis. He is also new in this country; his cultural background is identical with Strauss's. Come. But first we must step down to the corner drugstore and purchase what I believe is termed a comic book."

Mr. Quilter, his eyes agleam, hardly apologized for their intrusion into the home of the Viennese writer. He simply pointed at a picture in the comic book and demanded, "Tell me, sir. What character is that?"

The bemused Viennese smiled. "Why, that is Mikki Maus."

Mr. Quilter's finger rested on a pert little drawing of Minnie.

Philip Newton sat in the cold jail cell, but he was oblivious of the cold. He was holding his wife's hands through the bars and she was saying, "I could come to you now, dear, where I couldn't before. Then you might have thought it was just because you were successful, but now I can tell you how much I love you and need you—need you even when you're in disgrace. . . ."

They were kissing through the bars when Michaels came with the good news. "She's admitted it, all right. It was just the way Smith reconstructed it. She'd destroyed the paste replica and was trying to use us to pull off an insurance frame. She cracked when we had Strauss point out a picture of what he called 'Mikki Maus.' So you're free again, Newton. How's that for a Christmas present?"

"I've got a better one, officer. We're getting married again."

"You wouldn't need a new wedding ring, would you?" Michaels asked with filial devotion. "Michaels, Fifth between Spring and Broadway—fine stock."

Mr. Quilter laid down the final draft of Tom Smith's story, complete now with ending, and fixed the officer with a reproachful gaze. "You omitted, sir, the explanation of why such a misunderstanding should arise."

Tom Smith shifted uncomfortably. "I'm afraid, Mr. Quilter, I couldn't remember all that straight."

"It is simple. The noun *Maus* in German is of feminine gender. Therefore a *Mikki Maus* is a female. The male, naturally, is a *Mikki Mäserich*. I recall a delightful Viennese song of some seasons ago, which we once employed as background music, wherein the singer declares that he and his beloved will be forever paired, '*wie die Mikki Mikki Mikki Mikki Mikki Maus und der Mikki Mäserich*.' "

"Gosh," said Tom Smith. "You know a lot of things."

Mr. Quilter allowed himself to beam. "Between us, sir, there should be little that we do not know."

"We sure make a swell team as a detective."

The beam faded. "As a detective? Damme, sir, do you think I cared about your robbery? I simply explained the inevitable denouement to this story."

"But she didn't confess and make a gesture. Michaels had to prove it on her."

"All the better, sir. That makes her mysterious and deep. A Bette Davis role. I think we will first try for a magazine sale on this. Studios are more impressed by matter already in print. Then I shall show it to F.X., and we shall watch the squirmings of that genius Aram Melekian."

Tom Smith looked out the window, frowning. They made a team, all right; but which way? He still itched to write, but the promotion Michaels had promised him sounded good, too. Were he and this strange lean old man a team for writing or for detection?

The friendly red and green lights of the neighborhood Christmas trees seemed an equally good omen either way.

Margery Allingham

THE CASE IS ALTERED

$\mathbf{M}$r. Albert Campion, sitting in a first-class smoking compartment, was just reflecting sadly that an atmosphere of stultifying decency could make even Christmas something of a stuffed-owl occasion, when a new hogskin suitcase of distinctive design hit him on the knees. At the same moment a golf bag bruised the shins of the shy young man opposite, an armful of assorted magazines burst over the pretty girl in the far corner, and a blast of icy air swept round the carriage. There was the familiar rattle and lurch which indicates that the train has started at last, a squawk from a receding porter, and Lance Feering arrived before him apparently by rocket.

"Caught it," said the newcomer with the air of one confidently expecting congratulations, but as the train bumped jerkily he teetered back on his heels and collapsed between the two young people on the opposite seat.

"My dear chap, so we noticed," murmured Campion, and he smiled apologetically at the girl, now disentangling herself from the shellburst of newsprint. It was his own disarming my-poor-friend-is-afflicted variety of smile that he privately considered infallible, but on this occasion it let him down.

The girl, who was in the early twenties and was slim and fair, with eyes like licked brandy-balls, as Lance Feering inelegantly put it afterward, regarded him with grave interest. She stacked the magazines into a neat bundle and placed them on the seat opposite before returning to her own book. Even Mr. Feering, who was in one of his more exuberant moods, was aware of that chilly protest. He began to apologize.

Campion had known Feering in his student days, long before he had become one of the foremost designers of stage decors in Europe, and was used to him, but now even he was impressed. Lance's apologies were easy but also abject. He collected his bag, stowed it on a clear space on the rack above the shy young man's head, thrust his golf things under the seat, positively blushed when he claimed his magazines, and regarded the girl with pathetic humility. She glanced at him when he spoke, nodded coolly with just enough graciousness not to be gauche, and turned over a page.

Campion was secretly amused. At the top of his form Lance was reputed to be irresistible. His dark face with the long mournful nose and bright eyes were unhandsome enough to be interesting, and the quick gestures of his short painter's hands made his conversation picturesque. His singular lack of success on this occasion clearly astonished him and he sat back in his corner eyeing the young woman with covert mistrust.

Campion resettled himself to the two hours' rigid silence which etiquette demands from firstclass travelers who, although they are more than probably going to be asked to dance a reel together if not to share a bathroom only a few hours hence, have not yet been introduced.

There was no way of telling if the shy young man and the girl with the brandy-ball eyes knew each other, and whether they too were en route for Underhill, Sir Philip Cookham's Norfolk place. Campion was inclined to regard the coming festivities with a certain amount of lugubrious curiosity. Cookham himself was a magnificent old boy, of course, "one of the more valuable pieces in the Cabinet," as someone had once said of him, but Florence was a different kettle of fish. Born to wealth and breeding, she had grown blasé towards both of them and now took her delight in notabilities, a dangerous affectation in Campion's experience. She was some sort of remote aunt of his.

He glanced again at the young people, caught the boy unaware, and was immediately interested.

The illustrated magazine had dropped from the young man's hand and he was looking out of the window, his mouth drawn down at the corners and a narrow frown between his thick eyebrows. It was not an unattractive face, too young for strong character but decent and open enough in the ordinary way. At that particular moment, however, it wore a revealing expression. There was recklessness in the twist of the mouth and sullenness in the eyes, while the hand which lay upon the inside arm rest was clenched.

Campion was curious. Young people do not usually go away for Christmas in this top-step-at-the-dentist's frame of mind. The girl looked up from her book.

"How far is Underhill from the station?" she inquired.

"Five miles. They'll meet us." The shy young man turned to her so easily and with such obvious affection that any romantic theory Campion might have formed was knocked on the head instantly. The youngster's troubles evidently had nothing to do with love.

Lance had raised his head with bright-eyed interest at the gratuitous information and now a faintly sardonic expression appeared upon his lips. Campion sighed for him. For a man who fell in and out of love with the abandonment of a seal round a pool, Lance Feering was an impossible optimist. Already he was regarding the girl with that shy despair which so many ladies had found too piteous to be allowed to persist. Campion washed his hands of him and turned away just in time to notice a stranger glancing in at them from the corridor. It was a dark and arrogant young face and he recognized it instantly, feeling at the same time a deep wave of sympathy for old Cookham. Florence, he gathered, had done it again.

Young Victor Preen, son of old Preen of the Preen Aero Company, was certainly notable, not to say notorious. He had obtained much publicity in his short life for his sensational flights, but a great deal more for adventures less creditable; and when angry old gentlemen in the armchairs of exclusive clubs let themselves go about the blackguardliness of the younger generation, it was very often of Victor Preen that they were thinking.

He stood now a little to the left of the compartment window, leaning idly against the wall, his chin up and his heavy lids drooping. At first sight he did not appear to be taking any interest in the occupants of the compartment, but when the shy young man looked up, Campion happened to see the swift glance of recognition, and of something else, which passed between them. Presently, still with the same elaborate casualness, the man in the corridor wandered away, leaving the other staring in front of him, the same sullen expression still in his eyes.

The incident passed so quickly that it was impossible to define the exact nature of that second glance, but Campion was never a man to go imagining things, which was why he was surprised when they arrived at Minstree station to hear Henry Boule, Florence's private secretary, introducing the two and to notice that they met as strangers.

It was pouring with rain as they came out of the station, and Boule, who, like all Florence's secretaries, appeared to be suffering from an advanced case of nerves, bundled them all into two big Daimlers, a smaller car, and a shooting-brake. Campion looked round him at Florence's Christmas bag with some dismay. She had surpassed herself. Besides Lance there were at least half a dozen celebrities: a brace of political highlights, an angry looking lady novelist, Madja from the ballet, a startled R. A., and Victor Preen, as well as some twelve or thirteen unfamiliar faces who looked as if they might belong to Art, Money, or even mere Relations.

Campion became separated from Lance and was looking for him anxiously when he saw him at last in one of the cars, with the novelist on one side and the girl with brandy-ball eyes on the other, Victor Preen making up the ill-assorted four.

Since Campion was an unassuming sort of person he was relegated to the brake with Boule himself, the shy young man, and the whole of the luggage. Boule introduced them awkwardly and collapsed into a seat, wiping the beads from off his forehead with a relief which was a little too blatant to be tactful.

Campion, who had learned that the shy young man's name was Peter Groome, made a tentative inquiry of him as they sat jolting shoulder to shoulder in the back of the car. He nodded.

"Yes, it's the same family," he said. "Cookham's sister married a brother of my father's. I'm some sort of relation, I suppose."

The prospect did not seem to fill him with any great enthusiasm and once again Campion's curiosity was piqued. Young Mr. Groome was certainly not in seasonable mood.

In the ordinary way Campion would have dismissed the matter from his mind, but there was something about the youngster which attracted him, something indefinable and of a despairing quality, and moreover, there had been that curious intercepted glance in the train.

They talked in a desultory fashion throughout the uncomfortable journey. Campion learned that young Groome was in his father's firm of solicitors, that he was engaged to be married to the girl with the brandy-ball eyes, who was a Miss Patricia Bullard of an old north country family, and that he thought Christmas was a waste of time.

"I hate it," he said with a sudden passionate intensity which startled even his mild inquisitor. "All this sentimental good-will-to-all-men business is false and sickening. There's no such thing as good will. The world's rotten."

He blushed as soon as he had spoken and turned away.

"I'm sorry," he murmured, "but all this bogus Dickensian stuff makes me writhe."

Campion made no direct comment. Instead he asked with affable inconsequence, "Was that young Victor Preen I saw in the other car?"

Peter Groome turned his head and regarded him with the steady stare of the willfully obtuse.

"I was introduced to someone with a name like that, I think," he said carefully. "He was a little baldish man, wasn't he?"

"No, that's Sir George." The secretary leaned over the luggage to give the information. "Preen is the tall young man, rather handsome, with the very curling hair. He's *the* Preen, you know." He sighed. "It seems very young to be a millionaire, doesn't it?"

"Obscenely so," said Mr. Peter Groome abruptly, and returned to his despairing contemplation of the landscape.

Underhill was *en fête* to receive them. As soon as Campion observed the preparations, his sympathy for young Mr. Groome increased, for to a jaundiced eye Lady Florence's display might well have proved as dispiriting as Preen's bank balance. Florence had "gone all Dickens," as she said herself at the top of her voice, linking her arm through Campion's, clutching the R. A. with her free hand, and capturing Lance with a bright birdlike eye.

The great Jacobean house was festooned with holly. An eighteen-foot tree stood in the great hall. Yule logs blazed on iron dogs in the wide hearths and already the atmosphere was thick with that curious Christmas smell which is part cigar smoke and part roasting food.

Sir Philip Cookham stood receiving his guests with pathetic bewilderment. Every now and again his features broke into a smile of genuine welcome as he saw a face he knew. He was a distinguished-looking old man with a fine head and eyes permanently worried by his country's troubles.

"My dear boy, delighted to see you. Delighted," he said, grasping Campion's hand. "I'm afraid you've been put over in the Dower House. Did Florence tell you? She said you wouldn't mind, but I insisted that Feering went over there with you and also young Peter." He sighed and brushed away the visitor's hasty reassurances. "I don't know why the dear girl never feels she has a party unless the house is so overcrowded that our best friends have to sleep in the annex," he said sadly.

The "dear girl," looking not more than fifty-five of her sixty years, was clinging to the arm of the lady novelist at that particular moment and the two women were emitting mirthless parrot cries at each other. Cookham smiled.

"She's happy, you know," he said indulgently. "She enjoys this sort of thing. Unfortunately I have a certain amount of urgent work to do this weekend, but we'll get in a chat, Campion, some time over the holiday. I want to hear your news. You're a lucky fellow. You can tell your adventures."

The lean man grimaced. "More secret sessions, sir?" he inquired.

The cabinet minister threw up his hands in a comic but expressive little gesture before he turned to greet the next guest.

As he dressed for dinner in his comfortable room in the small Georgian dower house across the park, Campion was inclined to congratulate himself on his quarters. Underhill itself was a little too much of the ancient monument for strict comfort.

He had reached the tie stage when Lance appeared. He came in very elegant indeed and highly pleased with himself. Campion diagnosed the symptoms immediately and remained irritatingly incurious.

Lance sat down before the open fire and stretched his sleek legs.

"It's not even as if I were a goodlooking blighter, you know," he observed invitingly when the silence had become irksome to him. "In fact, Campion, when I consider myself I simply can't understand it. Did I so much as speak to the girl?"

"I don't know," said Campion, concentrating on his dressing. "Did you?"

"No." Lance was passionate in his denial. "Not a word. The hard-faced female with the inky fingers and the walrus mustache was telling me her life story all the way home in the car. This dear little poppet with the eyes was nothing more than a warm bundle at my side. I give you my dying oath on that. And yet—well, it's extraordinary, isn't it?"

Campion did not turn round. He could see the artist quite well through the mirror in front of him. Lance had a sheet of notepaper in his hand and was regarding it with that mixture of feigned amusement and secret delight which was typical of his eternally youthful spirit.

"Extraordinary," he repeated, glancing at Campion's unresponsive back. "She had nice eyes. Like licked brandy-balls."

"Exactly," agreed the lean man by the dressing table. "I thought she seemed very taken up with her fiancé, young Master Groome, though," he added tactlessly.

"Well, I noticed that, you know," Lance admitted, forgetting his professions of disinterest. "She hardly recognized my existence in the train. Still, there's absolutely no accounting for women. I've studied 'em all my life and never understood 'em yet. I mean to say, take this case in point. That kid ignored me, avoided me, looked through me. And yet look at this. I found it in my room when I came up to change just now."

Campion took the note with a certain amount of distaste. Lovely women were invariably stooping to folly, it seemed, but even so he could not accustom himself to the spectacle. The message was very brief. He read it at a glance and for the first time that day he was conscious of that old familiar flicker down the spine as his experienced nose smelled trouble. He re-read the three lines.

"There is a sundial on a stone pavement just off the drive. We saw it from the car. I'll wait ten minutes there for you half an hour after the party breaks up tonight."

There was neither signature nor initial, and the summons broke off as baldly as it had begun.

"Amazing, isn't it?" Lance had the grace to look shamefaced.

"Astounding." Campion's tone was flat. "Staggering, old boy. Er—fishy."

"Fishy?"

"Yes, don't you think so?" Campion was turning over the single sheet thoughtfully and there was no amusement in the pale eyes behind his horn-rimmed spectacles. "How did it arrive?"

"In an unaddressed envelope. I don't suppose she caught my name. After all, there must be some people who don't know it yet." Lance was grinning impudently. "She's batty, of course. Not safe out and all the rest of it. But I liked her eyes and she's very young."

Campion perched himself on the edge of the table. He was still very serious.

"It's disturbing, isn't it?" he said. "Not nice. Makes one wonder."

"Oh, I don't know." Lance retrieved his property and tucked it into his pocket. "She's young and foolish, and it's Christmas."

Campion did not appear to have heard him. "I wonder," he said. "I should keep the appointment, I think. It may be unwise to interfere, but yes, I rather think I should."

"You're telling me." Lance was laughing. "I may be wrong, of course," he added defensively, "but I think that's a cry for help. The poor girl evidently saw that I looked a dependable sort of chap and—er—having her back against the wall for some reason or other she turned instinctively to the stranger with the kind face. Isn't that how you read it?"

"Since you press me, no. Not exactly," said Campion, and as they walked over to the house together he remained thoughtful and irritatingly uncommunicative.

Florence Cookham excelled herself that evening. Her guests were exhorted "to be young again," with the inevitable result that Underhill contained a company of irritated and exhausted people long before midnight.

One of her ladyship's more erroneous beliefs was that she was a born organizer, and that the real secret of entertaining people lay in giving everyone something to do. Thus Lance and the R. A.—now even more startled-looking than ever—found themselves superintending the decoration of the great tree, while the girl with the brandy-ball eyes conducted a small informal dance in the drawing room, the lady novelist scowled over the bridge table, and the ballet star refused flatly to arrange amateur theatricals.

Only two people remained exempt from this tyranny. One was Sir Philip himself, who looked in every now and again, ready to plead urgent work awaiting him in his study whenever his wife pounced upon him, and the other was Mr. Campion, who had work to do on his own account and had long mastered the difficult art of self-effacement. Experience had taught him that half the secret of this maneuver was to keep discreetly on the move and he strolled from one part to another, always ready to look as if he belonged to any one of them should his hostess's eye ever come to rest upon him inquiringly.

For once his task was comparatively simple. Florence was in her element as she rushed about surrounded by breathless assistants, and at one period the very air in her vicinity seemed to have become thick with colored paper wrappings, yards of red ribbons, and a colored snowstorm of little address tickets as she directed the packing of the presents for the Tenants' Tree, a second monster which stood in the ornamental barn beyond the kitchens.

Campion left Lance to his fate, which promised to be six or seven hours' hard labor at the most moderate estimate, and continued his purposeful meandering. His lean figure drifted among the company with an apparent aimlessness which was deceptive. There was hidden urgency in his lazy movements and his pale eyes behind his spectacles were inquiring and unhappy.

He found Patricia Bullard dancing with Preen, and paused to watch them as they swung gracefully by him. The man was in a somewhat flamboyant mood, flashing his smile and his noisy witticisms about him after the fashion of his kind, but the girl was not so content. As Campion caught sight of her pale face over her partner's sleek shoulder his eyebrows rose. For an instant he almost believed in Lance's unlikely suggestion. The girl actually did look as though she had her back to the wall. She was watching the doorway nervously and her shiny eyes were afraid.

Campion looked about him for the other young man who should have been present, but Peter Groome was not in the ballroom, nor in the great hall, nor yet among the bridge tables in the drawing room, and half an hour later he had still not put in an appearance.

Campion was in the hall himself when he saw Patricia slip into the anteroom which led to Sir Philip's private study, that holy of holies which even Florence treated with a wholesome awe. Campion had paused for a moment to enjoy the spectacle of Lance, wild eyed and tight lipped, wrestling with the last of the blue glass balls and tinsel streamers on the Guests' Tree, when he caught sight of the flare of her silver skirt disappearing round a familiar doorway under one branch of the huge double staircase.

It was what he had been waiting for, and yet when it came his disappointment was unexpectedly acute, for he too had liked her smile and her brandy-ball eyes. The door was ajar when he reached it, and he pushed it open an inch or so farther, pausing on the threshold to consider the scene within. Patricia was on her knees before the paneled door which led into the inner room and was trying somewhat ineffectually to peer through the keyhole.

Campion stood looking at her regretfully, and when she straightened herself and paused to listen, with every line of her young body taut with the effort of concentration, he did not move.

Sir Philip's voice amid the noisy chatter behind him startled him, however, and he swung round to see the old man talking to a group on the other side of the room. A moment later the girl brushed past him and hurried away.

Campion went quietly into the anteroom. The study door was still closed and he moved over to the enormous period fireplace which stood beside it. This particular fireplace, with its carved and painted front, its wrought iron dogs and deeply recessed inglenooks, was one of the showpieces of Underhill.

At the moment the fire had died down and the interior of the cavern was dark, warm and inviting. Campion stepped inside and sat down on the oak set-tee, where the shadows swallowed him. He had no intention of being unduly officious, but his quick ears had caught a faint sound in the inner room and Sir Philip's private sanctum was no place for furtive movements when its master was out of the way. He had not long to wait.

A few moments later the study door opened very quietly and someone came out. The newcomer moved across the room with a nervous, unsteady tread, and paused abruptly, his back to the quiet figure in the inglenook. Campion recognized Peter Groome and his thin mouth narrowed. He was sorry. He had liked the boy.

The youngster stood irresolute. He had his hands behind him, holding in one of them a flamboyant parcel wrapped in the colored paper and scarlet rib-bon which littered the house. A sound from the hall seemed to fluster him for he spun round, thrust the parcel into the inglenook which was the first hiding place to present itself, and returned to face the new arrival. It was the girl again. She came slowly across the room, her hands outstretched and her face raised to Peter's.

In view of everything, Campion thought it best to stay where he was, nor had he time to do anything else. She was speaking urgently, passionate sinceri-ty in her low voice.

"Peter, I've been looking for you. Darling, there's something I've got to say and if I'm making an idiotic mistake then you've got to forgive me. Look here, you wouldn't go and do anything silly, would you? Would you, Peter? Look at me."

"My dear girl." He was laughing unsteadily and not very convincingly with his arms around her. "What on earth are you talking about?"

She drew back from him and peered earnestly into his face.

"You wouldn't, would you? Not even if it meant an awful lot. Not even if for some reason or other you felt you *had* to. Would you?"

He turned from her helplessly, a great weariness in the lines of his sturdy back, but she drew him round, forcing him to face her.

"Would he what, my dear?"

Florence's arch inquiry from the doorway separated them so hurriedly that she laughed delightedly and came briskly into the room, her gray curls a trifle disheveled and her draperies flowing.

"Too divinely young, I love it!" she said devastatingly. "I must kiss you both. Christmas is the time for love and youth and all the other dear charming things, isn't it? That's why I adore it. But my dears, not here. Not in this silly poky little room. Come along and help me, both of you, and then you can slip away and dance together later on. But don't come in this room. This is Philip's dull part of the house. Come along this minute. Have you seen my precious tree? Too incredibly distinguished, my darlings, with two great artists at work on it. You shall both tie on a candle. Come along."

She swept them away like an avalanche. No protest was possible. Peter shot a single horrified glance towards the fireplace, but Florence was gripping his arm; he was thrust out into the hall and the door closed firmly behind him.

Campion was left in his corner with the parcel less than a dozen feet away from him on the opposite bench. He moved over and picked it up. It was a long flat package wrapped in holly-printed tissue. Moreover, it was unexpectedly heavy and the ends were unbound.

He turned it over once or twice, wrestling with a strong disinclination to interfere, but a vivid recollection of the girl with the brandy-ball eyes, in her silver dress, her small pale face alive with anxiety, made up his mind for him and, sighing, he pulled the ribbon.

The typewritten folder which fell on to his knees surprised him at first, for it was not at all what he had expected, nor was its title, "Report on Messrs. Anderson and Coleridge, Messrs. Saunders, Duval and Berry, and Messrs. Birmingham and Rose," immediately enlightening, and when he opened it at random a column of incomprehensible figures confronted him. It was a scribbled pencil note in a precise hand at the foot of one of the pages which gave him his first clue.

"These figures are estimated by us to be a reliable forecast of this firm's full working capacity,"

he read, and after that he became very serious indeed.

Two hours later it was bitterly cold in the garden and a thin white mist hung over the dark shrubbery which lined the drive when Mr. Campion, picking his way cautiously along the clipped grass verge, came quietly down to the sundial walk. Behind him the gabled roofs of Underhill were shadowy against a frosty sky. There were still a few lights in the upper windows, but below stairs the entire place was in darkness.

Campion hunched his greatcoat about him and plodded on, unwonted severity in the lines of his thin face.

He came upon the sundial walk at last and paused, straining his eyes to see through the mist. He made out the figure standing by the stone column, and heaved a sigh of relief as he recognized the jaunty shoulders of the Christmas tree decorator. Lance's incurable romanticism was going to be useful at last, he reflected with wry amusement.

He did not join his friend but withdrew into the shadows of a great clump of rhododendrons and composed himself to wait. He intensely disliked the situation in which he found himself. Apart from the extreme physical discomfort involved, he had a natural aversion towards the project on hand, but little fairhaired girls with shiny eyes can be very appealing.

It was a freezing vigil. He could hear Lance stamping about in the mist, swearing softly to himself, and even that supremely comic phenomenon had its unsatisfactory side.

They were both shivering and the mist's damp fingers seemed to have stroked their very bones when at last Campion stiffened. He had heard a rustle behind him and presently there was a movement in the wet leaves, followed by the sharp ring of feet on the stones. Lance swung round immediately, only to drop back in astonishment as a tall figure bore down.

"Where is it?"

Neither the words nor the voice came as a complete surprise to Campion, but the unfortunate Lance was taken entirely off his guard.

"Why, hello, Preen," he said involuntarily. "What the devil are you doing here?"

The newcomer had stopped in his tracks, his face a white blur in the uncertain light. For a moment he stood perfectly still and then, turning on his heel, he made off without a word.

"Ah, but I'm afraid it's not quite so simple as that, my dear chap."

Campion stepped out of his friendly shadows and as the younger man passed, slipped an arm through his and swung him round to face the startled Lance, who was coming up at the double.

"You can't clear off like this," he went on, still in the same affable, conversational tone. "You have something to give Peter Groome, haven't you? Something he rather wants?"

"Who the hell are you?" Preen jerked up his arm as he spoke and might have wrenched himself free had it not been for Lance, who had recognized Campion's voice and, although completely in the dark, was yet quick enough to grasp certain essentials.

"That's right, Preen," he said, seizing the man's other arm in a bear's hug. "Hand it over. Don't be a fool. Hand it over."

This line of attack appeared to be inspirational, since they felt the powerful youngster stiffen between them.

"Look here, how many people know about this?"

"The world—" Lance was beginning cheerfully when Campion forestalled him.

"We three and Peter Groome," he said quietly. "At the moment Sir Philip has no idea that Messr. Preen's curiosity concerning the probable placing of government orders for aircraft parts has overstepped the bounds of common sense. You're acting alone, I suppose?"

"Oh, lord, yes, of course." Preen was cracking dangerously. "If my old man gets to hear of this I—oh, well, I might as well go and crash."

"I thought so." Campion sounded content. "Your father has a reputation to consider. So has our young friend Groome. You'd better hand it over."

"What?"

"Since you force me to be vulgar, whatever it was you were attempting to use as blackmail, my precious young friend," he said. "Whatever it may be, in fact, that you hold over young Groome and were trying to use in your attempt to force him to let you have a look at a confidential government report concerning the orders which certain aircraft firms were likely to receive in the next six months. In your position you could have made pretty good use of them, couldn't you? Frankly, I haven't the faintest idea what this incriminating document may be. When I was young, objectionably wealthy youths accepted I. O. U.'s from their poorer companions, but now that's gone out of fashion. What's the modern equivalent? An R. D. check, I suppose?"

Preen said nothing. He put his hand in an inner pocket and drew out an envelope which he handed over without a word. Campion examined the slip of pink paper within by the light of a pencil torch.

"You kept it for quite a time before trying to cash it, didn't you?" he said. "Dear me, that's rather an old trick and it was never admired. Young men who are careless with their accounts have been caught out like that before. It simply wouldn't have looked good to his legal-minded old man, I take it? You two seem to be hampered by your respective papas' integrity. Yes, well, you can go now."

Preen hesitated, opened his mouth to protest, but thought better of it. Lance looked after his retreating figure for some little time before he returned to his friend.

"Who wrote that blinking note?" he demanded.

"He did, of course," said Campion brutally. "He wanted to see the report but was making absolutely sure that young Groome took all the risks of being found with it."

"Preen wrote the note," Lance repeated blankly.

"Well, naturally," said Campion absently. "That was obvious as soon as the report appeared in the picture. He was the only man in the place with the necessary special information to make use of it."

Lance made no comment. He pulled his coat collar more closely about his throat and stuffed his hands into his pockets.

All the same the artist was not quite satisfied, for, later still, when Campion was sitting in his dressing gown writing a note at one of the little escritoires which Florence so thoughtfully provided in her guest bedrooms, he came padding in again and stood warming himself before the fire.

"Why?" he demanded suddenly. "Why did I get the invitation?"

"Oh, that was a question of luggage," Campion spoke over his shoulder.

"That bothered me at first, but as soon as we fixed it onto Preen that little mystery became blindingly clear. Do you remember falling into the carriage this afternoon? Where did you put your elegant piece of gent's natty suitcasing? Over young Groome's head. Preen saw it from the corridor and assumed that the chap was sitting *under his own bag*! He sent his own man over here with the note, told him not to ask for Peter by name but to follow the nice new pigskin suitcase upstairs."

Lance nodded regretfully. "Very likely," he said sadly. "Funny thing. I was sure it was the girl."

After a while he came over to the desk. Campion put down his pen and indicated the written sheet.

"Dear Groome," it ran, "I enclose a little matter that I should burn forthwith. The package you left in the inglenook is still there, right at the back on the left-hand side, cunningly concealed under a pile of logs. It has not been seen by anyone who could possibly understand it. If you nipped over very early this morning you could return it to its appointed place without any trouble. If I may venture a word of advice, it is never worth it."

The author grimaced. "It's a bit avuncular," he admitted awkwardly, "but what else can I do? His light is still on, poor chap. I thought I'd stick it under his door."

Lance was grinning wickedly. "That's fine," he murmured. "The old man does his stuff for reckless youth. There's just the signature now and that ought to be as obvious as everything else has been to you. I'll write it for you. 'Merry Christmas. Love from Santa Claus.'"

"You win," said Mr. Campion.

Thomas Larry Adcock

CHRISTMAS COP

By the second week of December, when they light up the giant fir tree behind the statue of a golden Prometheus overlooking the ice-skating rink at Rockefeller Center, Christmas in New York has got you by the throat.

Close to five hundred street-corner Santas (temporarily sober and none too happy about it) have been ringing bells since the day after Thanksgiving; the support pillars on Macy's main selling floor have been dolled up like candy canes since Hallowe'en; the tipping season arrives in the person of your apartment-house super, all smiles and open-palmed and suddenly available to fix the leaky pipes you've complained about since July; total strangers insist not only that you have a nice day but that you be of good cheer on top of it; and your Con Ed bill says HAPPY HOLIDAYS at the top of the page in a festive red-and-green dot-matrix.

In addition, New York in December is crawling with boosters, dippers, yokers, smash-and-grabbers, bindlestiffs on the mope, aggressive pros offering special holiday rates to guys cruising around at dusk in station wagons with Jersey plates, pigeon droppers and assorted other bunco artists, purveyors of all manner of dubious gift items, and entrepreneurs of the informal branch of the pharmaceutical trade. My job is to try and prevent at least some of these fine upstanding perpetrators from scoring against at least some of their natural Yuletide prey—the seasonal hordes of out-of-towners, big-ticket shoppers along Fifth Avenue, blue-haired Wednesday matinee ladies, and wide-eyed suburban matrons lined up outside Radio City Music Hall with big, snatchable shoulder bags full of credit cards.

I'm your friendly neighborhood plainclothesman. *Very* plain clothes. The guy in the grungy overcoat and watch cap and jeans and beat-up shoes and a week's growth of black beard shambling along the street carrying something in a brown paper bag—that ubiquitous New York bum you hurry past every day while holding your breath—might be me.

101

The name is Neil Hockaday, but everybody calls me Hock, my fellow cops and my snitches alike. And that's no pint of muscatel in my paper bag, it's my point-to-point shortwave radio. I work out of a boroughwide outfit called Street Crimes Unit-Manhattan, which is better known as the befitting S.C.U.M. patrol.

For twelve years, I've been a cop, the last three on S.C.U.M. patrol, which is a prestige assignment despite the way we dress on the job. In three years, I've made exactly twice the collars I did in my first nine riding around in precinct squad cars taking calls from sector dispatch. It's all going to add up nicely when I go for my gold shield someday. Meanwhile, I appreciate being able to work pretty much unsupervised, which tells you I'm at least a half honest cop in a city I figure to be about three-quarters crooked.

Sometimes I do a little bellyaching about the department—and who doesn't complain along about halfway through the second cold one after shift? —but mainly I enjoy the work I do. What I like about it most is how I'm always up against the elements of chance and surprise, one way or another.

That's something you can't say about most careers these days. Not even a cop's, really. Believe it or not, you have plenty of tedium if you're a uniform sealed up in a blue-and-white all day, even in New York. But the way my job plays, I'm out there on the street mostly alone and it's an hour-by-hour proposition: fifty-eight minutes of walking around with my pores open so I don't miss anything and two minutes of surprise.

No matter what, I've got to be ready because surprise comes in several degrees of seriousness. And when it does, it comes out of absolutely nowhere.

On the twenty-fourth of December, I wasn't ready.

To me, it was a day like any other. That was wishful thinking, of course. To a holiday-crazed town, it was Christmas Eve and the big payoff was on deck—everybody out there with kids and wives and roast turkeys and plenty of money was anxious to let the rest of us know how happy they were.

Under the circumstances, it was just as well that I'd pulled duty. I wouldn't have had anyplace to go besides the corner pub, as it happened—or, if I could stand it, the easy chair in front of my old Philco for a day of *Christmas in Connecticut* followed by *Miracle on Thirty-fourth Street* followed by *A Christmas Carol* followed by *March of the Wooden Soldiers* followed by Midnight Mass live from St. Patrick's.

Every year since my divorce five years ago, I'd dropped by my ex-wife's place out in Queens for Christmas Eve. I'd bring champagne, oysters, an expensive gift, and high hopes of spending the night. But this year she'd wrecked my plans. She telephoned around the twentieth to tell me about this new boyfriend of hers—some guy who wasn't a cop and whose name sounded like a respiratory disease, Flummong—and how he was taking her out to some rectangular state in the Middle West to meet his parents, who grow wheat. Swell.

So on the twenty-fourth, I got up at the crack of noon and decided that the only thing that mattered was business. Catching bad guys on the final, frantic shopping day—that was the ticket. I reheated some coffee from the day before, then poured some into a mug after I picked out something small, brown, and dead. I also ate a week-old piece of babka and said, "Bah, humbug!" right out loud.

I put on my quilted longjohns and strapped a lightweight .32 automatic Baretta Puma around my left ankle. Then I pulled on a pair of faded grey corduroys with holes in the knees, a black turtleneck sweater with bleach stains to wear over my beige bulletproof vest and my patrolman's badge on a chain, a New York Knicks navy-blue stocking cap with a red ball on top, and Army-surplus boots. The brown-paper bag for my PTP I'd saved from the past Sunday when I'd gotten bagels down on Essex Street and shaved last.

I strapped on my shoulder holster and packed away the heavy piece, my .44 Charter Arms Bulldog. Then I topped off my ensemble with an olive-drab officer's greatcoat that had seen lots of action in maybe the Korean War. One of the side pockets was slashed open. Moths and bayonet tips had made holes in other places. I dropped a pair of nickel-plated NYPD bracelets into the good pocket.

By half past the hour, I was in the Bleecker Street subway station near where I live in the East Village. I dropped a quarter into a telephone on the platform and told the desk sergeant at Midtown South to be a good guy and check me off for the one o'clock muster. A panhandler with better clothes than mine and a neatly printed plywood sandwich sign hanging around his shoulders caught my eye. The sign read, TRYING TO RAISE $1,000,000 FOR WINE RESEARCH. I gave him a buck and caught the uptown D train.

When I got out at Broadway and Thirty-fourth Street, the weather had turned cold and clammy. The sky had a smudgy grey overcast to it. It would be the kind of afternoon when everything in Manhattan looks like a black-and-white snapshot. It wasn't very Christmaslike, which suited me fine.

Across the way, in a triangle of curbed land that breaks up the Broadway and Sixth Avenue traffic flow at the south end of Herald Square, winos stood around in a circle at the foot of a statue of Horace Greeley. Greeley's limed shoulders were mottled by frozen bird dung and one granite arm was forever pointed toward the westward promise. I thought about my ex and the Flummong guy. The winos coughed, their foul breath hanging in frosted lumps of exhaled air, and awaited a ritual opening of a large economy-sized bottle of Thunderbird. The leader broke the seal and poured a few drops on the ground, which is a gesture of respect to mates recently dead or imprisoned. Then he took a healthy swallow and passed it along.

On the other side of the statue, a couple of dozen more guys carrying the stick (living on the street, that is) reclined on benches or were curled up over heating grates. All were in proper position to protect their stash in the event of sleep: money along one side of their hat brims, one hand below as a sort of pillow. The only way they could be robbed was if someone came along and cut off their hands, which has happened.

Crowds of last-minute shoppers jammed the sidewalks everywhere. Those who had to pass the bums (and me) did so quickly, out of fear and disgust, even at this time of goodwill toward men. It's a curious thing how so many comfortable middle-class folks believe vagrants and derelicts are dangerous, especially when you consider that the only people who have caused them any serious harm have been other comfortable middle-class folks with nice suits and offices and lawyers.

Across Broadway, beyond the bottle gang around the stone Greeley, I recognized a mope I'd busted about a year ago for boosting out of a flash clothes joint on West Fourteenth street. He was a scared kid of sixteen and lucky I'd gotten to him first. The store goons would have broken his thumbs. He was an Irish kid who went by the street name Whiteboy and he had nobody. We have lots of kids like Whiteboy in New York, and other cities, too. But we don't much want to know about them.

Now he leaned against a Florsheim display window, smoking a cigarette and scoping out the straight crowd around Macy's and Gimbels. Whiteboy, so far as I knew, was a moderately successful small-fry shoplifter, purse snatcher, and pickpocket.

I decided to stay put and watch him watch the swarm of possible marks until he got up enough nerve to move on somebody he figured would give him the biggest return for the smallest risk, like any good businessman. I moved back against a wall and stuck out my hand and asked passers-by for spare change. (This is not exactly regulation, but it guarantees that nobody will look at my face and it happens to be how I cover the monthly alimony check.) A smiling young fellow in a camel topcoat, the sort of guy who might be a Jaycee from some town up in Rockland County, pressed paper on me and whispered, "Bless you, brother." I looked down and saw that he'd given me a circular from the Church of Scientology in the size, color, and shape of a dollar bill.

When I looked up again, Whiteboy was crossing Broadway. He tossed his cigarette into the street and concentrated on the ripe prospect of a mink-draped fat lady on the outside of a small mob shoving its way into Gimbels. She had a black patent-leather purse dangling from a rhinestone-studded strap clutched in her hand. Whiteboy could pluck it from her pudgy fingers so fast and gently she'd be in third-floor housewares before she noticed.

I followed after him when he passed me. Then, sure enough, he made the snatch. I started running down the Broadway bus lane toward him. Whiteboy must have lost his touch because the fat lady turned and pointed at him and hollered "Thief!" She stepped right in front of me and I banged into her and she shrieked at me, "Whyn't you sober up and get a job, you bum you?"

Whiteboy whirled around and looked at me full in the face. He made me. Then he started running, too.

He darted through the thicket of yellow taxicabs, cars, and vans and zigzagged his way toward Greeley's statue. There was nothing I could do but chase him on foot. Taking a shot in such a congestion of traffic and pedestrians would get me up on IAD charges just as sure as if I'd stolen the fat lady's purse myself.

Then a funny thing happened.

Just as I closed in on Whiteboy, all those bums lying around on the little curbed triangle suddenly got up and blocked me as neatly as a line of zone defensemen for the Jets. Eight or ten big, groggy guys fell all over me and I lost Whiteboy.

I couldn't have been more frustrated. A second collar on a guy like Whiteboy would have put him away for two years' hard time, minimum. Not to mention how it would get me a nice commendation letter for my personal file. But in this business, you can't spend too much time crying over a job that didn't come off. So I headed east on Thirty-second toward Fifth Avenue.

At mid-block, I stopped to help a young woman in a raggedy coat with four bulging shopping bags and three shivering kids. She set the bags on the damp sidewalk and rubbed her bare hands as I neared her. Two girls and a boy, the oldest maybe seven, huddled around her. "How much farther?" one of the girls asked.

I didn't hear an answer. I walked up and asked the woman, "Where you headed, lady?" She looked away, embarrassed because of the tears in her eyes. She was small and slender, with light-brown skin and black hair pulled straight back from her face and held with a rubber band. A gust of dry wind knifed through the air.

"Could you help me?" she finally asked. "I'm just going up to the hotel at the corner. These bags are cutting my hands."

She meant the Martinique. It's a big dark hulk of a hotel, possibly grand back in the days when Herald Square was nearly glamorous. Now it's peeling and forbidding and full of people who have lost their way for a lot of different reasons—most of them women and children. When welfare families can't pay the rent anymore and haven't any place to go, the city puts them up "temporarily" at the Martinique. It's a stupid deal even by New York's high standards of senselessness. The daily hotel rate amounts to a monthly tab of about two grand for one room and an illegal hotplate, which is maybe ten times the rent on the apartment the family just lost.

"What's your name?" I asked her.

She didn't hesitate, but there was a shyness to her voice. "Frances. What's yours?"

"Hock." I picked up her bags, two in each hand. "Hurry up, it's going to snow," I said. The bags were full of children's clothes, a plastic radio, some storybooks, and canned food. I hoped they wouldn't break from the sidewalk dampness.

Frances and her kids followed me and I suppose we looked like a line of shabby ducks walking along. A teenage girl in one of those second-hand men's tweed overcoats you'd never find at the Goodwill took our picture with a Nikon equipped with a telephoto lens.

I led the way into the hotel and set the bags down at the admitting desk. Frances's three kids ran off to join a bunch of other kids who were watching a couple of old coots with no teeth struggling with a skinny spruce tree at the entry of what used to be the dining room. Now it was dusty and had no tables, just a few graffiti-covered vending machines.

Frances grabbed my arm when I tried to leave her. "It's not much, I know that. But maybe you can use it all the same." She let me go, then put out a hand like she wanted to shake. I slipped off my glove and took hold of her small, bone-chilled fingers. She passed me two dimes. "Thanks, and happy Christmas."

She looked awfully brave and awfully heartsick, too. Most down-and-outers look like that, but people who eat regularly and know where their next dollar will likely come from make the mistake of thinking they're stupid and confused, or maybe shiftless or crazy.

I tried to refuse the tip, but she wouldn't have any of that. Her eyes misted up again. So I went back out to the street, where it was starting to snow.

The few hours I had left until the evening darkness were not productive. Which is not to say there wasn't enough business for me. Anyone who thinks crooks are nabbed sooner or later by us sharp-witted, hard-working cops probably also thinks there's a tooth fairy. Police files everywhere bulge with unfinished business. That's because cops are pretty much like everybody else in a world that's not especially efficient. Some days we're inattentive or lazy or hungover—or in my case on Christmas Eve, preoccupied with the thought that loneliness is all it's cracked up to be.

For about an hour after leaving Frances and the kids at the Martinique, I tailed a mope with a big canvas laundry sack, which is the ideal equipment when you're hauling off valuables from a place where nobody happens to be home. I was practically to the Hudson River before I realized the perp had made me a long time back and was just having fun giving me a walk-around on a raw, snowy day. Perps can be cocky like that sometimes. Even though I was ninety-nine percent sure he had a set of lock picks on him, I didn't have probable cause for a frisk.

I also wasted a couple of hours shadowing a guy in a very uptown cashmere coat and silk muffler. He had a set of California teeth and perfect sandy-blond hair. Most people in New York would figure him for a nice simple TV anchorman or maybe a GQ model. I had him pegged for a shoulder-bag bus dipper, which is a minor criminal art that can be learned by anyone who isn't moronic or crippled in a single afternoon. Most of its practitioners seem to be guys who are too handsome. All you have to do is hang around people waiting for buses or getting off buses, quietly reach into their bags, and pick out wallets.

I read this one pretty easily when I noticed how he passed up a half empty Madison Avenue bus opposite B. Altman's in favor of the next one, which was overloaded with chattering Lenox Hill matrons who would never in a thousand years think such a nice young man with nice hair and a dimple in his chin and so well dressed was a thief.

Back and forth I went with this character, clear up to Fifty-ninth Street, then by foot over to Fifth Avenue and back down into the low Forties. When I finally showed him my tin and spread him against the base of one of the cement lions outside the New York Public Library to pat him down, I only found cash on him. This dipper was brighter than he looked. Somewhere along the line, he'd ditched the wallets and pocketed only the bills and I never once saw the slide. I felt fairly brainless right about then and the crowd of onlookers that cheered when I let him go didn't help me any.

So I hid out in the Burger King at Fifth and Thirty-eighth for my dinner hour. There aren't too many places that could be more depressing for a holiday meal. The lighting was so oppressively even that I felt I was inside an ice cube. There was a plastic Christmas tree with plastic ornaments chained to a wall so nobody could steal it, with dummy gifts beneath it. The gifts were strung together with vinyl cord and likewise chained to the wall. I happened to be the only customer in the place, so a kid with a bad complexion and a broom decided to sweep up around my table.

To square my pad for the night, I figured I had to make some sort of bust, even a Mickey Mouse. So after my festive meal (Whopper, fries, Sprite, and a toasted thing with something hot and gummy inside it), I walked down to Thirty-third Street and collared a working girl in a white fake-fox stole, fish-net hose, and a red-leather skirt. She was all alone on stroll, a freelance, and looked like she could use a hot meal and a nice dry cell. So I took her through the drill. The paperwork burned up everything but the last thirty minutes of my tour.

When I left the station house on West Thirty-fifth, the snow had become wet and heavy and most of midtown Manhattan was lost in a quiet white haze. I heard the occasional swish of a car going through a pothole puddle. Plumes of steam hissed here and there, like geysers from the subterranean. Everybody seemed to have vanished and the lights of the city had gone off, save for the gauzy red-and-green beacon at the top of the Empire State Building. It was rounding toward nine o'clock and it was Christmas Eve and New York seemed settled down for a long winter's nap.

There was just one thing wrong with the picture. And that was the sight of Whiteboy. I spotted him on Broadway again, lumbering down the mostly blackened, empty street with a big bag on his back like he was St. Nicholas himself.

I stayed out of sight and tailed him slowly back a few blocks to where I'd lost him in the first place, to the statue of Greeley. I had a clear view of him as he set down his bag on a bench and talked to the same bunch of grey, shapeless winos who'd cut me off the chase. Just as before, they passed a bot-tle. Only this time Whiteboy gave it to them. After everyone had a nice jolt, they talked quickly for a couple of minutes, like they had someplace impor-tant to go.

I hung back in the darkness under some scaffolding. Snow fell between the cracks of planks above me and piled on my shoulders as I stood there try-ing to figure out their act. It didn't take me long.

When they started moving from the statue over to Thirty-second Street, every one of them with a bag slung over his shoulder, I hung back a little. But my crisis of conscience didn't last long. I followed Whiteboy and his unlikely crew of elves—and wasn't much surprised to find the blond shoulder-bag dip-per with the cashmere coat when we got to where we were all going. Which was the Martinique. By now, the spindly little spruce I'd felt sorry for that after-noon was full of bright lights and tinsel and had a star on top. The same old coots I'd seen when I helped Frances and her kids there were standing around playing with about a hundred more hungry-looking kids.

Whiteboy and his helpers went up to the tree and plopped down all the bags. The kids crowded around them. They were quiet about it, though. These were kids who didn't have much experience with Norman Rockwell Christmases, so they didn't know it was an occasion to whoop it up.

Frances saw me standing in the dimly lit doorway. I must have been a sight, covered in snow and tired from walking my post most of eight hours. "Hock!" she called merrily.

And then Whiteboy spun around like he had before and his jaw dropped open. He and the pretty guy stepped away from the crowd of kids and mothers and the few broken-down men and walked quickly over to me. The kids looked like they expected all along that their party would be busted up. Frances knew she'd done something very wrong hailing me like she had, but how could she know I was a cop?

"We're having a little Christmas party here, Hock. Anything illegal about that?" Whiteboy was a cool one. He'd grown tougher and smarter in a year and talked to me like we'd just had a lovely chat the other day. We'd have to make some sort of deal, Whiteboy and me, and we both knew it.

"Who's your partner?" I asked him. I looked at the pretty guy in cashmere who wasn't saying anything just yet.

"Call him Slick."

"I like it," I said. "Where'd you and Slick get all the stuff in the bags?"

"Everything's bought and paid for, Hock. You got nothing to worry about."

"When you're cute, you're irritating, Whiteboy. You know I can't turn around on this empty-handed."

Then Slick spoke up. "What you got on us, anyways? I've just about had my fill of police harassment today, Officer. I was cooperative earlier, but I don't intend to cooperate a second time."

I ignored him and addressed Whiteboy. "Tell your friend Slick how we all appreciate discretion and good manners on both sides of the game."

Whiteboy smiled and Slick's face grew a little red.

"Let's just say for the sake of conversation," Whiteboy suggested, "that Slick and me came by a whole lot of money some way or other we're unwilling to disclose since that would tend to incriminate us. And then let's say we used that money to buy a whole lot of stuff for those kids back of us. And let's say we got cash receipts for everything in the bags. Where's that leave us, Officer Hockaday?"

"It leaves you with one leg up, temporarily. Which can be a very uncomfortable way of standing. Let's just say that I'm likely to be hard on your butts from now on."

"Well, that's about right. Just the way I see it." He lit a cigarette, a Dunhill. Then he turned back a cuff and looked at his wristwatch, the kind of piece that cost him plenty of either nerve or money. Whiteboy was moving up well for himself.

"You're off duty now, aren't you, Hock? And wouldn't you be just about

out of overtime allowance for the year?"

"Whiteboy, you better start giving me something besides lip. That is, unless you want forty-eight hours up at Riker's on suspicion. You better believe there isn't a judge in this whole city on straight time or overtime or any kind of time tonight or tomorrow to take any bail application from you."

Whiteboy smiled again. "Yeah, well, I figure the least I owe you is to help you see this thing my way. Think of it like a special tax, you know? Around this time of year, I figure the folks who can spare something ought to be taxed. So maybe that's what happened, see? Just taxation."

"Same scam as the one Robin Hood ran?"

"Yeah, something like that. Only Slick and me ain't about to start living out of town in some forest."

"You owe me something more, Whiteboy."

"What?"

"From now on, you and Slick are my two newest snitches. And I'll be expecting regular news."

There is such a thing as honor among thieves. This is every bit as true as the honor among Congressmen you read about in the newspapers all the time. But when enlightened self-interest rears its ugly head, it's also true that rules of gallantry are off.

"Okay, Hock, why not?" Whiteboy shook my hand. Slick did, too, and when he smiled his chin dimple spread flat. Then the three of us went over to the Christmas tree and everybody there seemed relieved.

We started pulling merchandise out of the bags and handing things over to disbelieving kids and their parents. Everything was the best that money could buy, too. Slick's taste in things was top-drawer. And just like Whiteboy said, there were sales slips for it all, which meant that this would be a time when nobody could take anything away from these people.

I came across a pair of ladies' black-leather gloves from Lord & Taylor, with grey-rabbit-fur lining. These I put aside until all the kids had something, then I gave them to Frances before I went home for the night. She kissed me on the cheek and wished me a happy Christmas again.

Edward D. Hoch

THE THEFT OF THE CHRISTMAS STOCKING

It always seemed more like Christmas with snow in the air, even if there were only fat white flakes that melted as they hit the sidewalk. Walking briskly along Fifth Avenue at noon on Christmas Eve, Nick Velvet was aware of the last-minute crowds clutching red-and-green shopping bags that must have delighted the merchants. When he turned in at the building on the corner of Fifty-fourth Street, he wasn't surprised to see that the pre-Christmas festivities had spread even here, within the confines of one of Manhattan's most exclusive private clubs.

The slender, sour-faced man behind the desk inside the door eyed Nick for an instant and asked, "Are you looking for the Dellon-Simpson Christmas party?"

"Mr. Charles Simpson," Nick confirmed. "I have an appointment with him here."

The guardian of the door consulted his list. "You'd be Mr. Velvet?"

"That's right."

"You'll find Mr. Simpson in the library, straight ahead. He's expecting you."

Nick crossed the marble floor, past a curving staircase that led up to a surprisingly noisy party, and entered the library through tall oak doors that shut out virtually all sound. Inside was a club-room from a hundred years ago, complete with an elderly member dozing in front of the fireplace.

"Mr. Velvet?" a voice asked, and Nick turned and saw a figure rising from the shadow of an oversized wing chair.

"That's correct. You'd be Charles Simpson?"

"I would be." By the flickering firelight, Nick could make out a tall man with a noble face and furry white sideburns. He looked to be a vigorous sixty or so and his handshake was a grip of steel. "Thank you for coming."

"I'm keeping you from your firm's Christmas party."

"Nonsense. Business before pleasure, even on Christmas Eve. I want you to steal something for me, Mr. Velvet."

"That's my business. You understand the conditions? Nothing of value, and my fee—"

"I was told in advance. But it must be done tonight. Is that a problem?"

"No. What's the object?"

Simpson's face crinkled into a tight-lipped smile. "A Christmas stocking. I want you to steal the Christmas stocking hanging from the fireplace at my granddaughter's. Any time after midnight."

"Does it contain something valuable?"

"The gift inside will be valueless, but I want that, too."

"Where does she live?"

"With her mother in a duplex apartment on upper Fifth Avenue." He produced a piece of paper from his pocket. "Here's the address. I warn you, the building has tight security. "

"I'll get in."

"Phone me at this number if you're successful." He walked Nick to the lobby, and as Nick started for the door he said, "Oh, and Mr. Velvet—"

Nick turned. "Yes?"

"Merry Christmas. "

After explaining on the phone to Gloria why he wouldn't be home until well after midnight, Nick journeyed up Fifth Avenue to the address he'd been given. It proved to be a fine old building with a doorman, and a security guard seated behind a bank of television monitors. There would be a TV camera in each of the elevators, at the service entrance, and probably in the stairwell.

Nick walked around the block and thought about it. The most likely way to gain access to the building would be to pose as a delivery man. He could rent a uniform, buy a poinsettia, and walk right past the doorman as if he were delivering it to one of the apartments. It wouldn't work after midnight, of course. He'd have to gain access to the building much earlier and find a hiding place out of range of the TV cameras.

Surprisingly—or not—as Nick again approached the front of the building, a florist's van pulled up in front of the building. A young man got out, walked quickly around to the rear, and opened the doors. He brought out a huge poinsettia that almost hid his face and walked into the lobby with it. Nick stopped on the sidewalk to light a cigarette and pause as if in thought.

The doorman immediately took the plant from the young man, checked the address tag, and sent him on his way. He picked up the house phone and presently one of the building employees appeared to complete the plant's delivery. Through it all, the security man never left his post behind the TV monitors.

112

Nick sighed and strolled away. A delivery wouldn't gain him access to the apartment, not even on Christmas Eve. It would have to be something else. He glanced again at the note he carried in his pocket: Florence Beaufeld, it read. Apt. 501.

The name was not Simpson, he'd noticed at once. If the child was his granddaughter, that meant the mother she lived with was probably Charles Simpson's daughter, separated, widowed, or divorced. Nick wondered why Simpson couldn't go to the apartment himself on Christmas Day and perform his own stocking theft.

Nick wasn't paid to think too much about the motives of his clients—that had gotten him into trouble enough in the past—but he did feel he should know whether Florence was the mother's or the daughter's name. The phonebook showed only one Beaufeld at that address: Beaufeld, F. It seemed likely that Florence was the child's mother, Florence Simpson Beaufeld.

None of which would help him gain entrance to the apartment after midnight. He crossed Fifth Avenue and tried to get a better view of the building from Central Park. Assuming Apartment 501 was on the fifth floor, it had to face either the side street or the park. The other two sides of the building abutted adjoining buildings on Fifth Avenue and the side street. But the top stories of all three buildings were set back, so there was no access between them across the rooftops. No one could have reached the top of any of the buildings except Santa Claus.

The more Nick thought about it, the more convinced he became that it would have to be Santa Claus.

At eleven-thirty that night, he approached the front door of the building. The padding of the Santa Claus suit was warm and uncomfortable, smelling faintly of scented powder, and the bag of fancily wrapped gifts he'd slung over his shoulder weighed more than he'd expected. The doorman saw him coming and held open the portals for him. That was the first good sign. Santa was expected.

"Ho ho ho!" Nick thundered in the heartiest voice he could manage.

The doorman smiled good-naturedly. "Got a gift for me, Santa?"

"Ho ho ho!" Nick took out one of the gifts he'd bought to fill the top of the sack. "Right here, sonny!"

The doorman smiled and accepted the slim flat box. "Looks like a necktie to me. Thanks a lot, Santa. Which party do you want, the Brewsters or the Trevensons?"

"Brewsters," Nick decided.

"Seventeenth floor."

Nick glanced toward the security guard and saw him looking through the

early edition of the following morning's *Times*. He entered the nearest elevator and pressed the button for seventeen. As soon as the door closed and the
elevator started to rise, he hit the fifth-floor button, too. The TV camera might
spot him getting off at the wrong floor, but it was less of a risk than being seen
running down the stairwell with his bag of tricks.

The corridor on the fifth floor was silent and deserted, lit only by an indi-
rect glow from unseen fixtures near the ceiling. There were only three doors,
so he knew 501 was going to be a large apartment. He glanced at his watch
and saw that it wasn't yet midnight. Then he listened at the door of 501.
Hearing nothing, he reached deep into his bag and extracted a leather case of
lock picks. It took him just forty-five seconds to unlock the door. He was mildly surprised that the chain lock wasn't latched, but the reason quickly became
obvious. The woman of the house, Florence Beaufeld, was preparing to go
out.

By the glow of a twelve-foot Christmas tree standing near the spiral staircase in the duplex, he saw a handsome brown-haired woman of around forty
adjusting a glistening earring. It was her hair, done in an unusual style that
evoked the idea of a layered helmet, that caught his attention. She finished
adjusting the earring, straightened the neckline of her red-velvet dress, and
picked up a sequined purse.

Nick slipped into the dining area, taking shelter in the shadows behind
a china cabinet, as the woman stepped to the foot of the staircase and called
out, "I'm going up to the Brewsters' party, Michelle. Go to bed now, it's almost
midnight. And don't peek at your gifts!" There was a mumbled reply from
upstairs as Mrs. Beaufeld let herself out of the apartment.

Nick waited, sweating in his Santa suit, until he heard a grandfather clock
chime midnight. Then he left his hiding place and moved silently across the
carpeted floor toward the lighted Christmas tree. A fireplace was beyond the
tree, along an inside wall, and above it was an oil portrait of Florence Beaufeld
seated with a protective arm around a lovely young girl about eight years old.
Below it, taped to the mantel, was a single red Christmas stocking, bulging
with an unseen gift.

Carefully setting down the bag, Nick moved to the mantel. He reached
out and took the stocking in his hand, carefully pulling the tape away from the
wood. As he did, he heard the slightest of sounds behind him and turned to
see a young woman in a short nightgown and bare legs standing at the foot
of the staircase, a tiny automatic held firmly in her right hand.

"Get your hand off my stocking, Santa," she said, "or I'll send you back
to the North Pole in a wooden box . . ."

Nick did as he was told. "Come now," he said gruffly, "you don't want
to point that thing at Santa."

She motioned slightly with the pistol. "Take off the hat and beard. I like to see who I'm talking to."

He tossed the red hat on the floor and pulled the sticky beard away from his skin.

"Satisfied now?" he asked in his normal voice.

"Say, you're not bad-looking. Who are you?"

"Do you mind if I take off this coat and padding before we talk? It's really quite uncomfortable."

"Sure, but don't try anything. I've seen all the movies." She watched him while he dropped the coat on the floor with the rest and then pulled the padding from his pants. He'd worn jeans and a black turtleneck under the Santa suit in case he had to shed it to make his escape. With the padding out, the red pants fell by themselves and he stepped out of them.

"Now, what was your question?"

"Who are you?"

She spoke with an educated, private-school voice, even when her words were tough and gritty. Nick guessed Michelle Beaufeld was now in her late teens.

"I'm a friend of your grandfather," he told her.

"Charles Simpson?" The truth seemed to dawn on her. "Oh, no!" She started to laugh. "He wanted you to steal the gift!"

"Well, the stocking the gift is in."

She shook her head. "Santa Claus, the thief! Won't that make a story for the papers? Grandpa Tries To Steal Child's Christmas Gift."

"You're no child," Nick pointed out. "Why don't you put away that gun? I'm not going to hurt you."

She motioned toward the Santa Claus outfit on the floor. "Put your pants back on."

"They're too big for me without the padding."

"That's the idea. If you try to rush me, they'll trip you up."

When he'd done as she ordered, she sat in an easy chair and carefully set the pistol down on an end table by her side. "Now we can talk," she said. "I know Grandpa wouldn't send anyone to harm me, but I can understand his wanting to get his hands on that gift. Let's have a look at it—toss the stocking over here. No funny business now!"

Nick did as he was told, convinced now that she wouldn't think of shooting him any more than he'd think of harming her. The stocking landed on the chair by her side and she picked it up, withdrawing the gift in its holiday wrapping. As she worked at unwrapping it, she reminded Nick of her mother adjusting the earring earlier. She had her mother's high cheekbones and pouting lips, and was well on her way to becoming a great beauty. Putting aside

115

the wrapping, she held up a little plastic pig for Nick to see. It was a gift more suitable for a child of five or six. "There we go! I'll put it with the others."

"What others?"

"Didn't Grandpa tell you? They're gifts from my father. He sends one every Christmas."

"Does he know how old you are?"

"Of course he does. They have a special meaning."

"Oh?"

"*That's* what Grandpa's dying to find out—what their special meaning is."

"Do *you* know?" he asked.

"Well—not yet," she admitted. "It's about something I'm supposed to get when I'm eighteen."

"How old are you now?"

"Seventeen. My birthday's next month."

"Does your father ever come to see you?"

She shook her head. "Not since I was twelve. The only time I hear from him is at Christmas, and then it's just the gift in the stocking. There hasn't been a note since the first time."

"How does he deliver them? I know you don't believe in Santa Claus."

That brought a genuine smile. "I don't know. I suppose Mother must put them there, although she's always denied it."

"What does your grandfather have to do with any of this?"

Her face showed exasperation, then uncertainty. "Why am I telling you my family history when I should be calling the police?"

"Because you wouldn't want to call the police and implicate your grandfather. You told me yourself how funny the headline would look. Besides, I might be able to help you."

"How?"

"It seems to me you've got a real mystery on your hands. If I can solve it for you, there'd be no need for you to keep this little pig, would there?"

"What do you mean?"

"You'd have the answer to your mystery and I'd have the gift to deliver to your grandfather in the stocking."

"He's paying you for this, isn't he?"

"Yes," Nick admitted.

"How much?"

"A great deal. It's how I make my living."

She picked up the automatic and for a split second he thought she was going to shoot him, after all. "Take off those foolish red pants," she said, "and let's have a beer."

*   *   *

116

The kitchen had a sleek contemporary look that clashed with the rest of the apartment. Michelle opened the refrigerator and brought out two bottles of a popular German beer. "Aren't you a bit young to be drinking beer?" Nick asked as she poured two glasses.

"Aren't you a bit old to be a thief?"

"All right," he agreed with a smile, "let's get down to business. Tell me about your father."

"His name is Dan Beaufeld. When I was a child, he ran a charterboat business in Florida. He was away from New York most of the time, especially in the winter when he had a lot of tourist business. Sometimes my mother would take me down to visit him and we'd get to ride on one of his deep-sea-fishing boats. I was twelve the last time I saw him, five years ago. That was when my mother divorced him. At the time I had no idea what it was all about. Somehow I blamed myself, which I guess a lot of kids do. My mother had bought this apartment with her own money, so she stayed here. My father moved to Florida year-round."

"Did you understand what caused the divorce?"

"Not at first. I knew my grandfather had been part of it. I thought he'd poisoned my mother's mind against my father. Once when he found me sobbing in my room, he told me I shouldn't cry over my father because he was a bad man—an evil man."

Charter boats in Florida in the mid-1980s suggested only one thing to Nick. "Could your father have been involved in drug traffic?"

"That's what Grandpa finally told me, just last year. He said he'd made a lot of money using his boats for drug smuggling and that the police were still looking for him. That was why Grandpa forced my mother to divorce him. He was afraid the family would be tainted or something."

"What about these mysterious gifts?"

"They started when I was thirteen. There was a note attached to the first one. It was from my father and he said I was always in his thoughts. He said to keep the gifts, and when I was eighteen they'd make me wealthy. The gifts have appeared in my stocking every Christmas, but there were never any more notes."

"What were the gifts?"

"The first was a little toy bus with a greyhound on the side. Then there was a copy of Poe's poem 'The Raven,' which I loved when I was fourteen. The third year was an apple, and I ate that. Last year there was a snapshot of Mother my father had taken when they were still married. Now there's this plastic pig."

"An odd combination of gifts," Nick admitted. "I can't see—"

"Who the hell are *you*?" a voice asked from the doorway.

Nick turned to see Florence Beaufeld standing wide-eyed at the kitchen door, taking in the scene before her.

He stood up, more as a reflex action than from any real fear of attack. "I'm pleased to meet you, Mrs. Beaufeld. My name is Nick Velvet."

"What are you doing here with my daughter?"

"Mother—"

"Were you sent by her father? Are you this year's Christmas gift?"

"He was sent to steal the gift, Mother! I caught him by the fireplace dressed up like Santa Claus."

"And you're sitting here chatting with him? Where are the police?"

"I didn't call them."

"My God, Michelle!"

"I'm perfectly all right, Mother. Please."

"Go upstairs and put on some clothes. I'll attend to Mr. Velvet."

Michelle hesitated and then decided to obey her mother's command. She left the kitchen without a word and went up the staircase, taking the automatic with her. Florence Beaufeld turned back to Nick. "Now tell me the truth. What are you doing here?"

"I was hired by your father, Mrs. Beaufeld."

"I should have guessed as much. Whenever I mentioned those Christmas gifts from Dan it threw him into a frenzy. I vowed not to tell him if there was one this year, but he had to know. He said Dan was planning to give Michelle a large sum of illegal drug money."

"Why would he do that?"

Mrs. Beaufeld shook her head. "Only because he loves her, I suppose, and she's his daughter. He's been hiding out from the police for over five years now, and he's never seen her in all that time."

"What do *you* make of these gifts?"

"I suppose they're a message of some sort, like a child's puzzle, but I haven't been able to read it. Was there another gift tonight?"

"A plastic pig. But perhaps I don't have to tell you that—your daughter suspects you're the one who leaves them for her."

"I swear I'm not! I have no contact with Dan. That stocking was empty earlier this evening. I looked."

"At what time?"

"Shortly before ten, I think."

"Who was in the apartment after that?"

"Only Michelle and me."

"No one else?"

"I have a woman who cooks and cleans for us. She left at about that time. I can't remember whether I looked at the stocking before or after she let herself out."

"Would you give me her name and address?"

"Are you a detective of some sort?"

"Only a professional trying to earn some money. I was hired to bring your father the stocking with the latest gift. Maybe if I solve the riddle for your daughter, she'll let me have it. Then everyone will be happy."

"Well, I'm certain Agnes isn't involved, but you can have her address if you want." She wrote it on a piece of notepaper.

"One other thing. Before I leave, could I see the gifts your daughter received? She told me she ate the apple, but the others?"

She studied him through narrowed eyes. "You have a way with you, Mr. Velvet. For all I know you're nothing but a common thief, yet you charmed my daughter and now you seem to be doing the same with me. Come upstairs. I'll ask Michelle to show you the gifts."

He followed her up the staircase and waited discreetly in the hallway while she checked to see that her daughter was wearing a robe. Then he entered the girl's bedroom. All seventeen years of her life seemed to be crammed haphazardly into it. Michelle led him to a bookcase where a rock star's poster dominated shelves of alphabet books and stuffed toys. There the four objects were lined up, just as she had described them—the toy bus, the Poe poem, the snapshot of Mrs. Beaufeld, and now the pig.

"Michelle will be eighteen next month," Nick said. "It's my understanding the message must be complete, whatever it is, if it's to direct her to a fortune by then."

"But how is he able to get in here to leave these things?"

"I'm hoping Agnes can tell me that," Nick said.

The clock was chiming one as he left the apartment.

Downstairs, a different doorman and security guard were on duty. Nick slipped the doorman a ten-dollar bill. "Merry Christmas."

"Thank you, sir. Are you a resident here?"

"Only a visitor. I was wondering if you've worked here long enough to remember Dan Beaufeld. He was in Apartment 501 before his divorce about five years ago."

"Sorry, I just started last year." He called over to the security guard watching the television monitors. "Larry, were you here five years ago?"

The man shook his head. "Just over four years. The old-timers get the day and evening shifts."

"Thanks anyway," Nick said. He went out into the cold night air and took a cab home. Gloria was waiting up for him, to exchange gifts over a bottle of champagne.

*   *   *

The Beaufeld maid and cook, Agnes Wilson, lived on Fifth Avenue, too, but far uptown in Harlem. It was noon on Christmas Day when Nick visited the housing project where her apartment was located. Her husband eyed him suspiciously and asked, "What do you want with Agnes?"

"I just have a couple of questions. It won't take a minute."

"You a cop?"

"Do I look like one? I'm a friend of the Beaufeld family. "

Agnes Wilson was small and pretty, with deep-brown eyes and a friendly smile. "I never knew Mr. Beaufeld," she said. "They were still married when I started there, but he was always in Florida. I never saw him. "

"Mrs. Wilson, someone left a Christmas toy in Michelle's stocking by the fireplace last night. Do you know anything about it?"

"No."

"You didn't leave it? You weren't paid to leave it?"

"No one paid me to do anything."

"Not Dan Beaufeld?"

"Not him or anyone else."

Nick leaned forward in his chair. "Michelle has received gifts in her stocking for five years now—a toy bus, a poem, an apple, a photograph, and a plastic pig. Do these mean anything to you?"

"No, they don't." She seemed genuinely surprised. "I didn't know about the gifts. A couple of years back I mentioned to Mrs. Beaufeld that I thought Michelle was pretty old to be hanging a stocking on the fireplace Christmas Eve, but she just shrugged it off. It wasn't any of my business, so I shut up. Maybe it wasn't so odd, after all. I worked for a German family once that hung stockings on the fireplace for St. Nicholas every Christmas—all of them, even the parents."

"Did any strangers come to the door this week when Michelle or her mother were out?"

"No strangers get by the doorman in that building. They've got TV cameras in the elevators and everything."

Nick got up to leave, handing her a folded ten-dollar bill. "Thank you for your time, Mrs. Wilson. I hope you and your husband have a Merry Christmas."

Agnes's husband saw him to the door. "You always go calling on Christmas Day?"

"Just like Santa Claus," Nick told him with a smile.

He telephoned Charles Simpson from a pay phone at the corner. "Are you having a good holiday?" he asked.

"Is that you, Velvet? What luck have you had?"

"Fair. I had the stocking in my hands, but I don't have it now."

"What was in it?"

"If I tell you, do I get paid?"

"A partial payment. I won't know if I need the stocking and the gift until I see them."

"All right. I'll try to have them tonight, or tomorrow morning for sure."

He hung up and grabbed a bus heading downtown. Ten minutes later he was back at the Beaufelds' building. The doorman was the same one who'd been on duty the previous day when he'd first scouted the building. Nick asked him if he'd known Dan Beaufeld.

The doorman told him he'd only been there three years.

Nick asked the security guard the same question. "Me? I've been here a year. I know the mother and daughter, not the ex-husband. He never comes around, does he?"

"Not lately," Nick agreed. "Do you have keys to all the apartments?"

"We have one set of master keys, but they never leave this locked desk unless they have to be used in an emergency."

"And there's always someone on duty here?"

"Always," the guard said, beginning to look suspiciously at Nick. "The doorman and I are never away at the same time."

"That certainly speaks well for the security here. No one gets in who isn't expected."

"Including you," the doorman said. "Who are you here to see, anyway?"

"Florence Beaufeld."

The doorman called up on the phone and then sent Nick up on the elevator.

Florence Beaufeld met him at the door with word that they'd be leaving soon to have Christmas dinner with her father. "He'll be picking us up in his car."

"This won't take long. Are you likely to discuss the gift in Michelle's Christmas stocking?"

"No chance of that."

Michelle came down the stairs. "Are *you* back again?" She was wearing a sparkling green party dress with a flared skirt. "Have you solved the riddle yet?"

"I may have. But first I'd like to see a picture of your father. A snapshot, anything."

"I threw them all away after the divorce," Florence said.

"I have one," Michelle told him and went off to get it. She returned with a snapshot of a handsome man with a moustache and a broad grin, squinting into the camera.

Nick studied it for a moment and nodded. "Now I can tell you about the gifts. It's just a theory, but I think it's correct. Here's my proposition. If I'm right, you give me the stocking and the latest gift to deliver to your grandfather."

"All right," Michelle agreed, and her mother nodded, gripping her hands together.

"I had no idea what the five gifts meant until I glimpsed those old alphabet books in your room, Michelle. I imagine your dad used to read to you from those when you were learning the alphabet." Michelle nodded silently. "Those books always use simple objects or animals to stand for the letters. Many of them start out 'A is for Apple.' "

Her mother took it up. "Of course! 'B is for Bus,' 'R is for Raven,' 'A is for Apple'—but then there was the photo of me."

"Mother?" Nick said. " 'M is for Mother,' 'P is for Pig.' "

"Bramp?" Michelle laughed. "What does that mean?"

"That stumped me, too, until I remembered it wasn't just any bus. It had a greyhound on the side. 'G is for Greyhound.' That would give us gramp."

"Gramp," Florence Beaufeld said.

"Gramp!" her daughter repeated. "You mean Grandpa? The money was to come from him?"

"Obviously out of the question," Nick agreed. "He'd never act as a channel for your father's money, not when he opposed the whole thing so vigorously. He even hired me in the hope of learning the location of the money before you found it."

"But gramp certainly means grandfather," Florence pointed out. "It has no other meaning that I know of."

"True enough. But remember that your former husband was limiting himself to a five-letter word by using this system of symbolic Christmas gifts. The word had to be completed by today, a month before Michelle's eighteenth birthday. If gramp stands for grandfather, could the word grandfather itself signify something other than Michelle's flesh-and-blood grandfather?"

He saw the light dawn on Michelle's face first. "The grandfather clock!"

Nick smiled. "Let's take a look."

In the base of the clock, below the window where the pendulum swung, they found the package. Inside were neatly banded packages of hundred-dollar bills.

Florence Beaufeld stood up, breathing hard. "There's close to a half million dollars here."

"He couldn't risk entering this apartment too many times, so he hid the money in advance. If you hadn't found it, he'd probably have found a way to give you a more obvious hint."

"You mean Dan has been in this apartment?"

Nick nodded. "For the last five Christmas Eves."

"But—"

She was interrupted by the buzzer, and the doorman's voice announced the arrival of Mr. Simpson's car.

"Go on," Nick urged them. "I'll catch you up on the rest later. "

It was shortly before midnight when Nick stepped from the shadows near the building and intercepted the man walking quickly toward the entrance. "Larry?"

The night-security man turned to stare at Nick. "You're the fellow who was asking all those questions."

"That's right. I finally got some answers. You're Dan Beaufeld, aren't you?"

"I—"

"There's no point in denying it. I've seen your picture. You shaved off your moustache, but otherwise you look pretty much the same."

"Where did I slip up? Or was it just the photo?" There was a tone of resignation in his voice.

"There were other things. If Dan Beaufeld was leaving those Christmas gifts himself, he had to have a way into the apartment. A building employee seemed likely in view of the tight security, and one of the security men seemed most likely. There are master keys in the security desk and it would have been easy for you to have one duplicated. The gifts were always left shortly before midnight on Christmas Eve, and that implied someone who might start work on the midnight shift. You couldn't leave your post after midnight. Last night as I was leaving, you told me you'd been here just over four years—enough to cover the last five Christmases. You also said old-timers got the day and evening shifts, yet the day security man told me he's only been here a year. That made me wonder if you preferred the midnight shift so you'd be less likely to be seen and recognized by people who might know you. Of course you spent most of your time in Florida, even before the divorce, and without the moustache it was doubtful any of the other employees or residents would recognize you. On those occasions when Michelle or her mother came in after midnight, you could simply hide your face behind a newspaper or bend down behind the TV monitors."

"I had to be close to her," Dan Beaufeld admitted. "I had to watch my daughter growing up, even if it meant risking arrest. I'd see her going off to school or to parties, watching from across the street, and that was enough.

Working here made me feel close to them both. Michelle had a custom of hanging up her Christmas stocking, so I started leaving the gifts every year to let her know I was near and to prepare her for the money she'd get when she turned eighteen.

"I knew the maid let herself out around ten o'clock, and Florence never bothered to relatch the chain lock until bedtime. I entered with my master key, making certain they weren't in the downstairs rooms, and left the gift in the stocking before midnight. Last year I had to come back twice because they were sitting by the fireplace, but usually Florence was out at someone's Christmas party and it was all clear."

"Last night you left the money, too—in the grandfather clock."

Beaufeld grinned. "So they read the clues properly."

"It's drug money, isn't it?"

"Some of it, but I'm out of that now. I used some fake ID to start a new life, a clean life."

"Charles Simpson still wants you in prison."

Dan Beaufeld took a deep breath. "Sometimes I think about turning myself in. Some of the crimes are beyond the statute of limitations now, and a lawyer told me that if I surrendered I'd probably get off with a lenient sentence."

"Why don't you talk it over with Florence and Michelle? They don't want your money, they want you. They're waiting up there for you now."

Dan Beaufeld turned his eyes skyward, toward the lighted windows he must have looked at hundreds of times before. "What are *you* getting out of this?" he asked.

Nick Velvet, who had serious doubts about collecting his fee from Charles Simpson, merely answered, "I don't need to get anything out of this one. It's Christmas."

Herbert Resnicow

THE CHRISTMAS BEAR

"Up there, Grandma," Debbie pointed, all excited, tugging at my skirt, "in the top row. Against the wall. See?" I'm not really her grandma, but at six and a half the idea of a great-grandmother is hard to understand. All her little friends have grandmothers, so she has a grandmother. When she's a little older, I'll tell her the whole story.

The firehouse was crowded this Friday night, not like the usual weekend where the volunteer firemen explain to their wives that they have to polish the old pumper and the second-hand ladder truck. They give the equipment a quick lick-and-a-promise and then sit down to an uninterrupted evening of pinochle. Not that there's all that much to do in Pitman anyway—we're over fifty miles from Pittsburgh, even if anyone could afford to pay city prices for what the big city offers—but still, a man's first thought has to be of his wife and family. Lord knows I've seen too much of the opposite in my own generation and all the pain and trouble it caused, and mine could've given lessons in devotion to this new generation that seems to be interested only in fun. What they call fun.

Still, they weren't all bad. Even Homer Curtis, who was the worst boy of his day, always full of mischief and very disrespectful, didn't turn out all that bad. That was after he got married, of course; not before. He was just voted fire chief and, to give him credit, this whole Rozovski affair was his idea, may God bless him.

Little Petrina Rozovski—she's only four years old and she's always been small for her age—her grandfather was shift foreman over my Jake in the mine while we were courting. We married young in those days because there was no future and you grabbed what happiness you could and that's how I came to be the youngest great-grandmother in the county, only sixty-seven, though that big horse-faced Mildred Ungaric keeps telling everybody I'm over seventy. Poor Petrina has to have a liver transplant, and soon. Real soon. You wouldn't believe what that costs, even if you could find the right liver in the first place. Seventy-five thousand dollars, and it could go to a lot more than that, depending. There isn't that much money in the whole county.

There was talk about going to the government—as if the government's got any way to just give money for things like this or to make somebody give her baby's liver to a poor little girl—or holding a raffle, or something, but none of the ideas was worth a tinker's dam. Then Homer, God bless him, had this inspiration. The volunteer firemen—they do it every year—collect toys for the poor children, which, these days, is half the town, to make sure every child gets *some* present for Christmas. And we all, even if we can't afford it, we all give something. Then one of them dresses up as Santa Claus and they all get on the ladder truck and, on Christmas Eve, they ride through the town giving out the presents. There's a box for everyone, so nobody knows who's getting a present, but the boxes for the families where the father is still working just have a candy bar in them or something like that. And for the littlest kids, they put Santa on top of the ladder and two guys turn the winch and lift him up to the roof as though he's going to go down the chimney and the kids' eyes get all round and everybody feels the way a kid should on Christmas Eve.

We had a town meeting to discuss the matter. "Raffles are no good," Homer declared, "because one person wins and everybody else loses. This year we're going to have an auction where everybody wins. Everybody who can will give a good toy—it can be used, but it's got to be good—in addition to what they give for the poor kids. Then the firemen will auction off those extra toys and the idea of that auction is to pay as *much* as possible instead of as little." That was sort of like the Indian potlatches they used to have around here that my grandfather told me about. Well, you can imagine the opposition to that one. But Homer overrode them all. Skinny as he is, when he stands up and raises his voice—he's the tallest man in town by far—he usually gets his way. Except with his wife, and that's as it should be. "Anyway," he pointed out, "it's a painless way of getting the donations Rozovski needs to get a liver transplant for Petrina."

Shorty Porter, who never backed water for anyone, told Homer, "Your brain ain't getting enough oxygen up there. Even if every family in town bought something for ten dollars on the average, with only twelve hundred families in town, we'd be short at least sixty-three thousand dollars, not to mention what it would cost for Irma Rozovski to stay in a motel near the hospital. And not everybody in town can pay more than what the present he bids on is worth. So you better figure on getting a lot less than twelve thousand, Homer, and what good that'll do, I fail to see." Levi Porter always had a good head for figures. One of these days we ought to make him mayor, if he could take the time off from busting his butt in his little back yard farm which, with his brood, he really can't.

"I never said," Homer replied, "that we were going to raise enough money this way to take care of the operation and everything. The beauty of my plan is . . . I figure we'll raise about four thousand. Right, Shorty?"

"That's about what I figured," Shorty admitted.

"We give the money to Hank and Irma and they take Petrina to New York. They take her to a TV station, to one of those news reporters who are always looking for ways to help people. We have a real problem here, a real emergency, and Petrina, with that sweet little face and her big brown eyes, once she appears on TV, her problems are over. If only ten percent of the people in the U.S. send in one cent each, that's all, just one cent, we'd get two hundred fifty thousand dollars. That would cover everything and leave plenty over to set up an office, right here in Pitman, for a clearing house for livers for all the poor little kids in that fix. And the publicity would remind some poor unfortunate mother that her child—children are dying in accidents every day and nobody knows who or where, healthy children—her child's liver could help save the life of a poor little girl."

Even Shorty had to admit it made sense. "And to top it all," Homer added, "if we do get enough money to set up a liver clearing house, we've brought a job to Pitman, for which I'd like to nominate Irma Rozovski, to make up for what she's gone through. And if it works out that way, maybe even two jobs, so Hank can have some work too." Well, that was the clincher. We all agreed and that's how it came about that I was standing in front of the display of the auction presents in the firehouse on the Friday night before Christmas week while Deborah was tugging and pointing at that funny-looking teddy bear, all excited, like I'd never seen her before.

Deborah's a sad little girl. Not that she doesn't have reason, what with her father running off just before the wedding and leaving Caroline in trouble; I never did like that Wesley Sladen in the first place. The Social Security doesn't give enough to support three on, and nobody around here's about to marry a girl going on twenty-nine with another mouth to feed, and I'm too old to earn much money, so Carrie's working as a waitress at the Highway Rest. But thanks to my Jake, we have a roof over our heads and we always will. My father was against my marrying him. I was born a Horvath, and my father wanted me to marry a nice Hungarian boy, not a damn foreigner, but I was of age and my mother was on my side and Jake and I got married in St. Anselm's and I wore a white gown, and I had a right to, not like it is today.

That was in '41 and before the year was out we were in the war. Jake volunteered and, not knowing I was pregnant, I didn't stop him. He was a good man, made sergeant, always sent every penny home. With me working in the factory, I even put a little away. After Marian was born, the foreman was nice enough to give me work to do at home on my sewing machine, so it was all right. Jake had taken out the full G.I. insurance and, when it happened, we got ten thousand dollars, which was a lot of money in those days. I bought the house, which cost almost two thousand dollars, and put the rest away for the bad times.

My daughter grew up to be a beautiful girl and she married a nice boy, John Brodzowski, but when Caroline was born, complications set in and Marian never made it out of the hospital. I took care of John and the baby for six months until John, who had been drinking, hit a tree going seventy. The police said it was an accident. I knew better but I kept my mouth shut because we needed the insurance.

So here we were, quiet little Deborah pulling at me and pointing at that teddy bear, all excited, and smiling for the first time I can remember. "That's what I want, Grandma," she begged. "He's my bear."

"You have a teddy bear," I told her. "We can't afford another one. I just brought you to the firehouse to look at all the nice things."

"He's not a teddy bear, Grandma, and I love him."

"But he's so funny looking," I objected. And he was, too. Black, sort of, but shining blueish when the light hit the right way, with very long hair. Ears bigger than a teddy bear's, and a longer snout. Not cute at all. Some white hairs at the chin and a big crescent-shaped white patch on his chest. And the eyes, not round little buttons, but slanted oval pieces of purple glass. I couldn't imagine what she saw in him. There was a tag, with #273 on it, around his neck. "Besides," I said, "I've only got eighteen dollars for all the presents, for everything. I'm sure they'll want at least ten dollars for him on account of it's for charity."

She began crying, quietly, not making a fuss; Deborah never did. Even at her age she understood, children do understand, that there were certain things that were not for us, but I could see her heart was broken and I didn't know what to do.

Just then the opening ceremonies started. Young Father Casimir, of St. Anselm's, gave the opening benediction, closing with "It is more blessed to give than to receive." I don't know how well that set with Irma Rozovski and the other poor people there, but he'll learn better when he gets older. Then Homer brought up Irma, with Petrina in her arms looking weaker and yellower than ever, to speak. "I just want to thank you all, all my friends and neighbors, for being so kind and . . ." Then she broke down and couldn't talk at all. Petrina didn't cry, she never cried, just looked sad and hung onto her mother. Then Homer came and led Irma away and said a few words I didn't even listen to. I knew what I had to do and I'd do it. Christmas is for the children, to make the children happy, that's the most important part. The children. I'd just explain to Carrie, when she got home, that I didn't get her anything this year and I didn't want her to get me anything. She'd understand.

I got hold of Homer in a corner and told him, "Look, Homer, for some reason Deborah's set on that teddy bear in the top row. Now all I've got is eighteen dollars, and I don't think you'd get anywhere near that much for it at the auction, but I don't want to take a chance on losing it and break Deborah's heart. I'm willing to give it all to you right now, if you'll sell it to me."

"Gee, I'd like to, Miz Sophie," he said, "but I can't. I have to go according to the rules. And if I did that for you, I'd have to do it for everybody, then with everybody picking their favorites, nobody would bid on anything and we couldn't raise the money for Petrina to go to New York."

"Come on, Homer, this ain't the first time you've broken some rules. Besides, I wouldn't tell anyone; I'd just take it off the shelf after everybody's left and no one would know the difference. It's an ugly looking teddy bear anyway."

"I'm real sorry, Mrs. Slowinski," he said, going all formal on me, "but I can't. Besides, there's no way to get it now. Those shelves, they're just boxes piled up with boards across them. You look at them crooked, and the whole thing'll fall down. There's no way to get to the top row until you've taken off the other rows. That's why the numbers start at the bottom."

"You're a damned fool, Homer, and I'm going to get that bear for Deborah anyway. I'm going to get him for a lot less than eighteen dollars too, so your stubbornness has cost the fund a lot of money and you ought to be ashamed of yourself."

We didn't go back to the firehouse until two days before Christmas Eve, Monday, when Carrie was off. Deborah had insisted on showing the bear to her mother to make sure we knew exactly which bear it was she wanted, but when we got there the bear was gone. Poor Deborah started crying, real loud this time, and even Carrie couldn't quiet her down. I picked her up and told her, swore to her, that I would get that bear back for her, but she just kept on sobbing.

I went right up to Homer to tell him off for selling the bear to somebody else instead of to me but before I could open my mouth, he said, "That wasn't right, Mrs. Slowinski, but as long as it's done, I won't make a fuss. Just give me the eighteen dollars and we'll forget about it."

That was like accusing me of stealing, and Milly Ungaric was standing near and she had that nasty smile on her face, so I knew who had stolen the bear. I ignored what Homer said and asked, "Who was on duty last night?" We don't have a fancy alarm system in Pitman; one of the firemen sleeps in the firehouse near the phone.

"Shorty Porter," Homer said, and I went right off.

I got hold of him on the side. "Levi, did you see anyone come in last night?" I asked. "I mean late."

"Only Miz Mildred," he said. "Just before I went to sleep."

Well, I knew it was her, but that wasn't what I meant. "I mean after you went to sleep. Did any noise wake you up?"

"When I sleep, Miz Sophie, only the phone bell wakes me up."

She must have come back later, the doors are never locked, and taken the bear. She's big enough, but how could she reach it? She couldn't climb over the shelves, everything would be knocked over. And she couldn't reach it from the floor. So how did she do it? Maybe it wasn't her, though I would have liked it to be. I went back to Homer. He was tall enough and had arms like a chimpanzee. "Homer," I said, "I'm going to forget what you said if you'll just do one thing. Stand in front of the toys and reach for the top shelf."

He got red, but he didn't blow. After a minute he said, sort of strangled, "I already thought of that. If I can't reach it by four feet, nobody can. Tell you what; give me seventeen dollars and explain how you did it, and I'll pay the other dollar out of my own pocket."

"You always were a stupid, nasty boy, Homer, and you always will be. Well, if you won't help me, I'll have to find out by myself, start at the beginning and trace who'd want to steal a funny-looking bear like that. Who donated the bear?"

"People just put toys in the boxes near the door. We pick out the ones for the auction and the ones for the Santa Claus boxes. No way of knowing who gave what."

I knew he wouldn't be any help, so I got Carrie and Debbie and went to the one man in town who might help me trace the bear, Mr. Wong. He doesn't have just a grocery, a *credit* grocery, thank God; he carries things you wouldn't even find in Pittsburgh. His kids were all grown, all famous scientists and doctors and professors, but he still stayed here, even after Mrs. Wong died. Mrs. Wong never spoke a word of English, but she understood everything. Used to be, her kids all came here for Chinese New Year—that's about a month after ours—and they'd have a big feast and bring the grandchildren. Funny how Mrs. Wong was able to raise six kids in real hard times, but none of her children has more than two. Now, on Chinese New Year, Mr. Wong closes the store for a week and goes to one of his kids. But he always comes back here.

"Look I have for you," he said, and gave Debbie a little snake on a stick, the kind where you turn it and the snake moves like it's real. She was still sniffling, but she smiled a little. The store was chock full of all kinds of Chinese things; little dragons and fat Buddhas with bobbing heads and candied ginger. I knew I was in the right place.

"Did you ever sell anyone a teddy bear?" I asked. "Not a regular teddy bear, but a black one with big purple eyes."

"No sell," he said. "Give."

"Okay." I had struck gold on the first try. "Who'd you give it to?"

"Nobody. Put in box in firehouse."

"You mean for the auction?"

"Petrina nice girl. Like Debbie. Very sick. Must help."

"But . . ." Dead end. I'd have to find another way to trace the bear so I could find out who'd want to steal it. "All right, where'd you get the teddy bear?"

"Grandmother give me. Before I go U.S. Make good luck. Not teddy bear. Blue bear. From Kansu."

"You mean there's a bear that looks like this?"

"Oh yes. Chinese bear. Moon bear. Very danger. Strong. In Kansu."

"Your grandmother *made* it? For you?"

"Not *make*, make. Grandfather big hunter, kill bear. Moon bear very big good luck. Eat bear, get strong, very good. Have good luck in U.S."

"That bear is real bearskin?"

"Oh yes. Grandmother cut little piece for here," he put his hand under his chin, "and for here," he put his hand on his chest. "Make moon." He moved his hand in the crescent shape the bear had on its chest. "Why call moon bear."

"You had that since you were a little boy?" I was touched. "And you gave it for Petrina? Instead of your own grandchildren?"

"Own grandchildren want sportcar, computer, skateboard, not old Chinese bear."

Well, that was typical of all modern kids, not just Chinese, but it didn't get me any closer to finding out who had stolen the teddy bear, the moon bear. Deborah, though, was listening with wide eyes, no longer crying. But what was worse, that romantic story would make it all the harder on her if I didn't get that bear back. She went up to the counter and asked, "Did it come in?"

"Oh yes." He reached down and put a wooden lazy tongs on top of the counter.

"I got it for you, Grandma," Debbie said, "for your arthritis, so you don't have to bend down. I was going to save it for under the tree, but you looked so sad . . ."

God bless you, Deborah, I said in my heart, that's the answer. I put my fingers in the scissor grip and extended the tongs. They were only about three feet long, not long enough, and they were already beginning to bend under their own weight. No way anyone, not even Mildred Ungaric, could use them to steal the moon bear. Then I knew. For sure. I turned around and there it was, hanging on the top shelf. I turned back to Mr. Wong and said, casually, "What do you call that thing grocers use to get cans from the top shelf? The long stickhandle with the grippers at the end?"

"Don't know. In Chinese I say, 'Get can high shelf.' "

"Doesn't matter. Why did you steal the bear back? Decided to sell it to a museum or something?"

"No. Why I steal? If I want sell, I no give." He was puzzled, not insulted. "Somebody steal moon bear?"

He was right. But so was I. At least I knew *how* it was stolen. You didn't need a "get can high shelf." All the thief needed was a long thing with a hook on the end. Or a noose. Like a broomstick. Or a fishing rod. Anything that would reach from where you were standing to the top of the back row so you could get the bear without knocking over the shelves or the other toys. It had to be Mildred Ungaric; she might be mean, but she wasn't stupid. Any woman had enough long sticks in her kitchen, and enough string and hooks to make a bear-stealer, though she'd look awful funny walking down the street carrying one of those. But it didn't have to be that way. There was something in the firehouse that anyone could use, one of those long poles with the hooks on the end they break your windows with when you have a fire. All you'd have to do is get that hook under the string that held the number tag around the moon bear's neck and do it quietly enough not to wake Levi Porter. Which meant that anyone in town could have stolen the moon bear.

But who would? It would be like stealing from poor little Petrina herself. Mildred was mean, but even she wouldn't do that. Homer was nasty; maybe he accused me to cover up for himself. Mr. Wong might have changed his mind, in spite of what he said; you don't give away a sixty-year-old childhood memory like that without regrets. Levi Porter was in the best position to do it; there was only his word that he slept all through the night and he has eight kids he can hardly feed. Heck, anyone in town could have done it. All I knew was that I didn't.

So who stole the moon bear?

That night I made a special supper for Carrie, and Deborah served. There's nothing a waitress enjoys so much on her time off as being served. I know; there was a time I waitressed myself. After supper, Carrie put Deborah to bed and read to her, watched TV for a while, then got ready to turn in herself. There's really nothing for a young woman to do in Pitman unless she's the kind that runs around with the truckers that stop by, and Carrie wasn't that type. She had made one mistake, trusted one boy, but that could have happened to anybody. And she did what was right and was raising Deborah to be a pride to us all.

I stayed up and sat in my rocker, trying to think of who would steal that bear, but there was no way to find that out. At least it wasn't a kid, a little kid, who had done it; those firemen's poles are heavy. Of course it could have been a teenager, but what would a teenager want with a funny-looking little bear like that? There were plenty of better toys in the lower rows to tempt a teenager, toys that anyone could take in a second with no trouble at all. But none of them had been stolen. No, it wasn't a teenager; I was pretty sure of that.

Finally, I went to sleep. Or to bed, at least. I must have been awake for half the night and didn't come up with anything. But I did know one thing I had to do.

That night being the last night before Christmas Eve, they were going to hold the auction for Petrina in the firehouse. I didn't want to get there too early; no point in making Deborah feel bad seeing all the other presents bought up and knowing she wasn't going to get her moon bear. But I did want her to know it wasn't just idle talk when I promised I'd get her bear back.

Debbie and I waited until the last toy was auctioned off and Porter announced the total. Four thousand, three hundred seventy-two dollars and fifty cents. More than we had expected and more than enough to send the Rozovskis to New York. Then I stood up and said, "I bid eighteen dollars, cash, for the little black bear, Number 273."

Homer looked embarrassed. "Please, Mrs. Slowinski, you know we don't have that bear anymore.

"I just want to make sure, *Mr.* Curtis, that when I find that bear, it's mine. Mine and Deborah's. So you can just add eighteen dollars to your total, *Mr.* Porter, and when that bear turns up, it's mine." Now if anyone was seen with the bear, everybody'd know whose it was. And what's more, if the thief had a guilty conscience, he'd know where to return the bear.

That night I stayed in my rocking chair again, rocking and thinking, thinking and rocking. I was sure I was on the right track. Why would anyone want to take the moon bear? That had to be the way to find the thief; to figure out why anyone would take the bear. But as much as I rocked, much as I thought, I was stuck right there. Finally, after midnight, I gave up. There was no way to figure it out. Maybe if I slept on it . . . Only trouble was, tomorrow was Christmas Eve, and even if I figured out who took the bear, there was no way I could get it back in time to put it under the tree so Debbie would find it when she woke up Christmas morning. For all I knew, the bear was in Pittsburgh by now, or even back in China. Maybe I shouldn't have warned the thief by making such a fuss when I bought the missing bear.

Going to bed didn't help. I lay awake, thinking of everything that had happened, from the time we first stood behind the firetrucks and saw the bear, to the time in Mr. Wong's store when I figured out how the bear had been stolen. Then all of a sudden it was clear. I knew who had stolen the bear. That is I knew *how* it had been stolen and that told me *who* had stolen it which told me how, which . . . What really happened was I knew it all, all at once. Of course, I didn't know *where* the bear was, not exactly, but I'd get to that eventually. One thing I had to remember was not to tell Deborah what I had figured out. Not that I was wrong— I *wasn't* wrong; everything fit too perfectly—but I might not be able to get the bear back. After all, how hard would it be to destroy the bear, to burn it or throw it in the dump, rather than go to jail?

The next morning Deborah woke me. "It's all right, Grandma," she said. "I didn't really want that old moon bear. I really wanted a wetting doll. Or a plain doll. So don't cry." I wasn't aware I was crying, but I guess I was. Whatever else I had done in my life, whatever else Carrie had done, to bring to life, to bring up such a sweet wonderful human being, a girl like this, one to be so proud of, that made up for everything. I only wished Jake could have been here with me to see her. And Wesley Sladen, the fool, to see what he'd missed.

I didn't say anything during breakfast—we always let Carrie sleep late because of her hours but right after we washed up, I dressed Deborah warmly. "We're going for a long walk," I told her. She took my hand and we started out.

I went to the garage where he worked and motioned Levi Porter to come out. He came, wiping his hands on a rag. Without hesitating, I told him what I had to tell him. "You stole the teddy bear. You swiveled the ladder on the ladder truck around, pointing in the right direction, and turned the winch until the ladder extended over the bear. Then you crawled out on the flat ladder and stole the bear. After you put everything back where it was before, you went to sleep."

Well, he didn't bat an eye, just nodded his head. "Yep, that's the way it was," he said, not even saying he was sorry. "I figured you knew something when you bought the missing bear. Nobody throws away eighteen dollars for nothing." Deborah just stared up at him, not understanding how a human being could do such a thing to her. She took my hand for comfort, keeping me between her and Shorty Porter.

"Well, that's *my* bear," I said. "I bought it for Deborah; she had her heart set on it." He wasn't a bit moved. "She loved that bear, Porter. You broke her heart."

"I'm sorry about that, Miz Sophie," he said, "I really didn't want to hurt anybody. I didn't know about Debbie when I stole the bear."

"Well, the least you could do is give it back. If you do, I might consider, just *consider*, not setting the law on you." I didn't really want to put a man with eight children in jail and, up till now, he'd been a pretty good citizen, but I wasn't about to show him that. "So you just go get it, *Mr.* Porter. Right now, and hop to it."

"Okay, Miz Sophie, but it ain't here. We'll have to drive over." He stuck his head in the shop and told Ed Mahaffey that he had to go someplace, be back soon, and we got in his pickup truck.

I wasn't paying attention to where we were going and when he stopped, my heart stopped too. Petrina was lying on the couch in the living room, clutching the moon bear to her skinny little chest. Irma was just standing there wondering what had brought us. "It's about the teddy bear," Levi Porter apologized. "It belongs to Debbie. I have to take it back."

We went over to the couch. "You see," he explained to me, "on opening night, Petrina fell in love with the bear. I wanted to get it for her, but I didn't have any money left. So I took it, figuring it wasn't really stealing; everything there was for Petrina anyway. If I'd knowed about Debbie, I would've worked out something else, maybe."

He leaned over the couch and gently, very gently, took the moon bear out of Petrina's hands. "I'm sorry, honey," he told the thin little girl, "it's really Debbie's. I'll get you a different bear soon." The sad little girl let the bear slip slowly out of her hands, not resisting, but not really letting go either. She said nothing, so used to hurt, so used to disappointment, so used to having everything slip away from her, but her soft dark eyes filled with tears as Shorty took the bear. I could have sworn that the moon bear's purple glass eyes looked full of pain, too.

Shorty put the bear gently into Debbie's arms and she cradled the bear closely to her. She put her face next to the bear's and kissed him and whispered something to him that I didn't catch, my hearing not being what it used to be. Then she went over to the couch and put the bear back into Petrina's hands. "He likes you better," she said. "He wants to stay with you. He loves you."

We stood there for a moment, all of us, silent. Petrina clutched the bear to her, tightly, lovingly, and almost smiled. Irma started crying and I might've too, a little. Shorty picked Deborah up and kissed her like she was his own. "You're blessed," he said to me. "From heaven."

He drove us home, and on the way back I asked Debbie what she said to the bear. "I was just telling him his name," she said innocently, "and he said it was exactly right."

"What is his name?" I asked.

"Oh, that was *my* name for him, Grandma. Petrina told him *her* name; he has a different name now," and that's all she would say about it.

I invited Shorty in but he couldn't stay; had to get back to the garage. If he took too long—well, there were plenty of good mechanics out of work. He promised he'd get Deborah another gift for Christmas, but he couldn't do it in time for tonight. I told him not to worry; I'd work out something.

When we got home, I got started making cookies with chocolate sprinkles, the kind Deborah likes. She helped me. After a while, when the first batch of cookies was baking, her cheeks powdered with flour and her pretty face turned away, she said, quietly, "It's all right not to get a present for Christmas. As long as you know somebody *wanted* to give it to you and spent all her money to get it."

My heart was so full I couldn't say anything for a while. Then I lifted her onto my lap and hugged her to my heart. "Oh, Debbie my love, you'll understand when you're older, but you've just gotten the best Christmas present of all: the chance to make a little child happy."

I held her away and looked into her wise, innocent eyes and wondered if, maybe, she already understood that.

Francis M. Nevins, Jr.

THE SHAPE OF THE NIGHTMARE

On the afternoon of the second day before Christmas, just before the terror swept the airport, Loren Mensing was studying the dispirited and weaving line in front of the ticket counter and wishing fervently that he were somewhere else.

He had turned in his exam grades at the law school, said goodbye to the handful of December graduates among his students, and wasted three days moping, with the dread of spending the holidays alone again festering inside him like an untreated wound. The high-rise apartment building he'd lived in for years was being converted to condominiums, dozens of tenants had moved out and dozens more had flown south for the holidays, and the isolation in the building reinforced his sense of being alone in the world.

He had called a travel agent and booked passage on a week-long Caribbean cruise where, if he was lucky, he might find someone as seasonally lonely as he was himself. A *Love Boat* fantasy that he tried desperately to make himself believe. He drove to the airport through swirling snow that froze to ice on the Volkswagen's windshield. He checked his bags, went through security at the lower level, and was lounging near the departure gate for Flight 317, nonstop to Miami, when he heard his name over a microphone.

And learned that he'd been bumped.

"I'm very sorry, Mr. Mensing." The passenger service rep seemed to look bored, solicitous, and in charge all at once. "We have to overbook flights because so many reserved-seat holders don't cancel but don't show up either. Today everyone showed up! You have a right to compensatory cash payment plus a half-fare coupon for the next Miami flight." His racing fingers leafed through the schedule book. "Which departs in just five hours. If you'll take this form to the counter on the upper level they'll write you a fresh ticket."

If he took the next flight he'd miss connections with the excursion ship. He kept his rage under control, detached himself from the horde of travelers at the departure gate, and stalked back upstairs to find a supervisor and demand a seat

136

on the flight he was scheduled to take. When he saw the length of the line at the upper level he almost decided to go home and forget the cruise altogether.

A large metropolitan airport two days before Christmas. Men, women, children, bundled in overcoats and mufflers and down jackets and snowcaps, pushing and jostling and shuffling in the interminable lines that wove and shifted in front of the ticket counters like multicolored snakes. Thousands of voices merging into an earsplitting hum. View through panoramic windows of snow sifting through the gray afternoon, of autos and trucks and taxis crawling to a halt. Honeyed robot voices breaking into the recorded Christmas carols to make flight announcements no one could hear clearly.

Loren was standing apart from the line, trying to decide whether to join it or surrender his fantasy and go home, when it happened.

He heard a voice bellowing something through the wall of noise in the huge terminal. "Bon! Bonreem!" That was what it sounded like in the chaos. It was coming from a man standing to one side of the line like himself. A short sandy-haired man wearing jeans and a down jacket and red ski cap, shouting the syllables in a kind of fury. "Bonreem!"

A man standing in the line turned his head to the right, toward the source of the shout, as if he were hearing something that related to him. A woman in a tan all-weather coat with a rain hood, just behind the man in the line, began to turn her head in the same direction.

The sandy-haired man dropped into a combat crouch, drew a pistol from the pocket of his down jacket, and fired four times at the two who were turning. In the bedlam of the airport the shots sounded no louder than coughs. The next second the face of the man in the line was blown apart. Someone screamed. Then everyone screamed. The man with the shattered face fell to the tiled floor, his fingers still moving, clutching air. The line in front of the ticket counter dissolved into a kaleidoscope of figures running, fainting, shrieking. Instinctively Loren dropped to the floor.

The killer raced for the exit doors, stumbled over Loren's outstretched feet, fell on one knee, hard, cried out in pain, picked himself up, and kept running. John Wilkes Booth flashed through Loren's mind. He saw uniformed figures racing toward them, city and airport police, pistols drawn. Two of them blocked the exit doors. The killer wheeled left, stumbled down the main concourse out of sight, police rushing after him.

In the distance Loren heard more screams, then one final shot.

The public-address system was still playing "White Christmas."

At first they put Loren in with the other witnesses, all of them herded into a large auditorium away from the public areas of the airport. Administrative people brought in doughnuts and urns of coffee on wheeled carts. The witnesses sat or stood in small knots—friends, family groups, total strangers, talking compulsively and pacing and clinging to each other. A few stood or sat alone. Loren was one of them. He was still stunned and he knew no one there to talk to.

After a while he pulled out of shock and looked around the room at the other loners. An old man with a wispy white mustache, probably a widower on his way to visit grandchildren for Christmas. A thin dour man with a cleft chin who blinked continually behind steel-rimmed glasses as if the sun were shining in his eyes. In a folding chair in a corner of the auditorium he saw the woman in the tan hooded coat, her head bowed, eyes indrawn, hugging herself and trying not to shudder. He started to get out of his chair and move toward her.

Another woman flung back the swing doors of the auditorium and stood in the entranceway, a tall fortyish woman in a pantsuit, her hair worn long and straight and liberally streaked with gray. "Loren Mensing?" she called out. Her strong voice cut through the hubbub of helpless little conversations in the vast room. "Is there a Loren Mensing here?"

Loren raised his hand and the woman came over to him. "I'm Gene Holt," she said. "Sergeant Holt, city police, Homicide. You're wanted in the conference room."

He followed her to a room down the hall with a long oak table in the center, flanked by chairs. The air was thick with smoke from cigarettes and a few pipes. He counted at least twenty men in the room—airport police, local police, several in plainclothes. The man at the head of the conference table stood up and beckoned. "Lou Belford," he introduced himself. "Special Agent in charge of the F.B.I. office for the area. The locals just told me you're a sort of detective yourself in an oddball way."

"I used to be deputy legal adviser on police matters for the mayor's office," Loren said. "A part-time position. I teach law for a living."

"And you've helped crack some weird cases, right?"

"I've helped a few times," Loren conceded.

"Well, we've got a weird one here, Professor," Belford grunted. "And you're our star witness. Tell me what you saw."

As Loren told his story Belford scrawled notes on a pad. "It all fits," he said finally. "The guy tripped over your feet and hurt his knee. When he saw he couldn't get out the front exit he headed for the side doors that lead to the underground parking ramps. If he hadn't stumbled over you he could have made it out of the building. Bad luck for him."

"You caught him then? Who was he, and why did he kill that man?"

"We didn't catch him," Belford said. "Cornered him in the gift shop. He saw he was trapped and ate his gun. One shot, right through the mouth. Dead on the spot."

Loren clenched his teeth.

"He wasn't carrying ID," Belford went on, "but we made him a while ago. His name was Frank Wilt. Vietnam vet, unemployed for the last three years. He couldn't hold a job, claimed his head and body were all screwed up from exposure to that Agent Orange stuff they used in the war. The VA couldn't do a thing to help him."

"The man he killed worked for the Veterans Administration?" Loren guessed.

"No, no." Belford shook his head impatiently. "Wilt was obviously desperate for money. It looks as if he took a contract to waste somebody. We just learned he put twenty-five hundred dollars in a bank account Monday. That part of the case is easy. It's the other end we need help with."

"Other end? You mean the victim?" Loren's mind sped to a conclusion from the one fact he knew for certain. "So that's why the F.B.I. are involved! Murder in an airport isn't a Federal crime, and neither is murder by a veteran. So there must be something special about the victim." He leaned forward, elbows on the conference table. "Who was he?"

"The accountant who testified against Lo Scalzo and Pollin in New York last year," Belford said. "John Graham. We gave him and his family new identities under the Witness Relocation Program. They've been living in the city for eighteen months. And now, Professor, we've got an exam for you. Question one: How did the mob find out who and where Graham was? Question two: Why did they hire a broken-down vet to waste him instead of sending in a professional hit man?"

Loren had a sudden memory of one of his own law-school professors who had delighted in posing impossible riddles in class. The recollection made him distinctly uncomfortable.

He stayed with the investigators well into the evening, helping Lieutenant Krauzer of Homicide and Sergeant Holt and the F.B.I. agents interrogate all the actual and possible witnesses. Shortly before midnight, bone-weary and almost numb with the cold, he excused himself, trudged out into the public area of the airport, retrieved his luggage, and grabbed a tasteless snack in the terminal coffee shop. He found his VW in the underground parking garage and drove through hard-packed snow back to his high-rise.

He was unlocking his apartment door when he heard footsteps behind him and whirled, then relaxed. It was the woman, the one in the tan hooded coat who had been standing in the line directly behind John Graham at the time of the murder. "Please let me in, Mr. Mensing," she said. Her voice was soft but filled with desperation, her face taut with tension and fatigue. Loren was afraid she'd collapse at any moment. "Come on in," he nodded. "You need a drink worse than I do."

Ten minutes later they were sitting on the low-backed blue couch, facing the night panorama of the city studded with diamond lights, a pot of coffee, a bottle of brandy, and a plate of cheese and crackers on the cocktail table in front of them. Slowly the warmth, the drinks, and the presence of someone she could trust dissipated the tightness from the woman. Loren guessed that she was about thirty, and that not too long ago she had been lovely.

"Thank you," she said. "I haven't eaten since early this morning, I mean yesterday morning."

"Let me make you a real meal." Loren got up from the couch. "I don't have much in the refrigerator but I think I could manage some scrambled eggs."

"No." She reached out with her hand to stop him. "Maybe later. I'd like to talk now if you don't mind. You may want to kick me out when I'm through." She gave a nervous high-pitched giggle, and Loren sat down again and held her hand, which still felt all but frozen.

"My name is Donna," she began. "Donna Keever. That's my maiden name. I'm married. No, I was married. My husband died just about a year ago. His name was Greene, Charles Greene." Her eyes filled with tears. "It was a year ago last week," she mumbled. "You must have read about it."

Loren groped in the tangle of his memory. Yes, that was it, last year's Christmas heartbreak story in the media. Charles Greene and his six-year-old daughter had been driving home from gift shopping, going west on U.S. 47, when a car traveling east on the same highway hit a rut. The eastbound lane at that point was slightly higher than the westbound because of the shape of a hill on which U.S. 47 was built. The eastbound auto had bounced up into the air, literally flown across the median, and landed nose first on top of Greene's car. Then it had bounced off, flown over the roofs of other passing cars, and landed in the ditch at the side of the highway. Greene, his child, and the other driver, who turned out to be driving on an expired license and with his blood full of alcohol, all died instantly. "I remember," Loren said softly.

"I was ill that day," Donna Greene said, "or I'd have been shopping with Chuck and Cindy. That's the only reason I'm still alive while my family's dead. Isn't life wonderful?"

"It was just chance," Loren told her. "You can't feel guilty about it and ruin the rest of your life."

"No!" Her voice rose to the pitch of a scream. "It wasn't chance. That accident didn't just happen. Someone wanted to kill Chuck or Cindy or me. Or all of us!"

She broke then, and Loren held her while she sobbed. When she could talk again he asked her the obvious question. "Have you told the police what you think?"

"Not the police, not the lawyer who's handling the wrongful death claim for me, not anyone. It was only last week that I knew. A burglar broke into my house a week ago Monday night, came into my bedroom. He was wearing a stocking mask and he—he put his hands on me. I screamed my head off and scared him away. The police said it was just a burglar, but I knew. That man was going to kill me! The police think I'm exaggerating, that I'm still crazy with grief because of the accident."

"How about family? Friends? Have you told them of your suspicions?"

"My parents and Chuck's are all dead. My older brother ran away from home about fifteen years ago, when I was fifteen and he was twenty, and no one's heard from him since. I don't work, I don't have a boyfriend and I just couldn't go to my women friends with something like this."

"What made you come to me?" he asked gently.

"Out at the airport auditorium, when that policewoman or whatever she was paged you, I recognized your name. I've read how you've helped people in trouble. When they let me go I looked up where you live in the phone book and came up here to wait for you."

"Why were you at the airport?"

"I had to get away. If I stayed here I knew that burglar would come back and kill me, if I didn't kill myself first. And I was right! You were there, you saw that man, that gunman standing a few feet from me and he called my name, Donna Greene, and I started to turn and he shot at me and hit the man next to me in the line. Oh, God, somebody, help me!" She broke again, terror and despair poured out of her, and Loren held her and made comforting sounds while his mind raced.

Yes, the two names, John Graham and Donna Greene, sounded just enough alike that in the crowded terminal, with noises assaulting the ears from every side, both of them might have thought their name was being called and turned. To Loren, less than a dozen feet away, the name had sounded like "Bonreem." But which of the two *had* Frank Wilt been paid to kill? If Donna was right, the double-barreled question posed by Agent Belford became meaningless. And if she was the intended victim, what would the person who had hired Wilt do next?

All the time he was soothing Donna Greene he fought with himself. "Don't get involved again," something inside told him. "The last time you saved someone he went out later and killed a bunch of innocent people. This time you're already partly responsible for Wilt's death. And for all you know this woman may be a raving paranoid."

And then all at once he knew what to do, something that would reconcile the conflicting emotions within him and make his Christmas a lot brighter too. He waited until Donna was under control again before he explained.

"I've been thinking," he said. "I don't think I'm qualified to judge whether

141

you're right or wrong about being the target at the airport. But I know someone who is—a woman private detective up in Capital City named Val Tremaine. She's fantastically good at her work. I'm going to ask her to come down and spend a couple of days on your case, getting to know you, talking with you, forming judgments. You'll like her. Her husband died young too and she had to start life over." He disengaged himself gently and rose to his feet. "I'll make the call from my study. You'll be all right?"

"I'm better now. I just needed someone I could open up to who wouldn't treat me like a fool or a lunatic. Look, Mr. Mensing, I'm not a charity case. My lawyer is suing the estate of that other driver for three million dollars. He was rich, his attorneys already offered to settle for three-quarters of a million. I'm not asking you or your detective friend to work for nothing."

"Don't worry about money now," Loren said, and went down the inner hall to the second bedroom that was fixed up as his study, closing the door behind him. He had to check his address book for the number of Val's house, the lovely house nestled on the side of a mountain forty miles from the capital's center, the house she had built as therapy after her husband had died. God, had it been that long since he'd called her? He wondered what had made their relationship taper off, his choice or hers or just the natural drifting of two people who cared deeply for each other but were hundreds of miles apart. He hoped she wouldn't mind his calling in the middle of the night. He hoped very much that she'd be alone.

On the fourth ring she answered, her voice heavy with sleep and bewilderment and a touch of anger.

"Hi, Val, it's me . . . Yes, much too long. I've missed you too. Want to make up for lost time?" He told her about his involvement in the airport murder which she'd heard reported on the evening's TV newscasts, and about the riddle of the intended target which Donna Greene had dropped in his lap. "So if you haven't any other plans for the holidays, why not spend Christmas here? Check her story, be her bodyguard if she needs one, help her start functioning again. Take her to the police with me if you believe she's right." He knew better than to hold out the prospect of a substantial fee. That wasn't the way Val operated.

"You've got yourself a guest," she said. "You know, I was going to invite you up to my place for Christmas but—well, I wasn't sure you'd come."

"I'd have come," he told her softly. If she had invited him he wouldn't have been at the airport this afternoon, and maybe Frank Wilt would be alive and able to tell who had hired him, and maybe Donna Greene would be dead. Chance.

"I'll have to get someone to run the office and I'll need an hour to pack. No way I can get a plane reservation this time of year, so I'll drive. See you around, oh, say eight in the morning if I don't get stuck in the snow."

"I hope you like quiche for breakfast," Loren said.

*   *   *

A soft rapping on the front door jerked him out of a doze on the blue couch. Sullen gray light filling the living room told him it was morning. His watch on the end table read 7:14. "Yes?" he called in the door's direction.

"Me." He recognized Val's voice, undid the deadbolt and the chain lock. The second she was inside with her suitcase he kissed her. It was their first kiss in months and they both made it last. Then they just looked at each other. Val's cheeks were red from the cold and her eyes showed the strain of a long drive through snow-haunted darkness. She was beautiful as ever.

"I missed you," he whispered. "Mrs. Greene's asleep in the bedroom."

They talked quietly in the kitchen while they grated some cheddar, cut a strip of pepper and an onion and ham slices into bits, beat two eggs in cream and melted butter, poured the ingredients into a ready-made pie crust, seasoned them with salt and nutmeg, and popped the quiche into the oven. Loren reported on the murder and Donna's story as the aroma of hot melted cheese filled the kitchen.

"The first step isn't hard to figure," Val said, cutting the quiche into thirds as Loren poured orange juice and coffee. "She'll have to look at pictures of Wilt and tell us if he was her Monday-night burglar. If she identifies him we'll know she was the target at the airport."

"But if she can't identify him," Loren pointed out, "it's not conclusive the other way. Maybe two guys were after her, maybe she didn't get a good look at the burglar . . . We do make a delicious quiche, partner."

"And I'm glad we saved a third of it for our client," Val said, "because the minute she gets up I'm borrowing your bed. I can't take sleepless nights the way I used to."

They left Val asleep and drove downtown through the snow in Loren's VW and entered the office of the homicide detail a little after eleven. Lieutenant Krauzer was in his cubicle, and from his rumpled red-eyed look he'd been working through the night. He was a balding soft-spoken overweight man in his fifties who never seemed to react to anything but, like a human sponge, absorbed whatever came before him.

The lieutenant listened to Loren's story and to Donna Greene's, then picked up his phone handset, and twirled the dial. "Gene, you still have the Wilt photos? Yeah, bring them in, please."

"We've learned a bunch about Frank Wilt since you hung it up last night, Professor," Krauzer said. "He spent most of his time in bars, one joint in particular that's owned by a guy with mob connections. That could explain how he was hired for the hit if the target was John Graham, but it doesn't explain why. Damn it, the mob just doesn't pay washed-up vets to waste a top man on their hit list.

"Your story reads better on that score, Mrs. Greene. An amateur hires Wilt for a private killing. He messes it up at your house last week and runs. He follows you to the airport yesterday, tries again, and messes it up again, because the guy next to you in line happened to have a name that sounds a little like yours, turned faster than you did, and took the bullets meant for you. But, ma'am, you just can't ask me to believe that there's a plot to wipe out your family, because there's no way on earth the freak accident that killed your husband and daughter could have been anything but—"

A knock sounded on the cubicle door and a woman entered. Loren recognized her as Sergeant Holt from last night. She placed a sheaf of photos on Krauzer's desk and left after the lieutenant thanked her. Loren handed the pictures to Donna and watched her face as she squinted and studied the shots with intense deliberation. In the outer office phones were ringing constantly, voices rising and falling, doors slamming, and in the street Loren heard the wail of sirens. Violent crime seemed to thrive on holidays.

There was a hunted look in Donna Greene's eyes when she handed the photos back to Krauzer. "I can't tell," she said in almost a whisper. "I think the burglar was taller but with that stocking mask he wore and in the dark I couldn't see his face well enough to be sure. Oh, I'm sorry!" She began to cry again and Loren reached out for her. Krauzer lifted the phone and a minute later Sergeant Holt came back in, put her arm around the other woman, and led her away.

Leaving Loren alone with Krauzer and free to ask the lieutenant for a large favor.

The Homicide specialist kept shaking his head sadly. "I can't spare the personnel to put a twenty-four-hour watch on her, Professor. Not short-handed the way we are around Christmas. Not without more proof she's really in danger. I like the lady, I think she was totally honest with us, and I know she's scared half to death, but—"

"But she's paranoid?" Loren broke in. "Like all the dissidents in the Sixties and Seventies who thought the government was persecuting them? Look, suppose she's right the way they were right?"

"Then you've got Val Tremaine to protect her," Krauzer said, "and we both know they don't come better." He gave Loren a bleak but knowing smile. "Go on, get out of here with your harem, and have a merry Christmas. Call me if something should happen."

If something should happen . . .

He decided to let Val sleep at the apartment and take Donna shopping so that he and his unexpected guests could have some sort of Christmas. After weaving through downtown streets in a crazy-quilt pattern to throw off any possible followers, he swung the VW onto the Interstate and drove out to the tri-leveled Cherrywood Mall. On the day before Christmas there was more safety among the crowds of frantic last-minute shoppers than behind fortress walls.

The excursion seemed to take Donna out of herself, erase some of the hunted look from her eyes. It was after four and their arms were full of brightly wrapped packages when they slipped into a dark quiet bar on the mall's third level.

"Feeling better?" Loren asked as they sipped Alexanders.

"Much." She smiled hesitantly in the dimness. "Mr. Mensing, these are the happiest few hours I've had since, well, since last year. I can never repay you. You've even made me begin to feel different about everything that's happened to me."

"Different how?"

"I've decided it wasn't just blind chance that I didn't go in the car with Chuck and Cindy that day and that the man next to me was shot and not me. I think I'm meant to live awhile yet. And, oh, God, there's so much I've got to do after the holidays to put my life back in order. The house is a hopeless mess and the tires on my car are getting bald and I need a new will—Chuck and I had mutual wills, we each left everything to the other—and, you know, I may start dating again." She looked into her glass and then into Loren's eyes. "You're, ah, not available, right?"

"I'm honestly not sure," Loren said. "Val and I have been out of touch for months and we've been sort of preoccupied since she got in this morning." He paused, blinked behind his glasses, bewildered as he habitually was by the thought that any young woman could find a bear-bodied, unaggressive, overly learned intellectual in his late thirties even slightly desirable. "But look. However that turns out, I'm your friend. Val and I both are."

"To friendship," she said as they touched glasses. "To a new life."

It was the strangest Christmas Eve he'd ever spent. To an outsider it would have seemed that an exotic fantasy had become real—a man and two lovely women, a high-rise well stocked with food and drink. As night fell and with it fresh snow, Loren made a bowl of hot mulled wine and played the new recording of the Dvorak Piano Quintet No. 5 that he'd bought as his Christmas present to himself. Later he turned on the radio to an FM station and they listened to traditional carols as he gave Val and Donna the gifts he'd purchased at Cherrywood. Their squeals of delight warmed him more than the wine.

Part of him felt relaxed and at peace and part of him stayed alert like an animal in fear of predators. But as midnight approached he found it harder and harder to believe there was danger. Not with the snow outside turning to ice as it fell, not behind the deadbolt and chain lock in a haven twenty stories high.

A little after 12:30 they exchanged good-night kisses and Loren surrendered his bedroom to the women. When they'd closed the door behind them he made a last ritual concession to security by tugging the massive blue couch over against the front door before arranging its cushions on the living-room rug in a makeshift bed.

He was fitting a spare sheet over the couch cushions when Val came back, her blonde hair falling soft and loose over the shoulders of the floor-length caftan he'd given her for Christmas. She smiled and helped him smooth the sheets. "Now you'll sleep better," she said. "I feel like a toad kicking you out of your bed on Christmas Eve."

"Can't be helped. Donna's asleep?"

"Out like a light. You were right to serve decaffeinated coffee." She sat on a sheet-draped cushion. "And thanks to that nap I had before the sergeant dropped by, I'm not tired in the least—"

"Sergeant?" Loren asked. He was suddenly alert.

Her face dropped slightly. "Oh, rats, I wasn't supposed to tell you. Lieutenant Krauzer sent a man over this afternoon just in case Donna was in danger. He came while you were shopping, showed me his ID, looked this place over, and set up a stakeout in 20-B, the vacant apartment across the hall. He said not to tell you and Donna so you'd act natural and not scare any suspects away. But it's good to know Sergeant Holt is standing guard."

Loren leaped to his feet. "Sergeant *who?*" he shouted.

"Gene Holt, Lieutenant Krauzer's assistant. He's been in 20-B since midafternoon. The couple that lives there is in Florida—"

"Describe him." Loren's face was white, and wet fear crawled down his spine.

"A tall man in his middle thirties, thin face, cleft chin. He wears glasses and blinks a lot as if his eyes were weak."

In that moment Loren saw the shape of the nightmare. "That's it," he muttered, and stood there frozen with understanding. He could hear clocks ticking, the night stirrings of the building, the plock-plock of icy snow falling on the outdoor furniture on his balcony. Every sound was magnified now, transformed into menace.

Val shook his shoulders, fear twisting her own face. "Loren, what in God's name is the matter?"

"Sergeant Gene Holt," Loren told her, "is a woman. And now I know who Weak Eyes is too."

"He had a badge and identification!" she protested.

"And if you know the right document forger you can have stuff like that made to order while you wait." He pushed her aside, headed for the phone on a stand in the corner. "I'm calling Krauzer and getting some real cops here."

The phone exploded into sound before he'd crossed the room and he jumped as if shot. A second ring, a third. He picked it up as if it were a cobra, forced it to his ear. Silence. Then a voice, smooth, low, calm. "Unfortunately, Professor, I can't let you call for reinforcements," it said.

Loren slammed the phone down, held it in its cradle for a count of ten, then lifted the handset. He didn't hear a dial tone. He punched the hook furiously. Still no dial tone. He whirled to Val. "Him," he whispered. "He must have planted a bug here while he was pretending to check the place out for security. He heard every word we said all evening and was just waiting for all of us to go to bed. We can't phone outside—he's tying up the line by keeping the phone in 20-B off the hook."

"We can phone for help from one of the other apartments on this floor!"

"We can't. 20-C moved out when the building converted to condo and 20-D's out of town. Besides, he's at the front door of 20-B. If you try to go out in the hall he's got you."

"Let's get out on the balcony and scream for help!"

"Who'd hear us in that storm?"

Val swung around, raced down the inner hall to the bedroom. Loren knew why. To throw on street clothes and get her gun. If she'd brought one with her. Loren hadn't asked.

The phone shrilled again. Loren stared at it as if hypnotized. He let it ring six times, nine. Over the rings he heard Donna's sobs of terror from the bedroom. Oh, God, if only it were Krauzer on the other end, or Belford the F.B.I. man, or anyone in the world except Weak Eyes, anyone Loren could ask to call the police! On the twelfth ring he picked up the receiver.

"Mensing," the low calm voice said, "I have just placed a charge of plastic explosive on the outside of your door. You have two minutes to take down that barricade I heard you put up and send Donna across the hall. Do that and you and Tremaine live."

Loren slammed the phone down. Val in a dark gray jumpsuit ran back into the living room. There was no gun in her hand. Loren almost cried out with frustration. "Donna's in your closet," she whispered. "I pushed the dresser against the door."

Loren nodded, held her close, and spoke feverishly into her ear. Time slipped away into nothingness. Val went down the inner hall, turning off lights, opened the fusebox, and cut the master switch. The apartment was pitch-dark now. Loren found the hall closet, put on rubbers, and his heaviest overcoat. Then he tugged the couch away from the front door, undid the deadbolt and chain, and ran across the room.

He slipped on the couch cushions in the middle of the floor and pain shot through his ankle. He bit down on his lower lip, hobbled the rest of the way across the room, threw open the door leading to his balcony. Sudden cold stunned him, made him shake uncontrollably as he stood outside, behind the curtained balcony door, and watched through the thin elongated crack.

The front door was flung back and Weak Eyes leaped in, using a combat crouch like Wilt at the airport. In his hand there was a gun. His eyes focused on the patch of light across the dark room, the light coming from the balcony. He stalked across the room like a wolf. Loren tensed, waiting. Yes, he was close enough to the balcony now, time for Val to make her move.

There she went, crawling across the wall-to-wall carpet in the dark, all but invisible in her jumpsuit, making the front door and then for the firestairs.

Weak Eyes heard nothing, didn't turn. He kicked the balcony door all the way open, looked down the long balcony. There was nothing to see but a white-painted cast-iron outdoor table and three matching chairs. He took a cautious step out onto the balcony, his eyes trying to pierce the deeper shadows at the far end.

Loren brought the fourth iron chair down hard on the back of the killer's neck. Weak Eyes howled, flung his arms up for balance. The gun flew out of his hand into the slush. He skidded halfway down the balcony, his belly slammed into the outdoor table.

Loren kept hitting him with the chair until Weak Eyes wasn't moving. It was all Loren could do to keep from hurling him over the balcony rail and down twenty stories to the street.

Loren was still standing there, his teeth chattering in the cold, his ankle throbbing, sweat pouring down him, when a few minutes later Val and two uniformed patrolmen rushed out to the balcony.

"What a world," Lieutenant Krauzer grunted eight hours later. "Her own brother."

Weak Eyes was in a cell, Donna had been taken to the hospital under sedation, and they were gathered in Loren's apartment. He sat on the blue couch with his right leg raised on a kitchen chair and the ankle bandaged tightly. Val sat on a hassock at his side, refilling his coffee cup, handing him tissues when he sneezed. Outside, Christmas morning dawned in shades of smoky gray.

"It had to be her brother," Loren said. "Once Val described the fake Gene Holt it all clicked, because I remembered seeing a man of that exact description in the airport auditorium after the Graham murder. And then I remembered three things Donna had mentioned in passing: that she and her late husband had had mutual wills, that she hadn't gotten around to making a new will yet, and that her wrongful-death suit against the driver of the car that killed her family was going to net her a lot of money.

"Now suppose she'd been killed by that burglar, or at the airport? Who would have wound up with that money? Obviously if she died intestate it would go to her next of kin. Who's her next of kin? Her parents are dead, her only child is dead—*but she had a brother who dropped out of sight fifteen years ago.*

"Now the picture clears up," he went on. "Charles and Cindy Greene die in a tragic accident that gets heavy coverage in the media. Wherever he was at the time, Donna's brother hears of it, sees huge financial possibilities, comes to the city quietly, and begins shadowing her. He satisfied himself that the wrongful-death action is going to produce big money and that his sister hasn't made out a new will. He had to get rid of her before she does. He looks around—the forged ID and bugging equipment and plastique show he has underworld connections—and hires Frank Wilt for the hit.

"Wilt breaks into her house a week ago Monday night and bungles the job. Brother gives him another chance. Wilt follows her to the airport, makes his move—and by blind chance a man with a name similar to Donna's is next to her in line, turns faster than she does, and dies instead of her.

"Brother has gone to the airport too, as a backup in case Wilt blew it again. He and Donna are both rounded up as witnesses and taken to the auditorium but either she doesn't see him in the crowd or just doesn't recognize him after fifteen years. When she's let go he follows her to my place and works out a plan to kill her here, doing the job himself this time. He reads the newspaper stories about the airport murder, picks up the name of Sergeant Gene Holt, and uses it as his cover identity but makes the big mistake of assuming from the name that the sergeant is a man."

"And that bit of chauvinism's going to cost him twenty years in the slam." Krauzer yawned and lumbered wearily to his feet. "Well, if you'll excuse me it's Christmas morning and I've got grandkids to play Santy for." He winked broadly at Val. "Remember he's a sick man and needs his rest."

When he had let himself out Val slid off the hassock to sit on the floor. "Funny," Loren said as he ran his hand through her hair. "The way Christmas turned out isn't anything like what I either was afraid of or hoping for. I can't walk, I haven't slept in two nights, I've got the chills, but all in all I feel good. The crazy way this world goes, I'll be damned if I know if it's all chance or if it's meant."

"I'll take the world either way if you're part of it," Val told him softly.

Robert Turner

CHRISTMAS GIFT

There was no snow and the temperature was a mild sixty-eight degrees and in some of the yards nearby the shrubbery was green, along with the palm trees, but still you knew it was Christmas Eve. Doors on the houses along the street held wreaths, some of them lighted. A lot of windows were lighted with red, green, and blue lights. Through some of them you could see the lighted glitter of Christmas trees. Then, of course, there was the music, which you could hear coming from some of the houses, the old familiar songs, "White Christmas," "Ave Maria," "Silent Night."

All of that should have been fine because Christmas in a Florida city is like Christmas anyplace else, a good time, a tender time. Even if you're a cop. Even if you pulled duty Christmas Eve and can't be home with your own wife and kid. But not necessarily if you're a cop on duty with four others and you're going to have to grab an escaped con and send him back, or more probably have to kill him because he was a lifer and just won't *go* back.

In the car with me was McKee, a Third-Grade, only away from a beat a few months. Young, clear-eyed, rosy-cheeked All-American-boy type, and very, very serious about his work. Which was fine; which was the way you should be. We were parked about four houses down from the rented house where Mrs. Bogen and her three children were living.

At the same distance the other side of the house was a sedan in which sat Lieutenant Mortell and Detective First-Grade Thrasher. Mortell was a bitter-mouthed, needle-thin man, middle-aged and with very little human expression left in his eyes. He was in charge. Thrasher was a plumpish, ordinary guy, an ordinary cop.

On the street behind the Bogen house was another precinct car with two other Firsts in it, a couple of guys named Dodey and Fischman. They were back there in case Earl Bogen got away from us and took off through some yards to that other block. I didn't much think he'd get to do that.

After a while McKee said: "I wonder if it's snowing up north. I'll bet the hell it is." He shifted his position. "It don't really seem like Christmas, no snow. Christmas with palm trees, what a deal!"

"That's the way it was with the first one," I reminded him.

He thought about that. Then he said: "Yeah. Yeah. That's right. But I still don't like it."

I started to ask him why he stayed down here, then I remembered about his mother. She needed the climate; it was all that kept her alive.

"Y'know," McKee said then, "sarge, I been thinking; this guy Bogen must be nuts."

"You mean because he's human? Because he wants to see his wife and kids on Christmas?"

"Well, he must know there's a *chance* he'll be caught. If he is, it'll be worse for his wife and kids, won't it? Why the hell couldn't he just have *sent* them presents or something and then called them on the phone? Huh?"

"You're not married, are you, McKee?"

"No."

"And you don't have kids of your own. So I can't answer that question for you."

"I still think he's nuts."

I didn't answer. I was thinking how I could hound the stinking stoolie who had tipped us about Earl Bogen's visit home for Christmas, all next year, without getting into trouble. There was a real rat in my book, a guy who would stool on something like that, I was going to give him a bad time if it broke me.

Then I thought about what Lieutenant Mortell had told me an hour ago. "Tim," he said. "I'm afraid you're not a very good cop. You're too sentimental. You ought to know by now a cop can't be sentimental. Was Bogen sentimental when he crippled for life that manager of the finance company he stuck up on his last hit? Did he worry about *that* guy's wife and kids? Stop being a damned fool, will you, Tim?"

That was the answer I got to my suggestion that we let Earl Bogen get in and see his family and have his Christmas and catch him on the way out. What was there to lose, I'd said. Give the guy a break, I'd said. I'd known, of course, that Mortell wouldn't have any part of that, but I'd had to try anyhow. Even though I knew the lieutenant would think of the same thing I had—that when it came time to go, Bogen might be twice as hard to take.

McKee's bored young voice cut into my thoughts: "You think he'll really be armed? Bogen, I mean."

"I think so."

"I'm glad Mortell told us not to take any chances with him, that if he even makes a move that looks like he's going for a piece, we give it to him. He's a smart old cop, Mortell."

151

"That's what they say. But did you ever look at his eyes?"

"What's the matter with his eyes?" McKee said.

"Skip it," I said. "A bus has stopped."

We knew Earl Bogen had no car; we doubted he'd rent one or take a cab. He was supposed to be short of dough. A city bus from town stopped up at the corner. When he came he'd be on that, most likely. But he wasn't on this one. A lone woman got off and turned up the avenue. I let out a slight sigh and looked at the radium dial of my watch. Ten fifty. Another hour and ten minutes and we'd be relieved; it wouldn't happen on our tour. I hoped that was the way it would be. It was possible. The stoolie could have been wrong about the whole thing. Or something could have happened to change Bogen's plans, or at least to postpone his visit to the next day. I settled back to wait for the next bus.

McKee said: "Have you ever killed a guy, sarge?"

"No," I said. "I've never had to. But I've been there when someone else did."

"Yeah? What's it like?" McKee's voice took on an edge of excitement. "I mean for the guy who did the shooting? How'd he feel about it?"

"I don't know. I didn't ask him. But I'll tell you how he looked. He looked as though he was going to be sick to his stomach, as though he should've been but couldn't be."

"Oh," McKee said. He sounded disappointed. "How about the guy that was shot? What'd he do? I've never seen a guy shot."

"Him?" I said. "Oh, he screamed."

"Screamed?"

"Yeah. Did you ever hear a child scream when it's had a door slammed on its fingers? That's how he screamed. He got shot in the groin."

"Oh, I see," McKee said, but he didn't sound as though he really did. I thought that McKee was going to be what they called a good cop—a nice, sane, completely insensitive type guy. For the millionth time I told myself that I ought to get out. Not after tonight's tour, not next month, next week, tomorrow, but right now. It would be the best Christmas present in the world I could give myself and my family. And at the same time I knew I never would do that. I didn't know exactly why. Fear of not being able to make a living outside; fear of winding up a burden to everybody in my old age the way my father was—those were some reasons but not the whole thing. If I talk about how after being a cop so long it gets in your blood no matter how you hate it, that sounds phony. And it would sound even worse if I said one reason I stuck was in hopes that I could make up for some of the others, that I could do some good sometimes.

"If I get to shoot Bogen," McKee said, "he won't scream."

"Why not?"

"You know how I shoot. At close range like that, I'll put one right through his eyes."

"Sure, you will," I told him. "Except that you won't have the chance. We'll get him, quietly. We don't want any shooting in a neighborhood like this on Christmas Eve."

Then we saw the lights of the next bus stop up at the corner. A man and a woman got off. The woman turned up the avenue. The man, medium height but very thin, and his arms loaded with packages, started up the street.

"Here he comes," I said. "Get out of the car, McKee. "

We both got out, one on each side. The man walking toward us from the corner couldn't see us. The street was heavily shaded by strings of Australian pine planted along the walk.

"McKee," I said. "You know what the orders are. When we get up to him, Thrasher will reach him first and shove his gun into Bogen's back. Then you grab his hands and get the cuffs on him fast. I'll be back a few steps covering you. Mortell will be behind Thrasher, covering him. You got it?"

"Right," McKee said.

We kept walking, first hurrying a little, then slowing down some, so that we'd come up to Bogen, who was walking toward us, just right, before he reached the house where his family were but not before he'd passed Mortell and Thrasher's car.

When we were only a few yards from Bogen, he passed through an open space, where the thin slice of moon filtered down through tree branches. Bogen wore no hat, just a sport jacket and shirt and slacks. He was carrying about six packages, none of them very large but all of them wrapped with gaudily colored paper, foil, and ribbon. Bogen's hair was crew cut instead of long the way it was in police pictures and he'd grown a mustache; but none of that was much of a disguise.

Just then he saw us and hesitated in his stride. Then he stopped. Thrasher, right behind him, almost bumped into him. I heard Thrasher's bull-froggy voice say: "Drop those packages and put your hands up, Bogen. Right now!"

He dropped the packages. They tumbled about his feet on the sidewalk and two of them split open. A toy racing car was in one of them. It must have been still slightly wound up because when it broke out of the package, the little motor whirred and the tiny toy car spurted across the sidewalk two or three feet. From the other package, a small doll fell and lay on its back on the sidewalk, its big, painted eyes staring upward. It was what they call a picture doll, I think; anyhow, it was dressed like a bride. From one of the other packages a liquid began to trickle out onto the sidewalk and I figured that had been a bottle of Christmas wine for Bogen and his wife.

But when Bogen dropped the packages he didn't raise his hands. He spun around and the sound of his elbow hitting Thrasher's face was a sickening one. Then I heard Thrasher's gun go off as he squeezed the trigger in a reflex action, but the flash from his gun was pointed at the sky.

I raised my own gun just as Bogen reached inside his jacket but I never got to use it. McKee used his. Bogen's head went back as though somebody had jolted him under the chin with the heel of a hand. He staggered backward, twisted, and fell.

I went up to Bogen with my flash. The bullet from McKee's gun had entered Bogen's right eye and there was nothing there now but a horrible hole. I moved the flash beam just for a moment, I couldn't resist it, to McKee's face. The kid looked very white but his eyes were bright with excitement and he didn't look sick at all. He kept licking his lips, nervously. He kept saying: "He's dead. You don't have to be worrying about him, now. He's dead."

Front door lights began to go on then in nearby houses and people began coming out of them. Mortell shouted to them: "Go on back inside. There's nothing to see. Police business. Go on back inside."

Of course, most of them didn't do that. They came and looked, although we didn't let them get near the body. Thrasher radioed back to headquarters. Mortell told me: "Tim, go tell his wife. And tell her she'll have to come down and make final identification for us."

"Me?" I said. "Why don't you send McKee? He's not the sensitive type. Or why don't you go? This whole cute little bit was your idea, anyhow, lieutenant, remember?"

"Are you disobeying an order?"

Then I thought of something. "No," I told him. "It's all right. I'll go."

I left them and went to the house where Bogen's wife and kids lived. When she opened the door, I could see past her into the cheaply, plainly furnished living room that somehow didn't look that way now, in the glow from the decorated tree. I could see the presents placed neatly around the tree. And peering around a corner of a bedroom, I saw the eyes, big with awe, of a little girl about six and a boy about two years older.

Mrs. Bogen saw me standing there and looked a little frightened. "Yes?" she said. "What is it?"

I thought about the newspapers, then. I thought: "What's the use? It'll be in the newspapers tomorrow, anyhow." Then I remembered that it would be Christmas Day; there wouldn't *be* any newspapers published tomorrow, and few people would bother about turning on radios or television sets.

"Don't be alarmed," I told her, then. "I'm just letting the people in the neighborhood know what happened. We surprised a burglar at work, ma'am, and he ran down this street. We caught up with him here and had to shoot him. But it's all over now. We don't want anyone coming out, creating any more disturbance, so just go back to bed, will you please?"

Her mouth and eyes opened very wide. "Who—who was it?" she said in a small, hollow voice.

"Nobody important," I said. "Some young hood."

"Oh," she said then and I could see the relief come over her face and I knew then that my hunch had been right and Bogen hadn't let her know he was coming; he'd wanted to surprise her. Otherwise she would have put two and two together.

I told her good night and turned away and heard her shut the door softly behind me.

When I went back to Mortell I said: "Poor Bogen. He walked into the trap for nothing. His folks aren't even home. I asked one of the neighbors and she said they'd gone to Mrs. Bogen's mother's and wouldn't be back until the day after Christmas."

"Well, I'll be damned," Mortell said, watching the men from the morgue wagon loading Bogen onto a basket.

"Yes," I said. I wondered what Mortell would do to me when he learned what I'd done and he undoubtedly would, eventually. Right then I didn't much care. The big thing was that Mrs. Bogen and those kids were going to have their Christmas as scheduled. Even when I came back and told her what had happened, the day after tomorrow, it wouldn't take away the other.

Maybe it wasn't very much that I'd given them but it was something and I felt a little better. Not much, but a little.

James Powell

SANTA'S WAY

Lieutenant Field parked behind the Animal Protective League van. The night was cold, the stars so bright he could almost taste them. Warmer constellations of tree lights decorated the dark living rooms on both sides of the street. Field turned up his coat collar. Then he followed the footprints in the snow across the lawn and up to the front door of the house where a uniformed officer stood shuffling his feet against the weather.

Captain Fountain was on the telephone in the front hallway and listening so hard he didn't notice Field come in. "Yes, Commissioner," he said. "Yes, sir, Commissioner." Then he laid a hand over the mouthpiece, looked up at a light fixture on the ceiling, and demanded, "Why me, Lord? Why me?" (The department took a dim view of men talking to themselves on duty. So Fountain always addressed furniture or fixtures. He confided much to urinals. They all knew how hard-done-by Fountain was.) Turning to repeat his question to the hatrack he saw Field. "Sorry to bring you out on this of all nights, Roy," he said. He pointed into the living room and added cryptically, "Check out the fireplace, why don't you?" Then he went back to listening.

Field crossed to the cold hearth. There were runs of blood down the sides of the flue. Large, red, star-shaped spatters decorated the ashes.

A woman's muffled voice said, "I heard somebody coming down the chimney." A blonde in her late thirties sitting in a wing chair in the corner, her face buried in a handkerchief. She looked up at Field with red-rimmed eyes. "After I called you people I even shouted up and told him you were on your way. But he kept on coming."

Captain Fountain was off the telephone. From the doorway he said, "So Miss Doreen Moore here stuck her pistol up the flue and fired away."

"Ka-pow, ka-pow, ka-pow," said the woman, making her hand into a pistol and, in Field's opinion, mimicking the recoil quite well. But he didn't quite grasp the situation until men emerged from the darkness on the other side of the picture window and reached up to steady eight tiny reindeer being lowered down from the roof in a large sling.

"Oh, no!" said Field.

"Oh, yes," said Fountain. "Come see for yourself."

Field followed him upstairs to the third-floor attic where the grim-faced Animal Protective League people, their job done, were backing down the ladder from the trap door in the roof.

Field and Fountain stood out on the sloping shingles under the stars. Christmas music came from the radio in the dashboard of the pickle-dish sleigh straddling the ridge of the roof. Close at hand was Santa, both elbows on the lip of the chimney, his body below the armpits and most of his beard out of sight down the hole. He was quite dead. The apples in his cheeks were Granny Smiths, green and hard.

Only the week before Field had watched the PBS documentary "Santa's Way." Its final minutes were still fresh in his mind. Santa in an old tweed jacket sat at his desk at the Toy Works backed by a window that looked right down onto the factory floor busy with elves. Mrs. Claus, her eyes on her knitting, smiled and nodded at his words and rocked nearby. "Starting out all we could afford to leave was a candy cane and an orange," Santa had said. "The elves made the candy canes and it was up to me to beg or borrow the oranges. Well, one day the United Fruit people said, 'Old timer, you make it a Chiquita banana and we'll supply them free and make a sizable donation to the elf scholarship fund.' But commercializing Christmas wasn't Santa's way. So we made do with the orange. And look at us now." He lowered his hairy white head modestly. "The Toy Works is running three shifts making sleds and dolls and your paint boxes with your yellows, blues, and reds. The new cargo dirigible lets us restock the sleigh in flight." Santa gave the camera a sadder look. "Mind you, there's a down side," he acknowledged. "We've strip-mined and deforested the hell out of the North Pole for the sticks and lumps of coal we give our naughty little clients. And our bond rating isn't as good as it used to be. Still, when the bankers say, 'Why not charge a little something, a token payment for each toy?' I always answer, 'That isn't Santa's way.' "

An urgent voice from the sleigh radio intruded on Field's remembering. "We interrupt this program for a news bulletin," it said. "Santa is dead. We repeat, Santa is dead. The jolly old gentleman was shot several times in the chimney earlier this evening. More details when they are available." At that late hour all good little boys and girls were in bed. Otherwise, Field knew, the announcer would've said, "Antasay is eadday," and continued in pig Latin.

Field stood there glumly watching the street below where the A.P.L. people were chasing after a tiny reindeer which had escaped while being loaded into the van. Lights had come on all over the neighborhood and faces were appearing in windows. After a moment, he turned his attention to the corpse.

But Fountain was feeling the cold. "Roy," he said impatiently, "Santa came down the wrong chimney. The woman panicked. Ka-pow, ka-pow, ka-pow! Cut and dried."

Field shook his head. "Rooftops are like fingerprints," he reminded the Captain. "No two are alike. Santa wouldn't make a mistake like—" He frowned, leaned forward, and put his face close to the corpse's.

"It wasn't just the smell of whiskey on his lips, Miss Moore," said Field. "You see, if Santa'd been going down the chimney his beard would've been pushed up over his face. But it was stuck down inside. Miss Moore, when you shot Santa he was on his way up that chimney."

The woman twisted the handkerchief between her fingers. "All right," she snapped. Then in a quieter voice she said, "All right, Nicky and I go back a long way. Right around here is end of the line for his Christmas deliveries. I'll bet you didn't know that."

Field had guessed as much. Last year when his kids wondered why the treat they left on a tray under the tree was never touched he had suggested maybe Santa was milk-and-cookied out by the time he got to their house.

"Anyway," continued Miss Moore, "Nicky'd always drop by afterwards for a drink and some laughs and one thing would lead to another. But I'm not talking one-night stands," she insisted. "We took trips. We spent time together whenever he could get away. He said he loved Mrs. Claus but she was a saint. And I wasn't a saint, he said, and he loved me for that. And I was crazy about him. But tonight he tried to walk out on me. So I shot him."

In the distance Field heard the police helicopter come to take the sleigh on the roof to Impound.

Fountain said, "Better get Miss Moore down to the station before this place is crawling with reporters. I'll wait for the boys with the flue-extractor rig."

Field turned on his car radio to catch any late-breaking developments. "O Tannenbaum, O Tannenbaum, how beautiful your branches!" sang a small choir. They drove without speaking for a while. Then out of nowhere the woman said, "You know that business about Nicky having a belly that shook like a bowl full of jelly? Well, that was just the poet going for a cheap rhyme. Nicky took care of himself. He exercised. He jogged. And he had this twinkle in his eye that'd just knock my socks off."

"I heard about the twinkle," Field admitted.

"But underneath it all there was this deep sadness," she said. "It wasn't just the fund-raising, the making the rounds every year, hat in hand, for money to keep the North Pole going. And it wasn't the elves, although they weren't always that easy to deal with. 'They can be real short, Doreen,' he told me once. 'Hey, I know elves are short, Nicky. Give me credit for some brains,' I said. He said, 'No, Doreen, I mean abrupt.'

"One time I asked him why he got so low and he said, 'Doreen, when I look all those politicians, bankers, lawyers, and captains of industry in the eye do you know who I see staring back at me? Those same naughty little boys and girls I gave the sticks and lumps of coal to. Where did I go wrong, Doreen? How did they end up running the show?'

"Well, a while back Nicky got this great idea how he could walk away from the whole business. Mr. Santa franchises. He'd auction the whole operation off country by country. Mr. Santa U.S.A. gets exclusive rights to give free toys to American kids and so on, country by country. 'And the elves'd take care of Mrs. Claus,' he said. 'They love her. She's a saint. And with the money I'll raise you and me'll buy a boat and sail away. We'll live off my patented Mr. Santa accessories. You know, my wide belt and the metered tape recorder of my laugh at a buck a 'ho!' "

Suddenly a voice on the radio said, "We now take you to New York where Leviathan Cribbage, elf observer to the United Nations, is about to hold a press conference." After the squeal of a microphone being adjusted downward a considerable distance, a high-pitched little voice said, "The High Council of Elves has asked me to issue the following statement: 'Cast down as we are by the murder of our great leader, Santa Claus, we are prepared, as a memorial to the man and his work, to continue to manufacture and distribute toys on the night before Christmas. In return we ask that our leader's murderer, whom we know to be in police custody, be turned over to elf justice. If the murderer is not in our hands within twenty-four hours the Toy Works at the North Pole will be shut down permanently.' " The room erupted into a hubbub of voices.

"Turn me over to elf justice?" said Miss Moore with a shudder. "That doesn't sound so hot."

"It won't happen," Field assured her as he parked the car. "Even a politician couldn't get away with a stunt like that."

Four detectives were crowded around the squad room television set. Field took Miss Moore into his office. Gesturing her into a chair, he sat down at his desk and said, "Now where were we?"

"With a buck a 'ho!' and me waiting there tonight with my bags packed," she said. "And here comes Nicky down the chimney. 'Doreen,' he says. 'I've only got a minute. I've still deliveries to make. Honey, I told Mrs. Claus about us. She's forgiven me, as I knew she would. But I can't see you again.'

" 'What about the Mr. Santa auction?' said I.

" 'Some auction,' he said. 'Everybody wanted America or Germany. Nobody wanted to be the Bangladeshi or the Ethiopian Mr. Santa. Crazy, isn't it? Everybody wants to load up the kids who've already got everything when giving to kids with nothing is the real fun.' Then he looked at me and said, 'It got me thinking about where I went wrong, Doreen. Maybe I should have given my naughty little clients toys, too. Maybe then they wouldn't have grown up into the kinds of people they did. Anyway, I'm going to give it a try. From now on, I'll be Santa of all the children, naughty or nice. Good-bye, Doreen,' he said and turned to go.

"That's when I pulled out the revolver I keep around because I'm alone so much. I was tired of men who put their careers ahead of their women. I swore I'd kill him if he tried to leave. He went 'ho-ho-ho!' and took the gun out of my hand. He knew I couldn't shoot. I burst into tears. He gathered me in his arms and gave me a good-bye kiss. Emptying the bullets onto the rug, he tossed the pistol aside and walked over to the fireplace. 'You're a nice girl, Doreen,' he said with a twinkle in his eye. 'Don't let anybody ever tell you different.' But just before he ducked his head under the mantel I saw the twinkle flicker."

"Flicker?" asked Field.

"Like he was thinking maybe he'd figured me wrong," she explained. "Like maybe I'd reload the gun. Well, up the chimney he went, hauling ass real fast. And suddenly, I was down on my knees pushing those bullets back into that pistol, furious that I'd wasted my whole life just to be there any time that old geezer in his red wool suit with that unfashionably wide belt could slip his collar and be with me, furious that he was dumping me just so he could give toys to naughty little boys and girls. I was trembling with rage. But every bullet I dropped I picked up again. When I'd gotten them all I went over and emptied the pistol up the chimney. Then I called you people."

Field's telephone rang. "Roy," said his wife, "I just heard the news about Santa. Roy, there aren't any presents under our tree. What are we going to do?"

"Lois, I can't talk now," said Field. "Don't worry. I'll think of something." He hung up the phone. Maybe if he worked all night he could cobble together some toys out of that scrap lumber in the basement.

Fountain was signaling from the doorway. He had an efficient-looking young woman with him. Field stepped outside. "Roy, this is Agent Mountain, Federal Witness Protection Program," he said. "I just got off the phone with the Commissioner. We're not bringing charges."

"Captain, we could be talking premeditated murder here," insisted Field, telling the part about her putting the bullets back into the pistol.

Fountain shrugged. "You want a trial? You want all the nice little boys and girls finding out that Santa was murdered and why? No way, Roy. She walks. But we can't let those damn knee-highs get her."

"You mean elves?" asked Field, who had never heard elves referred to in that derogatory way before.

"You got it," said Fountain. "So Agent Mountain's here to relocate her, give her a whole new identity."

Agent Mountain waved through the door at Doreen Moore. "Hi, honey," she said cheerily. "It looks like it's back to being a brunette."

*   *   *

Field put on his overcoat and closed his office door behind him. He stopped for a moment in front of the squad room television set. Somebody from the State Department was saying, "Peter, let's clear up one misconception right now. Elves are not short genetically. Their growth has been stunted by smoking and other acts of depravity associated with a perverse lifestyle. Can we let such twisted creatures hold our children's happiness hostage? I think not. I refer the second part of your question to General Frost."

A large man in white camouflage placed a plan of the Toy Works at the North Pole on an easel. "In case of a military strike against them, the elves intend to destroy the Toy Works with explosive charges set here, here, and here," he said, tapping with a pointer. "As I speak, our airborne forces, combined with crack RCMP dogsled units, have moved to neutralize—"

Field's phone was ringing. He hurried back to his office. "Hey, Lieutenant," said Impound, "we found presents in Santa's sleigh, some with your kids' names on them. Want to come by and pick them up?"

Field came in with the presents trapped between his chin and his forearm, closing the door quietly behind him. His wife was rattling around in the kitchen. He didn't call out to her, not wanting to wake the children. The light from the kitchen would be enough to put the presents under the tree. He was halfway across the living room when the lights came on. His children were staring down at him from the top of the stairs. Zack and Lesley, the eldest, exchanged wise glances. Charlotte was seven. She'd lost her first baby tooth that afternoon and her astonished mouth had a gap in it.

Field smiled up at them. "Santa got held up in traffic," he lied. "So he deputized a bunch of us as Santa's little helpers to deliver his presents." Charlotte received this flimsy nonsense with large, perplexed eyes. It was the first time he had ever told her anything she didn't believe instantly.

Ordering the children back to bed, Field went into the kitchen. Lois was watching a round-table discussion called "Life After Santa" on the little television set. When he told her about the presents from Impound she said, "Thank God." He didn't tell her what had just happened with the kids. Maybe one of these days he'd be able to sit down and give them the straight scoop, how there really had been this nice guy called Santa Claus who went around in a sleigh pulled by reindeer giving kids presents because he loved them, so, of course, we had to shoot him.

He turned on the kettle to make himself a cup of instant coffee and sat down beside his wife. On the screen a celebrated economist was saying, "Of course, we'll have to find an alternate energy source. Our entire industrial base has always depended on Santa's sticks and lumps of coal."

"But what a golden opportunity to end our kids' dependence on free toys," observed a former National Security advisor. "That's always smelled like socialism to me. Kids have to learn there's no free lunch. We should hand the Toy Works over to private enterprise. I hear Von Clausewitz Industries are interested in getting into toys."

"What about distribution?" asked someone else.

"Maybe we could talk the department stores into selling toys for a week or two before Christmas."

"Selling toys?" asked someone in disbelief.

The National Security advisor smiled. "We can hardly expect the Von Clausewitz people to pick up the tab. No, the toys'll have to be sold. But the play of the marketplace will hold prices—"

Field heard a sound. Someone had raised an upstairs window. Footsteps headed down the hall toward the children's rooms. He took the stairs two at a time, reaching the top with his service revolver drawn. Someone was standing in the dark corner by Charlotte's door. Crouching, pistol at the ready, Field snapped on the hall light. "Freeze!" he shouted.

The woman turned and gave him a questioning look. She had immense rose-gossamer wings of a swallow-tail cut sprouting from her shoulder-blades and a gown like white enamel shimmering with jewels. He didn't recognize who it was behind the surgical mask until she tugged at the wrists of her latex gloves, took a shiny quarter from the coin dispenser at her waist and stepped into Charlotte's room.

Field came out of his crouch slowly. Returning his weapon to its holster he went back down to the kitchen. He turned off the kettle, found the whiskey bottle in the cupboard and poured himself a drink with a trembling hand. "Lois," he said, "I almost shot the Tooth Fairy."

"Oh, Roy," she scolded in a tired voice.

On the television screen someone said, "Of course, we'll need a fund to provide toys for the children of the deserving poor."

"Don't you mean 'the deserving children of the poor'?" someone asked.

" 'Deserving children of the deserving poor,' " suggested another.

Lois shook her head. "Store-bought toys, Roy?" she asked. "We've got mortgage payments, car payments, Lesley's orthodontist, and saving for the kids' college. How can we afford store-bought toys?"

It'd been a hard day. He didn't want to talk about next year's toys. "Lois, please—" he started to say a bit snappishly. But here the program broke for a commercial and a voice said, "Hey, Mom, hey, kids, is Dad getting a little short? (And we don't mean abrupt). Why not send him along to see the folks at Tannenbaum Savings and Loan. All our offices have been tastefully decorated for the season. And there's one near you. So remember—" here a choir chimed in "—Owe Tannenbaum, Owe Tannenbaum, how beautiful their branches!"

George Baxt

I SAW MOMMY KILLING
SANTA CLAUS

W̶e buried my mother yesterday, so I feel free to tell the truth. She lived to be ninety-three because, like the sainted, loyal son I chose to be, I didn't blab to the cops. I'm Oscar Leigh and my mother was Desiree Leigh. That's right—Desiree Leigh, inventor of the Desiree face cream that promised eternal youth to the young and rejuvenation to the aged. It was one of the great con games in the cosmetics industry. I suppose once this is published, it'll be the end of the Desiree cosmetics empire, but frankly, my dears, I don't give a damn. Desiree Cosmetics was bought by a Japanese combine four years ago, and my share (more than two billion) is safely salted away. I suppose I inherit Mom's billions, too, but what in heaven's name will I do with it all? Count it, I guess.

Desiree Leigh wasn't her real name. She was born Daisy Ray Letch, and who could go through life with a surname like Letch? For the past fourteen years she's been entertaining Alzheimer's and that was when I began to take an interest in her past. She was always very mysterious about her origins and equally arcane about the identity of my father. She said he was killed in North Africa back in 1943 and that his name was Clarence Kolb. I spent a lot of money tracing Clarence, until one night, in bed watching an old movie, the closing credits rolled and one of the character actors was named Clarence Kolb. I mentioned this to Mother the next morning at breakfast, but she said it was a coincidence and she and my father used to laugh about it.

She had no photos of my father, which I thought was strange. When they married a few months before the war, they settled in Brooklyn, in Coney Island. Surely they must have had their picture taken in one of the Coney Island fun galleries? But no, insisted Mother, they avoided the boardwalk and the amusement parks—they were too poor for such frivolities. How did Father make his living? He was a milkman, she said—his route was in Sheepshead Bay. She said he worked for the Borden Company. Well, let me tell you this; there is no record of a Clarence Kolb ever having been employed by the Borden Milk

Company. It cost an ugly penny tracking that down.

Did Mom work, too, perhaps? "Oh, yes," she told me one night in Cannes where our yacht was berthed for a few days, "I worked right up until the day before you were born."

"What did you do?" We were on deck playing honeymoon bridge in the blazing sunlight so Mom could keep an eye on the first mate, with whom she was either having an affair or planning to have one.

"I worked in a laboratory." She said it so matter of factly while collecting a trick she shouldn't have collected that I didn't believe her. "You don't believe me." (She not only conned, stole, and lied, she was a mind-reader.)

"Sure I believe you." I sounded as convincing as an East Berlin commissar assuring would-be emigrés they'd have their visas to freedom before sundown.*

"It was a privately owned laboratory," she said, sneaking a look at the first mate, who was sneaking a look at the second mate. "It was a couple of blocks from our apartment."

"What kind of a laboratory was it?" I asked, mindful that the second mate was sneaking a look at me.

"It was owned by a man named Desmond Tester. He fooled around with all kinds of formulas."

"Some sort of mad scientist?"

She chuckled as she cheated another trick in her favor. "I guess he *was* kind of mad in a way. He had a very brilliant mind. I learned a great deal from him."

"Is that where you originated the Desiree creams and lotions?"

"The seed was planted there."

"How long were you with this—"

"Desmond Tester. Let me see now. Your daddy went into the Army in February of '42. I didn't know I was pregnant then or he'd never have gone. On the other hand, I suppose if I *had* known, I would have kept it to myself so your dad could go and prove he was a hero and not just a common everyday milkman."

"I don't see anything wrong in delivering milk."

"There's nothing heroic about it, either. Where was I?"

"Taking my king of hearts, which you shouldn't be."

She ignored me and favored the first mate with a seductive smile, and I blushed when the second mate winked at me. "Anyway, I took time off to give birth to you and then I went right back to work for Professor Tester. A nice lady in the neighborhood looked after you. Let me think, what was her name? Oh, yes—Blanche Yurka."

*Ed. note: A joyful note to anachronism—shortly after this story was written.

164

"Isn't that the name of the actress who played Ma Barker in a gangster movie we saw on the late show?"

"I don't know, is it? That's my ten of clubs you're taking," she said sharply.

"I've captured it fair and square with the queen of clubs," I told her. "How come you never married again?"

"I guess I was too busy being a career woman. I was assisting Professor Tester in marketing some of his creams and lotions by then. I had such a hard time cracking the department stores."

"When did you come up with your own formulas?"

"That was after the professor met with his unfortunate death."

Unfortunate, indeed. I saw her kill him.

It was Christmas of 1950—in fact, it was Christmas Day. Mom was preparing to roast a turkey at the professor's house—our apartment was much too small for entertaining—and I remember almost everyone who was there. It was mostly kids from the neighborhood, the unfortunate ones whose families couldn't afford a proper Christmas dinner. There must have been about ten of them. Mother and the professor were the only adults, although Mom still insists there was a woman there named Laurette with whom the professor was having an affair. Mom says this woman was jealous of her because she thought Mom and the professor were having a little ding-dong of their own. (I've always suspected my mother of doing quite a bit of dinging and donging in the neighborhood when she couldn't meet a grocery bill or a butcher bill or satisfy the landlord or Mr. Kumbog, who owned the liquor store.)

Mom says it was Laurette who shot the professor in the heart and ran away (and was never heard of again, need I tell you?) —but I'm getting ahead of myself. It happened like this: Mom was in the kitchen stuffing the turkey when Professor Tester appeared in the doorway dressed in the Santa Claus suit. He had stuffed his stomach but still looked no more like Santa Claus than Monty Woolley did in *Life Begins at Eight-Thirty*.

"Daisy Ray, I have to talk to you," he said.

"Just let me finish stuffing this turkey and get it in the oven," she told him. "I'd like to feed the kids by around five o'clock when I'm sure they'll be tired of playing Post Office and Spin the Bottle and Doctor." I remember her asking me, "Sonny, have you been playing Doctor?"

"As often as I can," I replied with a smirk. And I still do. Now I'm a specialist.

"Daisy Ray, come with me to the laboratory," Tester insisted.

"Oh, really, Desmond," Mother said, "I don't understand your tone of voice."

"There are a lot of things going on around here that are hard to understand," the professor said ominously. "Daisy Ray!" He sounded uncannily like Captain Bligh summoning Mr. Christian.

I caught a very strange and very scary look on my mother's face. And then she did something I now realize should have made the professor realize that something unexpected and undesirable was about to befall him. She picked up her handbag, which was hanging by its strap on the back of a chair, and followed him out of the room. "Sonny, you stay here." Her voice sounded as though it was coming from that echo chamber I heard on the spooky radio show, *The Witch's Tale*.

"Yes, Mama."

I watched her follow Professor Tester out of the kitchen. I was frightened. I was terribly frightened. I had a premonition that something awful was going to happen, so I disobeyed her orders and tiptoed after them.

The laboratory was in the basement. I waited in the hall until I heard them reach the bottom of the stairs and head for the main testing room, then I tiptoed downstairs, praying the stairs wouldn't squeak and betray me. But I had nothing to worry about. They were having a shouting match that would have drowned out the exploding of an atom bomb.

The door to the testing room was slightly ajar and I could hear everything.

"What have you done with the formula?" he raged.

"I don't know what you're talking about." Mama was quite cool, subtly underplaying him. It was one of those rare occasions when I almost admired her.

"You damn well know what I'm talking about, you thief!"

"How dare you!" What a display of indignation—had she heard it, Norma Shearer would have died of envy.

"You stole the formula for my rejuvenating cream! You've formed a partnership with the Sibonay Group in Mexico!"

"You're hallucinating. You've been taking too many of your own drugs."

"I've got a friend at Sibonay—he's told me everything! I'm going to put you behind bars unless you give me back my formula!"

Although I didn't doubt for one moment that my mother had betrayed him, I still had to put my hand over my mouth to stifle a laugh. I mean, have you ever seen Santa Claus blowing his top? It's a scream in red and white.

"Don't you touch me! Don't you lay a hand on me!" Mother's handbag was open and she was fumbling for something in it. He slapped her hard across the face. Then I heard the *pop* and the professor was clutching at his chest. Through his fingers little streams of blood began to form.

Mom was holding a tiny pearl-handled pistol in her hand, the kind Kay

Francis used to carry around in a beaded bag. My God, I remember saying to myself, I just saw Mommy killing Santa Claus.

I turned tail and ran. I bolted up the stairs and into the front of the house, where the other kids who couldn't possibly have heard what had gone on in the basement were busy choosing up sides for a game called Kill the Hostess. I joined in and there wasn't a peep out of Mom for at least half an hour.

I began to wonder if maybe I had been hallucinating, if maybe I hadn't seen Mom slay the professor. I left the other kids and—out of curiosity and I suppose a little anxiety—I went to the kitchen.

You've got to hand it to Mom (you might as well, she'd take it anyway): the turkey was in the oven, roasting away. She had prepared the salad. Vegetables were simmering, timed to be ready when the turkey was finished roasting. She was topping a sweet-potato pie with little round marshmallows. She looked up when I came in and asked, "Enjoying yourself, Sonny?"

I couldn't resist asking her. "When is Santa Claus coming with his bag of presents for us?"

"Good Lord, when indeed! Now, where could Santa be, do you suppose?"

Dead as a doornail in the testing room, I should have responded, but instead I said, "Shucks, Mom, it beats me."

She thought for a moment and then said brightly, "I'll bet he's downstairs working on a new formula. Go down and tell him it's time he put in his appearance."

Can you top that? Sending her son into the basement to discover the body of the man she'd just assassinated?

Well, I dutifully discovered the body and started yelling my head off, deciding that was the wisest course under the circumstances. Mom and the kids came running. When they saw the body, the kids began shrieking, me shrieking the loudest so that maybe Mom would be proud of me, and Mom hurried and phoned the police.

What ensued after the police arrived was sheer genius on my mother's part. I don't remember the detective's name—by now he must be in that Big Squadroom in the Sky—but I'm sure if he was ever given an I.Q. test he must have ended up owing them about fifty points. Mom was saying hysterically, "Oh, my God, to think there was a murderer in the house while I was in the kitchen preparing our Christmas dinner and the children were in the parlor playing guessing games!" She carried the monologue for about ten minutes until the medical examiner came into the kitchen to tell the detective the professor had been done in by a bullet to the heart.

"Any sign of the weapon?" asked the detective.

"It's not *my* job to look for one," replied the examiner testily.

So others were dispatched to look for a weapon. Knowing Mom, it wouldn't be in her handbag, but where, I wondered, could she have stashed it? I stopped in mid-wonder when I heard her say, "It might have been Laurette."

"Who's she?" asked the detective.

Mom folded her hands, managing to look virtuous and sound scornful. "She was the professor's girl friend, if you know what I mean. He broke it off with her last week and she wasn't about to let him off so easy. She's been phoning and making threats, and this morning he told me she might be coming around to give him his Christmas present." She added darkly, "That Christmas present was called—*death!*"

"Did you see her here today?" the detective asked. Mom said she hadn't. He asked us all if we'd seen a strange lady come into the house. I was tempted to tell him the only strange lady I saw come into the house was my mother, but I thought of that formula and how wealthy we'd become and I became a truly loving son.

"She could have come in by the cellar door," I volunteered.

It was the first time I saw my mother look at me with love and admiration. "It's on the other side of the house, and with all the noise we were making—"

"And I had the radio on in the kitchen, listening to the *Make Believe Ballroom,*" was the fuel Mother added to the fire I had ignited. The arson was successful. The police finally left—without finding the weapon—taking the body with them, and Mom proceeded with Christmas dinner as though killing a man was an everyday occurrence.

The dinner was delicious, although some of us kids noted the turkey had a slightly strange taste to it.

"Turkey can be gamey," Mama trilled—and within the next six months she was on her way to becoming one of the most powerful names in the cosmetics industry.

I remained a bachelor. I worked alongside Mother and her associates and watched as, one by one over the years, she got rid of all of them. She destroyed the Sibonay people in Mexico by proving falsely and at great cost, that they were the front for a dope-running operation. She thought it would be fun if I could become a mayor of New York City, but a psychic told me to forget about it and go into junk bonds—which I did and suffered staggering losses. (The psychic died a mysterious death, which she obviously hadn't foretold herself.)

Year after year, Christmas after Christmas, I was sorely tempted to tell Mama I saw her kill Santa Claus. Year after year, Christmas after Christmas, I was aching to know where she had hidden the weapon.

And then I found out. It was Christmas Day fourteen years ago.

The doctors, after numerous tests, had assured me that Mom was showing signs of Alzheimer's. Such as when applying lipstick, she ended up covering her chin with rouge. And wearing three dresses at the same time. And filing her shoes and accessories in the deep freeze. It was sad, really, even for a murderess who deserved no mercy. Yet she insisted on cooking the Christmas dinner herself that year.

"It's going to be just like that Christmas Day when we had that wonderful dinner with the neighborhood kiddies," she said. "And Professor Tester dressed up as Santa Claus and brought in that big bag of games and toys. And he gave me the wonderful gift of the exclusive rights to the formula for the Desiree Rejuvenating Lotion."

There were twenty for dinner and, believe it or not, Mother cooked it impeccably. The servants were a bit nervous, but the guests were too drunk to notice. Then, while eating the turkey, Mother asked me across the table, "Does the turkey taste the same way it did way back when, Sonny?"

And then I remembered how the turkey had tasted that day forty years ago when Mama had said something about turkey sometimes tasting gamey. I looked at her and, ill or not, there was mockery in her eyes. It was then that I said to her, not knowing if she would understand what I meant: "Mama, I saw what you did."

There was a small smile on her face. Slowly her head began to bob up and down. "I had a feeling you did," she said. "But you haven't answered me. Does the turkey taste the same way it did then?"

I spoke the truth. "No, Mama, it doesn't. It's very good."

She was laughing like a madwoman. Everyone at the table looked embarrassed and there was nowhere for me to hide. "Is this a private joke between you and your mother?" the man at my right asked me. But I couldn't answer. Because my mother had reached across the table and shoved her hand into the turkey's cavity, obscenely pulling out gobs of stuffing and flinging it at me.

"Don't you know why the turkey tasted strange? Can't you guess why, Sonny? Can't you guess what I hid in the stuffing so those damn fool cops wouldn't find it? Can't you guess, Sonny? Can't you?"

Peter Lovesey

SUPPER WITH MISS SHIVERS

The door was stuck. Something inside was stopping it from opening, and Fran was numb with cold. School had broken up for Christmas that afternoon—"Lord dismiss us with Thy blessing"—and the jubilant kids had given her a blinding headache. She'd wobbled on her bike through the London traffic, two carriers filled with books suspended from the handlebars. She'd endured exhaust fumes and maniac motorists, and now she couldn't get into her own flat. She cursed, let the bike rest against her hip, and attacked the door with both hands.

"It was quite scary, actually," she told Jim when he got in later. "I mean, the door opened perfectly well when we left this morning. We could have been burgled. Or it could have been a body lying in the hall."

Jim, who worked as a systems analyst, didn't have the kind of imagination that expected bodies behind doors. "So what was it—the doormat?"

"Get knotted. It was a great bundle of Christmas cards wedged under the door. Look at them. I blame you for this, James Palmer."

"Me?"

Now that she was over the headache and warm again, she enjoyed poking gentle fun at Jim. "Putting our address book on your computer and running the envelopes through the printer. This is the result. We're going to be up to our eyeballs in cards. I don't know how many you sent, but we've heard from the plumber, the dentist, the television repairman, and the people who moved us in, apart from family and friends. You must have gone straight through the address book. I won't even ask how many stamps you used."

"What an idiot," Jim admitted. "I forgot to use the sorting function."

"I left some for you to open."

"I bet you've opened all the ones with checks inside," said Jim. "I'd rather eat first."

"I'm slightly mystified by one," said Fran. "Do you remember sending to someone called Miss Shivers?"

170

"No. I'll check if you like. Curious name."

"It means nothing to me, but she's invited us to a meal."

Fran handed him the card—one of those desolate, old-fashioned snow scenes of someone dragging home a log. Inside, under the printed greetings, was the signature *E. Shivers (Miss)* followed by *Please make my Christmas— come for supper seven next Sunday, 23rd.* In the corner was an address label.

"Never heard of her," said Jim. "Must be a mistake."

"Maybe she sends her cards by computer," said Fran, and added, before he waded in, "I don't think it's a mistake, Jim. She named us on the envelope. I'd like to go."

"For crying out loud—Didmarsh is miles away. Berkshire or somewhere. We're far too busy."

"Thanks to your computer, we've got time in hand," Fran told him with a smile.

The moment she'd seen the invitation, she'd known she would accept. Three or four times in her life she'd felt a similar impulse and each time she had been right. She didn't think of herself as psychic or telepathic, but sometimes she felt guided by some force that couldn't be explained scientifically. A good force, she was certain. It had convinced her that she should marry no one else but Jim, and after three years together she had no doubts. Their love was unshakable. And because he loved her, he would take her to supper with Miss Shivers. He wouldn't understand *why* she was so keen to go, but he would see that she was in earnest, and that would be enough . . .

"By the way, I checked the computer," he told her in front of the destinations board on Paddington Station next Sunday. "We definitely didn't send a card to anyone called Shivers."

"Makes it all the more exciting, doesn't it?" Fran said, squeezing his arm.

Jim was the first man she had trusted. Trust was her top requirement of the opposite sex. It didn't matter that he wasn't particularly tall and that his nose came to a point. He was loyal. And didn't Clint Eastwood have a pointed nose?

She'd learned from her mother's three disastrous marriages to be ultra-wary of men. The first—Fran's father, Harry—had started the rot. He'd died in a train crash just a few days before Fran was born. You'd think he couldn't be blamed for that, but he could. Fran's mother had been admitted to hospital with complications in the eighth month, and Harry, the rat, had found someone else within a week. On the night of the crash he'd been in London with his mistress, buying her expensive clothes. He'd even lied to his pregnant wife, stuck in hospital, about working overtime.

For years Fran's mother had fended off the questions any child asks about a father she has never seen, telling Fran to forget him and love her stepfather instead. Stepfather the First had turned into a violent alcoholic. The divorce had taken nine years to achieve. Stepfather the Second—a Finn called Bengt (Fran called him Bent)—had treated their Wimbledon terraced house as if it were a sauna, insisting on communal baths and parading naked around the place. When Fran was reaching puberty, there were terrible rows because she wanted privacy. Her mother had sided with Bengt until one terrible night when he'd crept into Fran's bedroom and groped her. Bengt walked out of their lives the next day, but, incredibly to Fran, a lot of the blame seemed to be heaped on her, and her relationship with her mother had been damaged forever. At forty-three, her mother, deeply depressed, had taken a fatal overdose.

The hurts and horrors of those years had not disappeared, but marriage to Jim had provided a fresh start. Fran nestled against him in the carriage and he fingered a strand of her dark hair. It was supposed to be an Intercity train, but B.R. were using old rolling-stock for some of the Christmas period and Fran and Jim had this compartment to themselves.

"Did you let this Shivers woman know we're coming?"

She nodded. "I phoned. She's over the moon that I answered. She's going to meet us at the station."

"What's it all about, then?"

"She didn't say, and I didn't ask."

"You didn't? Why not, for God's sake?"

"It's a mystery trip—a Christmas mystery. I'd rather keep it that way."

"Sometimes, Fran, you leave me speechless."

"Kiss me instead, then."

A whistle blew somewhere and the line of taxis beside the platform appeared to be moving forward. Fran saw no more of the illusion because Jim had put his lips to hers.

Somewhere beyond Westbourne Park Station, they noticed how foggy the late afternoon had become. After days of mild, damp weather, a proper December chill had set in. The heating in the carriage was working only in fits and starts and Fran was beginning to wish she'd worn trousers instead of opting decorously for her corduroy skirt and boots.

"Do you think it's warmer farther up the train?"

"Want me to look?"

Jim slid aside the door. Before starting along the corridor, he joked, "If I'm not back in half an hour, send for Miss Marple."

"No need," said Fran. "I'll find you in the bar and mine's a hot cuppa."

She pressed herself into the warm space Jim had left in the corner and rubbed a spy-hole in the condensation. There wasn't anything to spy. She shivered and wondered if she'd been right to trust her hunch and come on this trip. It was more than a hunch, she told herself. It was intuition.

It wasn't long before she heard the door pulled back. She expected to see Jim, or perhaps the man who checked the tickets. Instead, there was a fellow about her own age, twenty-five, with a pink carrier bag containing something about the size of a box file. "Do you mind?" he asked. "The heating's given up altogether next door."

Fran gave a shrug. "I've got my doubts about the whole carriage."

He took the corner seat by the door and placed the bag beside him. Fran took stock of him rapidly, hoping Jim would soon return. She didn't feel threatened, but she wasn't used to these old-fashioned compartments. She rarely used the trains these days except the tube occasionally.

She decided the young man must have kitted himself in an Oxfam shop. He had a dark-blue car coat, black trousers with flares, and crepe-soled ankle boots. Around his neck was one of those striped scarves that college students wore in the sixties, one end slung over his left shoulder. And his thick, dark hair matched the image. Fran guessed he was unemployed. She wondered if he was going to ask her for money.

But he said, "Been up to town for the day?"

"I live there." She added quickly, "With my husband. He'll be back presently."

"I'm married, too," he said, and there was a chink of amusement in his eyes that Fran found reassuring. "I'm up from the country, smelling the wellies and cowdung. Don't care much for London. It's crazy in Bond Street this time of year."

"Bond Street?" repeated Fran. She hadn't got him down as a big spender.

"This once," he explained. "It's special, this Christmas. We're expecting our first, my wife and I."

"Congratulations."

He smiled. A self-conscious smile. "My wife, Pearlie—that's my name for her—Pearlie made all her own maternity clothes, but she's really looking forward to being slim again. She calls herself the frump with a lump. After the baby arrives, I want her to have something glamorous, really special. She deserves it. I've been putting money aside for months. Do you want to see what I got? I found it in Elaine Ducharme."

"I don't know it."

"It's a very posh shop. I found the advert in some fashion magazine." He had already taken the box from the carrier and was unwrapping the pink ribbon.

"You'd better not. It's gift-wrapped."

"Tell me what you think," he insisted, as he raised the lid, parted the tissue, and lifted out the gift for his wife. It was a nightdress, the sort of night-dress, Fran privately reflected, that men misguidedly buy for the women they adore. Pale-blue, in fine silk, styled in the empire line, gathered at the bodice, with masses of lace interwoven with yellow ribbons. Gorgeous to look at and hopelessly impractical to wash and use again. Not even comfortable to sleep in. His wife, she guessed, would wear it once and pack it away with her wedding veil and her love letters.

"It's exquisite."

"I'm glad I showed it to you." He started to replace it clumsily in the box.

"Let me," said Fran, leaning across to take it from him. The silk was irresistible. "I know she'll love it."

"It's not so much the gift," he said as if he sensed her thoughts. "It's what lies behind it. Pearlie would tell you I'm useless at romantic speeches. You should have seen me blushing in that shop. Frilly knickers on every side. The girls there had a right game with me, holding these nighties against themselves and asking what I thought."

Fran felt privileged. She doubted if Pearlie would ever be told of the gauntlet her young husband had run to acquire the nightdress. She warmed to him. He was fun in a way that Jim couldn't be. Not that she felt disloyal to Jim, but this guy was devoted to his Pearlie, and that made him easy to relax with. She talked to him some more, telling him about the teaching and some of the sweet things the kids had said at the end of the term.

"They value you," he said. "They should."

She reddened and said, "It's about time my husband came back." Switching the conversation away from herself, she told the story of the mysterious invitation from Miss Shivers.

"You're doing the right thing," he said. "Believe me, you are."

Suddenly uneasy for no reason she could name, Fran said, "I'd better look for my husband. He said I'd find him in the bar."

"Take care, then."

As she progressed along the corridor, rocked by the speeding train, she debated with herself whether to tell Jim about the young man. It would be difficult without risking upsetting him. Still, there was no cause really.

The next carriage was of the standard Intercity type. Teetering toward her along the center aisle was Jim, bearing two beakers of tea, fortunately capped with lids. He'd queued for ten minutes, he said. And he'd found two spare seats.

They claimed the places and sipped the tea. Fran decided to tell Jim what had happened. "While you were getting these," she began—and then stopped, for the carriage was plunged into darkness.

Often on a long train journey, there are unexplained breaks in the power supply. Normally, Fran wouldn't have been troubled. This time, she had a horrible sense of disaster, a vision of the carriage rearing up, thrusting her sideways. The sides seemed to buckle, shattered glass rained on her, and people were shrieking. Choking fumes. Searing pain in her legs. Dimly, she discerned a pair of legs to her right, dressed in dark trousers. Boots with crepe soles. And blood. A pool of blood.

"You've spilt tea all over your skirt!" Jim said.

The lights came on again, and the carriage was just as it had been. People were reading the evening paper as if nothing at all had occurred. But Fran had crushed the beaker in her hand—no wonder her legs had smarted.

The thickness of the corduroy skirt had prevented her from being badly scalded. She mopped it with a tissue. "I don't know what's wrong with me— I had a nightmare, except that I wasn't asleep. Where are we?"

"We went through Reading twenty minutes ago. I'd say we're almost there. Are you going to be okay?"

Over the public-address system came the announcement that the next station stop would be Didmarsh Halt.

So far as they could tell in the thick mist, they were the only people to leave the train at Didmarsh.

Miss Shivers was in the booking hall, a gaunt-faced, tense woman of about fifty, with cropped silver hair and red-framed glasses. Her hand was cold, but she shook Fran's firmly and lingered before letting it go.

She drove them in an old Maxi Estate to a cottage set back from the road not more than five minutes from the station. Christmas-tree lights were visible through the leaded window. The smell of roast turkey wafted from the door when she opened it. Jim handed across the bottle of wine he had thoughtfully brought.

"We're wondering how you heard of us."

"Yes, I'm sure you are," the woman answered, addressing herself more to Fran than Jim. "My name is Edith. I was your mother's best friend for ten years, but we fell out over a misunderstanding. You see, Fran, I loved your father."

Fran stiffened and turned to Jim. "I don't think we should stay."

"Please," said the woman, and she sounded close to desperation, "we did nothing wrong. I have something on my conscience, but it isn't adultery, whatever you were led to believe."

They consented to stay and eat the meal. Conversation was strained, but the food was superb. And when at last they sat in front of the fire sipping coffee, Edith Shivers explained why she had invited them. "As I said, I loved your father Harry. A crush, we called it in those days when it wasn't mutual. He was kind to me, took me out, kissed me sometimes, but that was all. He really loved your mother. Adored her."

"You've got to be kidding," said Fran grimly.

"No, your mother was mistaken. Tragically mistaken. I know what she believed, and nothing I could say or do would shake her. I tried writing, phoning, calling personally. She shut me out of her life completely."

"That much I can accept," said Fran. "She never mentioned you to me."

"Did she never talk about the train crash—the night your father was killed, just down the line from here?"

"Just once. After that it was a closed book. He betrayed her dreadfully. She was pregnant, expecting me. It was traumatic. She hardly ever mentioned my father after that. She didn't even keep a photograph."

Miss Shivers put out her hand and pressed it over Fran's. "My dear, for both their sakes I want you to know the truth. Thirty-seven people died in that crash, twenty-five years ago this very evening. Your mother was shocked to learn that he was on the train, because he'd said nothing whatsoever to her about it. He'd told her he was working late. She read about the crash without supposing for a moment that Harry was one of the dead. When she was given the news, just a day or two before you were born, the grief was worse because he'd lied to her. Then she learned that I'd been a passenger on the same train, as indeed I had, and escaped unhurt. Fran, that was chance—pure chance. I happened to work in the City. My name was published in the press, and your mother saw it and came to a totally wrong conclusion."

"That my father and you—"

"Yes. And that wasn't all. Some days after the accident, Harry's personal effects were returned to her, and in the pocket of his jacket they found a receipt from a Bond Street shop for a nightdress."

"Elaine Ducharme," said Fran in a flat voice.

"You *know?*"

"Yes."

"The shop was very famous. They went out of business in 1969. You see—"

"He'd bought it for her," said Fran, "as a surprise."

Edith Shivers withdrew her hand from Fran's and put it to her mouth. "Then you know about me?"

"No."

Their hostess drew herself up in her chair. "I must tell you. Quite by chance on that night twenty-five years ago, I saw him getting on the train. I still loved him and he was alone, so I walked along the corridor and joined him. He was carrying a bag containing the nightdress. In the course of the journey he showed it to me, not realizing that it wounded me to see how much he loved her still. He told me how he'd gone into the shop—"

"Yes," said Fran expressionlessly. "And after Reading, the train crashed."

"He was killed instantly. The side of the carriage crushed him. But I was flung clear—bruised, cut in the forehead, but really unhurt. I could see that Harry was dead. Amazingly, the box with the nightdress wasn't damaged." Miss Shivers stared into the fire. "I coveted it. I told myself if I left it, someone would pick it up and steal it. Instead, I did. *I* stole it. And it's been on my conscience ever since."

Fran had listened in a trancelike way, thinking all the time about her meeting in the train.

Miss Shivers was saying, "If you hate me for what I did, I understand. You see, your mother assumed that Harry bought the nightdress for me. Whatever I said to the contrary, she wouldn't have believed me."

"Probably not," said Fran. "What happened to it?"

Miss Shivers got up and crossed the room to a sideboard, opened a drawer, and withdrew a box—the box Fran had handled only an hour or two previously. "I never wore it. It was never meant for me. I want you to have it, Fran. He would have wished that."

Fran's hands trembled as she opened the box and laid aside the tissue. She stroked the silk. She thought of what had happened, how she hadn't for a moment suspected that she had seen a ghost. She refused to think of him as that. She rejoiced in the miracle that she had met her own father, who had died before she was born—met him in the prime of his young life, when he was her own age.

Still holding the box, she got up and kissed Edith Shivers on the forehead. "My parents are at peace now, I'm sure of it. This is a wonderful Christmas present," she said.

Jacqueline Vivelo

APPALACHIAN BLACKMAIL

$\mathbf{M}$y great-aunt Molly Hardison was a wealthy woman. By the standards of the coal mining town that was home to my family, she was fabulously rich. We didn't have any particular claim on her; she had nearer relatives. Still, she never forgot us children—and there were eight of us—at Christmastime. Once in every two or three years, she would come and spend the holiday with us.

Mama said Christmas with us was more like Aunt Molly's own childhood holidays than Christmas at her grand house or with her sons and their snooty wives.

We were poor all the time, and some years we were poorer than others. Nevertheless, at Christmas our house would be filled with evergreen boughs, pine cones, and red ribbons. Mama would keep hot cider simmering on the back of the woodstove so the house always smelled of cinnamon and cloves. No matter how bad things were Papa could take his hunting dog, first Ol' Elsie and then later her son Ol' Ben, and bring in game. He brought home quail by the dozens, deer, wild turkeys.

Sometimes he'd be the only person we knew who had found a turkey, but he'd always get ours for the holiday. I think he was smart in the ways of turkeys. I was his tomboy and counted myself in on his discussions about hunting with my brothers. Papa would follow a goodsized turkey gobbler for weeks, learning its ways and finding its roosts. Turkeys like to move around, which is why they fool so many hunters, and they almost always have more than one roost.

I listened to all my father could tell us about hunting and would have gone with him when he began to take Joe and Cliff, but Mama put her foot down. I had to content myself with taking care of the hunting dog.

"Maybe someday, Betsy," Papa consoled me. "You'd make a fine hunter."

In any case, our house looked and smelled good at Christmas. It was filled with all the food a resourceful country family could provide. In our neck of the woods that was better than most city families, poor or rich, could do.

So, fairly regularly Aunt Molly would come and spend Christmas in our bustling, over-crowded house. Whether she was there or not, she always sent presents. Her sister, our own grandmother, was dead, which made her something of a stand-in. But we children understood that presents for Christmas and our birthdays would be all we could expect from Aunt Molly, except, of course, for my sister Molly.

I don't think any scheming was involved on my mother's part. I think she just liked the name Molly. She named her first daughter for her mother and her second daughter for her aunt. It didn't hurt that both Mollys happened to be green-eyed redheads. Our Molly was the only redhead among the eight of us and the only one with green eyes. We understood, all of us from oldest to youngest, that our Molly was special to Aunt Molly.

Aunt Molly made it clear that something more than seasonal presents would come Molly's way. I was five the Christmas that Aunt Molly first brought her ruby and diamond necklace with her. Molly was twelve that year when our great-aunt put that magnificent necklace on her for the first time.

"It isn't yours yet, but it will be. I'm not having it go to either of my daughters-in-law. It'll be yours."

We were all in awe of those old stones that glowed with fire. Even the boys took a look, rolled their eyes, and murmured, "Wowee."

"When?" my sister Amanda, oldest of all and most practical, asked.

Aunt Molly fairly cackled.

"When? Well, you see, she'll get to keep it when she marries. Marriage," Great-aunt Molly said, "is the only choice open to a girl. It's the only way to live."

From then on, every Christmas that Aunt Molly spent with us included another look at the necklace and another review of what Molly had to do to get it.

When my sister Amanda was nineteen, she married Dr. Harvey Brittaman, a young G.P. who had just taken up practice in our area. Great-aunt Molly gave them a full set of fine dishes, a hundred and two pieces.

Everybody agreed that none of the rest of us girls was likely to do any better than Amanda had. After all, a doctor!

Sister Molly was seventeen that year. I always thought she was the best-looking of all of us, though later on my little sister Cindy turned out to be a beauty, too. Molly had creamy fair skin without freckles and deep dark red hair. She was slim and tall and wore her hair long. She liked nothing in the world better than reading and carried a book with her everywhere. She would sit on a damp hillside and read until someone, usually me, went and told her to come home.

She had lots of admirers in high school, but two were the frontrunners. Malcolm Bodey was a football player, and Jerry Rattagan edited the school newspaper. Malcolm was planning to go into the mines like the rest of his family. Jerry was going on to the state university.

"You wait for the older men," Aunt Molly told sister Molly when she came for Amanda's wedding. "These boys are fine, but someone better will come along."

That wedding started me thinking. I was ten at the time. I thought about losing Amanda. I thought about marrying in general. I thought about me. I tried to picture me marrying one of the boys I knew, and it was an awful thought. I decided to try again to persuade Mama to let Papa teach me to hunt. I figured what I'd really like was to be a woodsman and live alone in a cabin in the woods. In our house I never had any time or any place alone.

Then I thought about Molly, Molly and the ruby and diamond necklace. For the first time I saw that the necklace hadn't been anything but trouble. For one thing, it had turned my sister Amanda bitter. Here she was, the oldest and the first married, but she wasn't getting the necklace. Aunt Molly had given her Royal Doulton china worth a king's ransom, but it didn't take away the sting. Amanda bore the brunt of the sense of rejection, but I suddenly saw that it was there for all of us, boys as well as girls.

A year later Molly graduated from high school and went to work at Lacy's drugstore. She didn't talk to any of us about what she wanted, but it was easy to see she was unhappy. Malcolm was determined to marry her, and it seemed to me she was weakening.

I felt like there was something about Molly I was missing, so out on the hillside one day I just asked her outright, "How do you really feel about that necklace Aunt Molly's going to give you when you get married?"

Well, she told me. I guess nobody had ever asked her that question before. She spilled out her feelings, her hopes, her wishes—everything in one long outburst. "Didn't you know?" she asked. "Didn't you guess? You're the one who's always watching everybody. I thought you didn't miss a thing—not that I expected anybody else to guess. But I thought you would."

I felt pretty stupid. Once she told me, it seemed obvious.

That next Christmas was one that Aunt Molly spent with us. She showed up two days before Christmas, in time to put her presents under the tree and to help with some of the cooking. Her coming brought back all the things I'd been thinking about when Amanda was married. When you're eleven-going-on-twelve, you're plagued by weighty thoughts.

My brother Cliff was my confidant in the family, but he'd picked that moment to have a chest cold or flu of some sort. He had been moved into the little room at the head of the stairs that was used as a sickroom whenever Mama suspected one of us had something contagious. We were only supposed to pass notes to each other, sending them in on the food trays.

I stood my serious thoughts all on my own for as long as I could, then went and knocked on the sickroom door.

"Who is it?" If a toad had a voice, it might sound all croupy like Cliff's that day.

"It's Betsy. I'm coming in."

I went to the far end of the bed and sat by Cliff's feet. He didn't say you shouldn't be here. He just said, "I can't talk so good."

"Well, you can listen." And I told him all the things I had thought about marriage, about the necklace, and about Molly. While I was talking, some things that had never entered my mind before seemed clear. Cliff croaked that since he wasn't the marrying type and I wasn't either, maybe we could both be hunters.

I felt a lot better after that. I wasn't weird after all. I slipped out of his room before Mama showed up with his lunch.

After supper that night we all gathered in the parlor. Cliff, his chest wrapped with flannel cloths that smelled of camphor, was bundled into a chair by the fireplace, Ol' Ben asleep at his feet. Even Amanda was with us. Her husband Harvey was there, too, but the two youngest children didn't know that because Harvey was dressed as Santa Claus and carried a big bag of toys.

He distributed presents, and we all opened them. There would be more in the morning under the tree, but we liked to spread Christmas out as far as we could.

Christmas Eve was always the time Aunt Molly asked Molly to wear the ruby and diamond necklace, "for a while, so I can see it on you, child." Aunt Molly laid it out on the table, and we all saw that it was still as impressive as ever. It seemed to catch the lights of the Christmas tree and the glow of the candles, not only reflecting but matching with light of its own.

Just as Aunt Molly said, "Come here, my dear, and let me put this on you," Cliff had a fit of coughing. Everyone's attention turned from the necklace to Cliff.

Aunt Molly laid the necklace down and stood up to look over the back of Cliff's chair. One younger child climbed on each arm of the chair, Cindy on one side and Tommy on the other. Harvey, who was a doctor first and Santa second, tossed his sack to one side and clumped across the room in oversized shoes. Someone tramped on Ol' Ben's tail in an effort to get to Cliff, and I led the dog, drugged by food and the warmth of the fire, toward the door.

"He's all right. Move back, everyone," Papa said. "Don't open that door," he added to me. "I don't want a draft through here until I get another blanket."

I slapped Ol' Ben on the bottom and sent him off to his box in the kitchen.

The little ones scrambled back to their presents. Aunt Molly, with a hand pressed to her bosom, turned back to the table. Mama picked up a bottle of cough medicine and then almost dropped it as Aunt Molly screamed.

"Who picked up the necklace? Molly, do you have it already?"

Looks of bewilderment met her questions. "Don't go out!" she commanded Santa Claus, who was trying to slip out the door with his empty sack to change back into his identity as Dr. Brittaman. "Don't anyone move out of this room until I find the necklace."

"You can't suspect Santa Claus!" my brother James shouted, which was a cue for a good bit of silly chatter that had a bad effect on Aunt Molly's temper. She was much more thorough and more demanding in her search than she might have been otherwise.

Mama and Papa kept trying to make light of it. Of course the necklace was there. It had to be. None of us would take it. Aunt Molly said she would have granted that an hour earlier but the fact was someone *had*.

Our Santa Claus suggested we quarter the room and search it inch by inch with Aunt Molly supervising each stage of the search until the necklace turned up. That search was classic, something to pass into legend within our family. First, there were twelve people in the room, counting Aunt Molly herself, and someone insisted she should not be exempt from being searched. Santa and his sack were checked. Even Cliff agreed to be searched, his chair, his blankets, his clothes, his flannel wraps, every inch of the space around him.

Every branch of the tree was examined, every present inspected for signs of tampering. Two of them had to be opened and then repackaged because young hands had been scrabbling at them. But neither one contained the necklace. Chairs were overturned. The hanging light fixture was checked. It became a game to suggest new possibilities.

Maybe because he had been caught trying to get out the door, Harvey went to extremes to see that he and his props were cleared of suspicion. He also made sure every suggestion, no matter how unreasonable, was followed up. The windows were tested, even though everyone knew no one had opened a door or window. An icy wind was blowing, and it was snowing outside. Opening up just long enough to toss something out would have let in a blast the rest would have noticed, not to mention that the necklace would have been lost in the snow.

Aunt Molly had never seemed the least bit pitiful to anyone before that night. Now she looked like a broken woman. Her face was blotchy, and her shoulders sagged. I felt truly sorry for her. Like everyone else that night, I wanted to find her necklace and restore it to her, but it just wasn't possible.

Mama put her arm around her and told her she'd walk her up to her room. At the door, Aunt Molly turned and, looking at Molly, said, "I'm sorry, dear."

"We'll find it," Mama told Aunt Molly. "We'll still find it."

Papa, Amanda, and Dr. Brittaman were all shaking their heads behind Mama and Aunt Molly's backs. I knew what they were thinking. That necklace had just plain vanished, and it didn't seem likely it could ever be found. If it wasn't in that room, well, it just wasn't anywhere.

Papa carried Cliff back to his bed. The rest of us also began to get ready to sleep. Somehow no one knew quite what to say to Molly.

We shuffled through nighttime rituals in uneasy silence. This was no way to go to bed on Christmas Eve. Aunt Molly was hurt, and to all appearances, we had a thief in our family. A dull misery settled around my heart.

You wouldn't think a holiday could recover from a disaster like that, but the next day was one of the best Christmases of our lives. Strangely enough, it was all due to Aunt Molly, too. Several times during breakfast I saw her fingering a small piece of folded paper. She opened her presents with the rest of us and sounded sincerely grateful for her box of handkerchiefs, bottle of toilet water, book of poetry, and the handmade gifts from the younger children. If she was grieving, she was doing it bravely. It seemed to me she just looked thoughtful.

In the middle of the afternoon when the younger children were playing and Amanda and Harvey had gone home, Aunt Molly said she had something to say. She gathered Mama and Papa and Molly around the table. I hung around to hear what was going on.

"I've been doing some thinking since last night," she told them. "No, don't interrupt," she cautioned as my mother began to speak. "I think I wanted to arrange for my namesake to have my life all over again, a thing that's not possible, not even reasonable." She stopped and sighed.

"It's all right about the necklace. I mean, it isn't all right that you lost it," Molly told her, "but it's all right that it isn't coming to me."

Aunt Molly ignored her and continued, "I'd like to see this young woman go on with her studies. Toward that end, I want to pay her way to college." At a sign of protest from my father, Aunt Molly said dryly, "Believe me, four years' tuition will be less than the value of that necklace. You will not, of course, get the necklace," she added to Molly.

"Thank you," said Molly, her eyes wet and shining.

Molly walked on air for the rest of the day. Aunt Molly beamed. My parents kept exchanging smiles. The rest of us were infected by their joy, so it felt like Christmas morning all day and half the night.

I worked it out the other day that Aunt Molly on that Christmas was about the age I am now. I, of course, am not old at all, though she seemed old to me then. She just recently died, having lived into her nineties. Her large estate was divided among her children and grandchildren, but her will made provision for a sealed manila envelope to be delivered to me.

When I opened the envelope, I found a correctly folded letter on thick creamy stationery together with a yellowed slip of paper folded into a square. I opened the slip of paper first and read the message:

> You can have you mizerable necklace back if you promise Molly don't
> haf to git married. She don't want a husban. She wants to go to collige.

I wouldn't have believed the spelling could have been that bad. I unfolded the accompanying letter and read:

> Dear Betsy,
> I don't know how many years will pass before you get this back, but I want to return your note to you.
> For days I was baffled by the disappearing stunt you pulled. No one had left the room, yet the necklace wasn't in the room, I told myself. Continuing to puzzle over the problem, I repeated that paradox endlessly. Finally I varied it a bit and said, "Not one creature went out of the room." I stopped as I reached that point because I realized a "creature" had left—that smelly old hound. Then I knew my ruby and diamond necklace must have gone out of the room with the dog. He was wearing it there in his box by the kitchen stove all the time we were searching, wasn't he? Of course, I also remembered that you were the one who sent the dog out of the room while Cliff kept the rest of us distracted. What a determined child you must have been to hold out against all that adult energy!
> You always were a clever child, Betsy.

Aunt Molly'd gone home that year with her necklace. Late on Christmas afternoon, it showed up without explanation on her bed. She made sure everyone saw it one last time, then after that holiday never mentioned it again.

When the new semester began a few weeks after Christmas, my sister Molly started college.

Margery Allingham

ON CHRISTMAS DAY IN
THE MORNING

Sir Leo Persuivant, the Chief Constable, had been sitting in his comfortable study after a magnificent lunch and talking shyly of the sadness of Christmas while his guest, Mr. Albert Campion, most favored of his large house party, had been laughing at him gently.

It was true, the younger man had admitted, his pale eyes sleepy behind his horn-rimmed spectacles, that, however good the organization, the festival was never quite the same after one was middle-aged, but then only dear old Leo would expect it to be, and meanwhile, what a truly remarkable bird that had been!

But at that point the Superintendent had arrived with his grim little story and everything had seemed quite spoiled.

At the moment their visitor sat in a highbacked chair, against a paneled wall festooned with holly and tinsel, his round black eyes hard and preoccupied under his short gray hair. Superintendent Bussy was one of those lean and urgent countrymen who never quite lose their fondness for a genuine wonder. Despite years of experience and disillusion, the thing that simply can't have happened and yet indubitably *has* happened, retains a place in their cosmos. He was holding forth about one now. It had already ruined his Christmas and had kept a great many other people out in the sleet all day; but nothing would induce him to leave it alone even for five minutes. The turkey sandwiches, which Sir Leo had insisted on ordering for him, were disappearing without him noticing them and the glass of scotch and soda stood untasted.

"You can see I had to come at once," he was saying for the third time. "I had to. I don't see what happened and that's a fact. It's a sort of miracle. Besides," he eyed them angrily, "fancy killing a poor old *postman* on Christmas morning! That's inhuman, isn't it? Unnatural."

Sir Leo nodded his white head. "Horrible," he agreed. "Now, let me get this clear. The man appears to have been run down at the Benham-Ashby crossroads . . ."

Bussy took a handful of cigarettes from the box at his side and arranged them in a cross on the table.

"Look," he said. "Here is the Ashby road with a slight bend in it, and here, running at right angles slap through the curve, is the Benham road. As you know as well as I do, Sir Leo, they're both good wide main thoroughfares, as roads go in these parts. This morning the Benham postman, old Fred Noakes, a bachelor thank God and a good chap, came along the Benham Road loaded down with Christmas mail."

"On a bicycle?" asked Campion.

"Naturally. On a bicycle. He called at the last farm before the crossroads and left just about 10 o'clock. We know that because he had a cup of tea there. Then his way led him over the crossing and on towards Benham proper."

He paused and looked up from his cigarettes.

"There was very little traffic early today, terrible weather all the time, and quite a bit of activity later; so we've got no skid marks to help us. Well, to resume: no one seems to have seen old Noakes, poor chap, until close on half an hour later. Then the Benham constable, who lives some 300 yards from the crossing and on the Benham road, came out of his house and walked down to his gate to see if the mail had come. He saw the postman at once, lying in the middle of the road across his machine. He was dead then."

"You suggest he'd been trying to carry on, do you?" put in Sir Leo.

"Yes. He was walking, pushing the bike, and had dropped in his tracks. There was a depressed fracture in the side of his skull where something—say, a car mirror—had struck him. I've got the doctor's report. I'll show you that later. Meanwhile there's something else."

Bussy's finger turned to his other line of cigarettes.

"Also, just about 10, there were a couple of fellows walking here on the *Ashby* road, just before the bend. They report that they were almost run down by a wildly driven car which came up behind them. It missed them and careered off out of their sight round the bend towards the crossing. But a few minutes later, half a mile farther on, on the other side of the crossroads, a police car met and succeeded in stopping the same car. There was a row and the driver, getting the wind up suddenly, started up again, skidded and smashed the car into the nearest telephone pole. The car turned out to be stolen and there were four half-full bottles of gin in the back. The two occupants were both fighting drunk and are now detained."

Mr. Campion took off his spectacles and blinked at the speaker.

"You suggest that there was a connection, do you? —that the postman and the gin drinkers met at the crossroads? Any signs on the car?"

Bussy shrugged his shoulders. "Our chaps are at work on that now," he said. "The second smash has complicated things a bit, but last time I 'phoned they were hopeful."

"But my dear fellow!" Sir Leo was puzzled. "If you can get expert evidence of a collision between the car and the postman, your worries are over. That is, of course, if the medical evidence permits the theory that the unfortunate fellow picked himself up and struggled the 300 yards towards the constable's house."

Bussy hesitated.

"There's the trouble," he admitted. "If that were all we'd be sitting pretty, but it's not and I'll tell you why. In that 300 yards of Benham Road, between the crossing and the spot where old Fred died, there is a stile which leads to a footpath. Down the footpath, the best part of a quarter of a mile over very rough going, there is one small cottage, and at that cottage letters were delivered this morning. The doctor says Noakes might have staggered the 300 yards up the road leaning on his bike, but he puts his foot down and says the other journey, over the stile and so on, would have been absolutely impossible. I've talked to the doctor. He's the best man in the world on the job and we won't shake him on that."

"All of which would argue," observed Mr. Campion brightly, "that the postman was hit by a car *after* he came back from the cottage—between the stile and the constable's house."

"That's what the constable thought." Bussy's black eyes were snapping. "As soon as he'd telephoned for help he slipped down to the cottage to see if Noakes had actually called there. When he found he had, he searched the road. He was mystified though because both he and his missus had been at their window for an hour watching for the mail and they hadn't seen a vehicle of any sort go by either way. If a car did hit the postman where he fell, it must have turned and gone back afterwards."

Leo frowned at him. "What about the other witnesses? Did they see any second car?"

"No." Bussy was getting to the heart of the matter and his face shone with honest wonder. "I made sure of that. Everybody sticks to it that there was no other car or cart about and a good job too, they say, considering the way the smashed-up car was being driven. As I see it, it's a proper mystery, a kind of not very nice miracle, and those two beauties are going to get away with murder on the strength of it. Whatever our fellows find on the car they'll never get past the doctor's testimony."

Mr. Campion got up sadly. The sleet was beating on the windows, and from inside the house came the more cheerful sound of tea cups. He nodded to Sir Leo.

"I fear we shall have to see that footpath before it gets too dark. In this weather, conditions may have changed by tomorrow."

Sir Leo sighed. " 'On Christmas day in the morning!' " he quoted bitterly. "Perhaps you're right."

They stopped their dreary journey at the Benham police station to pick up the constable. He proved to be a pleasant youngster with a face like one of the angel choir and boots like a fairy tale, but he had liked the postman and was anxious to serve as their guide.

They inspected the crossroads and the bend and the spot where the car had come to grief. By the time they reached the stile, the world was gray and freezing, and all trace of Christmas had vanished, leaving only the hopeless winter it had been invented to refute.

Mr. Campion negotiated the stile and Sir Leo followed him with some difficulty. It was an awkward climb, and the path below was narrow and slippery. It wound out into the mist before them, apparently without end.

The procession slid and scrambled on in silence for what seemed a mile, only to encounter a second stile and a plank bridge over a stream, followed by a brief area of what appeared to be simple bog. As he struggled out of it, Bussy pushed back his dripping hat and gazed at the constable.

"You're not having a game with us, I suppose?" he inquired.

"No, sir." The boy was all blush. "The little house is just here. You can't make it out because it's a bit low. There it is, sir. There."

He pointed to a hump in the near distance which they had all taken to be a haystack. Gradually it emerged as the roof of a hovel which squatted with its back towards them in the wet waste.

"Good Heavens!" Sir Leo regarded its desolation with dismay. "Does anybody really live there?"

"Oh, yes, sir. An old widow lady. Mrs. Fyson's the name."

"Alone?" He was aghast. "How old?"

"I don't rightly know, sir. Quite old. Over 75, must be."

Sir Leo stopped in his tracks and a silence fell on the company. The scene was so forlorn, so unutterably quiet in its loneliness, that the world might have died.

It was Campion who broke the spell.

"Definitely no walk for a dying man," he said firmly. "Doctor's evidence completely convincing, don't you think? Now that we're here, perhaps we should drop in and see the householder."

Sir Leo shivered. "We can't *all* get in," he objected. "Perhaps the Superintendent . . ."

"No. You and I will go." Campion was obstinate. "Is that all right with you, Super?"

Bussy waved them on. "If you have to dig for us we shall be just about here," he said cheerfully. "I'm over my ankles now. What a place! Does anybody ever come here *except* the postman, Constable?"

Campion took Sir Leo's arm and led him firmly round to the front of the cottage. There was a yellow light in the single window on the ground floor and, as they slid up a narrow brick path to the very small door, Sir Leo hung back. His repugnance was as apparent as the cold.

"I hate this," he muttered. "Go on. Knock if you must."

Mr. Campion obeyed, stooping so that his head might miss the lintel. There was a movement inside, and at once the door was opened wide, so that he was startled by the rush of warmth from within.

A little old woman stood before him, peering up without astonishment. He was principally aware of bright eyes.

"Oh, dear," she said unexpectedly, and her voice was friendly. "You *are* damp. Come in." And then, looking past him at the skulking Sir Leo, "Two of you! Well, isn't that nice. Mind your poor heads."

The visit became a social occasion before they were well in the room. Her complete lack of surprise, coupled with the extreme lowness of the ceiling, gave her an advantage from which the interview never entirely recovered.

From the first she did her best to put them at ease.

"You'll have to sit down at once," she said, laughing as she waved them to two little chairs, one on either side of the small black stove. "Most people have to. I'm all right, you see, because I'm not tall. This is my chair here. You must undo that," she went on, touching Sir Leo's coat. "Otherwise you may take cold when you go out. It is so very chilly, isn't it? But so seasonable and that's always nice."

Afterwards it was Mr. Campion's belief that neither he nor Sir Leo had a word to say for themselves for the first five minutes. They were certainly seated and looking round the one downstairs room which the house contained before anything approaching a conversation took place.

It was not a sordid room, yet the walls were unpapered, the furniture old without being in any way antique, and the place could hardly have been called neat. But at the moment it was festive. There was holly over the two pictures and on the mantle above the stove, and a crowd of bright Christmas cards.

Their hostess sat between them, near the table. It was set for a small tea party and the oil lamp with the red and white frosted glass shade, which stood in the center of it, shed a comfortable light on her serene face.

She was a short, plump old person whose white hair was brushed tightly to her little round head. Her clothes were all knitted and of an assortment of colors, and with them she wore, most unsuitably, a maltese-silk lace collarette and a heavy gold chain. It was only when they noticed she was blushing that they realized she was shy.

"Oh," she exclaimed at last, making a move which put their dumbness to shame. "I quite forgot to say it before. A Merry Christmas to you! Isn't it wonderful how it keeps coming round? Very quickly, I'm afraid, but it is so nice when it does. It's such a *happy* time, isn't it?"

Sir Leo pulled himself together with an effort which was practically visible.

"I must apologize," he began. "This is an imposition on such a day. I . . ." But she smiled and silenced him again.

"Not at all," she said. "Oh, not at all. Visitors are a great treat. Not everybody braves my footpath in the winter."

"But some people do, of course?" ventured Mr. Campion.

"Of course." She shot him her shy smile. "Certainly every week. They send down from the village every week and only this morning a young man, the policeman to be exact, came all the way over the fields to wish me the compliments of the season and to know if I'd got my post!"

"And you had!" Sir Leo glanced at the array of Christmas cards with relief. He was a kindly, sentimental, family man, with a horror of loneliness.

She nodded at the brave collection with deep affection.

"It's lovely to see them all up there again, it's one of the real joys of Christmas, isn't it? Messages from people you love and who love you and all so *pretty*, too."

"Did you come down bright and early to meet the postman?" Sir Leo's question was disarmingly innocent, but she looked ashamed and dropped her eyes.

"I wasn't up! Wasn't it dreadful? I was late this morning. In fact, I was only just picking the letters off the mat there when the policeman called. He helped me gather them, the nice boy. There were such a lot. I lay lazily in bed this morning thinking of them instead of moving."

"Still, you heard them come." Sir Leo was very satisfied. "And you knew they were there."

"Oh, yes." She sounded content. "I knew they were there. May I offer you a cup of tea? I'm waiting for my party . . . just a woman and her dear little boy; they won't be long. In fact, when I heard your knock I thought they were here already."

Sir Leo excused them, but not with any undue haste. He appeared to be enjoying himself. Meanwhile, Mr. Campion, who had risen to inspect the display on the mantle shelf more closely, helped her to move the kettle so that it should not boil too soon.

The Christmas cards were splendid. There were nearly 30 of them in all, and the envelopes which had contained them were packed in a neat bundle and tucked behind the clock, to add even more color to the whole.

In design, they were mostly conventional. There were wreaths and firesides, saints and angels, with a secondary line of gardens in unseasonable bloom and Scotch terriers in tam-o'shanter caps. One magnificent card was entirely in ivorine, with a cutout disclosing a coach and horses surrounded by roses and for-get-me-nots. The written messages were all warm and personal, all breathing affection and friendliness and the out-spoken joy of the season:

The very best to you, Darling, from all at The Limes.

To dear Auntie from Little Phil.

Love and Memories. Edith and Ted.

There is no wish like the old wish. Warm regards, George.

For dearest Mother.

Cheerio. Lots of love. Just off. Writing. Take care of yourself. Sonny.

For dear little Agnes with love from us all.

Mr. Campion stood before them for a long time but at length he turned away. He had to stoop to avoid the beam and yet he towered over the old woman who stood looking up at him.

Something had happened. It had suddenly become very still in the house. The gentle hissing of the kettle sounded unnaturally loud. The recollection of its lonely remoteness returned to chill the cosy room.

The old lady had lost her smile and there was wariness in her eyes.

"Tell me." Campion spoke very gently. "What do you do? Do you put them all down there on the mat in their envelopes before you go to bed on Christmas Eve?"

While the point of his question and the enormity of it was dawning upon Sir Leo, there was silence. It was breathless and unbearable until old Mrs. Fyson pierced it with a laugh of genuine naughtiness.

"Well," she said, "it does make it more fun!" She glanced back at Sir Leo whose handsome face was growing steadily more and more scarlet.

"Then . . . ?" He was having difficulty with his voice. "Then the postman did *not* call this morning, ma'am?"

She stood looking at him placidly, the flicker of the smile still playing round her mouth.

"The postman never calls here except when he brings something from the Government," she said pleasantly. "Everybody gets letters from the Government nowadays, don't they? But he doesn't call here with *personal* letters because, you see, I'm the last of us." She paused and frowned very faintly. It rippled like a shadow over the smoothness of her quiet, careless brow. "There's been so many wars," she said sadly.

"But, dear lady . . ." Sir Leo was completely overcome. There were tears in his eyes and his voice failed him.

She patted his arm to comfort him.

"My dear man," she said kindly. "Don't be distressed. It's not sad. It's Christmas. We all loved Christmas. They sent me their love at Christmas and you see *I've still got it*. At Christmas I remember them and they remember me . . .

wherever they are." Her eyes strayed to the ivorine card with the coach on it. "I do sometimes wonder about poor George," she remarked seriously. "He was my husband's elder brother and he really did have quite a shocking life. But he once sent me that remarkable card and I kept it with the others. After all, we ought to be charitable, oughtn't we? At Christmas time . . ."

As the four men plodded back through the fields, Bussy was jubilant.

"That's done the trick," he said. "Cleared up the mystery and made it all plain sailing. We'll get those two crooks for doing in poor old Noakes. A real bit of luck that Mr. Campion was here," he added generously, as he squelched on through the mud. "The old girl was just cheering herself up and you fell for it, eh, Constable? Oh, don't worry, my boy. There's no harm done, and it's a thing that might have deceived anybody. Just let it be a lesson to you. I know how it happened. You didn't want to worry the old thing with the tale of a death on Christmas morning, so you took the sight of the Christmas cards as evidence and didn't go into it. As it turned out, you were wrong. That's life."

He thrust the young man on ahead of him and came over to Mr. Campion.

"What beats me is how you cottoned to it," he confided. "What gave you the idea?"

"I merely read it, I'm afraid." Mr. Campion sounded apologetic. "All the envelopes were there, sticking out from behind the clock. The top one had a ha'penny stamp on it, so I looked at the postmark. It was 1914."

Bussy laughed "Given to you," he chuckled. "Still, I bet you had a job to believe your eyes."

"Ah." Mr. Campion's voice was thoughtful in the dusk. "That, Super, that was the really difficult bit."

Sir Leo, who had been striding in silence, was the last to climb up onto the road. He glanced anxiously towards the village for a moment or so, and presently touched Campion on the shoulder.

"Look there." A woman was hurrying towards them and at her side, earnest and expectant, trotted a small, plump child. They scurried past and as they paused by the stile, and the woman lifted the boy onto the footpath, Sir Leo expelled a long sighing breath.

"So there was a party," he said simply. "Thank God for that. Do you know, Campion, all the way back here I've been wonderin'."

Rex Stout

SANTA CLAUS BEAT

"Christmas Eve," Art Hipple was thinking to himself, "would be a good time for the murder."

The thought was both timely and characteristic. It was 3 o'clock in the afternoon of December 24, and though the murder would have got an eager welcome from Art Hipple any day at all, his disdainful attitude toward the prolonged hurly-burly of Christmas sentiment and shopping made that the best possible date for it. He did not actually turn up his nose at Christmas, for that would have been un-American; but as a New York cop not yet out of his twenties who had recently been made a precinct dick and had hung his uniform in the back of the closet of his furnished room, it had to be made clear, especially to himself, that he was good and tough. A cynical slant on Christmas was therefore imperative.

His hope of running across a murder had begun back in the days when his assignment had been tagging illegally parked cars, and was merely practical and professional. His biggest ambition was promotion to Homicide, and the shortest cut would have been discovery of a corpse, followed by swift, brilliant, solo detection and capture of the culprit. It had not gone so far as becoming an obsession; as he strode down the sidewalk this December afternoon he was not sniffing for the scent of blood at each dingy entrance he passed; but when he reached the number he had been given and turned to enter, his hand darted inside his jacket to touch his gun.

None of the three people he found in the cluttered and smelly little room one flight up seemed to need shooting. Art identified himself and wrote down their names. The man at the battered old desk, who was twice Art's age and badly needed a shave, was Emil Duross, proprietor of the business conducted in that room—Duross Specialties, a mail-order concern dealing in gimcrack jewelry. The younger man, small, dark and neat, seated on a chair squeezed in between the desk and shelves stacked with cardboard boxes, was II. E. Koenig, adjuster, according to a card he had proffered, for the Apex Insurance

193

Company. The girl, who had pale watery eyes and a stringy neck, stood backed up to a pile of cartons the height of her shoulder. She had on a dark brown felt hat and a lighter brown woolen coat that had lost a button. Her name was Helen Lauro, and it could have been not rheum in her eyes but the remains of tears.

Because Art Hipple was thorough it took him twenty minutes to get the story to his own satisfaction. Then he returned his notebook to his pocket, looked at Duross, at Koenig, and last at the girl. He wanted to tell her to wipe her eyes, but what if she didn't have a handkerchief?

He spoke to Duross. "Stop me if I'm wrong," he said. "You bought the ring a week ago to give to your wife for Christmas and paid sixty-two dollars for it. You put it there in a desk drawer after showing it to Miss Lauro. Why did you show it to Miss Lauro?"

Duross turned his palms up. "Just a natural thing. She works for me, she's a woman, and it's a beautiful ring."

"Okay. Today you work with her—filling orders, addressing packages, and putting postage on. You send her to the post office with a bag of the packages. Why didn't she take all of them?"

"She did."

"Then what are those?" Art pointed to a pile of little boxes, addressed and stamped, on the end of a table.

"Orders that came in the afternoon mail. I did them while she was gone to the post office."

Art nodded. "And also while she was gone you looked in the drawer to get the ring to take home for Christmas, and it wasn't there. You know it was there this morning because Miss Lauro asked if she could look at it again, and you showed it to her and let her put it on her finger, and then you put it back in the drawer. But this afternoon it was gone, and you couldn't have taken it yourself because you haven't left this room. Miss Lauro went out and got sandwiches for your lunch. So you decided she took the ring, and you phoned the insurance company, and Mr. Koenig came and advised you to call the police, and—"

"Only his stock is insured," Koenig put in. "The ring was not a stock item and is not covered."

"Just a legality," Duross declared scornfully. "Insurance companies can't hide behind legalities. It hurts their reputation."

Koenig smiled politely but noncommittally.

Art turned to the girl. "Why don't you sit down?" he asked her. "There's a chair we men are not using."

"I will never sit down in this room again," she declared in a thin tight voice.

"Okay." Art scowled at her. She was certainly not comely. "If you did take the ring you might—"

"I didn't!"

"Very well. But if you did you might as well tell me where it is because you won't ever dare to wear it or sell it."

"Of course I wouldn't. I knew I wouldn't. That's why I didn't take it."

"Oh? You thought of taking it?"

"Of course I did. It was a beautiful ring." She stopped to swallow. "Maybe my life isn't much, but what it is, I'd give it for a ring like that, and a girl like me, I could live a hundred years and never have one. Of course I thought of taking it—but I knew I couldn't ever wear it."

"You see?" Duross appealed to the law. "She's foxy, that girl. She's slick."

Art downed an impulse to cut it short, get out, return to the station house, and write a report. Nobody here deserved anything, not even justice— especially not justice. Writing a brief report was all it rated, and all, ninety-nine times out of a hundred, it would have got. But instead of breaking it off, Art sat and thought it over through a long silence, with the three pairs of eyes on him. Finally he spoke to Duross:

"Get me the orders that came in the afternoon mail."

Duross was startled. "Why?"

"I want to check them with that pile of boxes you addressed and stamped."

Duross shook his head. "I don't need a cop to check my orders and ship- ments. Is this a gag?"

"No. Get me the orders."

"I will not!"

"Then I'll have to open all the boxes." Art arose and headed for the table. Duross bounced up and got in front of him and they were chest to chest.

"You don't touch those boxes," Duross told him. "You got no search war- rant. You don't touch anything!"

"That's just another legality." Art backed off a foot to avoid contact. "And since I guessed right, what's a little legality? I'm going to open the boxes here and now, but I'll count ten first to give you a chance to pick it out and hand it to me and save both of us a lot of bother. One, two, three—"

"I'll phone the station house!"

"Go ahead. Four, five, six, seven, eight, nine . . ."

Art stopped at nine because Duross had moved to the table and was fin- gering the boxes. As he drew away with one in his hand Art demanded, "Gimme." Duross hesitated but passed the box over, and after a glance at the address Art ripped the tape off, opened the flap of the box, took out a wad of tissue paper, and then a ring box. From that he removed a ring, yellow gold, with a large greenish stone. Helen Lauro made a noise in her throat. Koenig let out a grunt, evidently meant for applause. Duross made a grab, not for the ring but for the box on which he had put an address, and missed.

"It stuck out as plain as your nose," Art told him, "but of course my going for the boxes was just a good guess. Did you pay sixty-two bucks for this?"

Duross's lips parted, but no words came. Apparently he had none. He nodded, not vigorously.

Art turned to the girl. "Look, Miss Lauro. You say you're through here. You ought to have something to remember it by. You could make some trouble for Mr. Duross for the dirty trick he tried to play on you, and if you lay off I expect he'd like to show his appreciation by giving you this ring. Wouldn't you, Mr. Duross?"

Duross managed to get it out. "Sure I would."

"Shall I give it to her for you?"

"Sure." Duross's jaw worked. "Go ahead."

Art held out the ring and the girl took it, but not looking at it because she was gazing incredulously at him. It was a gaze so intense as to disconcert him, and he covered up by turning to Duross and proffering the box with an address on it.

"Here," he said, "you can have this. Next time you cook up a plan for getting credit with your wife for buying her a ring, and collecting from the insurance company for its cost, and sending the ring to a girl friend—all in one neat little operation—don't do it. And don't forget you gave Miss Lauro that ring before witnesses."

Duross gulped and nodded.

Koenig spoke. "Your name is not Hipple, officer, it's Santa Claus. You have given her the ring she would have given her life for, you have given him an out on a charge of attempted fraud, and you have given me a crossoff on a claim. That's the ticket! That's the old yuletide spirit! Merry Christmas!"

"Nuts," Art said contemptuously, and turned and marched from the room, down the stairs, and out to the sidewalk. As he headed in the direction of the station house he decided that he would tone it down a little in his report. Getting a name for being tough was okay, but not too damn tough. That insurance guy sure was dumb, calling him Santa Claus—him, Art Ripple, feeling as he did about Christmas.

Which reminded him, Christmas Eve would be a swell time for the murder.

Dan Stumpf

WHITE LIKE THE SNOW

Lieutenant Mayhew brought one of the rookies upstairs to the detective bureau last week, I guess to show where he could go in a few years if he kept his pants clean. I did my bit to make an impression by hiding the magazine I was reading under a report I closed out six weeks ago. Not for Nicky-New-Guy, you understand, but more for Mayhew's benefit. Anyway, the kid got to looking at some of the old photos we hang around the place and damn if he didn't spot an old one of Sergeant Sughrue, smiling at the camera like a clean shotgun, and ask who it was.

"Someone before my time." Mayhew's one of the chief's five-year wonders. He looked at the picture closer, then half turned to me. "How 'bout it, Jake? You know this guy?"

Yeah, I knew him; time was when half the folks in town lived in mortal fear of Sergeant "Sugar" Sughrue and the rest of us just worried about him a lot. But nobody remembers him much these days, and the picture'd hung there so long I quit seeing it myself. So I said, "That's just some guy I killed once." The kid hesitated, laughed; Mayhew laughed, then pushed him down the hall and I got back to my magazine.

Not that I actually *did* kill Sughrue; that was just hype. Hell, I been here almost twenty years and never even shot anybody very much. But I was there when Sughrue died, and I maybe had something to do with it, so I guess what I told the kid wasn't too far off the mark at that.

It was Christmas morning, maybe ten years ago, maybe not that long. And it was snowing to beat hell; over a foot since midnight and no end in sight. I was supposed to take care of business in the detective bureau, but there wasn't much, this being Christmas in the suburbs, so I brought in a portable TV to pass the time. I was lugging it into the station and I passed Dibbs on the way out—he has the cubicle next to mine—and we wished each other "Merry Christmas" kind of automatically.

At least it was automatic for me; Dibbs took it serious, though, and stopped to look sorry for me. "Damn, Jake," he said, "nothing worse than working Christmas, is there?"

Well, there's lots of things worse than working Christmas at a suburban police department: young love and getting your foot stuck in a cannon are the two I know most about, but there's bound to be more. Actually, with not much work to do and all the food folks bring in, it's not bad at all. But I looked mournful for Dibbs's sake and went in to goof off for eight hours.

It should have been that simple. I wish it had been, sometimes. I mean, Sughrue was a pain all right, but what I went through was sure a tall price to get rid of him. And on Christmas, too.

I should tell you about Sergeant "Sugar" Sughrue. Lots of folks used to wonder what made him act so mean all the time, but I think he just figured if you got a God-given talent for something, you oughta use it, and he sure as hell had the touch for making folks around him unhappy. If not plain scared. See, Sughrue was big and fast and strong, and he could shoot good. Him and me, we were on the range one time and he put five shots in a playing card fifty feet away while I was still pulling my piece out of the holster and looking for the target. That's how good he was.

He was smart, too, and he liked to show it off. No one I ever saw at the station ever won an argument with Sughrue. Even if they were right. Sughrue'd just talk and argue and beat on them with words till they gave up. You win arguments that way, but you never convince anybody.

Being dangerous and capable like he was, it's no wonder Sughrue made sergeant fast. And it's no wonder he didn't go any farther. Once he got into a spot where he could give orders and chew folks out on a regular basis, the brass could see how much he liked it, which was way too much. And about that time, talk started about him and the crowd at Smokey's, and that was pretty much as far as his careeer ever went.

So that's all you need to know about Sughrue, except he shouldn't even have been in that day; sergeants get holidays off unless we call them in for something, and Sughrue being like he was, the building could burn down, no one would call him. But I hadn't been there more than an hour and in he comes, looking like hell's own hangover. He didn't even stop to rag me; just shuffled into his office and shut the door.

Well, it was good I didn't have to talk to him, but bad, too, because any minute he might come back out, so I couldn't get too laid back. No idea how long he'd be in there or even what he was doing here on Christmas. If Sughrue came out and saw me having fun, or not looking busy enough, or even just not looking miserable, he'd make sure I got that way in a hurry.

I sighed, turned off my TV, and went to the dispatch room to find a magazine I could hide under a report; old tricks are still the best.

It was quiet in there, too. Sometimes phones ring and guys yammer on the radio all the time, but this being Christmas, no one was doing much. Ed Rosemont turned from the radio console when I came in; his big swivel chair groaning under him made the only noise in the room. I gave him a look and jerked my thumb at Sughrue's office. "The hell's he doing here?"

"I will be damned if I know." Rosey's got one of those big, rich, pear-shaped voices, and a body to match—the kind I been working on all my life but never could get just right. Always struck me funny, hearing him swear in that important-sounding voice. "He said he had paperwork to catch up. What do you think?"

"Whoever he's sleeping with sobered up and kicked him out, is my theory," I said. Sughrue always had a reputation for acting nasty, but he never had any trouble getting women. Just keeping them. "Where's he hang his pants lately, anyway?"

Turned out neither me nor Rosey knew who Sughrue was jumping with since his last divorce. But that didn't keep us from tossing ideas around, and that led to a lively discussion about who else might be sleeping with who else, and what with one thing and another, we went on for nearly half an hour. Which is how I came to be there when we got the call. And saw Rosey's face go from polite to serious to scared as he sat upright and started jotting stuff down on the pad.

"Hold on the line," he said finally, and keyed the mike to alert the guys who were probably damn near asleep in their cars by now. "Eighteen and Twenty-Seven." He pushed each word slow and distinct, even for him. "Code Fifty-two—that's Code Five-two—at Smokey's—that's Smokey's—Seventy-seven Village Street. See Bob Gates, standing by in front."

"Damn," I said. "A stiff at Smokey's." It looked like I was going to have to go out in all that weather and act busy; *double damn*. But I didn't know the worst of it yet.

"Wuzzit?" I asked. "Some wino fall asleep in the door?" Smokey's is in a part of town where that happens some, so maybe I wouldn't have to do much besides take pictures.

But my life just ain't that pretty. Rosey looked up at me with no look at all in his eyes and said, "It is Mr. Smollett, Jake. And Bob says he was shot."

That was worth a whistle, and I gave it one. If you believe some folks, Fred "Smokey" Smollett just ran a real busy bar at the edge of town, where we border up on the city. If you believe others, he ran everything out of that bar that would run for money: games, women, drugs, and the occasional bit of stolen property. If you believe still other people, he paid us for the privilege.

Mind you, he never paid me anything. I never got that high up the ladder. Never even got high enough to know for certain he was paying off. But there was lots of talk, and it don't pay not to listen.

"Tell 'em just to hold the scene." If this was what it sounded like, I was going to have to get off my ass and do some detective work. But not much; once the brass learned who it was and what it was, they'd fall all over each other to get to Smokey's. "Call the lieutenant and see if we can get a real photographer out there. See if he'll let us call Dibbs." Dibbs wouldn't much like that after working all night, but he'd been to more evidence schools than me, so he was the man for an important job. And this was one. Talk was, Smollett had his hooks in some pretty major people here in the department, and that would include—

"What's up?" Sergeant Sughrue was leaning on the doorframe, still looking bad hungover but talking casual. Rosey told him and he nodded, still leaning, still talking casual. "Cancel those calls," he said. "Marley and me can take a look and see what has to be done before we go dragging everyone out on Christmas overtime." He turned to me. "Fetch the car, Jake; I'll get the kit." And he slouched off.

Rosey and I traded looks. We both of us knew I was a bad photographer and even worse handling evidence. Any other day of the year, there'd be brass hats enough around the place to make sure a job like this got handled by the best—or carefulest—we had. But this was Merry-dammit-Christmas, the brass was at home, and Sergeant Sughrue had just handed us a direct order. Rosey sure as hell wasn't going to cross him.

And me neither, I guess. I cursed the bones of old Kris Kringle and went out to get the car.

Traffic was light, and a good thing, too, because the streets were godawful. We saw just one snow plow on our way across town, slumping through the snow drifts like a whipped dog. The rest of the way, it was find the road and try to stay on it.

After a while, though, I got into the tracks made by the cruisers already on the scene ahead of us, and I figured this might be my chance. Now that I could drive with one hand, I reached out and got the radio mike.

"I'll just make sure Rosey called the lieutenant—"

That was as far as I got with it before Sughrue's big left hand jerked out and knocked the mike clean from my fingers.

That was a funny moment, right then. I mean, Sughrue had a temper, all right, and he was fast and mean and looked to be hungover bad, but hitting my hand like that was past the edge, even for him. I looked over—real quick because I had to pay attention to the road—and just for a second he was bent over, his face screwed up like he was mad as hell. Then his eyes opened up and locked on mine.

It couldn't have been more than a quarter of a second, that glance, because I had to look right back at the road, but it was long enough for something to pass between us. Something really ugly.

"I'll call him from Smokey's." Sughrue slumped back in the seat, his voice softer than I expected. I thought he was going to say more, and I think he thought so, too, but we were both quiet the rest of the way.

And that thing that passed between us, whatever it was, kept biting my butt.

I wasn't long figuring it out, either. It didn't take a real educated nose to smell the stink around this business pretty quick, and by the time we got to Smokey's, I'd pretty much put it together.

I saw it like this: Smollett, who probably has more dirt on the department in general and Sughrue in particular than was safe for anyone, gets shot dead. And it happens on Christmas, when the senior detectives and the brass hats are all at home with the kiddies. And here's Sughrue, he just comes tripping into work on Christmas morning looking like slime on a shingle and insisting him and me are going to investigate this all by ourselves—him that supposedly Smollett was paying off, and me . . .

Some folks say I became a cop because I'm too lazy to work and not smart enough to steal, but they're only half right. I could see this one coming down Main Street. And I was getting scared, because when Sughrue knocked that mike out of my hand and we looked at each other, I could tell he didn't *want* anyone at that crime scene who'd act like he gave a damn. And maybe in my eyes he saw I'd figured that out. And if he *did* see it, my life wasn't worth dryer lint, because Sughrue was that much faster and stronger and meaner than me that if he got worried about me giving him up, and decided to do something about it, I was damn sure to finish second.

That's what I was thinking when we walked into Smokey's that Christmas day, and it was pretty damn grim, if you ask me. Of course, Sughrue's dead now, and maybe I killed him, and I for sure didn't have it all figured out like I thought I did. But you can understand, maybe, why I was sweating like a crack-head when Sughrue told the uniforms at the scene to secure the area and take a statement from old Bob Gates, who used to sweep up the place, while he and I went into the office where Smollett was laying around dead.

It looked like the office of every bar everywhere. Maybe bigger than some, but with the same battered desk, cheap paneling, and old steel safe you see in all of them. Only here the safe hung open; a dead man sat behind the desk, white like the snow, leaning way back in his chair, with a raunchy cigar still clenched in his teeth; and there was blood all over.

And I mean, There Was Blood All Over; it was on the wall behind

Smollett's body in big splash patterns, it was soaked into the carpet under his chair, it was spritzed across the top of his desk, and it dribbled from his private toilet—a closet-sized deal off to one side—clear to the front of the desk.

"Let's check out the bathroom," Sughrue said, and I followed him quick. It wasn't quite as gross as the rest of the place, but there was plenty of blood on the floor by the sink, and like I said, the trail of drops to the front of the desk.

"This is where it started," Sughrue said when we'd looked around a little. "Smollett got shot here, went to his desk, tried to call for help, then fell back in his chair and bled to death. I'll call the coroner." He took a couple of slow steps back to the office and dialed the dead man's phone.

And if I had any doubts about the smell around this thing, I stopped having them right then. Because we never call the coroner till we're completely through gathering evidence. Last thing we want is those guys coming in with their jumpsuits and body bags, stepping all over everything. But here Sughrue calls them first thing.

I didn't say a word, though. No sense letting on I knew any more than he already thought I did. *Just stay quiet, act dumb, and maybe you'll get out of this better than Smollett did*, I told myself.

So I took pictures, knowing that no better than I am, and in this light, they'd be worthless. I got shots of Smollett in his chair, supposedly showing how he'd sat down, leaned back against the wall where his blood was spattered, and bled to death. I took pictures of the empty safe, thinking whoever shot him also took all the incriminating records *(that's how long ago this was; nowadays there'd be computer disks and backup files and all, but back then, if it wasn't on paper, it wasn't there, period)*, and just as the guys from the coroner's came clomping in, I got pictures of the blood on Smollett's desk and the drips running from his toilet into the office. And like I say, I knew every damn one of them was worthless: The way I handled a camera, no one'd even recognize it was Smollett unless they saw the cigar stuck in his mouth, and the other shots would be too light or too dark, or just not pointed right to show which way the blood was splattered—

So maybe I'm not bright, after all. It took me all the while they were moving Smollett to figure out what that blood was telling me. And to tie it in with how Sughrue was sitting heavy in a spare seat off to one side while the coroner's boys made their haul. But by the time they left, I was almost curious about all this.

"You collect, Marley," Sughrue sighed. "I'll tag. Start in the toilet where it started, and work out to the desk."

The toilet where it started? Well, that was one theory. Of course, it wouldn't explain how so much of Smollett got splattered back against the wall behind his chair, or why there wasn't more of him spilled over the desk he supposedly leaned across. It wouldn't even account for why the blood drops on the carpet were *in front* of the desk, and trailed toward the toilet, not away from it. No, the only story that would explain all that was one where Smollett and whoever killed him got up in each other's face over his desk and one of them pulled a gun but didn't do it quick enough to keep the other one from shooting him. Or shooting him back.

But I had a feeling that wasn't how Sughrue wanted things to look, and they damn well weren't going to look like that when we left. Well, I sure as hell wasn't going to stick my foot in his story just now. I got down on my knees—not much fun for a guy of my build—and started scraping half-dried blood from the floor onto little sterile pieces of paper that went into little sterile envelopes for Sughrue to put labels on.

Sughrue didn't get up. Just sat there with his pen out and wrote down what part of the room each envelope came from before putting it carefully in the kit.

That's another thing shows how long ago this was: Nowadays you can get DNA identification from a blood smear and know whose it was and what he ate last Thursday. But back then, all you could get was blood type. So if Sughrue was fiddling with the envelopes like I thought he was, all the blood that got to the lab would be from behind the desk. The envelopes might say this sample or that sample was from the toilet or the front of the desk, but . . .

Then I thought of one other thing, and it almost got me killed right there. Which shows where thinking will get you. I was picking up blood from behind the desk, and when I got up I sort of routinely opened and closed the desk drawers. There was the usual clutter of coin wrappers, old receipts, and business cards, but "No gun," I said, and then kicked myself for saying it, because Sughrue turned to me real fast—fast like when he'd knocked the mike out of my fingers—and I couldn't see where his right hand was, which scared me so that I tried to cover.

"I mean" —I said it slow and dumb-like— "I was thinking there'd be one. Guess not, though; I never heard of him to pack." Fact is, you could look in a million back-room offices in bars like this and find a gun in every one of them. It's like bar owners think they're supposed to have one, or maybe they come with the liquor license or something. And considering Smollett's reputation, it was damn funny there *wasn't* one here. Maybe it was with the records gone from the safe. But I could see I wasn't going to get much older by saying that in front of Sughrue, so I just stood there looking stupid till he finally untensed and moved his hand out where I could see it empty.

"That's enough," he said. What with pictures and samples and the coroner's boys, we'd been there maybe two hours. "Let's get this to the station and ready for the lab." He got to his feet, slow, wincing a little.

So here I was with a guy who I thought had done the murder we were investigating, a guy who was also maybe roping me in as his accomplice, and who might just put me out of my misery if he thought I'd figured that out. And all I could think was, *I wonder how he plans to keep anyone else from looking over the scene and reading it right.* And I never did find that out.

Funny how your mind works. I mean, I should've been thinking a lot of other stuff, about Smollett and Sughrue, and if my guesses were right—about both of them—and whether Sughrue thought I was going along with whatever his plans were, and what ideas he might have about my future. But what I remember most was worrying about how he was going to keep everyone else from seeing what I saw in the back room there at Smokey's.

So this next part nobody believes. I must've told it a hundred times in the week after it happened and never got anything but funny looks, but it's true just like I'm going to say: We were walking out the back of Smokey's, to the car. And the snow hadn't let up a bit, but it'd been packed down by the uniforms standing around holding the scene for us. So as I followed Sughrue out the back door, onto the little landing there, I stepped onto that smooth-packed snow and my foot slid out from under me, and I lurched up to keep from falling and bumped into Sughrue, and he went down. Hard. Into the snow.

And he yelped.

Like I say, most folks don't think it happened that way. I could see on their faces when I got to that part, they all figured I pushed Sughrue on purpose. But it ain't so; I was there, I seen it, and it was pure luck, good or bad.

Anyway, Sughrue hit the snow and he yelped and laid there. After a second, I reached down to help him up, but he kind of half swung at me so I pulled back.

He rolled over then and got to his feet, but it wasn't like anything I ever saw before. You know how sometimes you get hurt and feel like you're moving in slow motion? Well, now I saw just that. Sughrue moving in slow motion. It was almost like he floated onto his side, holding his coat shut real tight, then got to his knees, then his feet, and I swear I wouldn't have been surprised if he drifted up into the falling snow and vanished in the gray clouds.

He might as well have.

We looked at each other again. We both knew now that he'd got shot last night, and I knew that the guy who'd done it just went to the morgue. And Sughrue knew I knew, and there wasn't a damn thing he could do about it but walk back to the car with me.

And I mean to tell you, that ride back was weird. We had this thing between us now, and we both knew what it was, and neither one of us said a word all the way back to the station. I wasn't worried about Sughrue anymore, I wasn't even thinking what I should do about this sorry mess. I just kept trying to remember a word I read in a book once about something the Greeks call it, when fear turns to pity.

I never did think of that word. I don't think I had one other clear thought in my head all the time I fought the car through the snow-drifted streets. I parked and followed Sughrue across the parking lot to the station, seeing his steps get stiff and lurchy. And slow. I followed him up the stairs to the second floor even slower, hearing his breath get loud and raspy as he pulled himself up the steps one at a time, and I mean, One. At. A. Time.

I never saw his face again. Not while he was alive, anyway. I stood there at the top of the stairs and watched the back of him ooze down the hall to his office and get the door closed. Then I figured it was safe and I told Rosey to call the lieutenant.

Lieutenant Franklin retired a few years back, then died or something. So no one but me remembers pushing open the door to Sughrue's office and seeing him sprawled back in his chair, white like Smollett was, white like the snow, with his coat hanging open and red blood spread all over his shirt and down on the floor. The same blood that was trailed from the front of Smollett's desk into the bathroom where last night he'd gone to stop the bleeding and thought he had till he went down in the snow and opened up the wound again.

But all that was a long time ago, and nobody remembers Sughrue much anymore, and us who were there reported what we had to and covered up the rest and never talked about it after. In a few years it was like it never happened at all. Like I say, I'd even quit seeing Sughrue's picture on the wall till the new kid made a point of it.

And even though I looked at it again on the way out that night, it didn't mean much to me; just some guy I killed once, that's all.

John Mortimer

RUMPOLE AND THE CHAMBERS PARTY

Christmas comes but once a year. Once a year I receive a gift of socks from She Who Must Be Obeyed; each year I add to her cellar of bottles of lavender water, which she now seems to use mainly for the purpose of "laying down" in the bedroom cupboard (I suspect she has only just started on the 1980 vintage).

Tinseled cards and sprigs of holly appear at the entrance to the cells under the Old Bailey and a constantly repeated tape of "God Rest Ye Merry Gentlemen" adds little zest to my two eggs, bacon, and sausage on a fried slice in the Taste-Ee-Bite, Fleet Street; and once a year the Great Debate takes place at our December meeting. Should we invite solicitors to our Chambers party?

"No doubt at the season of our Savior's birth we should offer hospitality to all sorts and conditions of men," "Soapy" Sam Ballard, q.c., our devout Head of Chambers, opened the proceedings in his usual manner, that of a somewhat backward bishop addressing Synod on the wisdom of offering the rites of baptism to non-practicing, gay Anglican converts of riper years.

"All conditions of men and *women*." Phillida Erskine-Brown, q.c., nee Trant, the Portia of our Chambers, was looking particularly fetching in a well fitting black jacket and an only slightly flippant version of a male collar and tie. As she looked doe-eyed at him, Ballard, who hides a ridiculously susceptible heart beneath his monkish exterior, conceded her point.

"The question before us is, does all sorts and conditions of men, and women, too, of course, include members of the junior branch of the legal profession?"

"I'm against it!" Claude Erskine-Brown had remained an aging junior whilst his wife Phillida fluttered into silk, and he was never in favor of radical change. "The party is very much a family thing for the chaps in Chambers, and the clerk's room, of course. If we ask solicitors, it looks very much as though we're touting for briefs."

"I'm very much in favor of touting for briefs." Up spake the somewhat grey barrister, Hoskins. "Speaking as a man with four daughters to educate. For heaven's sake, let's ask as many solicitors as we know, which, in my case, I'm afraid, is not many."

"Do you have a view, Rumpole?" Ballard felt bound to ask me, just as a formality.

"Well, yes, nothing wrong with a bit of touting, I agree with Hoskins. But I'm in favor of asking the people who really provide us with work."

"You mean solicitors?"

"I mean the criminals of England. Fine conservative fellows who should appeal to you, Ballard. Greatly in favor of free enterprise and against the closed shop. I propose we invite a few of the better-class crooks who have no previous engagements as guests of Her Majesty, and show our gratitude."

A somewhat glazed look came over the assembly at this suggestion and then Mrs. Erskine-Brown broke the silence with: "Claude's really being awfully stuffy and old-fashioned about this. I propose we invite a smattering of solicitors, from the better-class firms."

Our Portia's proposal was carried *nem con*, such was the disarming nature of her sudden smile on everyone, including her husband, who may have had some reason to fear it. Rumpole's suggestion, to nobody's surprise, received no support whatsoever.

Our clerk, Henry, invariably arranged the Chambers party for the night on which his wife put on the Nativity play in the Bexley Heath Comprehensive at which she was a teacher. This gave him more scope for kissing Dianne, our plucky but somewhat hit-and-miss typist, beneath the mistletoe which swung from the dim, religious light in the entrance hall of number three Equity Court.

Paper streamers dangled from the bookcase full of All England Law Reports in Ballard's room and were hooked up to his views of the major English cathedrals. Barristers' wives were invited, and Mrs. Hilda Rumpole, known to me only as She Who Must Be Obeyed, was downing sherry and telling Soapy Sam all about the golden days when her daddy, C. H. Wystan, ran Chambers. There were also six or seven solicitors among those present.

One, however, seemed superior to all the rest, a solicitor of the class we seldom see around Equity Court. He had come in with one hand outstretched to Ballard, saying, "Daintry Naismith, happy Christmas. Awfully kind of you fellows to invite one of the junior branch." Now he stood propped up against the mantelpiece, warming his undoubtedly Savile Row trousers at Ballard's gas fire and receiving the homage of barristers in urgent need of briefs.

He appeared to be in his well preserved fifties, with grey wings of hair above his ears and a clean-shaven, pink, and still single chin poised above what I took to be an old Etonian tie. Whatever he might have on offer, it wouldn't, I was sure, be a charge of nicking a frozen chicken from Safeways. Even his murders, I thought, as he sized us up from over the top of his gold-rimmed half glasses, would take place among the landed gentry.

He accepted a measure of Pommeroy's very ordinary white plonk from Portia and drank it bravely, as though he hadn't been used to sipping Chassagne-Montrachet all his adult life.

"Mrs. Erskine-Brown," he purred at her, "I'm looking for a hard-hitting silk to brief in the Family Division. I suppose you're tremendously booked up."

"The pressure of my work," Phillida said modestly, "is enormous."

"I've got the Geoffrey Twyford divorce coming. Pretty hairy bit of in-fighting over the estate and the custody of young Lord Shiplake. I thought you'd be just right for it."

"Is that the Duke of Twyford?" Claude Erskine-Brown looked suitably awestruck. In spite of his other affectations, Erskine-Brown's snobbery is completely genuine.

"Well, if you have a word with Henry, my clerk"—Mrs. Erskine-Brown gave the solicitor a look of cool availability—"he might find a few spare dates."

"Well, that is good of you. And you, Mr. Erskine-Brown, mainly civil work now, I suppose?"

"Oh, yes. Mainly civil." Erskine-Brown lied cheerfully; he's not above taking on the odd indecent assault when tort gets a little thin on the ground. "I do find crime so sordid."

"Oh, I agree. Look here. I'm stumped for a man to take on our insurance business, but I suppose you'd be far too busy."

"Oh, no. I've got plenty of time." Erskine-Brown lacked his wife's laid-back approach to solicitors. "That is to say, I'm sure I could make time. One gets used to extremely long hours, you know." I thought that the longest hours Erskine-Brown put in were when he sat, in grim earnest, through the *Ring* at Covent Garden, being a man who submits himself to Wagner rather as others enjoy walking from Land's End to John O'Groats.

And then I saw Naismith staring at me and waited for him to announce that the Marquess of Something or Other had stabbed his butler in the library and could I possibly make myself available for the trial. Instead he muttered, "Frightfully good party," and wandered off in the general direction of Soapy Sam Ballard.

"What's the matter with you, Rumpole?" She Who Must Be Obeyed was at my elbow and not sounding best pleased. "Why didn't you push yourself forward?" Erskine-Brown had also moved off by this time to join the throng.

"I don't care for divorce," I told her. "It's too bloodthirsty for me. Now if he'd offered me a nice gentle murder—"

"Go after him, Rumpole," she urged me, "and make yourself known. I'll go and ask Phillida what her plans are for the Harrods sale."

Perhaps it was the mention of the sale which spurred me toward that undoubted source of income, Mr. Daintry Naismith. I found him talking to Ballard in a way which showed, in my view, a gross overestimation of that old darling's forensic powers. "Of course the client would have to understand that the golden tongue of Samuel Ballard, q.c., can't be hired on the cheap," Naismith was saying. I thought that to refer to our Head of Chambers, whose voice in Court could best be compared to a rusty saw, as golden-tongued was a bit of an exaggeration.

"I'll have to think it over." Ballard was flattered but cautious. "One does have certain principles about"—he gulped, rather in the manner of a fish struggling with its conscience—"encouraging the publication of explicitly sexual material."

"Think it over, Mr. Ballard. I'll be in touch with your clerk." And then, as Naismith saw me approach, he said, "Perhaps I'll have a word with him now." So this legal Santa Claus moved away in the general direction of Henry and once more Rumpole was left with nothing in his stocking.

"By the way," I asked Ballard, "did *you* invite that extremely smooth solicitor?"

"No, I think Henry did." Our Head of Chambers spoke as a man whose thoughts are on knottier problems. "Charming chap, though, isn't he?"

Later in the course of the party I found myself next to Henry. "Good work inviting Mr. Daintry Naismith," I said to our clerk. "He seems set on providing briefs for everyone except me."

"I don't really know the gentleman," Henry admitted. "I think he must be a friend of Mr. Ballard's. Of course, we hope to see a lot of him in the future."

Much later, in search of a small cigar, I remembered the box, still in its special Christmas reindeer-patterned wrapping, that I had left in my brief tray. I opened the door of the clerk's room and found the lights off and Henry's desk palely lit by the old gas lamp outside in Equity Court.

There was a dark-suited figure standing beside the desk who seemed to be trying the locked drawers rather in the casual way that suspicious-looking youths test car handles. I switched on the light and found myself staring at our star solicitor guest. And as I looked at him, the years rolled away and I was in Court defending a bent house agent. Beside him in the dock had been an equally curved solicitor's clerk who had joined my client as a guest of Her Majesty.

"Derek Newton," I said, "Inner London Sessions. Raising mortgages on deserted houses that you didn't own. Two years."

"I knew you'd recognize me, Mr. Rumpole. Sooner or later."

"What the hell do you think you are doing?"

"I'm afraid—well, barristers' chambers are about the only place where you can find a bit of petty cash lying about at Christmas." The man seemed resolved to have no secrets from Rumpole.

"You admit it?"

"Things aren't too easy when you're knocking sixty, and the business world's full of wide boys up to all the tricks. You can't get far on one good suit and the Old Etonian tie nowadays. You always defend, don't you, Rumpole? That's what I've heard. Well, I can only appeal to you for leniency."

"But coming to our party," I said, staggered by this most confident of tricksters, "promising briefs to all the learned friends—"

"I always wanted to be admitted as a solicitor." He smiled a little wistfully. "I usually walk through the Temple at Christmastime. Sometimes I drop in to the parties. And I always make a point of offering work. It's a pleasure to see so many grateful faces. This is, after all, Mr. Rumpole, the season of giving."

What could I do? All he had got out of us, after all, was a couple of glasses of Pommeroy's Fleet Street white; that and the five-pound note he "borrowed" from me for his cab fare home. I went back to the party and explained to Ballard that Mr. Daintry Naismith had made a phone call and had to leave on urgent business.

"He's offered me a highly remunerative brief, Rumpole, defending a publisher of dubious books. It's against my principles, but even the greatest sinner has a right to have his case put before the Court."

"And put by your golden tongue, old darling," I flattered him. "If you take my advice, you'll go for it."

It was, after all, the season of goodwill, and I couldn't find it in my heart to spoil Soapy Sam Ballard's Christmas.

Edward D. Hoch

THE SPY AND THE CHRISTMAS CIPHER

It was just a few days before the Christmas recess at the University of Reading when Rand's wife Leila said to him over dinner, "Come and speak to my class on Wednesday, Jeffrey."

"What? Are you serious?" He put down his fork and stared at her. "I know nothing about archaeology."

"You don't have to. I just want you to tell them a Christmas story of some sort. Remember last year? The Canadian writer Robertson Davies was over here on a visit and he told one of his ghost stories."

"I don't know any good ghost stories."

"Then tell them a cipher story from before you retired. Tell them about the time you worked through Christmas Eve trying to crack the St. Ives cipher."

Ivan St. Ives. Rand hadn't thought of him in years.

Yes, he supposed it was a Christmas story of sorts.

It was Christmas Eve morning in 1974, when Rand was still head of Concealed Communications, operating out of the big old building overlooking the Thames. He remembered his superior, Hastings, making the rounds of the offices with an open bottle of sherry and a stack of paper cups, a tradition that no one but Hastings ever looked forward to. A cup of government sherry before noon was not something to warm the heart or put one in the Christmas spirit.

"It promises to be a quiet day," Hastings said, pouring the ritual drink. "You should be able to leave early and finish up your Christmas shopping."

"It's finished. I have no one but Leila to buy for." Rand accepted the cup and took a small sip.

"Sometimes I wish I was as well organized as you, Rand." Hastings seemed almost disappointed as he sat down in the worn leather chair opposite Rand's desk. "I was going to ask you to pick up something for me."

"On the day before Christmas? The stores will be crowded."

Hastings decided to abandon the pretense. "They say Ivan St. Ives is back in town."

"Oh? Surely you weren't planning to send him a Christmas gift?"

St. Ives was a double agent who'd worked for the British, the Russians, and anyone else willing to pay his price. There were too many like him in the modern world of espionage, where national loyalties counted for nothing against the lure of easy money.

"He's back in town and he's not working for us."

"Who, then?" Rand asked. "The Russians?"

"Perkins and Simplex, actually."

"Perkins and Simplex is a department store."

"Exactly. Ivan St. Ives has been employed over the Christmas season as their Father Christmas—red suit, white beard, and all. He holds little children on his knee and asks them what they want for Christmas."

Rand laughed. "Is the spying business in some sort of depression we don't know about? St. Ives could always pick up money from the Irish if nobody else would pay him."

"I just found out about it last evening, almost by accident. I ran into St. Ives's old girlfriend, Daphne Sollis, at the Crown and Piper. There's no love lost between the two of them and she was quite eager to tell me of his hard times."

"It's one of his ruses, Hastings. If Ivan St. Ives is sitting in Perkins and Simplex wearing a red suit and a beard it's part of some much more complex scheme."

"Maybe, maybe not. Anyway, this is his last day on the job. Why don't you drop by and take a look for yourself?"

"Is that what this business about last-minute shopping has been leading up to? What about young Parkinson—isn't this more his sort of errand?"

"Parkinson doesn't know St. Ives. You do."

There was no disputing the logic of that. Rand drank the rest of his sherry and stood up. "Do I have to sit on his lap?"

Hastings sighed. "Just find out what he's up to, Jeff."

The day was unseasonably warm, and as Rand crossed Oxford Street toward the main entrance of Perkins and Simplex he was aware that many in the lunchtime crowd had shed their coats or left them back at the office. The department store itself was a big old building that covered an entire block facing Oxford Street. It dated from Edwardian times, prior to World War I, and was a true relic of its age. Great care had been taken to maintain the exterior just as it had been, though the demands of modern merchandising had taken their toll with the interior. During the previous decade the first two floors had been gutted and transformed into a pseudo-atrium, surrounded by a balcony on which some of the store's regular departments had become little shops. The ceiling was frosted glass, lit from above by fluorescent tubes to give the appearance of daylight.

It was in this main atrium, near the escalators, that Father Christmas had been installed on his throne amidst sparkly white mountains of ersatz snow that was hardly in keeping with the outdoor temperature. The man himself was stout, but not as fat as American Santa Clauses. His white beard and the white-trimmed cowl of his red robe effectively hid his identity. It might have been Ivan St. Ives, but Rand wasn't prepared to swear to it. He had to get much closer if he wanted to be sure.

He watched for a time from the terrace level as a line of parents and tots wound its way up the carpeted ramp to Father Christmas's chair. There he listened carefully to each child's request, sometimes boosting the smallest of them to his knee and patting their heads, handing each one a small brightly wrapped gift box from a pile at his elbow.

After observing this for ten or fifteen minutes, Rand descended to the main floor and found a young mother approaching the end of the line with her little boy. "Pardon me, ma'am," Rand said. "I wonder if I might borrow your son and take him up to see Father Christmas."

She stared at him as if she hadn't heard him correctly. "No, I can take him myself."

Rand showed his identity card. "It's official business."

The woman hesitated, then stood firm. "I'm sorry. Roger would be terrified if I left him."

"Could I come along, then, as your husband?"

She stared at the card again, as if memorizing the name. "I suppose so, if it's official business. No violence or anything, though?"

"I promise."

They stood in line together and Rand took the little boy's hand. Roger stared up at him with his big brown eyes, but his mother was there to give him confidence. "I hate shopping on Christmas Eve," she told Rand. "I always spend too much when I wait until the last minute."

"I think most of us do that." He smiled at the boy. "Are you ready, Roger? We're getting closer to Father Christmas."

In a moment the boy was on the bearded man's knee, having his head patted as he told him what he wanted to find under the tree next day. Then he received his brightly wrapped gift box and they were on their way back down the ramp.

"Thank you," Rand told the woman. "You've been a big help." He went back up to the terrace level and spent the next hour watching Ivan St. Ives, double agent, passing out gifts to a long line of little children.

"It's St. Ives," Rand told Hastings when he returned to the office. "No doubt of it."

"Did he recognize you?"

"I doubt it." He explained how he'd accompanied himself with the woman and child. "If he did, he might have assumed I was with my family."

"So he's just making a little extra Christmas money?"

"I'm afraid it's more than that."

"You spotted something."

"A great deal, but I don't know what it means. I watched him for more than an hour in all. After he listened to each child, he handed them a small gift. I watched one little girl opening hers. It was a clear plastic ball to hang on a Christmas tree, with figures of cartoon characters inside."

"Seems harmless enough."

"I'm sure the store wouldn't be giving out anything that wasn't. The trouble is, while I watched him I noticed a slight deviation from his routine on three different occasions. In these cases, he chose the gift box from a separate pile, and handed it to the parent rather than the child."

"Well, some of the children are quite small, I imagine."

"In those three cases, none of the boxes were opened in the store. They were stowed away in shopping bags by the mother or father. One little boy started crying for his gift, but he didn't get it."

Hastings thought about it.

"Do you think an agent would take a position as a department store Father Christmas to distribute some sort of message to his network?"

"I think we should see one of those boxes, Hastings."

"If there *is* a message, it probably says 'Merry Christmas.' "

"St. Ives has worked for some odd people in the past, including terrorists. When I left the store, there were still seven or eight boxes left on his special pile. If I went back there now with a couple of men—"

"Very well," Hastings said. "But please be discreet, Rand. It's the day before Christmas."

It's not easy to be discreet when seizing a suspected spy in the midst of a crowd of Christmas shoppers. Rand finally decided he wanted one of the free gifts more than he wanted the agents at this point, so he took only Parkinson with him. As they passed through the Oxford Street entrance of Perkins and Simplex, the younger man asked, "Is this case likely to run through the holidays? I was hoping to spend Christmas and Boxing Day with the family."

"I hope there won't even be a case," Rand told him. "Hastings heard Ivan

St. Ives was back in the city, working as Father Christmas for the holidays. I confirmed the fact and that's why we're here."

"To steal a child's gift?"

"Not exactly steal, Parkinson. I have another idea."

They encountered a woman and child about to leave the store with the familiar square box. "Pardon me, but is that a gift from Father Christmas?" Rand asked her.

"Yes, it is."

"Then this is your lucky day. As a special holiday treat, Perkins and Simplex is paying every tenth person ten pounds for their gift." He held up a crisp new bill. "Would you like to exchange yours for a tenner?"

"I sure would!" The woman handed over the opened box and accepted the ten-pound note.

"That was easy," Parkinson commented when the woman and child were gone. "What next?"

"This might be a bit more difficult," Rand admitted. They retreated to a men's room where Rand fastened the festive paper around the gift box once more, resticking the piece of tape that held it together. "There, looks as good as new."

Parkinson got the point. "You're going to substitute this for one of the special ones."

"Exactly. And you're going to help."

They resumed Rand's earlier position on the terrace level, where he observed that the previous stack of boxes had dwindled to three. If he was right, they would be gone shortly, too. "How about that man?" Parkinson pointed out. "The one with the little boy."

"Why him?"

"He doesn't look that fatherly to me. And the boy seems a bit old to believe in Father Christmas."

"You're right," Rand said a moment later. "He's getting one of the special boxes. Come on!"

As the man and the boy came down off the ramp and mingled with the crowd, Rand moved in. The man was clutching the box just as the others had when Rand managed to jostle him. The box didn't come loose, so Rand jostled again with his elbow, this time using his other hand to yank it free. The man, in his twenties with black hair and a vaguely foreign look, muttered something in a language Rand didn't understand. There was a trace of panic in his face as he bent to retrieve the box. Rand pretended to lose his footing then, and came down on top of the man. The crowd of shoppers parted as they tumbled to the floor.

"Terribly sorry," Rand muttered, helping the man to his feet.

At the same moment, Parkinson held out the brightly wrapped package. "I believe you dropped this, sir."

Anyone else might have cursed Rand and made a scene, but this strange man merely grasped the box and hurried away without a word, the small boy trailing along behind. "Good work," Rand said, brushing off his jacket. "Let's get this back to the office."

"Aren't we going to open it?"

"Not here."

Thirty minutes later, Rand was carefully unwrapping the gift on Hastings' desk. Both Parkinson and Hastings were watching apprehensively, as if expecting a snake to spring out like a jack-in-the-box. "My money's on drugs," Parkinson said. "What else could it be?"

"Is the box exactly the same as the others?" Hastings asked.

"Just a bit heavier," Rand decided. "A few ounces."

But inside there seemed to be nothing but the same plastic tree ornament. Rand removed the tissue paper and stared at the bottom of the box.

"Nothing," Parkinson said.

"Wait a minute. Something had to make it heavier." Rand reached in and pried up the bottom piece of cardboard with his fingernails. It was a snugly fitted false bottom. Beneath it was a thin layer of a grey puttylike substance. "Better not touch it," Hastings cautioned.

"That's plastique—plastic explosive."

The man from the bomb squad explained that it was harmless without a detonator of some sort, but they were still relieved when he removed it from the office. "How much damage would that much plastic explosive do?" Rand wanted to know.

"It would make a mess of this room. That's about all."

"What about twelve or fifteen times that much?"

"Molded together into one bomb? It could take out a house or a small building."

They looked at each other glumly. "It's a pretty bizarre method for distributing explosives," Parkinson said.

"It has its advantages," Hastings said. "The bomb is of little use until enough of the explosive is gathered together. If one small box falls into government hands, as this one did, the rest is still safe. No doubt it was delivered to St. Ives only recently, and this served as the perfect method for getting it to his network—certainly better than the mails during the Christmas rush."

"Then you think it's to be reassembled into one bomb?" Rand asked.

"Of course. And it's to be used sometime soon."

"The IRA? Russians? Arabs?"

Hastings shrugged. "Take your pick. St. Ives has worked for all of them."

Rand held the box up to the light, studying the bottom. "This may be some writing, some sort of invisible ink that's beginning to become visible. Get one of the technicians up here to see if we can bring it out."

Heating the bottom of the box to bring out the message proved an easy task, but the letters that appeared were anything but easy to read: MPPMP MBSHG OEXAS-EWHMR AWPGG GBEBH PMBWE ALGHQ.

"A substitution cipher," Parkinson decided at once. "We'll get to work on it."

"Forty letters," Rand observed, "in the usual five-letter groups. There are five Ms, five Ps, and five Gs. Using letter frequencies, one of them could be E, but in such a short message you can't be sure."

"GHQ at the end could stand for General Headquarters," Hastings suggested.

Rand shook his head. "The entire message would be enciphered. Chances are that's just a coincidence."

Parkinson took the message off to the deciphering room and Rand confidently predicted he'd have the answer within an hour.

He didn't.

"It's tougher than it looks," Parkinson told them. "There may not be any Es at all."

"Run it through the computer," Rand suggested. "Use a program that substitutes various frequently used letters for the most frequently used letters in the message. See if you hit on anything."

Hastings glanced at the clock. "It's after six and my niece has invited me for Christmas Eve. Can you manage without me?"

"Of course. Merry Christmas."

After he'd gone, Rand picked up the phone and told Leila he'd be late. She was living in England now, and he'd planned to spend the holiday with her.

"How late?" she asked.

"These things have been known to last all night."

"Oh, Jeffrey. On Christmas Eve?"

"I'll call you later if I can," Rand promised. "It might not take that long."

He went down the hall and stood for a time watching the computer experts work on the message. They seemed to be having no better luck than Parkinson's people. "How long?" he asked one.

"In the worst possible case it could take us until morning to run all the combinations."

Rand nodded. "I'll be back."

They had to know what the message said, but they also had to find Ivan

St. Ives. The employment office at Perkins and Simplex would be closed now. His only chance was that pub where Hastings had spoken with Daphne Sollis. The Crown and Piper.

It was on a corner, as London pubs often are, and the night before Christmas didn't seem to have made much of a dent in the early-evening business. The bar was crowded and all the tables and booths were occupied. Rand let his eyes wander over the faces, seeking out either St. Ives or Daphne, but neither one seemed to be there. He didn't know either of them well, though he thought he would recognize St. Ives out of his Father Christmas garb. He was less certain about recognizing Daphne Sollis.

"Seen Daphne around?" he asked the bartender as he ordered a pint.

"Daphne Jenkins?"

"Daphne Sollis."

"Do I know her?"

"She was in here last night, talking to a grey-haired man wearing rimless glasses. He was probably dressed in a plaid topcoat."

"I don't— Wait a minute, you must mean Rusty. Does she have red hair?"

"Not the last time I knew her, but these things change."

"Well, if it's Rusty she comes in a couple of nights a week, usually alone. Once recently she was with a creepy-looking gent who kept laughing like Father Christmas. I sure wouldn't want *him* bringing gifts to my kids. He'd scare 'em half to death."

"Does she live around here?"

"No idea, mate." He went off to wait on another customer.

So whatever Daphne had told Hastings about her relationship with Ivan St. Ives, they were hardly enemies. He'd been with her recently in the Crown and Piper, apparently since he took on the job as Father Christmas.

Rand thought it unlikely that Daphne would visit the pub two nights in a row, but on the other hand she might stop by if she was lonely on Christmas Eve. He decided to linger over his pint and see if she appeared. Thirty minutes later he was about to give it up and head for Leila's flat when he heard the bartender say, "Hey, Rusty! Fellow here's been askin' after you."

Rand turned and saw Daphne Sollis standing not five feet behind him, unwrapping a scarf to reveal a tousled head of red hair. "Daphne!" She looked puzzled for a moment and he identified himself. "Ivan St. Ives introduced us a year or so back. He did some work for me."

She nodded slowly as it came back to her. "Oh, yes—Mr. Rand. I remember you now. Is this some sort of setup? The other one, Hastings, was here just last night."

"No setup, but I *would* like to talk with you, away from this noise. How about the lobby of the hotel next door?"

"Well—all right."

The hotel lobby was much quieter. They sat beneath a large potted palm and no one disturbed them. "What do you want?" she asked. "What did your friend Hastings want last night?"

"It was only happenstance that he met you, though I'll admit I came to the Crown and Piper looking for you. I need to locate Ivan St. Ives."

"I told Hastings we're on the outs."

"I saw him at Perkins and Simplex earlier today."

"Then you've already located him."

"No," Rand explained. "His Christmas job would have ended today. I need to know where he's living."

"I said we're on the outs."

"You were drinking with him at the Crown and Piper just a week or two ago."

She bit her lip and stared off into space. "I don't know where he's living. He rang me up and we had a drink for old times' sake. That's when he told me about the Christmas job. He talked about getting back together again, but I don't know. He works for a lot of shady people."

"Who's he working for now?"

"Just the store, so far as I know. He said he'd fallen on hard times."

Rand leaned forward. "It could be worth some money if you located him for us, told us who he's palling around with."

She seemed to consider the idea. "I could tell you plenty about who he's palled around with in the past. It wasn't just our side, you know."

"I know."

"But it would have to be after New Year's. I'm going to visit a girlfriend in Hastings, on the coast. Is your friend Hastings from there?"

"From Leeds, actually." Rand was frowning. "I need St. Ives now."

"I'm sorry, I can't help you. Perhaps the store has his address."

"I'll have to ask them." Rand stood up. "Can I buy you a pint back at the pub?"

"I'd better skip it now," she said, glancing at her watch. "I want to get home and change. I'm going to Midnight Mass with some friends."

"If you'll jot down your phone number I'd like to ring you up after New Year's."

"Fine," she agreed.

He'd intended to phone Leila after he left Daphne, but back at the Double-C office, Parkinson was in a state of dejection. "We've run every possible substitution of the letter E and there's still nothing. We're going down the letter-frequency list now, working on T, A, O, and N."

"Forty characters without a single E. Unusual, certainly. "

"Any luck locating St. Ives?"

"Not yet."

Rand worked with them for a time and then dozed on his office couch. It was long after midnight when Parkinson shook him awake. "I think we've got part of it."

"Let me see."

The younger man produced long folds of computer printout. "On this one we concentrated on the first six characters—the repetitive MPPMPM. We got nowhere substituting E, T, or A, but when we tried the next letters on the frequency list, O and N, look what came up."

Rand focused his sleepy eyes and read NOONON. "Noon on?"

"Exactly. And there's another ON combination later in the message."

"Just a simple substitution cipher after all," Rand marveled. "School children make them up all the time."

"And it took us all these hours to get this far."

"St. Ives didn't worry about making the cipher too complex because he was writing it in invisible ink. It was our good luck that the box warmed enough so that some of the message began to appear."

"A terrorist network armed with plastic explosives, and St. Ives is telling them when and where to set off the bomb. Do you think we should phone Hastings?"

Rand glanced at the clock. It was almost dawn on Christmas morning. "Let's wait till we get the rest of it.

He followed Parkinson down the hall to the computer room where the others were at work. Not bothering with the machines, he went straight to the old blackboard at the far end of the room. "Look here, all of you. The group of letters following *noon on* is probably a day of the week, or a date if it's spelled out. If it's a day of the week, three of these letters have to stand for *day.*"

As he worked, he became aware that someone had chalked the most common letter-frequency list down the left side of the board, starting with E, T, A, O, N, and continuing down to Q, X, Z. It was the list from David Kahn's massive 1967 book, *The Codebreakers*, which everyone in the department had on their shelves. He stared at it and noticed that M and P came together about halfway down the list. Together, just like N and O in the regular alphabet. Quickly he chalked the letters A to Z next to the frequency list. "Look here! The key is the standard letter-frequency list. ABCDE is enciphered as ETAON. There are no Ns in the message we found, so there are no Es in the plaintext."

220

The message became clear at once: NOONO NTHIS DAYCH ARING CROSS STATI ONTRA CKSIX. "Noon on this day, Charing Cross Station, Track six," Rand read.

"Noon on which day?" Parkinson questioned. "It was after noon yesterday before he distributed most of the boxes."

"He must mean today. Christmas Day. A Christmas Day explosion at Charing Cross Station."

"I'll phone Hastings," Parkinson decided. "We can catch them in the act."

Police and Scotland Yard detectives converged on the station shortly after dawn. Staying as unobtrusive as possible, they searched the entire area around track six. No bomb was found.

Noon came and went, and no bomb exploded.

Rand turned up at Leila's flat late that afternoon. "Only twenty-four hours late," she commented drily, holding the door open for him.

"And not in a good mood."

"You mean you didn't crack it after all this time?"

"We cracked it, but that didn't do us much good. We don't have the man who sent it, and we may be unable to prevent a terrorist bombing."

"Here in London?"

"Yes, right here in London." He knew a few police were still at Charing Cross Station, but he also knew it was quite easy to smuggle plastic explosives past the tightest security. They could be molded into any shape, and metal detectors were of no use against them.

He tried to put his mind at ease during dinner with Leila, and later when she asked if he'd be spending the night he readily agreed. But he awakened before dawn and walked restlessly to the window, looking out at the glistening streets where rain had started to fall. It would be colder today, more like winter.

The bomb hadn't gone off at Charing Cross Station yesterday. Either the time or the place was wrong.

But it hadn't gone off anywhere else in London, so he could assume the place was correct. It was the time that was off.

The time, or the day.

This day.

Noon on this day.

He went to Leila's telephone and called Parkinson at home. When he heard his sleepy voice answer, he said, "This is Rand. Meet me at the office in an hour."

"It's only six o'clock," Parkinson muttered. "And a holiday."

"I know. I'm sorry. But I'm calling Hastings, too. It's important."

He leaned over the bed to kiss Leila but left without awakening her.

An hour later, with Hastings and Parkinson seated before him in the office, Rand picked up a piece of chalk. "You see, we assumed the wrong meaning for the word 'this.' If someone wants to indicate 'today,' they say it—they don't say 'this day.' On the other hand, if I write the word 'this' on the desk in front of me—" he did so with the piece of chalk "—what am I referring to?"

"The desk," Parkinson replied.

"Right. If I wrote the word on a box, what would I be referring to?"

"The box."

"When St. Ives's message said, 'this day,' he wasn't referring to Christmas Eve or Christmas Day. He was telling them Boxing Day. Even if they were foreign, they'd know it was the day after Christmas here and a national holiday."

"That's today," Hastings said.

"Exactly. We need to get the men back to Charing Cross Station."

The station was almost deserted. The holiday travelers were at their destinations, and it was too soon for anyone to have started home yet. Rand stood near one of the newsstands looking through a paper while the detectives again searched unobtrusively around track six. It was nearly noon and time was running out.

"No luck," Hastings told him. "They can't find a thing."

"Plastique." Rand shook his head. "It could be molded around a girder and painted most any color. We'd better keep everyone clear from now until after noon." It was six minutes to twelve.

"Are you sure about this, Rand? St. Ives is using a dozen or more people. Perhaps they all didn't understand his message."

"They had to come together to assemble the small portions of explosive into a deadly whole. Most of them would understand the message even if a few didn't. I'm sure St. Ives trained them well."

"It's not a busy day. He's not trying to kill a great many people or he'd have waited until a daily rush hour."

"No," Rand agreed. "I think he's content to—" He froze, staring toward the street entrance to the station. A man and a woman had entered and were walking toward track six. The man was Ivan St. Ives and the woman was Daphne Sollis.

Rand had forgotten that the train to Hastings left from Charing Cross Station.

He ran across the station floor, through the beams of sunlight that had suddenly brightened it from the glass-enclosed roof. "St. Ives!" he shouted.

Ivan St. Ives had just bent to give Daphne a good-bye kiss. He turned suddenly at the sound of his name and saw Rand approaching. "What *is* this?" he asked.

"Get away from him, Daphne!" Rand warned.

"He just came to see me off. I told you I was visiting—"

"Get away from him!" Rand repeated more urgently.

St. Ives met his eyes, and glanced quickly away, as if seeking a safe exit. But already the others were moving in. His eyes came back to Rand, recognizing him. "You were at the store, in line for Father Christmas! I knew I'd seen you before!"

"We broke the cipher, St. Ives. We know everything."

St. Ives turned and ran, not toward the street from where the men were coming but through the gate to track six. A police constable blew his whistle, and the sound merged with the chiming of the station clock. St. Ives had gone about fifty feet when the railway car to his left seemed to come apart with a blinding flash and roar of sound that sent waves of dust and debris billowing back toward Rand and the others. Daphne screamed and covered her face.

When the smoke cleared, Ivan St. Ives was gone. It was some time later before they found his remains among the wreckage that had been blown onto the adjoining track. By then, Rand had explained it to Hastings and Parkinson. "Ivan St. Ives was a truly evil man. When he was hired to plan and carry out a terrorist bombing in London over the Christmas holidays, he decided quite literally to kill two birds with one stone. He planned the bombing for the exact time and place where his old girlfriend Daphne Sollis would be. To make certain she didn't arrive too early or too late, he even escorted her to the station himself. She knew too much about his past associations, and he wanted her out of his life for good. I imagine one of his men must have ridden the train into Charing Cross Station and hidden the bomb on board before he left."

But he didn't tell any of this to Daphne. She only knew that they'd come to arrest St. Ives and he'd been killed by a bomb while trying to flee. A tragic coincidence, nothing more. She never knew St. Ives had tried to kill her.

In a way Rand felt it was a Christmas gift to her.

Jeffry Scott

INSPECTOR TIERCE AND THE CHRISTMAS VISITS

Coppers are only human, Jill Tierce told herself, without much conviction, after Superintendent Haggard's invitation to a quiet drink after work. Actually he'd passed outside the open door of her broom-closet office, making Jill start by booming, "Heads up, girlie! Pub call, I'm buying. Back in five . . ." before bustling away, rubbing his hands.

Taking acceptance for granted was very Lance Haggard, and so was the empty, outward show of bonhomie, but there you were.

Unless forced to behave otherwise, Superintendent Haggard generally did no more than nod to Inspector Tierce in passing. This hadn't broken her heart. He had a reputation: it was whispered that he pulled strokes. Nothing criminal, he wasn't bent, but he had a knack of pilfering credit for ideas or successes, coupled with deft evasive action if his own projects went wrong.

Refusing to waste time on Jill Tierce owed less to sexism than to the fact that she was of no present use to him. Leg mangled on duty, she was recovering slowly. Fighting against being invalided out of the Wessex-Coastal Force, lying like a politician about miracles of surgery and physiotherapy, and disguising her limp by willpower, she had won a partial victory. Restricted to light duties on a part-time basis, she was assigned to review dormant cases —and Lance Haggard, skimming along the fast track, wasn't one to waste time on history.

It wasn't professional, then, and she doubted a pass. Superintendent Haggard was a notoriously faithful husband. Moreover, Inspector Tierce was clearsighted about her looks: too sharp-featured for prettiness, and the sort of pale hair that may deserve the label but escapes being called blonde.

What was he up to? Then she'd glanced out of the smeary window at her elbow and seen strings of colored lights doubly blurred by the glass and another flurry of snow. There was the explanation, Christmas spirit. She smiled wryly. The superintendent probably kept a checklist of seasonal tasks, so many off-duty hours per December week devoted to stroking inferiors who might mature into rivals or allies. She supposed she ought to feel flattered.

A police cadet messenger tapped at the door and placed a file on Jill's desk without leaving the corridor, by leaning in and reaching. He had a lipstick smudge in the lee of one earlobe. Mistletoe had been hung in the canteen at lunchtime, only five days to the twenty-fifth now.

Big deal, she thought sourly.

The new file was depressingly fat. She transferred it from the in tray to the bottom of the pending basket, noting that the covers were quite crisp though the buff cardboard jacket had begun to fade. More than a year old, Inspector Tierce estimated. Then Superintendent Haggard was back, jingling his car keys impatiently.

He drove a mile or so out of town, to a Dickensian pub by the river. The saloon bar evoked a sporting squire's den, Victorian-vintage trophy fish in glass cases on the walls, no jukebox, and just token sprigs of non-plastic holly here and there. "Quiet and a bit classy," Lance Haggard commented. "I stumbled on this place last summer, thought it would suit you."

Sure you did, she jeered, not aloud. Apart from an older man and younger woman murmuring in a snug corner (boss courting a soon-to-be-even-more-personal assistant, Jill surmised cattily) they had the bar to themselves. "Done all your Christmas shopping?" Haggard inquired. "Going anywhere for the break, or spending it with Mum and Dad?"

Satisfied that small-talk obligations were discharged, he continued before she could match banality with banality, "I've had a file passed to you, luv. Before you drown in details, seemed a good idea to talk you through it."

Despite a flick of irritation, Jill Tierce was vaguely relieved. It was upsetting when leopards changed their spots. Superintendent Haggard's were still in place, he wasn't dispensing Christmas cheer but attempting to spread blame; if she reviewed one of his setbacks, she assumed part of the responsibility.

"I'm listening," she said flatly.

To her surprise, Haggard was . . . what? Not hangdog exactly, yet defensive. Obviously shelving a prepared presentation, he said, "Forget so-called perfect crimes—untraceable poisons, trick alibis, some bright spark who's a master of disguise. *Im*perfect crimes are the bastards to deal with. Chap had a brainstorm, lashes out at a total stranger, and runs for his life. Unless he gets collared on the spot, blood still running, we've no chance. Or, say, this respectable housewife is getting messages from Mars, personal relay station in a flying saucer. Eh? Height of the rush hour, she's in a crowd and shoves a child under a bus. Goes on home, like normal. No planning, no sane motive, they don't even try that hard to get away, they just . . . go about their business.

"It gets to me," he admitted needlessly. "Well, this one instance does.

225

Prostitute killed, and what's a streetwalker but somebody in extra danger from crazies? Mitzi Field, twenty-four years old but looked younger. Mitzi was just her working name, mind."

"There's a surprise."

He didn't rise to the sarcasm. "Dorothy Field on the death certificate but we'll stick to Mitzi, that's what she was known as, to the few who did know her.

"She was found in Grand Drive ten days before Christmas three years ago. Dead of repeated blows from something with sharp angles, most likely a brick. I see her getting into some curb crawler's car, and he drove her to where she was attacked. Saw red—wanted what she wouldn't provide, she tried ripping him off, plenty of possible reasons—snatched the nearest weapon, bashed her as she turned to run, kept bashing." The theory was delivered with pointed lack of emotion, Superintendent Haggard back in full control.

"Drove her there . . . the car was seen?" Jill held up a hand. "Sorry, not thinking straight." Mount Wolfe was one of the city's best quarters, Grand Drive its best address.

"Exactly," said Haggard. "Mitzi had started living rough, so she looked tatty. She'd had a mattress in a squat, that old factory on Victoria Quay, but the council demolished it the week before her death. The docks were her beat. She was wearing those big boots, like the movie—"

"Pretty Woman," Jill suggested.

"Those're the jokers, long boots and hot-pants and a ratty leather jacket with her chest hanging out—in December! The boots were borrowed from another girl, too tight, had to be sliced off her feet. Walking two miles from the docks to where she was found would have crippled her. And okay, it was dark, but a feller and a blatantly obvious hooker didn't foot it all the way up the Mount and along to the end of Grand Drive without being noticed. Which they were not, house-to-house checks established that."

Taking another, rationed sip of champagne—the pub sold it by the glass, else Haggard might not have stood for the drink of her choice, she suspected—Inspector Tierce frowned doubtfully.

"Grand Drive's the last place a working girl would pick for business. It's a private road, and they're very territorial round there—sleeping policeman bumps every fifty yards to stop cars using it for a shortcut, and if a non-resident parks in the road, somebody rings us within minutes, wanting him shifted . . ."

"Stresses that the punter was a stranger here," Haggard argued. "Businessman on an overnight, or he tired of motorway driving, detoured into town for a meal and a change of scene. Mitzi wasn't a local, either. Londoner originally, family split up after she was sexually abused. Went on the game

226

after absconding from a council home when she was fifteen. Summer before her death she worked the transport cafes, Reading, Bath, Bristol, drifted far as here and stayed.

"For my money, the punter spotted her at the docks. Then they drove around. She had no crib, did the business in cars or alleys. Maybe this punter was scared of getting mugged if they stuck around the docks. Driving at random, they spot a quiet-looking street, plenty of deep shadow at the far end where the trees are. Must have seemed safe enough, and so it was—for him. Nobody saw them arrive or him leaving. Some pet lover daft enough to walk the dog in a hailstorm found Mitzi's body that night, but she could have lain there till morning otherwise.

"All known curb crawlers were interviewed and cleared. Ditto the Dodgy List." Superintendent Haggard referred to the extensive register of sex offenders whose misdeeds ranged from assaults to stealing underwear off washing lines. "Copybook imperfect crime: guy blew a gasket and got the hell out. Ensuring the perfect result for him."

"Thanks for hyping me up," Inspector Tierce responded dryly. She'd been right, ambitious Haggard wanted to distance himself from defeat. Cutting corners to achieve it; in theory, if not always in practice, the assistant chief decreed what files she studied. Unless she made a stand, final disposition of the Dorothy "Mitzi" Field case would rest with her rather than the superintendent.

"I haven't finished." But he stayed silent for a moment before seeming to digress. "Know the old wives' tale about a murderer having to return to the scene of the crime? Laughable! Only I've got a screwy notion that superstitions have a basis in fact. Anyway, a man has been hanging about in Grand Drive recently. Sitting in his car like he's waiting for somebody . . . right where the kid's body lay. He's a local, which blows my passing stranger stuff out of the water—still, I'm not proud, I am happy to take any loose end offered."

But that's the point, Jill parried mentally, keeping a poker face, you're not taking it. And a helpful colleague giving loose ends a little tug just might end up under the pile of rocks they release.

"This fellow," Superintendent Haggard continued doggedly, "has been haunting Grand Drive. Uniformed branch looked into it after several complaints from residents. They're a bit exclusive up there, not to mention paranoid about burglars, scared the bloke was casing their houses. What jumped out at me was one old girl being pretty certain the same chap, leastways somebody in an identical car, did the same thing at Christmastime last year. She was adamant that he was there for an hour or more every day for a week."

He treated her to a phony's smile. "Got to be interesting. Because whatever this man is, he's no burglar. A pest and a pain in the arse, but no record and a steady job, good references. Uniforms didn't have to trace him, they just waited, and sure enough, he rolled up and parked at the end of Grand Drive. Nowhere near his house, incidentally, and well off the route to it. He gave them a cock-and-bull yarn about birdwatching. They pressed him, and he mouthed off about police harassment, started teaching them the law."

The smile turned into a sneer. "The man is Noel Sarum, you'll have heard of him. Yes, *the* Noel Sarum. Spokesman for the Wessex chapter of Fight for Your Rights, does that disgraceful column in the local paper, born trouble-maker. Very useful cover if he happens to have a down on hookers and let it get the better of him three years ago."

Inspector Tierce set her flute of champagne aside. "You forgot your oven gloves. Ought to have them on, handing me a hot potato."

Lance Haggard spoke a laugh. "You can deal with it. Routine review of the Field case, search for possible witnesses overlooked in the original trawl. Sarum can't object to an approach on those terms—he's always banging on about being ready to do his civic duty without knuckling under to mindless bullying."

"You tell him that, then. It was your case."

"Ah." Superintendent Haggard took a long pull at his draught Guiness. "It wasn't, you see. I've kept myself *au fait*, but . . . no, it's not down to me."

Shifting restively, he went off on another tangent. "My daughter . . . Beth was nearly eighteen back then, but her mental age is nearer six or seven. Lovely girl, couldn't ask for a nicer, but never mind the current jargon, sim-pleminded. You knew about that," he accused edgily.

Jill hadn't, but she nodded and waited.

"Beth used to go to special school, homecraft and so forth. . . . She may have to look after herself when me and the wife have snuffed it. I couldn't give Beth a lift every day. No problem, bus stop outside our house. Nell sees the girl aboard, three stops later, out she gets. But one night a water main burst, and the bus went a different way. Beth was set down two streets from us. It confused her.

"Nell phoned me, frantic, when the girl was an hour overdue. I pulled rank, had the area cars searching. What we hadn't imagined was Beth getting on *another* bus, she thought they all went to our house. This one's terminus was the docks, and the driver made her get out. She was crying but he didn't want to know.

"Of course I shot home, and damned if a taxi didn't pull up behind me, with Nell and a young woman who'd found her: Mitzi Field. I recognized her from court, she was a regular. Cut a long story short, Beth was wandering the docks, running away if any male asked why she was crying; we'd drilled that into her, never talk to strange men. Mitzi twigged she needed help, looked us up in the phonebook, and flagged down a cab."

Haggard fiddled with his empty glass. "Nell made her come in for some grub and a cup of tea. God forgive me, grateful or no, I was pleased to see the back of her, the girl was dirty under the paint and dead cheap. Nell, my wife, isn't practical except round the house. Church on Sunday, says her prayers every night. She wanted to help Mitzi, give her a fresh start, once our girl was in bed and I'd explained what Mitzi was. I told Nell to forget it, the best help to her sort is leaving them alone. She'd still sleep rough and be on the game with a thousand quid in her purse.

"Easy to say when you don't want hassle—and how would it have looked, me taking a common prostitute, a dockside brass, under my wing? A month later she got herself killed."

He put a hand atop Jill Tierce's. "Comes back to me every Christmas, how we owed that girl and . . . we didn't let her down but . . . you follow? It was Len Poole's inquiry, I can't involve myself. You can. Christmas, and I'm asking for a present. Something isn't kosher about Noel Mr. Crusader Bloody Sarum; give him a spin, and help ease my blasted conscience."

Taking his hand back, he blustered, "Any of that personal stuff leaks out, I'll skin you alive." But it was appeal rather than threat. Oh yes, Jill reflected, coppers were human all right—even devoutly ambitious ones.

Noel Sarum lived in one of the Monopoly-board houses of a new estate, Larkspur Crest. For no good reason Inspector Tierce had expected a student-type flat festooned in Death to Tories banners, fragrant with pot fumes and dirty socks.

Like most police officers, she was aware of Sarum. His know-your-rights column in the weekly paper kept sniping at law enforcers. Jill had acknowledged that the diatribes were justified in general terms, yet still she felt resentful, attacked while denied another right—of defense. Somehow she'd formed a picture of an acrid character with a straggly beard and John Lennon glasses, spitting venom via his word processor. He was a teacher, too, probably indoctrinating whole generations of copper-baiters. Not that they needed encouragement.

She was taken aback by the man opening the glossy front door of pin-neat Number 30. Fifty, she judged, but relatively unlined, face open under a shock of silver-gray hair. Track suit and trainers reinforced the youthful, vigorous impression. Before she could speak, he beamed and exclaimed, "Why, it's the lame duck!"

Sensitive over her treacherous leg, she bristled, then recognized the face and decoded his remark. It was the Samaritan from that half-marathon in the happy time before she'd been hurt. Talked into running for charity, she'd not realized that the friendly fellow partnering her for the final miles was Sarum, scourge of the police.

Jill had been quite taken with him. He'd struck her as a man appreciating female company for its own sake. If he'd been ten years younger or she a decade older, she might have tried making something of it. As things were, when the event finished he'd wrapped her in a foil blanket and trotted away to help somebody else.

"You're a police, um, person," he said, returning Inspector Tierce's warrant card. "I wondered what you did for a living, never thought of *that*. Come on in."

The living room contrived to be homely and pristine, sealed woodblock floor reflecting carefully tended plants. "Passes inspection, huh? I lost my wife five years ago, but I try to maintain her standards. Must have known you were coming, that's the coffee perking, not my tummy rumbling. Take a pew, I'll get it—black, white, sugar, no sugar?"

He was just as he'd been on the charity run, chatting as if resuming a relationship after minutes instead of years. Some people did it naturally, and in her experience, the majority were as uncomplicated as their manner. He made reasonable coffee, as well . . . "What's the problem? Can't be anything too shattering, but you're a senior rank."

Disingenuous, Jill thought; he must have a shrewd idea what brought her.

"You've been seen in Grand Drive for extended periods over the last two years. Watching, hanging about. Spare me the stuff about a free country; you put the wind up the neighborhood, and no wonder. It's no-hawkers-no-lurkers territory. Storm in a teacup is your comeback, but the snag is a woman was done to death at your favorite haunt three years ago."

"Two and two makes me a murder suspect, is that it?" His tone was even. Sensing that Noel Sarum savored debate, she gained a better understanding of his newspaper column.

"No, you invited suspicion all on your own," she replied calmly. "Gave my uniformed colleagues some guff about wanting to confirm the presence of a rare bird in Grand Drive, a . . . can't read PC Harris's writing, but he told me the name and I remembered it long enough to make a phone call.

"It's your bad luck that a cousin of mine is an ornithologist—the bird you chose hasn't touched England since 1911, and even that sighting was doubted. However, it's something an intelligent amateur might pick to blind the cops with science. According to my expert." And she smiled cheekily.

Noel Sarum's mouth curved up at the corners, too. "Got me." Then his jaw set. "As a matter of fact, that was my *third* Christmas of going to Grand Drive. Breaking no law, causing no nuisance. Which is all you need from me."

"Believe it or not I'd agree if it weren't for Mitzi Field. The dead girl. Worthless girl, some might say, squalid little life, good riddance. But we don't agree, do we. I've got to account for loose ends, and you're flapping about in the wind, Mr. Sarum."

"Noel," he corrected abstractedly. "The kids call me First Noel, this time of year. Every class thinks it's being brilliantly original. . . ." Stubborn streak resurfacing, he grumbled. "After your pals pounced on me, I went to the *Gazaette* office and researched the murder in the back numbers. That winter I was supply-teaching at Peterborough, didn't get back to the city until the week after it happened. The night she was killed, I was chaperoning a Sixth Form dance more than a hundred miles away from Grand Drive."

"Bloody hell," Jill muttered. "What's the matter with you, why not tell the uniforms that?"

Taken aback by her impatience and the subtext of disgust, he shrugged helplessly. "I didn't think of it at the time."

Fair enough, Inspector Tierce granted. People didn't remember their whereabouts a week ago, let alone years later. Though Noel Sarum might be lying. . . .

Guessing the reaction, he brightened. "Hang on, I'm not escaping, just looking in the glory-hole."

She watched him delve in a cupboard under the stairs. Soon he returned, waving a pamphlet. "Here you are, Beacon School newsletter, date at the top of every page."

It was a slim, computer printed magazine. Sarum's finger jabbed at a poorly reproduced photograph in which he was recognizable, arm round the shoulders of a jolly, overweight woman in owl spectacles. " 'First Noel' got the Christmas spirit, Mrs. May got the grope, and the Sixth 'got down' with a vengeance last Thursday night," ran the disrespectful caption.

"Mrs. May's the head teacher, the kids loved that snap," he chuckled. Tuning him out, Jill found the first page of her notebook. Yes, the date was right, Mitzi Field had died at about nine P.M. that faraway Thursday night when Noel Sarum was hugging the head teacher. His tone hardened. "Sorry to disappoint you."

"Oh, drop it," she said crossly. "I liked you on that stupid run, I still like you, though what I'd really like is to shake you till your stupid teeth rattle."

Taken aback, he fiddled with the school magazine.

"You've got a bee in your bonnet about the police, fine. But that's no excuse for wasting two uniformed officers' time, and mine. Heaven knows what it is with you and Grand Drive, I don't care."

She broke off, eyes narrowing. "Hey! I think this was a setup. You have an ironclad alibi, so why not encourage the dim coppers to hassle you? Weeks and weeks of columns to be wrung out of that. Cancel the liking-you bit, you're sick. Feel free to complain about my attitude. I'll be happy to defend it, on the record."

Appalled, Noel Sarum protested. "It's not like that . . . *setup?* It never crossed my mind!" Cracking his knuckles, he glowered at the carpet. "It's strictly personal, can't you people get that through your heads?" After which, perversely (not only coppers are human), he told her the whole story.

Fifteen minutes later, Inspector Tierce said, "Why the heck didn't you press every bell and find her that way? Can't be that many flats in half a dozen houses."

"What would I say when each door opens?" Sarum demanded. "I don't even know if she's married, she was wearing gloves, I couldn't see if she had a wedding ring. Supposing her husband answered, imagine the trouble I could cause."

"I still can't make out how you chatted her up and didn't have the gumption to get her name, even a first name."

Still high-colored from enthusiasm and embarrassment, Sarum sputtered, "I didn't chat her up. It was . . . idyllic, a little miracle. We looked at each other and started talking as if we'd known each other forever. Somehow I couldn't bring myself to ask her name or give mine, it might have broken the spell."

"Yes, you told me," Jill butted in, lips tingling from the strain of keeping a straight line. The copper-bashing demon she had pictured snarling over his columns turned out to be a hopeless, helpless romantic. Noel Sarum, a widower well into middle age, patrolled Grand Drive once a year because he was suffering belated pangs of puppy love.

Having met his ideal woman one Christmas Eve, driven her home, and departed on air, he'd been unable to decide which house in Grand Drive was hers. Similar period and the same architect, and they looked different by daylight.

She could understand why he hadn't confided in a couple of constables patently ready to take him for some kind of weirdo. After all, he was the Know Your Rights fanatic, worried that they'd turn his romantic vigil into a mocking anecdote to belittle him. Inevitably he'd been combative.

It was already dark when Jill Tierce left Larkspur Crest. Fresh snow crunched under the tires. She slowed as her lights picked up a group of children crossing the road, dragging a muffled-up baby on the improvised sledge of a tin tray. At the foot of the hill a Rotary Club float blared canned carols, a squad of executive Santas providing harness-bells sound effects with their collecting tins.

Everything went a little scatty in this season, though nicely so, Inspector

Tierce mused. She'd bought no presents so far, that was scatty, dooming her to Christmas Eve panic.

Not the least of her scattiness, either. She thought: I can't believe I'm doing this, but stayed on course towards Grand Drive.

By six that evening, bad leg nagging savagely—it disapproved of stairs, and she had climbed a number of flights—Jill was showing her warrant card and saying with the glibness of practice, "This may sound odd, but bear with me. . . . Two Christmases ago, if you remember that far back, did you go Christmas Eve shopping at the Hi-Save in City Center?"

"I expect so." The woman's voice was unexpectedly deep and hoarse from such a slim body. "I use Hi-Save for all but deli stuff, it's loads cheaper."

"I mustn't lead you, put ideas in your head, but that Christmas Eve did you have help with your shopping, like your bags carried to the car?"

"I don't take the c— Oh, him, the knight errant!" She opened the door wider and stood aside. "Come in, you look chilled."

Constance—"Connie, please, the other's so prissy"—French remembered Noel Sarum, all right.

"He picked me up in the checkout line that Christmas Eve. Well, I picked him up, had he but known." Brown, almond eyes sparkled wickedly. "It was such a scrum, the line was endless, all the trolleys were taken so I was lugging three or four of those wretched baskets, and he did the polite, offered to share the load while we waited.

"Single men who aren't teenagers are so pathetic, aren't they? And he was kind and clean and cuddly, I really *took* to him." She'd insisted on making them mugs of hot chocolate ("with the teeniest spike of brandy to cheer it up") after Jill Tierce refused a cocktail.

And I could take to a pad like this, Inspector Tierce reflected a shade drowsily. Connie French had two floors of one of Grand Drive's former mansions. Her living room was spacious yet cosy, elegant antique pieces to dress it, costly modern furniture for wallowing.

Ms. French sat a little straighter. "What's this about, dear?"

"I'm glad you asked that." Jill pulled a face. "Officially I'm eliminating a loose end, confirming somebody's reason for . . . never mind, confirming a story. Don't quote me, but I was curious. A witness was terribly impressed by you and . . ."

Connie waited, and Jill said, "It's just that you knocked him for six, he hasn't got over it—and call it the Christmas syndrome, or downright nosiness, but I wondered if you'd felt the same."

"I have thought about him since." Connie smiled weakly, blushing. "A lot, on and off. Look, there is always enough for two when it's a casserole, and

233

a glass of wine can't put you over the limit for driving. Terrible thing to tell a woman, but you look exhausted. Stay for a meal."

They got on famously. A long while later, table cleared, dishwasher loaded, they'd put the world to rights and compared Most Terrible Male Traits (nasal fur, aggressive driving, and pointless untruths topping the painstakingly compiled list).

Inspector Tierce was deciding that she'd better go home by cab and pick her car up tomorrow—should have known she was unable to drink *one* glass of wine—when Connie French became fretful.

"What is it with that chap, Jill? I could tell he fancied me. Oh, not the flared nostrils and ripping the thin silk from my creamy shoulders, he wasn't that sort, but we really hit it off. Greek gods and toy boys are all very well, but what you need is a man who's comfy as old shoes. I've only met two or three, one was my brother and the others were friends' husbands. . . ."

"Tell me his name, I'll ring him." Connie reached for the phonebook on the end table at her side.

"I can't do that, I shouldn't be here anyway, certainly not gossiping. Christmas has a lot to answer for." It struck Jill that they were talking animatedly but with a certain precision over trickier words; perhaps the Beaujolais Villages in easy reach on the coffee table between them was not the first bottle.

"Wouldn't ring him anyway. My late husband, as in divorced, not RIP, said I had no pride but . . . is he gay? My supermarket chap, not the ex."

"Sarum? Certainly not." Frowning at the alliteration as much as the slip, Jill muttered, "I must make tracks."

"Night's young," Connie said on a pleading note. "He drove me home, I nearly asked him up for a drink—but something stopped me. I wanted him to at least introduce himself first, and after all that, he just took himself off."

"You'd stunned him," Jill said.

"Bull," Ms. French countered. But she was thoughtful. "Honest injun?"

"That's the impression I got. The twit's been keeping a vigil out there in the run-up to Christmas, ever since, hoping to pull the fancy-seeing-you-here bit."

Connie went to the bay window. "Typical of my luck, I never saw him."

"He stayed in his car, from up here he'd be an anonymous roof." Joining her, Inspector Tierce asked, "Were you questioned in the house-to-house sweep after Mitzi Field's body was found?"

"I was playing bridge that night, didn't get home till it was all over." Connie hugged herself. "Just as well. I couldn't bear it if I'd been up here watching some silly TV show while . . . ugh!"

"Looks pretty now." Snow crusted high walls and hedges, whiteness and moonlight giving Grand Drive a luminous quality.

"Christmas card," Connie French suggested, making the comment bleak. "I spend hours at this window sometimes, it's like a box seat for the seasonal stuff—carol singers from St. Stephen's in full Dickens costume, crinolines and caped coats and candle-lanterns. Then there are the children returning to the nest, back from boarding school, or a bit older, very proud of The Car and their university scarves.

"My daughter lives in California, she might ring on Christmas Day, probably will before New Year's. . . . Mummy's an afterthought."

To Jill's dismay, Connie French was crying silently, a single, fat tear sliding down the side of her elegant nose.

Inspector Tierce woke the next morning with the mildest of hangovers, little more than a nasty taste in the mouth, and a flinching sensation at the memory of her hostess.

The provoking thing was that she didn't pity Connie French. The sorrow had been alcohol-based and transitory; minutes afterwards they'd played an old Dory Previn album, whooping approval of the bitchy lyrics. Connie might have been briefly maudlin, but she was too sparky for extensive self-pity.

No, this was not about Connie, but something she had said or done kept niggling and scratching in the subconscious. Every time Jill recollected the profile etched against the window, decorated by a crystal tear—and the image was persistent, like that pop tune you cannot stop humming—an alarm went off.

"Think of something else," Inspector Tierce advised out loud, competing against the hair dryer's breathy roar. Nearly too late to post greetings cards, not that she'd bought them yet. She *had* bought some in good time one year. They were in A Safe Place to this day, waiting to be found.

Oh dear, she was better off thinking about the Mitzi Field case. Very well, Noel Sarum was in the clear. He could have printed that school magazine himself, or altered the date, but only in a Golden Age detective story. He'd been far away, and Connie French had confirmed his reason for haunting Grand Drive at a particular time of year. Further, while everyone was a potential life-taker, Noel Sarum belonged at the safest, last-resort end of the spectrum.

And that revived Superintendent Haggard's imperfect crime. She could picture a man on perhaps his first and last sojourn in the city, stopping at a street woman's signal and unrecognized, very likely unseen, driving away with her. To drive on, soon afterwards, taking care to stay away.

"Hopeless," Jill mumbled and, skipping breakfast, went off to her broom closet, cardboard-flavored coffee, and the case file.

It assured her that everything needful had been done. A fruitless check

235

for witnesses to the crime, an unrewarding search for tire tracks, footprints, any physical evidence apart from Mitzi Field's body. Local and then regional sexual offenders interrogated. Other prostitutes questioned, fellow tenants of her last known address, the demolished squat, traced and interviewed.

Nothing to go on; conscientious Detective-Inspector Poole, exactly the breed of plodder who catches most criminals, had demonstrated that if nothing else. Or had he?

Inspector Tierce stood up awkwardly, massaging scar tissue through her skirt. She hadn't thought the location significant, merely incongruous, when Superintendent Haggard told her of it. Previous reading of the file had left her cold. But now it was different because . . . because of Connie French. Something—*what?*—that she'd said last night.

She'd said so much, that was the snag. Squinting, lips moving silently, Jill talked herself through a lengthy and meandering conversation. Until reaching the point where Connie had lamented an uncaring daughter . . . bingo.

Children coming home for the holidays, of course. That's what families did at Christmas, families and friends of the family. Driven by nostalgia, tradition, the chance to purge year-long offenses during the annual truce, or (if mercenary souls) simply to collect presents, they headed for hearth and home.

She leafed through to a terse section of the dossier, the London end. A few discreet sentences covered Mitzi's life from just before her ninth birthday until she absconded from the council home six years later.

Lots of digging needed. Inspector Tierce felt sorry for Len Poole, and profoundly grateful that she did not have to follow up her idea.

Inspector Poole, a careworn, resigned character, took one look at the name on the file and groaned, "Haggard's got you at it as well, has he? Wish he'd mind his own business."

"Amen to that, but I'm stuck with it. Len, what was that girl doing on Grand Drive? Haggard thinks she took a client to a road full of snobs and busybodies because she didn't know any better. Or the punter was ignorant and Mitzi Field didn't care. Did you buy that?"

"No opinion—I'd need facts to form one, and the only certainty was that she was killed there." He wasn't being awkward, that was how his mind worked. "Long way to go for a quickie in a motor, right enough. Then again, Vice was chasing street prozzies at the time, she might have wanted to get well away from the redlight area."

"Supposing," said Jill, "she wasn't taken to Grand Drive and killed? Supposing she was *leaving* there, heading back to her beat, when it happened?"

"I'm not quite with you."

"She didn't walk all the way, wasn't dressed for it, therefore she went in a car, that's the conventional wisdom. Doesn't follow. A bus runs from dockland to a stop round the corner from Grand Drive every half hour. She could have taken herself there, right? Visited somebody, left again, and either her attacker was waiting, or he was the one she'd called on, and he chased her out of doors."

"Try reading the file," Inspector Poole urged. "No known sex offenders among the residents, remember. We grilled all Les Girls, whether or not they'd associated with Ms. Field, and none of them had a client in Grand Drive; far as they were aware, that is. Down-market hookers don't keep names and addresses. Her mates were sure Mitzi had never been up there before."

"Yes, but it was Christmas, Len. When we all get sudden urges to see Mum and Dad, look up Auntie Flo, send a card to that nice former neighbor who nursed us through whooping cough. Mitzi Field had a family of sorts, once upon a time."

Digesting the implications, Inspector Poole said, "Crumbs." He did not go in for bad language. "You do get 'em, the wild hunches. All right, she was Mitzi Field, but her mother remarried, to a man called, don't tell me . . . Edwardes. The stepfather who supposedly seduced the little girl. The mother died in 1984, Edwardes was never charged, lack of evidence, they just took the child away. He'd dropped off the radar screen by 1990, dead or gone abroad, certainly hasn't paid tax or claimed unemployment benefits for a long time. All in the file, dear. I may be slow but I ain't stupid."

"Perish the thought. But that still leaves Auntie Flo and the kindly neighbor."

"Crumbs," he repeated, even more feelingly, "you don't want much. We're talking ten, fifteen years back, and in London." Inspector Poole took possession of the file. "It's a thought, I can't deny it. More's the pity."

On Christmas Eve afternoon, Len Poole rapped jauntily at Jill's office door. "London doesn't get any better. I've had two days up there, and how those lads in the Met stand the life is beyond me. Noise, pollution, bad manners, homeless beggars everywhere. But I did find a helpful social worker, they do exist even if it's an endangered species, and this chap had a good memory.

"Great idea of yours—but I'm afraid James Edwardes, Mitzi's allegedly wicked stepfather, doesn't live at Grand Drive. He works the fairs in the Republic of Ireland, hasn't been in England for years."

Hitching half his skinny rump onto the corner of the desk, Inspector Poole added innocently, "No trace of Auntie Flo. But I'll tell you who did have a Grand Drive address until recently—Anthony Challis."

237

Since he had to have worked hard and fast and was full of himself over it, Jill Tierce played along. "Challis?"

"He lodged with Mitzi's family in the eighties. Freelance electrician, good earner, about to get married. But then Mitzi Field, only she was little Dorothy then, accused nice Mr. Challis of doing things to her. Her mother called the police, and then Dorothy admitted it wasn't Challis after all, it was her stepfather who kept raping her." Len Poole grimaced distastefully. "Ugly . . . my tame social worker said he'd never believed Challis had touched her. What it was, they discovered, Edwardes not only abused her, he practically brainwashed the poor kid, said she'd be struck down if she told on him. When it got too much for her, she accused Tony Challis—ironically enough, because he was kind, would never hurt her. She'd just wanted it out in the open, so the grownups would make it stop. Ruining Challis wasn't on her agenda, if she had such a thing, but that was the effect.

"After Dorothy-Mitzi was taken into council care, her mother threw Edwardes out, and Tony Challis went to other digs. No charges were brought in the end—the child was considered unreliable on account of changing her story. Rumors spread, mud stuck, Challis's fiancée told him to get lost, his regular customers followed suit . . ."

"Ugly," Jill agreed.

"Gets worse. Challis is a Wessex man, he talked a lot about this part of the world when he was lodging with Mitzi's folks. Maybe that's why she stuck around, having drifted here. Anyway, Challis took to drink, hit the gutter before he straightened up. Returned to his native heath, as posh books put it, found work as a janitor for Coastal Properties. They own several apartment houses on Grand Drive and gave him a basement flat in the end one on the left. Too dark and cramped for letting, and it gave them a good excuse to pay him peanuts.

"Mitzi Field wasn't looking for Challis—if she'd had a grain of sense she would have kept well clear—but she found him. Once a month he picked up supplies from a discount hardware store on her beat in dockland. He didn't notice her, which is natural; the last time he'd seen Dorothy, she was a child. But she must have seen him going in and out of the hardware place and pumped somebody there, discovered where he worked."

Len Poole sighed and shook his head. "Just as you said, it was Christmas. Tony Challis is watching TV in his basement one night, and suddenly this shabby little tart is at the side door, saying, I'm Dorothy, Mr. Challis, don't you remember me? Wanted to say sorry, hoped he was doing all right now, she hadn't wanted to make trouble for him. And so on.

"Challis says, and I believe him, he was in a daze while she talked to him. 'Noises, she was making noises,' he told me. She was dead when the actual words came back to him. Mitzi left, and for a minute—the chap's a drinker, mark you—he wondered whether he'd been hallucinating. Then he wished he had been. Challis hadn't hated *Dorothy*; he understood she was a victim who dragged him down with her, no malice involved. But she'd become Mitzi . . . ruining him and still ending up like that, that was past bearing.

"Next moment, it seemed to him, he was standing over her in the street, holding one of those little stone lions: half the big houses along the drive had them on either side of the porch. He had the lion by its head, the square base was allover blood.

"He accepted that he must have killed her, but he didn't feel like a murderer. All he felt was scared witless. He slipped back to his basement, washed the lion, and put it back in place. Then he prayed. Been praying ever since.

"From Met Police records and that social worker, I got the names of five people linked to Field when she was a child. Only one was among the residents of Grand Drive at the time she was killed. No problem finding him, he didn't move far, one of those new council flats near the marina. Soon as I said who I was, Challis goes, 'Thank God, now I can tell somebody.' "

Jill Tierce addressed her folded hands, almost inaudibly. "She wanted to make amends for what happened all those years ago, and he killed her for trying?"

Inspector Poole slid off the desk, his expression mixing wonder and compassion over her naivete. "If you can make sense of the why and wherefore, be sure to tell Challis. He can't sort it out. It's people, Jill . . . she was one of them that gets sentimental at Christmas, never considered she'd be opening a wound. As for him, he wasn't the kind man who'd lodged with her mum. Not anymore. She stirred up an embittered semialcoholic, temper overdue to snap."

Len Poole hesitated, cleared his throat. "Nobody's fault, luv, not even his. Though he'll go away for it."

"We got a result, which is all that matters."

"Not what I meant—though there is always that, at the end of the day."

Inspector Tierce's day, apparently over, had a postscript.

She'd wanted to watch the black and white movie of Scrooge for the fifth Christmas Eve in a row but went to bed instead. Her father would be calling "fairly early" to collect her for Christmas lunch, meaning crack of dawn.

The phone woke her. The caller sounded drunk, though on nothing more than girlish high spirits, it emerged.

"We've just got back from midnight Mass, now we can be the first to wish you Merry Christmas."

"Wha'? Who is it?" Jill pulled the alarm clock radio round on the bedside table, sending paperbacks, a bottle of cough mixture, and her pain tablets cascading to the floor. "It's twenty to two!" The voice's identity registered belatedly. "Connie, I'll kill you."

"Don't be like that. I rang him after all, you see. And I'm so *happy*."

"Bully for you. What in the world are you on about?"

"Noel, of course. You let his name slip the other night—"

"Did I, by gum." Fully awake and up on one elbow, Inspector Tierce rolled gummy eyes. "That was very unprofessional."

"Sarum's an unusual surname, only one in the local phonebook, and we talked for hours—" Following squeaks and a rattle, Noel Sarum came on the phone.

"And here I am! Well, I'll be leaving in a minute," he added sheepishly.

Another interlude of cryptic noises and then Connie French trilled, "He's so stuffy, of course he's not leaving at this time of the morning."

She said something aside, answering Noel in the background. "He wants you to know we're engaged and says I'm indiscreet, the idiot. I say, you must come to our wedding, it'll be February or March. You have to, you're the matchmaker."

"Let's talk about it next year. I'm pleased you are pleased, Connie. Tell Noel to go easy on the law in future; he owes me. 'Bye."

Lying back in the darkness, a phrase from the Bible popped into her head, a Sunday school fragment clear as if spoken for her benefit: "Out of the strong came forth sweetness." Something about bees using the remains of a savage lion as their hive. Why think of that? Mitzi Field was battered with a stone lion. Nothing sweet there, that was not the connection.

Connie was gorgeously happy, and Noel worshipped her. It couldn't last, euphoria didn't, yet it was a promising prelude to something better. They might fight eventually, but they would not be lonely.

That was what had triggered the parable of bees and a beast of prey. Out of evil, good can come. "Merry Christmas," Jill Tierce whispered to the pillow.

Martin Werner

CHRISTMAS PARTY

People in the advertising business said the Christmas party at French & Saunders was the social event of the year. For it wasn't your ordinary holiday office party. Not the kind where the staff gets together for a few mild drinks out of paper cups, some sandwiches sent in from the local deli, and a long boring speech by the company president. At F&S it was all very different: just what you'd expect from New York's hottest advertising agency.

The salaries there were the highest in town, the accounts were strictly blue chip, and the awards the agency won over the years filled an entire boardroom. And the people, of course, were the best, brightest, and most creative that money could buy.

With that reputation to uphold, the French & Saunders Christmas party naturally had to be the biggest and splashiest in the entire industry.

Year after year, that's the way it was. Back in the late Seventies, when discos were all the rage, the company took over Numero Uno, the club people actually fought over to get in. Another year, F&S hired half the New York Philharmonic to provide entertainment. And in 1989, the guest bartenders were Mel Gibson, Madonna, and the cast of *L.A. Law.*

There was one serious side to the party. That's when the president reviewed the year's business, announced how much the annual bonus would be, and then named the Board's choices for People of the Year, the five lucky employees who made the most significant contributions to the agency's success during the past twelve months.

The unwritten part to this latter (although everyone knew it, anyway) was that each one of the five would receive a very special individual bonus— some said as high as $50,000 apiece.

Then French & Saunders bought fifteen floors in the tallest, shiniest new office tower on Broadway, the one that had actually been praised by the *N.Y.*

Times architecture critic.

The original plan was to hold the party in the brand-new offices that were to be ready just before Christmas. A foolish idea, as it turned out, because nothing in New York is ever finished when it's promised. The delay meant the agency had to scramble and find a new party site—either that, or make do in the half finished building itself.

Amazingly—cleverly? —enough, that was the game plan the party committee decided to follow. Give the biggest, glitziest party in agency history amid half finished offices in which paneless windows looked out to the open skies, where debris and building supplies stood piled up in every corner, and where doors opened on nothing but a web of steel girders and the sidewalk seventy floors below.

Charlie Evanston, one of the company's senior vice-presidents (he had just reached the ripe old of age of fifty), was chosen to be party chairman. He couldn't have been happier. For Charlie had a deepdown feeling that this was finally going to be his year. After being passed over time and again for one of those five special Christmas bonuses, he just knew he was going to go home a winner.

Poor Charlie.

In mid-November—the plans for the party proceeding on schedule— the agency suddenly lost their multi-million-dollar Daisy Fresh Soap account, no reason given. Charlie had been the supervisor on the account for years, and although he couldn't be held personally responsible for the loss a few people (enemies!) shook their heads and wondered if maybe someone else, someone a little stronger—and younger—couldn't have held on to the business.

Two weeks later, another showpiece account—the prestigious Maximus Computer Systems—left the agency. Unheard of.

The trade papers gave away the reason in the one dreaded word "kickbacks." Two French & Saunders television producers who had worked on the account had been skimming it for years.

Again, Charlie's name came up. Not that he had anything remotely to do with the scandal. The trouble was that he personally had hired both offenders. And people remembered.

There's a superstition that events like these happen in threes, so it was only a question of time before the next blow. And, sure enough, two weeks before Christmas, it happened. A murder, no less. A F&S writer shot his wife, her lover, and himself.

With that, French & Saunders moved from front-page sidelines in the trade papers straight to screaming headlines in every tabloid in town. In less than a month, it had been seriously downgraded from one of New York's proudest enterprises to that most dreaded of advertising fates—an agency "in trouble."

It was now a week before Christmas and every F&S employee was carrying around his or her own personal lump of cold, clammy fear. The telltale signs were everywhere. People making secret telephone calls to headhunters and getting their resumes in order. Bitter jokes about the cold winter and selling apples on street corners told in the elevators and washrooms. Rumors that a buyout was in the making and *nobody* was safe.

And yet, strange as it sounds, there were those who still thought there would be a happy ending. At the Christmas party, perhaps. A last-minute announcement that everything was as before—the agency was in good shape and, just like always, everyone would get that Christmas bonus.

Charlie was one of the most optimistic. He didn't know why. Just a gut feeling that the world was still full of Christmas miracles and, bad times or not, he was going to be one of F&S's five magical People of the Year.

Poor Charlie.

A few days before the party, his phone rang. It was the voice of J. Stewart French, president and chairman of the board.

"Hi, Charlie. Got a minute?"

"Sure."

"I wonder if you'd mind coming up to my office. I've got a couple of things I'd like to talk to you about."

Nothing menacing about that, thought Charlie. J probably wants to discuss the party. The food. The caterers. The security measures that would be needed so that no one would be in any danger in those half finished offices.

Very neatly, very efficiently, Charlie got out his files and headed upstairs. When he arrived in the president's office—it was the only one that had been completely finished (vulgar but expensive, thought Charlie)—J was on the phone, his face pale and drawn, nothing like the way he usually looked, with that twelve-months-a-year suntan he was so proud of. He nodded over the phone. "Sit down, Charlie, sit down."

Charlie sank into one of the comfortable $12,000 chairs beside the desk and waited. After a minute the conversation ended and J turned to give him his full attention. Charlie had known J for fifteen years and had never seen him so nervous and ill at ease.

Then he spoke.

"Charlie, they tell me you've really got the Christmas party all together. Looks like it'll be a smash."

"We're hoping so, J."

"Well, we can certainly use some good times around here. I don't have to tell *you* that. It's been a bad, *bad* year."

"Things'll be better. I know it."

"Do you really think so, Charlie? Do you? I'd like to believe that, too. That's why this party means so much to me. To all of us. Morale—"

"I know."

"Well, you've certainly done your part. More than your part. That's why I called you in."

Here it comes, thought Charlie, here comes my special Christmas bonus! Ahead of time, before anyone else hears about it!

"I wanted you to be one of the first to know. The Board and I have agreed that, even with all our troubles, there'll be something extra in every-body's paycheck again this year. Nothing like before, of course, but it will be something."

"That's wonderful."

"Yeah. Wonderful. We monkeyed around with the budget and found we could come up with a few bucks. The *problem* is, we'll have to make some cuts here and there."

"Cuts?"

"Well, for one thing, I'm afraid there won't be any of those special bonus-es this year, Charlie. And I'll level with you—you were down for one. After all these years, you had really earned it. I can't tell you how sorry—"

Sure, thought Charlie. "It's not the end of the world, J," he said. "Maybe next year."

"No, Charlie, that's not all. With our losses and the cost of moving—I don't know how to tell you this, but we're doing something else. We're cutting back—some of our best people. I've never had to do anything like that in my life."

You bastard, Charlie thought. "Go on, J," he said. "I think I know what you're going to say."

J looked at him miserably. "You're one of the people we'll have to lose, Charlie. Wait a minute, please hear me out—it's nothing personal. I wanted to save you. After all, we've been together fifteen years. I talked and talked, I even threatened to resign myself. But no one wanted to listen."

Sure, Charlie thought.

"They said you hadn't produced anything worthwhile in years. And there was the business of those two crazies you hired. And—"

"Is that it?" Charlie asked.

"Don't get me wrong, Charlie. Please, let's do the Christmas party as we planned, just as if nothing happened. As for leaving, take your time. I got you a year's severance. And you can use your office to make calls, look around, and—"

"No problem, J." Charlie was moving to the door. "I understand. And don't worry about the party. Everything's all taken care of."

Not even a handshake.

Many people at some time or other have fantasized about killing the boss. In Charlie's case, it was different. From the minute he heard the bad news from J, he became a changed man. Not outwardly, of course. He wasn't about to become an overnight monster, buy a gun, make a bomb, sharpen an axe. No, he would be the same Charlie Evanston. Friendly. Smiling. Efficient. But now that he knew the worst, he began piling up all the long-suppressed injustices he had collected from J for fifteen years. The conversations that stopped abruptly when he entered an executive meeting. The intimate dinners at J's that he and his wife were never invited to. The countless other little slights. And, finally, this.

December 20. Party time! Everyone agreed it was the best bash French & Saunders had ever thrown.

The day was fair and warm. The milling crowds that drifted from the well stocked bars and refreshment tables didn't even notice there wasn't a heating system. The lack of carpets, the wide-open window spaces, the empty offices—it all added to the fun.

Carefully groomed waiters in white gloves and hard hats pressed their way from room to room, carrying silver trays laden with drinks and hors d'oeuvres. A heavy metal band blared somewhere. A troupe of strolling violinists pressed in and out. From the happy faces, laughter, and noise, you'd never know the agency had a care in the world.

But Charlie Evanston knew. He pushed his way over to a small crowd pressing around J. All of them were drunk, or on the way, and J, drink in hand, was swaying slightly. His laugh was louder than anybody's whenever one of the clients told a funny story. He spotted Charlie and shouted to him. "Charlie, c'mere a minute! Folks, you all know my old pal Charlie Evanston. We've been together since this place opened its doors. He's the guy who put this whole great party together."

There were murmurs of approval as J drew Charlie into his embrace.

"J," Charlie said, "I just came to ask you to come over here and let me show you something."

"Oh, Charlie, always business. Can't it wait till next week? After the holidays?"

"No, I think it's important. Please come over here. Let me show you."

"Oh, for Chrissakes, Charlie. What *is* it?"

"Just follow me. Won't take long."

J pulled away from the group with a back-in-a-minute wave of his hand and followed Charlie down a narrow hall to a room that would one day become the heart of the agency's computer operation.

It was empty. Even the floors hadn't been finished. Just some wooden planks, a few steel beams—and the sidewalk below. J glanced around the room and turned to Charlie. "So? What's the problem?"

"Don't you get it, J? There isn't a single Keep Out sign on that outside door. The workmen even forgot to lock it. Someone could walk in here and fall straight down to Broadway!"

"Oh, come on, Charlie, this place is off the beaten path—no one's going to be coming this way. Stop worrying."

"Yes, but—"

"No buts, Charlie. Just tell one of the security guards. My God, you drag me all the way out here just to see this. Jesus Christ, I'll bet I could even *walk* across one of these steel beams. The workmen do it every day."

It was uncanny. Charlie knew that was exactly what J would say. It was part of the macho, daredevil reputation he had cultivated so carefully. "Hey, wait a minute, J," he said.

"No. Serious. Watch me walk across this beam right here. It can't be more than twenty feet long. And I'll do it with a drink in each hand."

"Come on, J, don't be crazy."

But J had already taken his first tentative step on the beam—with Charlie directly behind him.

It was all so simple. Now all Charlie had to do was give J the tiniest of shoves in the back, watch him stagger and plunge over the side, and it would be all over.

As J continued to move along the beam, he seemed to grow more confident. Charlie continued to follow a few steps behind, his right arm outstretched. It was now or never. Suddenly he made his move. But J moved a couple of quick steps faster and Charlie missed J's back by an inch. Instead, he felt himself slipping over the side. He gasped. Then all he remembered was falling.

The hospital room was so quiet you could barely hear a murmur from the corridor outside.

On the single bed there lay what looked like a dead body. Every inch was covered in a rubbery casing and yards and yards of white gauze. All you could see of what was underneath was a little round hole where the mouth was supposed to be and another opening where a blood-shot blue eye stared up at the ceiling. Charlie Evanston.

The door opened slightly, admitting J, followed by one of Charlie's doctors.

J shuddered. He always did, every time he'd visited over the past six months. He turned to the doctor. "How's he doing today?"

"About the same. He tries to talk a little now and then."

"Can he hear me yet? Can he understand?"

"We think so. But don't try and get anything out of him."

"Yes. I know." He bent over the bed. "Charlie. Charlie. It's me, J. I just wanted you to know I'm here. And I want to thank you again—I guess I'll be thanking you for the rest of my life—for reaching out and trying to save me at that damn Christmas party."

The blue eye blinked. A tear began to tremble on the edge.

"I was a fool. Only a fool would have tried to do what I did. And you tried to stop me. I felt you grab my jacket and try to hold me back. Then you took the fall for me."

The blue eye stared.

"So what I came to say—what I hope you can understand—is that no matter how long it takes you're going to get the best care we can find. Just get well. Everything's going to be okay."

The blue eye continued to look at J without blinking.

"And, Charlie, here's the best news of all. The agency's just picked up three big accounts. Over a hundred million."

A light breeze blew the curtains from the window.

"So today the Board asked me to come up here and give you a special bonus. Not a Christmas bonus—more like Purple Heart. You deserve it, Charlie. You saved the old man's life, you bastard!"

Charlie tried to nod, but it was impossible.

"And just wait till you come back," J said enthusiastically. "You're a hero, Charlie! We've got all kinds of great things waiting for you. All kinds of plans. It's going to be a whole new ballgame, Charlie! Imagine!"

Yeah, thought Charlie. Imagine.

Sir Arthur Conan Doyle

THE ADVENTURE OF THE BLUE CARBUNCLE

I had called upon my friend Sherlock Holmes upon the second morning after Christmas, with the intention of wishing him the compliments of the season. He was lounging upon the sofa in a purple dressing-gown, a pipe-rack within his reach upon the right, and a pile of crumpled morning papers, evidently newly studied, near at hand. Beside the couch was a wooden chair, and on the angle of the back hung a very seedy and disreputable hard-felt hat, much the worse for wear, and cracked in several places. A lens and a forceps lying upon the seat of the chair suggested that the hat had been suspended in this manner for the purpose of examination.

"You are engaged," said I; "perhaps I interrupt you."

"Not at all. I am glad to have a friend with whom I can discuss my results. The matter is a perfectly trivial one"—he jerked his thumb in the direction of the old hat—"but there are points in connection with it which are not entirely devoid of interest and even of instruction."

I seated myself in his armchair and warmed my hands before his crackling fire, for a sharp frost had set in, and the windows were thick with the ice crystals. "I suppose," I remarked, "that, homely as it looks, this thing has some deadly story linked on to it—that it is the clue which will guide you in the solution of some mystery and the punishment of some crime."

"No, no. No crime," said Sherlock Holmes, laughing. "Only one of those whimsical little incidents which will happen when you have four million human beings all jostling each other within the space of a few square miles. Amid the action and reaction of so dense a swarm of humanity, every possible combination of events may be expected to take place, and many a little problem will be presented which may be striking and bizarre without being criminal. We have already had experience of such."

"So much so," I remarked, "that of the last six cases which I have added to my notes, three have been entirely free of any legal crime."

"Precisely. You allude to my attempt to recover the Irene Adler papers, to the singular case of Miss Mary Sutherland, and to the adventure of the man with the twisted lip. Well, I have no doubt that this small matter will fall into the same innocent category. You know Peterson, the commissionaire?"

"Yes."

"It is to him that this trophy belongs."

"It is his hat."

"No, no; he found it. Its owner is unknown. I beg that you will look upon it not as a battered billycock but as an intellectual problem. And, first, as to how it came here. It arrived upon Christmas morning, in company with a good fat goose, which is, I have no doubt, roasting at this moment in front of Peterson's fire. The facts are these: about four o'clock on Christmas morning, Peterson, who, as you know, is a very honest fellow, was returning from some small jollification and was making his way homeward down Tottenham Court Road. In front of him he saw, in the gaslight, a tallish man, walking with a slight stagger, and carrying a white goose slung over his shoulder. As he reached the corner of Goodge Street, a row broke out between this stranger and a little knot of roughs. One of the latter knocked off the man's hat, on which he raised his stick to defend himself, and swinging it over his head, smashed the shop window behind him. Peterson had rushed forward to protect the stranger from his assailants; but the man, shocked at having broken the window, and seeing an official-looking person in uniform rushing towards him, dropped his goose, took to his heels, and vanished amid the labyrinth of small streets which lie at the back of Tottenham Court Road. The roughs had also fled at the appearance of Peterson, so that he was left in possession of the field of battle, and also of the spoils of victory in the shape of this battered hat and a most unimpeachable Christmas goose."

"Which surely he restored to their owner?"

"My dear fellow, there lies the problem. It is true that 'For Mrs. Henry Baker' was printed upon a small card which was tied to the bird's left leg, and it is also true that the initials 'H.B.' are legible upon the lining of this hat; but as there are some thousands of Bakers, and some hundreds of Henry Bakers in this city of ours, it is not easy to restore lost property to any of them."

"What, then, did Peterson do?"

"He brought round both hat and goose to me on Christmas morning, knowing that even the smallest problems are of interest to me. The goose we retained until this morning, when there were signs that, in spite of the slight frost, it would be well that it should be eaten without unnecessary delay. Its finder has carried it off, therefore, to fulfil the ultimate destiny of a goose, while I continue to retain the hat of the unknown gentleman who lost his Christmas dinner."

"Did he not advertise?"

"No."

"Then, what clue could you have as to his identity?"

"Only as much as we can deduce."

"From his hat?"

"Precisely."

"But you are joking. What can you gather from this old battered felt?"

"Here is my lens. You know my methods. What can you gather yourself as to the individuality of the man who has worn this article?"

I took the tattered object in my hands and turned it over rather ruefully. It was a very ordinary black hat of the usual round shape, hard and much the worse for wear. The lining had been of red silk, but was a good deal discoloured. There was no maker's name; but, as Holmes had remarked, the initials "H.B." were scrawled upon one side. It was pierced in the brim for a hat-securer, but the elastic was missing. For the rest, it was cracked, exceedingly dusty, and spotted in several places, although there seemed to have been some attempt to hide the discoloured patches by smearing them with ink.

"I can see nothing," said I, handing it back to my friend.

"On the contrary, Watson, you can see everything. You fail, however, to reason from what you see. You are too timid in drawing your inferences."

"Then, pray tell me what it is that you can infer from this hat?"

He picked it up and gazed at it in the peculiar introspective fashion which was characteristic of him. "It is perhaps less suggestive than it might have been," he remarked, "and yet there are a few inferences which are very distinct, and a few others which represent at least a strong balance of probability. That the man was highly intellectual is of course obvious upon the face of it, and also that he was fairly well-to-do within the last three years, although he has now fallen upon evil days. He had foresight, but has less now than formerly, pointing to a moral retrogression, which, when taken with the decline of his fortunes, seems to indicate some evil influence, probably drink, at work upon him. This may account also for the obvious fact that his wife has ceased to love him."

"My dear Holmes!"

"He has, however, retained some degree of self-respect," he continued, disregarding my remonstrance. "He is a man who leads a sedentary life, goes out little, is out of training entirely, is middle-aged, has grizzled hair which he has had cut within the last few days, and which he anoints with lime-cream. These are the more patent facts which are to be deduced from his hat. Also, by the way, that it is extremely improbable that he has gas laid on in his house."

"You are certainly joking, Holmes."

"Not in the least. Is it possible that even now, when I give you these results, you are unable to see how they are attained?"

"I have no doubt that I am very stupid, but I must confess that I am unable to follow you. For example, how did you deduce that this man was intellectual?"

For answer Holmes clapped the hat upon his head. It came right over the forehead and settled upon the bridge of his nose. "It is a question of cubic capacity," said he; "a man with so large a brain must have something in it."

"The decline of his fortunes, then?"

"This hat is three years old. These flat brims curled at the edge came in then. It is a hat of the very best quality. Look at the band of ribbed silk and the excellent lining. If this man could afford to buy so expensive a hat three years ago, and has had no hat since, then he has assuredly gone down in the world."

"Well, that is clear enough, certainly. But how about the foresight and the moral retrogression?"

Sherlock Holmes laughed. "Here is the foresight," said he, putting his finger upon the little disc and loop of the hat-securer. "They are never sold upon hats. If this man ordered one, it is a sign of a certain amount of foresight, since he went out of his way to take this precaution against the wind. But since we see that he has broken the elastic and has not troubled to replace it, it is obvious that he has less foresight now than formerly, which is a distinct proof of a weakening nature. On the other hand, he has endeavored to conceal some of these stains upon the felt by daubing them with ink, which is a sign that he has not entirely lost his self-respect."

"Your reasoning is certainly plausible."

"The further points, that he is middle-aged, that his hair is grizzled, that it has been recently cut, and that he uses lime-cream, are all to be gathered from a close examination of the lower part of the lining. The lens discloses a large number of hair-ends, clean cut by the scissors of the barber. They all appear to be adhesive, and there is a distinct odour of lime-cream. This dust, you will observe, is not the gritty, gray dust of the street but the fluffy brown dust of the house, showing that it has been hung up indoors most of the time; while the marks of moisture upon the inside are proof positive that the wearer perspired very freely, and could therefore, hardly be in the best of training."

"But his wife—you said that she had ceased to love him."

"This hat has not been brushed for weeks. When I see you, my dear Watson, with a week's accumulation of dust upon your hat, and when your wife allows you to go out in such a state, I shall fear that you also have been unfortunate enough to lose your wife's affection."

"But he might be a bachelor."

"Nay, he was bringing home the goose as a peace-offering to his wife.

251

Remember the card upon the bird's leg."

"You have an answer to everything. But how on earth do you deduce that the gas is not laid on in his house?"

"One tallow stain, or even two, might come by chance; but when I see no less than five, I think that there can be little doubt that the individual must be brought into frequent contact with burning tallow—walks upstairs at night probably with his hat in one hand and a guttering candle in the other. Anyhow, he never got tallow-stains from a gas-jet. Are you satisfied?"

"Well, it is very ingenious," said I, laughing; "but since, as you said just now, there has been no crime committed, and no harm done save the loss of a goose, all this seems to be rather a waste of energy."

Sherlock Holmes had opened his mouth to reply, when the door flew open, and Peterson, the commissionaire, rushed into the apartment with flushed cheeks and the face of a man who is dazed with astonishment.

"The goose, Mr. Holmes! The goose, sir!" he gasped.

"Eh? What of it, then? Has it returned to life and flapped off through the kitchen window?" Holmes twisted himself round upon the sofa to get a fairer view of the man's excited face.

"See here, sir! See what my wife found in its crop!" He held out his hand and displayed upon the center of the palm a brilliantly scintillating blue stone, rather smaller than a bean in size, but of such purity and radiance that it twinkled like an electric point in the dark hollow of his hand.

Sherlock Holmes sat up with a whistle. "By Jove, Peterson!" said he, "this is treasure trove indeed. I suppose you know what you have got?"

"A diamond, sir? A precious stone. It cuts into glass as though it were putty."

"It's more than a precious stone. It is *the* precious stone."

"Not the Countess of Morcar's blue carbuncle!" I ejaculated.

"Precisely so. I ought to know its size and shape, seeing that I have read the advertisement about it in *The Times* every day lately. It is absolutely unique, and its value can only be conjectured, but the reward offered of one thousand pounds is certainly not within a twentieth part of the market price."

"A thousand pounds! Great Lord of mercy!" The commissionaire plumped down into a chair and stared from one to the other of us.

"That is the reward, and I have reason to know that there are sentimental considerations in the background which would induce the Countess to part with half her fortune if she could but recover the gem."

"It was lost, if I remember aright, at the Hotel Cosmopolitan," I remarked.

"Precisely so, on December 22nd, just five days ago. John Horner, a plumber, was accused of having abstracted it from the lady's jewel-case. The evidence against him was so strong that the case has been referred to the Assizes. I have some account of the matter here, I believe." He rummaged amid his newspapers, glancing over the dates, until at last he smoothed one out, doubled it over, and read the following paragraph:

"Hotel Cosmopolitan Jewel Robbery. John Horner, 26, plumber, was brought up upon the charge of having upon the 22d inst., abstracted from the jewel-case of the Countess of Morcar the valuable gem known as the blue carbuncle. James Ryder, upper-attendant at the hotel, gave his evidence to the effect that he had shown Horner up to the dressing-room of the Countess of Morcar upon the day of the robbery in order that he might solder the second bar of the grate, which was loose. He had remained with Horner some little time, but had finally been called away. On returning, he found that Horner had disappeared, that the bureau had been forced open, and that the small morocco casket in which, as it afterwards transpired, the Countess was accustomed to keep her jewel, was lying empty upon the dressing-table. Ryder instantly gave the alarm, and Horner was arrested the same evening; but the stone could not be found either upon his person or in his rooms. Catherine Cusack, maid to the Countess, deposed to having heard Ryder's cry of dismay on discovering the robbery, and to having rushed into the room, where she found matters as described by the last witness. Inspector Bradstreet, B division, gave evidence as to the arrest of Horner, who struggled frantically, and protested his innocence in the strongest terms. Evidence of a previous conviction for robbery having been given against the prisoner, the magistrate refused to deal summarily with the offence, but referred it to the Assizes. Horner, who had shown signs of intense emotion during the proceedings, fainted away at the conclusion and was carried out of the court.

"Hum! So much for the police-court," said Holmes thoughtfully, tossing aside the paper. "The question for us now to solve is the sequence of events leading from a rifled jewel-case at one end to the crop of a goose in Tottenham Court Road at the other. You see, Watson, our little deductions have suddenly assumed a much more important and less innocent aspect. Here is the stone; the stone came from the goose, and the goose came from Mr. Henry Baker, the gentleman with the bad hat and all the other characteristics with which I have bored you. So now we must set ourselves very seriously to finding this gentleman and ascertaining what part he has played in this little mystery. To do this, we must try the simplest means first, and these lie undoubtedly in an advertisement in all the evening papers. If this fails, I shall have recourse to other methods."

"What will you say?"

"Give me a pencil and that slip of paper. Now, then:

"Found at the corner of Goodge Street, a goose and a black felt hat. Mr. Henry Baker can have the same by applying at 6:30 this evening at 221B Baker Street.

That is clear and concise."

"Very. But will he see it?"

"Well, he is sure to keep an eye on the papers, since, to a poor man, the loss was a heavy one. He was clearly so scared by his mischance in breaking the window and by the approach of Peterson that he thought of nothing but flight, but since then he must have bitterly regretted the impulse which caused him to drop his bird. Then, again, the introduction of his name will cause him to see it, for everyone who knows him will direct his attention to it. Here you are, Peterson, run down to the advertising agency and have this put in the evening papers."

"In which, sir?"

"Oh, in the *Globe, Star, Pall Mall, St. James's, Evening News Standard, Echo,* and any others that occur to you."

"Very well, sir. And this stone?"

"Ah, yes, I shall keep the stone. Thank you. And, I say, Peterson, just buy a goose on your way back and leave it here with me, for we must have one to give to this gentleman in place of the one which your family is now devouring."

When the commissionaire had gone, Holmes took up the stone and held it against the light. "It's a bonny thing," said he. "Just see how it glints and sparkles. Of course it is a nucleus and focus of crime. Every good stone is. They are the devil's pet baits. In the larger and older jewels every facet may stand for a bloody deed. This stone is not yet twenty years old. It was found in the banks of the Amoy River in southern China and is remarkable in having every characteristic of the carbuncle, save that it is blue in shade instead of ruby red. In spite of its youth, it has already a sinister history. There have been two murders, a vitriol-throwing, a suicide, and several robberies brought about for the sake of this forty-grain weight of crystallized charcoal. Who would think that so pretty a toy would be a purveyor to the gallows and the prison? I'll lock it up in my strong box now and drop a line to the Countess to say that we have it."

"Do you think that this man Horner is innocent?"

"I cannot tell."

"Well, then, do you imagine that this other one, Henry Baker, had anything to do with the matter?"

"It is, I think, much more likely that Henry Baker is an absolutely innocent man, who had no idea that the bird which he was carrying was of considerably more value than if it were made of solid gold. That, however, I shall determine by a very simple test if we have an answer to our advertisement."

"And you can do nothing until then?"

"Nothing."

"In that case I shall continue my professional round. But I shall come back in the evening at the hour you have mentioned, for I should like to see the solution of so tangled a business."

"Very glad to see you. I dine at seven. There is a woodcock, I believe. By the way, in view of recent occurrences, perhaps I ought to ask Mrs. Hudson to examine its crop."

I had been delayed at a case, and it was a little after half-past six when I found myself in Baker Street once more. As I approached the house I saw a tall man in a Scotch bonnet with a coat which was buttoned up to his chin waiting outside in the bright semicircle which was thrown from the fanlight. Just as I arrived the door was opened, and we were shown up together to Holmes's room.

"Mr. Henry Baker, I believe," said he, rising from his armchair and greeting his visitor with the easy air of geniality which he could so readily assume. "Pray take this chair by the fire, Mr. Baker. It is a cold night, and I observe that your circulation is more adapted for summer than for winter. Ah, Watson, you have just come at the right time. Is that your hat, Mr. Baker?"

"Yes, sir, that is undoubtedly my hat."

He was a large man with rounded shoulders, a massive head, and a broad, intelligent face, sloping down to a pointed beard of grizzled brown. A touch of red in nose and cheeks, with a slight tremor of his extended hand, recalled Holmes's surmise as to his habits. His rusty black frock-coat was buttoned right up in front, with the collar turned up, and his lank wrists protruded from his sleeves without a sign of cuff or shirt. He spoke in a slow staccato fashion, choosing his words with care, and gave the impression generally of a man of learning and letters who had had ill-usage at the hands of fortune.

"We have retained these things for some days," said Holmes, "because we expected to see an advertisement from you giving your address. I am at a loss to know now why you did not advertise."

Our visitor gave a rather shamefaced laugh. "Shillings have not been plentiful with me as they once were," he remarked. "I had no doubt that the gang of roughs who assaulted me had carried off both my hat and the bird. I did not care to spend more money in a hopeless attempt at recovering them."

"Very naturally. By the way, about the bird, we were compelled to eat it."

"To eat it!" Our visitor half rose from his chair in his excitement.

"Yes, it would have been of no use to anyone had we not done so. But I presume that this other goose upon the sideboard, which is about the same weight and perfectly fresh, will answer your purpose equally well?"

"Oh, certainly, certainly," answered Mr. Baker with a sigh of relief.

"Of course, we still have the feathers, legs, crop, and so on of your own bird, so if you wish—"

The man burst into a hearty laugh. "They might be useful to me as relics of my adventure," said he, "but beyond that I can hardly see what use the *disjecta membra* of my late acquaintance are going to be to me. No, sir, I think that, with your permission, I will confine my attentions to the excellent bird which I perceive upon the sideboard."

Sherlock Holmes glanced sharply across at me with a slight shrug of his shoulders.

"There is your hat, then, and there your bird," said he. "By the way, would it bore you to tell me where you got the other one from? I am somewhat of a fowl fancier, and I have seldom seen a better grown goose."

"Certainly, sir," said Baker, who had risen and tucked his newly gained property under his arm. "There are a few of us who frequent the Alpha Inn, near the Museum—we are to be found in the Museum itself during the day, you understand. This year our good host, Windigate by name, instituted a goose club, by which, on consideration for some few pence every week, we were each to receive a bird at Christmas. My pence were duly paid, and the rest is familiar to you. I am much indebted to you, sir, for a Scotch bonnet is fitted neither to my years nor my gravity." With a comical pomposity of manner he bowed solemnly to both of us and strode off upon his way.

"So much for Mr. Henry Baker," said Holmes when he had closed the door behind him. "It is quite certain that he knows nothing whatever about the matter. Are you hungry, Watson?"

"Not particularly."

"Then I suggest that we turn our dinner into a supper and follow up this clue while it is still hot."

"By all means."

It was a bitter night, so we drew on our ulsters and wrapped cravats about our throats. Outside, the stars were shining coldly in a cloudless sky, and the breath of the passers-by blew out into smoke like so many pistol shots. Our footfalls rang out crisply and loudly as we swung through the doctors' quarter, Wimpole Street, Harley Street and so through Wigmore Street into Oxford Street. In a quarter of an hour we were in Bloomsbury at the Alpha

Inn, which is a small public-house at the corner of one of the streets which runs down into Holborn. Holmes pushed open the door of the private bar and ordered two glasses of beer from the ruddy-faced, white-aproned landlord.

"Your beer should be excellent if it is as good as your geese," said he.

"My geese!" The man seemed surprised.

"Yes. I was speaking only half an hour ago to Mr. Henry Baker, who was a member of your goose club."

"Ah! yes, I see. But you see, sir, them's not *our* geese."

"Indeed! Whose, then?"

"Well, I got the two dozen from a salesman in Covent Garden."

"Indeed? I know some of them. Which was it?"

"Breckinridge is his name."

"Ah! I don't know him. Well, here's your good health, landlord, and prosperity to your house. Good-night.

"Now for Mr. Breckinridge," he continued, buttoning up his coat as we came out into the frosty air. "Remember, Watson, that though we have so homely a thing as a goose at one end of this chain, we have at the other a man who will certainly get seven years' penal servitude unless we can establish his innocence. It is possible that our inquiry may but confirm his guilt; but, in any case, we have a line of investigation which has been missed by the police, and which a singular chance has placed in our hands. Let us follow it out to the bitter end. Faces to the south, then, and quick march!"

We passed across Holborn, down Endell Street, and so through a zigzag of slums to Covent Garden Market. One of the largest stalls bore the name of Breckinridge upon it, and the proprietor, a horsy-looking man, with a sharp face and trim side-whiskers, was helping a boy to put up the shutters.

"Good-evening. It's a cold night," said Holmes.

The salesman nodded and shot a questioning glance at my companion.

"Sold out of geese, I see," continued Holmes, pointing at the bare slabs of marble.

"Let you have five hundred to-morrow morning."

"That's no good."

"Well, there are some on the stall with the gas-flare."

"Ah, but I was recommended to you."

"Who by?"

"The landlord of the Alpha."

"Oh, yes; I sent him a couple of dozen."

"Fine birds they were, too. Now where did you get them from?"

To my surprise the question provoked a burst of anger from the salesman.

"Now, then, mister," said he, with his head cocked and his arms akimbo, "what are you driving at? Let's have it straight, now."

"It is straight enough. I should like to know who sold you the geese which you supplied to the Alpha."

"Well, then, I shan't tell you. So now!"

"Oh, it is a matter of no importance; but I don't know why you should be so warm over such a trifle."

"Warm! You'd be as warm, maybe, if you were as pestered as I am. When I pay good money for a good article there should be an end of the business; but it's 'Where are the geese?' and 'Who did you sell the geese to?' and 'What will you take for the geese?' One would think they were the only geese in the world, to hear the fuss that is made over them."

"Well, I have no connection with any other people who have been making inquiries," said Holmes carelessly. "If you won't tell us the bet is off, that is all. But I'm always ready to back my opinion on a matter of fowls, and I have a fiver on it that the bird I ate is country bred."

"Well, then, you've lost your fiver, for it's town bred," snapped the salesman.

"It's nothing of the kind."

"I say it is."

"I don't believe it."

"D'you think you know more about fowls than I, who have handled them ever since I was a nipper? I tell you, all those birds that went to the Alpha were town bred."

"You'll never persuade me to believe that."

"Will you bet, then?"

"It's merely taking your money, for I know that I am right. But I'll have a sovereign on with you, just to teach you not to be obstinate."

The salesman chuckled grimly. "Bring me the books, Bill," said he.

The small boy brought round a small thin volume and a great greasy-backed one, laying them out together beneath the hanging lamp.

"Now then, Mr. Cocksure," said the salesman, "I thought that I was out of geese, but before I finish you'll find that there is still one left in my shop. You see this little book?"

"Well?"

"That's the list of the folk from whom I buy. D'you see? Well, then, here on this page are the country folk, and the numbers after their names are where their accounts are in the big ledger. Now, then! You see this other page in red ink? Well, that is a list of my town suppliers. Now, look at that third name. Just read it out to me."

" 'Mrs. Oakshott, 117, Brixton Road—249,' " read Holmes.

"Quite so. Now turn that up in the ledger."

Holmes turned to the page indicated. "Here you are, 'Mrs. Oakshott, 117 Brixton Road, egg and poultry supplier.' "

"Now, then, what's the last entry?"

" 'December 22d. Twenty-four geese at 7s. 6d.' "

"Quite so. There you are. And underneath?"

" 'Sold to Mr. Windigate of the Alpha, at 12s.' "

"What have you to say now?"

Sherlock Holmes looked deeply chagrined. He drew a sovereign from his pocket and threw it down upon the slab, turning away with the air of a man whose disgust is too deep for words. A few yards off he stopped under a lamp-post and laughed in the hearty, noiseless fashion which was peculiar to him.

"When you see a man with whiskers of that cut and the 'Pink 'un' protruding out of his pocket, you can always draw him by a bet," said he. "I daresay that if I had put £100 down in front of him, that man would not have given me such complete information as was drawn from him by the idea that he was doing me on a wager. Well, Watson, we are, I fancy, nearing the end of our quest, and the only point which remains to be determined is whether we should go on to this Mrs. Oakshott tonight, or whether we should reserve it for tomorrow. It is clear from what that surly fellow said that there are others besides ourselves who are anxious about the matter, and I should—"

His remarks were suddenly cut short by a loud hubbub which broke out from the stall which we had just left. Turning round we saw a little rat-faced fellow standing in the centre of the circle of yellow light which was thrown by the swinging lamp, while Breckinridge, the salesman, framed in the door of his stall, was shaking his fists fiercely at the cringing figure.

"I've had enough of you and your geese," he shouted. "I wish you were all at the devil together. If you come pestering me any more with your silly talk I'll set the dog at you. You bring Mrs. Oakshott here and I'll answer her, but what have you to do with it? Did I buy the geese off you?"

"No; but one of them was mine all the same," whined the little man.

"Well, then, ask Mrs. Oakshott for it."

"She told me to ask you."

"Well, you can ask the King of Proosia, for all I care. I've had enough of it. Get out of this!" He rushed fiercely forward, and the inquirer flitted away into the darkness.

"Ha! this may save us a visit to Brixton Road," whispered Holmes. "Come with me, and we will see what is to be made of this fellow." Striding through the scattered knots of people who lounged round the flaring stalls, my companion speedily overtook the little man and touched him upon the shoulder. He sprang round, and I could see in the gas-light that every vestige of colour had been driven from his face.

"Who are you, then? What do you want?" he asked in a quavering voice.

"You will excuse me," said Holmes blandly, "but I could not help overhearing the questions which you put to the salesman just now. I think that I could be of assistance to you."

"You? Who are you? How could you know anything of the matter?"

"My name is Sherlock Holmes. It is my business to know what other people don't know."

"But you can know nothing of this?"

"Excuse me, I know everything of it. You are endeavoring to trace some geese which were sold by Mrs. Oakshott, of Brixton Road, to a salesman named Breckinridge, by him in turn to Mr. Windigate, of the Alpha, and by him to his club, of which Mr. Henry Baker is a member."

"Oh, sir, you are the very man whom I have longed to meet," cried the little fellow with outstretched hands and quivering fingers. "I can hardly explain to you how interested I am in this matter."

Sherlock Holmes hailed a four-wheeler which was passing. "In that case we had better discuss it in a cosy room rather than in this wind-swept marketplace," said he. "But pray tell me, before we go further, who it is that I have the pleasure of assisting."

The man hesitated for an instant. "My name is John Robinson," he answered with a sidelong glance.

"No, no; the real name," said Holmes sweetly. "It is always awkward doing business with an alias."

A flush sprang to the white cheeks of the stranger. "Well, then," said he, "my real name is James Ryder."

"Precisely so. Head attendant at the Hotel Cosmopolitan. Pray step into the cab, and I shall soon be able to tell you everything which you would wish to know."

The little man stood glancing from one to the other of us with half-frightened, half-hopeful eyes, as one who is not sure whether he is on the verge of a windfall or of a catastrophe. Then he stepped into the cab, and in half an hour we were back in the sitting-room at Baker Street. Nothing had been said during our drive, but the high, thin breathing of our new companion, and the claspings and unclaspings of his hands, spoke of the nervous tension within him.

"Here we are!" said Holmes cheerily as we filed into the room. "The fire looks very seasonable in this weather. You look cold, Mr. Ryder. Pray take the basketchair. I will just put on my slippers before we settle this little matter of yours. Now, then! You want to know what became of those geese?"

"Yes, sir."

"Or rather, I fancy, of that goose. It was one bird, I imagine, in which you were interested—white, with a black bar across the tail."

Ryder quivered with emotion. "Oh, sir," he cried, "can you tell me where it went to?"

"It came here."

"Here?"

"Yes, and a most remarkable bird it proved. I don't wonder that you should take an interest in it. It laid an egg after it was dead—the bonniest, brightest little blue egg that ever was seen. I have it here in my museum."

Our visitor staggered to his feet and clutched the mantelpiece with his right hand. Holmes unlocked his strongbox and held up the blue carbuncle, which shone out like a star, with a cold, brilliant, many-pointed radiance. Ryder stood glaring with a drawn face, uncertain whether to claim or to disown it.

"The game's up, Ryder," said Holmes quietly. "Hold up, man, or you'll be into the fire! Give him an arm back into his chair, Watson. He's not got blood enough to go in for felony with impunity. Give him a dash of brandy. So! Now he looks a little more human. What a shrimp it is, to be sure!"

For a moment he had staggered and nearly fallen, but the brandy brought a tinge of colour into his cheeks, and he sat staring with frightened eyes at his accuser.

"I have almost every link in my hands, and all the proofs which I could possibly need, so there is little which you need tell me. Still, that little may as well be cleared up to make the case complete. You had heard, Ryder, of this blue stone of the Countess of Morcar's?"

"It was Catherine Cusack who told me of it," said he in a crackling voice.

"I see—her ladyship's waiting-maid. Well, the temptation of sudden wealth so easily acquired was too much for you, as it has been for better men before you; but you were not very scrupulous in the means you used. It seems to me, Ryder, that there is the making of a very pretty villain in you. You knew that this man Horner, the plumber, had been concerned in some such matter before, and that suspicion would rest the more readily upon him. What did you do, then? You made some small job in my lady's room—you and your confederate Cusack—and you managed that he should be the man sent for. Then, when he had left, you rifled the jewel-case, raised the alarm, and had this unfortunate man arrested. You then—"

Ryder threw himself down suddenly upon the rug and clutched at my companion's knee. "For God's sake, have mercy!" he shrieked. "Think of my father! of my mother! It would break their hearts. I never went wrong before! I never will again. I swear it. I'll swear it on a Bible. Oh, don't bring it into court! For Christ's sake, don't!"

"Get back into your chair!" said Holmes sternly. "It is very well to cringe and crawl now, but you thought little enough of this poor Horner in the dock for a crime of which he knew nothing."

"I will fly, Mr. Holmes. I will leave the country, sir. Then the charge against him will break down."

"Hum! We will talk about that. And now let us hear a true account of the next act. How came the stone into the goose, and how came the goose into the open market? Tell us the truth, for there lies your only hope of safety."

Ryder passed his tongue over his parched lips. "I will tell you it just as it happened, sir," said he. "When Horner had been arrested, it seemed to me that it would be best for me to get away with the stone at once, for I did not know at what moment the police might not take it into their heads to search me and my room. There was no place about the hotel where it would be safe. I went out, as if on some commission, and I made for my sister's house. She had married a man named Oakshott, and lived in Brixton Road, where she fattened fowls for the market. All the way there every man I met seemed to me to be a policeman or a detective; and, for all that it was a cold night, the sweat was pouring down my face before I came to the Brixton Road. My sister asked me what was the matter, and why I was so pale; but I told her that I had been upset by the jewel robbery at the hotel. Then I went into the back yard and smoked a pipe, and wondered what it would be best to do.

"I had a friend once called Maudsley, who went to the bad, and has just been serving his time in Pentonville. One day he had met me, and fell into talk about the ways of thieves, and how they could get rid of what they stole. I knew that he would be true to me, for I knew one or two things about him; so I made up my mind to go right on to Kilburn, where he lived, and take him into my confidence. He would show me how to turn the stone into money. But how to get to him in safety? I thought of the agonies I had gone through in coming from the hotel. I might at any moment be seized and searched, and there would be the stone in my waistcoat pocket. I was leaning against the wall at the time and looking at the geese which were waddling about round my feet, and suddenly an idea came into my head which showed me how I could beat the best detective that ever lived.

"My sister had told me some weeks before that I might have the pick of her geese for a Christmas present, and I knew that she was always as good as her word. I would take my goose now, and in it I would carry my stone to Kilburn. There was a little shed in the yard, and behind this I drove one of the birds—a fine big one, white, with a barred tail. I caught it, and, prying its bill open, I thrust the stone down its throat as far as my finger could reach. The bird gave a gulp, and I felt the stone pass along its gullet and down into its crop. But the creature flapped and struggled, and out came my sister to know what was the matter. As I turned to speak to her the brute broke loose and fluttered off among the others.

" 'Whatever were you doing with that bird, Jem?' says she.

" 'Well,' said I, 'you said you'd give me one for Christmas, and I was feeling which was the fattest.'

" 'Oh,' says she, 'we've set yours aside for you—Jem's bird, we call it. It's the big white one over yonder. There's twenty-six of them, which makes one for you, and one for us, and two dozen for the market.'

" 'Thank you, Maggie,' says I; 'but if it is all the same to you, I'd rather have that one I was handling just now.'

" 'The other is a good three pound heavier,' said she, 'and we fattened it expressly for you.'

" 'Never mind. I'll have the other, and I'll take it now,' said I.

" 'Oh, just as you like,' said she, a little huffed. 'Which is it you want, then?'

" 'That white one with the barred tail, right in the middle of the flock.'

" 'Oh, very well. Kill it and take it with you.'

"Well, I did what she said, Mr. Holmes, and I carried the bird all the way to Kilburn. I told my pal what I had done, for he was a man that it was easy to tell a thing like that to. He laughed until he choked, and we got a knife and opened the goose. My heart turned to water, for there was no sign of the stone, and I knew that some terrible mistake had occurred. I left the bird, rushed back to my sister's, and hurried into the back yard. There was not a bird to be seen there.

" 'Where are they all, Maggie?' I cried.

" 'Gone to the dealer's, Jem.'

" 'Which dealer's?'

" 'Breckinridge, of Covent Garden.'

" 'But was there another with a barred tail?' I asked, 'the same as the one I chose?'

" 'Yes, Jem; there were two barred-tailed ones, and I could never tell them apart.'

"Well, then, of course I saw it all, and I ran off as hard as my feet would carry me to this man Breckinridge; but he had sold the lot at once, and not one word would he tell me as to where they had gone. You heard him yourselves tonight. Well, he has always answered me like that. My sister thinks that I am going mad. Sometimes I think that I am myself. And now—and now I am myself a branded thief, without ever having touched the wealth for which I sold my character. God help me! God help me!" He burst into convulsive sobbing, with his face buried in his hands.

There was a long silence, broken only by his heavy breathing, and by

263

the measured tapping of Sherlock Holmes's finger-tips upon the edge of the table. Then my friend rose and threw open the door.

"Get out!" said he.

"What, sir! Oh, Heaven bless you!"

"No more words. Get out!"

And no more words were needed. There was a rush, a clatter upon the stairs, the bang of a door, and the crisp rattle of running footfalls from the street.

"After all, Watson," said Holmes, reaching up his hand for his clay pipe, "I am not retained by the police to supply their deficiencies. If Horner were in danger it would be another thing; but this fellow will not appear against him, and the case must collapse. I suppose that I am commuting a felony, but it is just possible that I am saving a soul. This fellow will not go wrong again; he is too terribly frightened. Send him to jail now, and you make him a jail-bird for life. Besides, it is the season of forgiveness. Chance has put in our way a most singular and whimsical problem, and its solution is its own reward. If you will have the goodness to touch the bell, Doctor, we will begin another investigation, in which, also, a bird will be the chief feature."

Ennis Duling

THE EMBEZZLER'S CHRISTMAS PRESENT

Entire mornings could pass at the First National Bank without anyone speaking to Herb Cubbey about anything that wasn't business. Checks were cashed, and money was entered in personal accounts at the window where Herb worked. Customers were rewarded with a nod and a barely audible thank you. At the end of the day his records were always in perfect order.

Twenty-five-year-old Sue Rigney, who worked two windows away, thought that Herb moved around the bank as if he were a frightened herbivore (she liked the pun) in a jungle of meateaters. He might have blended into a paneled wall, his brown bow tie and the pattern of his remaining hair serving as protective coloration. Like a mouse at the cat's water dish, he poured water for tea, allowed it to steep weakly, and then darted away, leaving only the spore of the tea bag. Sue noticed that he used a tea bag more than once.

Sue had heard the other tellers and the secretaries discussing Herb's personal life. He spent his evenings at home with his widowed mother, and that was the sum of his life. Probably he kept a goldfish, watched the same television shows each week, and made his mother breakfast in bed on Sundays.

The secretaries made occasional jokes about Herb's saintly mother, but he was such little game that they usually found other targets such as the newly appointed assistant manager, Edward Bridgewright, who at thirty-three was exactly Herb's age. In fact, they had both entered the bank's employ at the same time, and while Herb remained at his original position, Bridgewright had risen to better things.

One morning before opening, a group of secretaries and tellers gathered near the coffee machine and talked about the Christmas presents they were giving their boyfriends and husbands. When Herb appeared, Sue, who at the moment had no boyfriend and wanted to keep the fact a secret, said, "What are you giving your mother for Christmas, Herb?"

Herb squeezed his tea bag between two spoons. "I really shouldn't say."

"Aw, come on, Herb," Dot Levin said. After twenty years at the bank, she liked to play mother to the younger employees. "Your mother is such a wonderful woman." Sue wished she hadn't said anything.

"I know I shouldn't tell you this," Herb said, "but I'm giving her ten thousand dollars." The water in his cup had turned a light amber. "Merry Christmas to you all." He looked down at his cup as he balanced it in retreat.

"Did he say ten thousand?" Dot asked.

"Where would the little man get that kind of money?" said Jan Washington, a strikingly beautiful black woman.

At that moment Mr. Bridgewright stepped out of the elevator and marched toward the conversation. "Girls, girls, girls, this is no time to stand around and talk. Back to work!"

"This is my break time, Mr. Bridgewright," Sue said.

He gave her one of his sincere smiles, the type she always saw before he asked her for a date.

"And Herb Cubbey has lots of money," Paula Kimble said.

"No, he doesn't. Work!"

Sue slipped away with the rest of them.

In the parking lot after closing, Herb's money was again the topic of conversation. "Maybe the man lied," Jan suggested.

"No!" Sue insisted. She thought that Herb deserved his privacy as much as anyone. She hated it when the others started to pry into her life.

"Herbert has never told a lie since he was born," Paula said. "He's afraid his mommy might slap his hand."

"Then he inherited it," Sue said.

John Franks from the trust department said, "I drove him home two years ago during the bus strike. He lives over in Bultman Village. You know those little bungalows built back in the Roaring Twenties. They looked better then, I imagine. He asked me in, and the old lady served me tea and biscuits. She looked like she was posing for a painting with her knitting. She kept telling me how hard it was to make ends meet and how her husband had been a wonderful man but didn't have a head for money. No, Herb didn't have any money then."

"A rich uncle," Sue said.

"A man like that with no idea in the world of how to spend money would be lucky enough to have an uncle leave him a bundle," Dot said.

"Worry not, ladies," John said. "I see Herb coming now. I'll just ask him."

As Herb walked by, he touched his hat. John said, "Sorry to hear about your relative dying like that, Mr. Cubbey. Your uncle, wasn't it?"

Herb glanced down. "You must be mistaken, Mr. Franks. My family has excellent health, except for my father, of course, and that was years ago. Good night all."

John watched him until he was out of sight and then he said, "He's a sly one. If he inherited the money, he's not telling."

"He seems to be a very private sort of person," Sue said.

"He has responsibilities," Jan said.

"He's not shy; he's just a Scrooge," Paula said.

"Goes home and counts it at night," Jan agreed. "Won't let anyone get any use out of it except his mother and what's she need with the cash?"

"Maybe he just saved that much and decided to give it to his mother," Sue suggested.

The next morning John steered Sue into Mr. Bridgewright's office. "Ed, I just want you to know how poorly trained your employee is," he said grinning.

"What?" Mr. Bridgewright gave his supervisor's frown.

"I was trying to explain to Susie here that Herb Cubbey could no more save up enough money to give his mom ten thousand dollars than I could convince the trust department to play the ponies. Now I don't want you giving away any state secrets, but let us put down a round figure for Herb's salary." He switched on a calculator and pushed Sue in front. "Look about right, Ed? Now let's subtract food and clothing for two, house maintenance, and taxes. We can multiply the small remainder by fifty-two weeks in a year. He could save that much, but the canary would have to go hungry. Women just don't have a head for money. That's one of the things that's so charming about them."

She twisted out of John's grasp and hurried to the door. "Maybe he made it on Wall Street!"

There was a long silence. "Maybe he did," Mr. Bridgewright said.

"Several hundred thousand," John added with awe in his voice.

At the coffee machine that noon Paula touched Herb's arm. "Would you be willing to give a poor girl like me a little advice, Herb?"

"I beg your pardon?"

"Advice. You know—good ideas from your storehouse of wisdom."

"Certainly," he said doubtfully.

"What percent of a portfolio should a small investor have in stocks?"

Herb backed away as if she had been making demands on him in a foreign language. "I don't understand."

By Christmas Eve most people had concluded that there had been a misunderstanding. Dot said that Herb was probably giving his mother "ten towels and a dollar."

"Weird present!" Jan said.

"But he can afford it," Dot said.

But Paula, who wouldn't let go, cornered him by the drinking fountain. "Is your mother's present all ready, Herb?" she said.

"All but the signature."

"Won't she be surprised by such a large sum of money?"

"Oh, I don't think so. She's used to it." And then Herb smiled. Nobody had seen him really smile before, but they were sure it made him look roguish.

So as Christmas passed, Sue noticed that people's attitude toward Herb had begun to change. His fearful movements around the bank were clear signs of the secretiveness that had made him his money. His near baldness reminded them of the complete baldness of a TV star. His bow tie was like that of a famous lawyer who had been in the news. His tea drinking was a sign of international tastes.

"How are you doing today, Herb honey?" Paula said each morning.

Jan put forward the theory that Herb was a gambler. "He couldn't admit to it and still work in a bank, could he?"

Once Sue met Herb by the candy machine in the basement. "I'm sorry for how the others are treating you," she said. "I feel like I started all this."

"I don't mind really, Sue, although I don't understand a lot that they say to me. John asked me today what I thought of a copper kettle in the third. I don't know anything about kettles."

"I wish I could make it up to you in some way," she said. "Maybe dinner. How about New Year's?" Then she realized that she was doing exactly what she was apologizing for.

"I appreciate the offer, but I'll have to check with my mother. She usually has some friends over, and she might need me." He had a surprised, cornered look on his face.

Sue wasn't sure she wanted to go out with Herb—she was certain she wasn't going to mention the possibility to anyone—but he was kind and polite, characteristics that made him a good deal more attractive than John Franks or Mr. Bridgewright.

Instead of the gambler's image fading, it grew, along with that of the Wizard of Wall Street and the fortunate heir. Only Mr. Bridgewright scoffed at the entire question. Later Sue figured that he would have continued to pay no attention if it hadn't been for her.

"I just want to give you one last opportunity to go out with me on New Year's, Susie," he said after calling her into his office.

"No, thank you. I have a date already." And then before she could clamp her mouth shut, she said, "With Herb!"

The word got around the bank fast. Paula said that Herb might not be much to look at and that his mother might be a millstone, but money made up for a lot of faults.

"We never took you for the greedy type," Dot teased.

"I'm not going out with him for his money."

"With a man like him, what else is there?" Paula said.

"I kind of feel sorry for him."

"You'll feel sorry for him all right when he starts giving you diamonds."

For the next two days, Sue noticed Mr. Bridgewright standing at the door to his office watching Herb. When Herb left his window for the men's room, Bridgewright would make a mark in a notebook. Jan noticed, too. "The man goes to the john more than anyone I've ever seen."

John whispered the conclusion first: "Embezzlement!"

"What an awful thing to say," Sue said.

"First thing you know he'll figure out a way to steal thousands at once, and he'll be off to South America," Paula said.

John laughed. "I can just picture him in a hotel room in Rio wishing he could understand what they were saying on TV."

"Are you serious?" Sue demanded.

"Bridgewright is," John said.

"He can't be."

"I expect the examiners to swoop down at any moment."

The next afternoon, December 31st, Bridgewright stepped over to Herb's cash drawer at the end of the day. "We're going to have someone else check your drawer tonight, Mr. Cubbey," he said. A grim-faced young man in a gray suit stood at his elbow.

"Certainly," Herb said in a voice filled with surprise.

"And Mr. Hamilton wants to see you in his office immediately." Mr. Hamilton was the bank president.

"Yes, sir." Herb walked a few steps away and stood looking out the plate glass window at the bustle on Main Street. Sue could see his shoulders slump in defeat.

Mr. Bridgewright came over to her. "Well, Miss Rigney, we're going to be at the bottom of the Herbert Cubbey case soon enough. Mr. Hamilton has been informed. We've played games far too long."

"I don't think Herb even knows what game we're playing," Sue said.

She went to where Herb stood and squeezed his arm. "Whatever happens, Herb, I know you're innocent."

"Am I in some sort of trouble?" He seemed terribly afraid, and she wanted to mother him.

"They say you stole the money."

"What money?"

"The ten thousand dollars you gave your mother for Christmas."

He swallowed hard. "You didn't really think I had all that money?"

"You said you did."

"If I did have that much, I'd take you out on New Year's to the best restaurant in town. You'd have flowers, and we'd drink champagne and dance all night."

"It doesn't take that much money to have a good time," Sue said. "I already lied and told Mr. Bridgewright we were going out."

"All right then," he said, straightening his shoulders. "We'll make some plans when we get back from talking to Mr. Hamilton. Will you come along with me?"

Sue followed him to the elevator.

"Could I have the opportunity to explain?" Herb said to President Hamilton.

"I expect you'd like one, Cubbey," Hamilton said. He was a short, heavy man with bushy eyebrows. "You should anyway! I'm an old man, so I don't need to be subtle. No time for it. So let's hear it. Bridgewright tells me you've been giving away thousands of dollars and the only explanation is you've got your hand in the till."

"I've honestly accounted for every cent that I've handled."

"Thought so. What about the gift?"

"I wrote my mother a check for ten thousand dollars at Christmas. I never should have told anyone."

"How's that again?"

"We haven't had much since my father passed away, so we pretend. Every year we write each other large checks. This year she gave me a check for two thousand. The year before I wrote one for five thousand, and she gave me one for eight thousand. *Checks* that is. We sit around and talk about what we'd like to buy until midnight, and then we burn the checks in the fireplace. We've always had a good time doing it. It must sound strange to outsiders."

Mr. Hamilton chuckled. "It's unusual, that's for sure, but not a bad idea. You get the pleasure of the money without the cost, which is not bad management at all. Not bad at all. Shows a good deal more sense than Mr. Bridgewright just exhibited."

"Do you have any further questions, sir?"

"Why hasn't an honest, imaginative young man like you received a promotion recently? Who's running this bank anyway? That's what I'd like to know."

Ron Goulart

BELIEVING IN SANTA

As it turned out, he didn't get a chance to murder anybody. He did make an impressive comeback, revitalizing his faltering career and saying goodbye to most of his financial worries. But in spite of all that, there are times when Oscar Sayler feels sad about not having been able to knock off his former wife.

Twenty-five years ago Oscar had been loved by millions of children. Well, actually, they adored his dummy, Screwy Santa, but they tolerated Oscar. For several seasons his early morning kid show was the most popular in the country, outpulling Captain Kangaroo and all the other competition. Multitudes of kids, and their parents, doted on Oscar's comic version of Santa Claus and tried to live by the show's perennial closing line—"Gang, try to act like it was Christmas every day!"

For the past decade and more, though, Oscar hadn't been doing all that well. In early December of last year, when he got the fateful phone call from the New York talent agency, he was scraping by on the $25,000 a year he earned from the one commercial voice job he'd been able to come up with lately. Oscar lived alone in a one-bedroom condo in a never-finished complex in New Beckford, Connecticut. He was fifty-five—well, fifty-seven actually—and he didn't look all that awful.

Since he'd given up drinking, his face was no longer especially puffy and it had lost that lobsterish tinge. His hair, which was nearly all his own, still had a nice luster to it. There was, really, no reason why he couldn't appear on television again.

When the agent called him at a few minutes after four P.M. on a bleak, chill Monday afternoon, Oscar was flat on his back in his small tan living room. He'd vowed to complete two dozen situps every day.

He crawled over to the phone on the coffee table. "Hello?"

"Is your son there?"

Oscar pulled himself up onto the sofa arm, resting the phone on his knees. "Don't have a son. My daughter, however, is the noted television actress Tish Sale, who stars in the *Intensive Care* soap opera, and hasn't set foot across dear old Dad's threshold for three, possibly four—"

"Spare me," requested the youthful, nasal voice. "You must be Oscar Sayler then. You sounded so old that I mistook you for your father."

"Nope, my dad sounded like this—'How about a little nip after dinner, my boy?' Much more throaty and with a quaver. Who the hell are you, by the way?"

"Vince Mxyzptlk. I'm with Mimi Warnicker & Associates, the crackerjack talent agency."

"Oops." Oscar sat on a cushion and straightened up. "That's a powerful outfit."

"You bet your ass it is," agreed the young agent. "You're not represented at the moment, are you?"

"No, because I find I can get all the acting jobs I want without—"

"C'mon, Oscar, old buddy, you ain't exactly rolling in work right now," cut in Vince disdainfully. "In fact, your only gig is doing the voice of the infected toe in those godawful Dr. Frankel's Foot Balm radio spots." He made a scornful noise.

"I do a very convincing itching toe, Vince. Fact is, there's talk of—"

"Listen, I can get you tons of work. Talk shows, commercials, lectures, TV parts, eventually some plum movie work. But first you—"

"How exactly are—"

"But first you have got to win your way back into the hearts and minds of the public."

"Just how do I accomplish that, Vince?"

"You just have to sit there with that lamebrained dummy on your knee."

"Screwy Santa? Hell, nobody's been interested in him for years."

"Let me do the talking for a bit, okay? Here's what's under way," continued the agent. *"Have a Good Day, USA!*, which has just become the top morning talk and news show, is planning a six-minute nostalgia segment for this Friday. The theme is 'Whatever happened to our favorite kids' shows?' Something they calculate'll have a tremendous appeal for the Boomers and Busters who make up their pea-brained audience. So far they've signed that old duffer who used to be Captain Buckeroo and—"

"Kangaroo."

"Oscar, are you more interested in heckling me than in making an impressive comeback? Would you prefer to go on living in squalor in that rural crackerbox, to voice tripe for Dr. Frankel throughout the few remaining years of your shabby life?"

"Okay, but his name is Captain Kangaroo, not—"

"Attend to me, Oscar. I assured Liz, who's putting this segment together, that I'd dig you up, wipe off the cobwebs, and have you there bright and early Friday. Can you drag yourself into Manhattan and meet me at the Consolidated Broadcasting headquarters building on Fifty-third no later than six A.M.?"

"Sure, that's no problem."

"Most importantly, can you bring that dimwitted dummy?"

Without more than a fraction of a second of hesitation Oscar answered, "Of course, yeah, absolutely." It didn't seem the right time to tell Mxyzptlk that his former wife, who currently loathed him and had ousted him eleven long years ago from the mansion they once shared, had retained custody of the only existing Screwy Santa dummy in the world. "We'll both see you on Friday, Vince."

It commenced snowing at dusk, a paltry, low-budget snow that didn't look as though it was up to blanketing the condo-complex grounds and masking its raw ugliness.

Glancing at his wristwatch once more, Oscar punched out his daughter's New York City number.

After four rings there came a twanging noise. "Merry Christmas," said Tish in her sexiest voice. "I'm not able to come to the phone right now, but if you'll leave your name and number, I'll get back to you real soon."

Oscar had been working all afternoon on the voice he was going to use. A mixture of paternal warmth and serious illness. "Patricia, my dear," he began, getting the quaver just about perfect, "this is your dad. Something quite serious has come up and I'd like very much to speak to you, my only child, in the hope that—"

"Holy Jesus," observed his daughter, coming onto the line. "What was that old television show you used to tell me about when I was little? Where they gave the contestants the gong for a rotten perf—"

"*The Amateur Hour.* Now, kid, I need—"

"Consider yourself gonged, Pop."

"Okay, all right, I overdid it a mite," he admitted. "Yet I do have a serious problem."

"My time is sort of limited, Dad. I'm getting ready for a date. You should've phoned me earlier."

"I assumed you were taping *Intensive Care.*"

She sighed. "Didn't you tell me you watched my soap faithfully?"

"I do, kid. It's on my must-see list every day."

"I've been in a coma for two weeks. So I don't have to show up at—"

"Sorry to hear that. Anything serious?"

"Near-fatal car crash. We killed that asshole, Walt Truett, thank God."

"But you'll survive?"

"Sure, with only a touch of amnesia."

Oscar asked, "When are you due to come out of your stupor?"

"Next Thursday."

"I'll start watching, I swear," he promised his daughter. "Now, as to the purpose of this call."

"It's Mom, isn't it?"

"Well, not exactly, kid." He filled her in about the offer from the talent agency and the upcoming appearance on *Have a Good Day, USA!* "This will revive my career."

"You think so? A couple of early morning minutes with a pack of over-the-hill doofers?"

"It's a shot. The only snag is—well, kid, they insist that I bring Screwy along."

"Obviously. You guys are a team."

"And your dear mother has custody of him."

Tish said, "She's not going to loan him to you."

"She might, if you were to—"

"Nope, she won't. A few months ago, when I noticed him up on a shelf in the mud room, I suggested that—"

"She keeps the most beloved dummy in America in the mud room?"

"In a shoe box," she answered. "And, Dad, Screwy Santa hasn't been beloved for a couple of decades now. "

"I know, neither have I," he said ruefully. "But, damn it, he helped pay for that mansion."

"Her romantic novels are paying for things now. Did you notice that *Kiss Me, My Pirate* was number two on the *Times*—"

"I extract the book section from the Sunday paper with surgical gloves and toss it immediately into the trash unopened. To make certain I never see so much as a mention of that slop she cranks out or, worse, a publicity photo of her mottled countenance."

"Let's get back to the point. I suggested to her back then that she return Screwy Santa to you."

"And?"

"You don't want to hear what she said," his daughter assured him. "It had, among other things, to do with Hell freezing over. But can't you dig up another dummy by Friday?"

"Impossible, that's the only one extant. We lost the backup copy during that ill-fated nostalgia tour through the Midwest years ago."

"Couldn't you carve another, since you built the others?"

"Kid, I may've fudged the truth a bit when I used to recount Screwy's history to you," he said. "In reality, the dummies were built by a prop man at the old WWAG-TV studios. And he, alas, is long in his grave."

"This is very disillusioning," Tish complained. "One of the few things I still admired about you, Dad, was your woodcarving ability."

"Listen, couldn't you call Mitzi and tell her that I'm expiring, that I want to be reunited with my dummy for one last time before I go on to glory?"

"She'd burst out laughing if I told her you were about to kick off, Dad. And probably dance a little jig."

"Okay, suppose we make a business deal with her? Offer the old shrew, say, fifteen percent of the take. "

"What take? *Have a Good Day, USA!* pays scale. I know, I did one last year to plug my abortion on *Intensive Care*."

"You looked terrific on that broadcast."

"You didn't even see it."

"Didn't I?"

"No, and you admitted as much at the time."

"Well, back to my immediate problem."

"Why don't you use one of the old Screwy Santa dolls? They look a lot like the dummy."

"Except they don't have movable mouths."

"It'd be better than nothing. I can loan you mine," she offered. "It's stuffed away in a closet."

"No, kid, I really have to have the real dummy."

"Afraid there's nothing I can do. I mean, if I so much as mention that you need Screwy Santa, Mom's liable to take an axe to him."

"Well, thanks anyway for listening to an old man's woes and—"

"Here comes the gong again," his daughter said. "Anyhow, I have to go put on some clothes. Bye."

After hanging up, he stayed on the sofa and brooded. After about ten minutes he said aloud, "I'll have to outwit Mitzi."

The snow improved the next morning, giving a Christmas-card gloss to the usually dismal view from his small living room window.

At ten A.M. he put the first phase of his latest plan into operation. He phoned his former wife's mansion over in Westport.

"Residence of Mitzi Sunsett Sayler," answered a crisp female voice.

"Yes, how are you?" inquired Oscar in a drawling, slightly British accent. "Ogden Brokenshire here."

"Yes?"

"Ogden Brokenshire of the Broadcasting Hall of Fame. Have I the honor of addressing the esteemed novelist Mitzi Sunsett Sayler herself?"

"Of course not, Mr. Brokenshire. I'm Clarissa Dempster, Mrs. Sayler's secretary."

"I see, my dear. Well, perhaps I can explain my mission to you, child, and you can explain the situation to your employer."

"That depends on—"

"We would like to enshrine Screwy Santa."

"Enshrine whom?"

"The ingenious dummy that Mrs. Sayler's one-time husband used in the days when he brought joy and gladness to the hearts of—"

"Oh, that thing," said the secretary. "My parents, wisely, never allowed me to watch that dreadful show when I was a child."

"Nonetheless, dear child, our board has voted, unanimously I might add, to place Screwy Santa on permanent display in the museum."

"Hold on a moment. I'll speak to Mrs. Sayler." The secretary went away.

In less than two minutes Mitzi started talking. "Who is this ?"

"Good morning, I'm Ogden Brokenshire. As I was explaining to your able secretary, my dear Mrs. Sayler, I'm an executive with the Broadcasting Hall of—"

"You haven't improved at all, you no-talent cheesehead."

"I beg your pardon, madam?"

"Oscar, love, you never could do a believable Brit."

"I don't happen to be British, dear lady. The fact that I was educated in Boston sometimes gives people that impression."

"Forget it, Oscar," advised his erstwhile wife. "I don't know why you want to get your clammy hands on that wooden dornick, but you'll never have him. And, dear heart, if you ever try to communicate with me again—in whatever wretched voice—I'll sic the law on you." She, rather gently, hung up on him.

"Looks like," decided Oscar, "I'm going to need a new plan."

He kept working on plans for nearly an hour, pacing his small living room, muttering, pausing now and then to gaze out at the falling snow.

Then the phone rang.

"Yeah?"

"We have hit a slight snag," announced Vince Mxyzptlk.

"Don't they want me?"

"Sure they want you, old buddy. Hell, they're prowling the lofty corridors at Consolidated crying out for you," said the youthful agent. "In fact, they can't wait until Friday."

"What do you mean—do they want me to do a separate segment on my own?"

"Not exactly. But Liz, *and* her boss, are very anxious to see you tomorrow."

Frowning, Oscar nodded. "An audition, huh?"

"Sort of, yeah," admitted the agent. "It has nothing, really, to do with you. But when one of their scouts unearthed the clunk who used to be Mr. Slimjim on that *Mr. Slimjim & Baby Gumdrop* turkey, he turned out to weigh three hundred pounds now and possess not a single tooth. So, as you can understand, Oscar, they want to see and hear all these wonderful stars of yesteryear in advance."

"Tomorrow?"

"At three P.M. Is that a problem for you?"

"Not exactly, but I—"

"I'm getting a lot of interest in you. Once you do well on Friday, the jobs will start rolling in."

"I understand, it's only—"

"I needn't remind you, Oscar, that a lot of talents in your present position would kill for this opportunity."

"You're absolutely right," he agreed. "See you tomorrow ."

He had a great new plan worked out by three that afternoon. But he had to wait until after dark to get going on it.

Dressed in dark clothes, Oscar slipped quietly out of his apartment and into the lean-to that passed for a garage. As usual, none of the roads in the sparsely inhabited complex had been plowed. The snow was soft, though, and not too high, and Oscar was able to drive down to the plowed lanes and byways of New Beckford without any serious delays.

He drove over to nearby Westport and parked in the lot behind Borneo's. There were only a few spaces left and he could see that the restaurant-bar was packed with people. The food and drink at Borneo's was just passable, but it sat only a half mile over the hill from Mitzi's mansion.

As he was crossing the lot a fire engine went hooting by, headed downhill.

Borneo himself was behind the bar. "Evening, Oscar."

He managed to elbow his way up to a narrow spot at the ebony bar. "The usual."

Borneo scratched at his stomach through the fabric of his bright tropical shirt. "Refresh my memory."

"Club soda, alas."

"Coming up."

Outside in the snowy night another fire engine went roaring by, followed by what sounded like a couple of police cars.

Oscar hoped all this activity wouldn't foul up his plan. So far everything was going well. People were seeing him, he was establishing an alibi. In another ten or fifteen minutes he'd go back to the john. Then he'd slip out the side door.

Once in the open, he'd make his way down to the mansion. Being careful, of course, that no one noticed him sneaking off.

Mitzi, being a skinflint, and in spite of her great wealth, had never bothered to put in a new alarm system. The original setup was still in place, and he knew how to disarm that.

Okay, once he got inside, after making certain that she was alone, he'd . . . well, he'd use the length of pipe he dug up in the garage this afternoon.

Once Mitzi was dead and done for, he'd gather up enough jewels and valuables to make it look like the usual burglary. Then he'd rescue Screwy Santa from the mud room and get the hell away.

Back here at the parking lot he'd stash the loot in his car, slip unobtrusively back into the place, and tell Borneo he'd had a sudden touch of stomach flu and had to stay back in the bathroom a few minutes.

It wasn't exactly foolproof, but it ought to work. He'd own Screwy again and Mitzi would be gone from his life.

He chuckled at the thought. Yeah, the idea of killing her off had come to him this afternoon and he'd taken to it immediately.

Tish might be a little suspicious about how he came by the dummy. He'd tell her something along the lines that he'd found the heirs of the old defunct prop man at the last minute and, gosh, they had a spare Screwy Santa. He'd always been a gifted liar and conning his daughter wouldn't be all that difficult.

"Don't worry about that now," he told himself.

"How's that?" inquired Borneo, setting a glass of sparkling water down in front of him.

"Nothing, I was just—"

"That must be some fire." Borneo paused to listen as yet another truck went howling by out in the night.

Oscar sipped the club soda, drumming the fingers of his free hand on the dark bar top. He'd make his move in about five minutes.

The phone behind the bar rang and Borneo caught it up. "Borneo's. Huh? Channel eight? Okay." Hanging up, he switched channels on the large television set mounted above the mirror.

And there was Mitzi, glowering out of the screen. Wearing a fuzzy bathrobe and not enough makeup, she was being interviewed by a slim black newswoman and gesturing at the mansion that was blazing behind her up across the wide night lawn.

"Good God," muttered Oscar.

"That's just downhill from us," observed Borneo.

"Yeah, I know."

The entire sprawling house was going up in flames.

"What exactly happened, Mrs. Sayler?" the reporter asked her.

"It was that goddamn cheesehead."

"Which cheesehead would that be?"

"Screwy Santa, that abominable dummy."

"I'm not certain that I quite under—"

"Aw, you're too damn young. Everybody is these days. I always knew that dornick would do me in eventually."

"You mean this was arson?"

"I mean, dear heart, that I decided to cremate that loathsome lump of wood. I took him and his shoebox, carried them into the living room, and tossed him into the fireplace."

Oscar pressed both hands to his chest. "There goes my comeback."

Mitzi continued, "Then . . . I don't know. His stupid beard seemed to explode . . . flames came shooting out of the fireplace. They hit the drapes and those caught fire . . . then the damn furniture started to go." She shook her head angrily. "Now the whole shebang is ablaze." Looking directly into the camera, she added, "If you're out there watching, Oscar . . ." She gave him the finger.

Borneo raised his shaggy eyebrows high. "Hey, is she talking to you, Oscar?"

"I'm not in the mood for conversation just now." Abandoning his club soda, he walked out into the night.

His daughter phoned a few minutes shy of midnight. "I didn't want you to worry."

"I'm way beyond worry, kid."

"When I caught the report about Mom's mansion on the news, I figured you'd assume that Screwy Santa was gone."

"Certainly I assumed that. There was Mitzi, fatter than ever, hollering for all the world to hear that my poor hapless creation was the cause of the whole blinking conflagration."

"It was a ringer, Dad."

"Eh?"

"I dropped by to visit Mom this afternoon and when she went away to yell at Clarissa, I substituted my old Screwy Santa doll for your dummy," explained Tish. "In a way, I may be responsible for that dreadful fire. The doll's a lot more flammable than—"

"No, there was some parent flap at the time, but we proved beyond a doubt that the dolls were perfectly safe if—"

"I have your dummy here in my apartment."

"You've really got Screwy?"

"Yes, he's sitting on my bed right this minute," she assured her father. "It's lucky I went out there when I did and saved him before Mom got going on her plan to destroy the little guy. Why did you go and telephone her and make it crystal clear that you were in desperate need of him? That was dippy, since it inspired her to destroy him."

"I didn't call her as myself. But somehow she penetrated my—"

"That's because, trust me, you do a terrible British voice. When do you need him?"

"Tomorrow."

"I thought you weren't doing the show until Friday."

"Well, and keep this to yourself, kid, there's a possibility they'll devote a separate seg all to me."

"That would be great."

"So can I pick him up tomorrow?"

"Sure, come by around one and I'll take you to lunch."

"Can't make lunch, because I have some people to see while I'm in the Apple. But I'll pop in, give you a paternal hug, and grab Screwy Santa," he said. "Thanks. You're a perfect daughter."

"Perfect for you, I guess. Bye."

Everything worked out well for Oscar. He did, in fact, do a segment of his own, which ran nearly four minutes, on *Have a Good Day, USA!* And Vince Mxyzptlk was able to get him an impressive batch of other jobs. At the moment there's also the possibility of a new kid show for Oscar and Screwy Santa on cable.

Oscar was able to leave his forlorn condo for a three-bedroom colonial in Brimstone, Connecticut, last month.

While he was packing, he came across the length of pipe he'd intended to use on Mitzi. He slapped it across the palm of his hand a few times, and, sighing, tossed it into a carton.

Peter Lovesey

PASS THE PARCEL

The roads were treacherous on Christmas Day and Andy and Gemma took longer than they expected to drive the twenty-five miles to Stowmarket. While Gemma concentrated on keeping the car from skidding, Andy complained about the party in prospect. "You and I must be crazy doing this. I mean, what are we putting our lives at risk for? Infantile games that your sister insists on playing simply because in her tiny mind that's the only permissible way of celebrating. The food isn't anything special. If Pauline produces those enormous cheese straws with red streaks like varicose veins, I'll throw up. I promise you. All over the chocolate log."

Gemma said, "We're not going for the food."

"The games?"

"The family."

"Your brother Reg, you mean? The insufferable Reg? I can't wait to applaud his latest stunt. What's he planning for this year, would you say? A stripogram? Or a police raid? He's a real bunch of laughs, is Reg."

Gemma negotiated a sharp bend and said, "Will you shut up about Reg? There are others in my family."

"Of course. There's Geoff. He'll be sitting in the most comfortable chair and speaking to nobody."

"Give it a rest, will you?" Gemma said through her teeth.

"I'd like to. They're showing *Apocalypse Now* on BBC2. I'd like to be giving it a rest in front of the telly with a large brandy in my fist."

Andy's grumbling may have been badly timed, but it was not unreasonable. Any fair-minded person would have viewed Christmas with this particular set of in-laws as an infliction. There were four in the current generation of Weavers, all in their thirties now, the sisters Gemma and Pauline and the brothers Reg and Geoff. Pauline, the hostess, eight years Gemma's junior, was divorced. She would have been devastated if the family had spent Christmas anywhere else but in Chestnut Lodge, the mansion she had occupied with her former husband and kept as her share of the settlement. No one risked devastating Pauline. As the youngest, she demanded and received everybody's cooperation.

"I could endure the food if it wasn't for the games," Andy started up again. "Why do we put up with them? Why not something intelligent instead of charades and—God help us—pass the parcel? I know, you're going to tell me it's a tradition in the family, but we don't have to be lumbered with traditions forevermore just because sweet little Pauline likes playing the games she did when she was a kid. She's thirty-one now, for Christ's sake. Does she sleep with a teddy bear?"

When they reached Stowmarket and swung left, Andy decently dipped into his reserve of bonhomie. "They probably dread it as much as we do, poor sods. Let's do our best to be convivial. You did bring the brandy?"

"On the backseat with the presents," said Gemma.

Chestnut Lodge had been built about 1840 for a surgeon. Not much had been done to the exterior since. The stonework wanted cleaning and there were weeds growing through the gravel drive.

Someone had left a parcel the size of a shoebox on the doorstep. Andy picked it up and carried it in with their presents.

"So sorry, darling," Gemma told Pauline. "The roads were like a rink in places. Are we the last?"

"No, Reg isn't here yet."

"Wanting to make the usual grand entrance?"

"Probably."

"You're wearing your pearls. And what a gorgeous dress."

Pauline always wore something in pink or yellow with layers of net. She was in competition with the fairy on the tree, according to Andy.

She smiled her thanks for the compliment. "Not very practical for the time of year, but I couldn't resist it. Let's take your coats. And Happy Christmas."

"First I'll park these under the tree," said Andy. "The brown paper one isn't from us, by the way. We found it on your doorstep. Doesn't feel heavy enough for booze, more's the pity."

"I do like surprises," said Pauline.

"A secret admirer?" said Gemma.

"At my age?"

"Oh, come on, what does that say for me, pushing forty?"

"You've got your admirer."

Gemma rolled her eyes upwards and said nothing.

"Come and say hello to Geoff." Pauline cupped her hand to her mouth as she added, "Hasn't had any work for three months, he told me."

"Oh, no."

Their accountant brother, short and fat, with half-glasses, greeted Gemma. "Merry Christmas" was likely to be the extent of his conversation for the day unless someone asked him about his garden.

Pauline brought in a tray of tea things.

Andy said, "Not for me, I'll help myself to a brandy, if you don't mind. Want one, Geoff?"

Geoff shook his head.

"Any trouble getting here?"

Geoff gave a shrug.

"Roads okay your way, then?"

Geoff thought about it and gave another shrug.

Pauline said, "It's nearly four. Reg ought to be here. It's not as if he has far to come. Geoff has a longer trip and was here by three-thirty."

"Knowing Reg of old, he could be planning one of his stunts," said Andy. "Remember the year of the ghost in the bathroom, Pauline?"

"Don't!" she said. "Will I ever forget it? It was so real, and he *knew* I was scared of living here alone."

Between them, they recalled Reg's party tricks in recent years: the time he arrived with his friend masquerading as an African bishop; the year the Queen's voice came out of the cocktail cabinet; and the live turkey in Geoff's car.

"You've got to give him full marks for trying," said Andy. "It would be a dull old Christmas without him."

"I'd rather have it dull," said Pauline.

"Me, too," said Gemma. "I may be his flesh and blood, but I don't share his sense of humor."

"Only because it could be your turn this time," said Andy. "Poor old Geoff got it last year. The sight of that turkey pecking your hand when you opened the door, Geoff, I'll never forget."

Geoff stared back without smiling.

Ten minutes later, Pauline said, "I've had the cocktail sausages warming for over an hour. They'll be burnt to a cinder. And we haven't even opened a single present."

"Want me to phone him, see if he's left?" Andy offered.

"Of course he's left," said Gemma. "He must have."

Pauline started to say, "I hope nothing's—"

Gemma said quickly, "He's all right. He wants to keep us in suspense. We're playing into his hands. I think we should get on with the party without him. Why don't we open some presents?"

"I think we ought to wait for Reg."

"You could open the one we found on the doorstep," Andy suggested to Pauline.

"Unless it *is* something personal," said Gemma.

That induced a change of mind from Pauline. "I've got nothing to hide from any of you."

Andy retrieved the parcel from under the tree, turned it over, and examined the brown paper wrapping. "There's nothing written on it. Maybe it isn't meant for Pauline after all."

"If it was left on her doorstep, it's hers," said Gemma.

Pauline sat in a chair with the parcel deep in the froth of her skirt and picked at the Sellotape. She was too fastidious to tear the paper.

"You want scissors," said Andy.

"I can manage." She eased open the brown paper. "It's gift-wrapped inside."

"Where's the tag?" said Gemma. "Who's it from?"

"There isn't one." Pauline examined the tinsel-tied parcel in its shiny red wrapper.

"Open it, then."

She worked at one edge of the paper with one of her long, lacquered fingernails. "Look, there's more wrapping inside."

"Just like pass the parcel," said Gemma.

Andy gave his wife a murderous look.

The paper yielded to Pauline's gentle probing. Underneath was yet another wrapping, with a design of holly and Christmas roses. She said, "I think you're right. This is meant for a game."

Andy swore under his breath.

"Let's all play, then," said Gemma with an amused glance at her husband's reaction.

"After tea."

"No, now. While we're waiting for Reg. Pull up a chair everyone and sit in a circle. I'll look after the music."

"Just three of us?" said Andy.

Gemma mocked him with a look. "You know how Pauline adores this game."

Andy and Pauline positioned themselves close to where Geoff was already seated, while Gemma selected a CD and placed it on the deck of the music center.

"What is it—'The Teddy Bears' Picnic'?" said Andy.

Pauline was impervious to sarcasm. " 'Destiny,' " she said as the sound of strings filled the room.

"That's an old one."

"Start passing it, then," said Gemma. "I'm not playing this for my amusement."

Pauline handed the parcel to Andy, who held it to his chest. "No cheating," said Pauline.

He passed it to Geoff and the music stopped. Geoff unwrapped a piece of pink paper and revealed a silver layer beneath.

"Tough," said Andy. "Play on, maestro."

As the game resumed, Pauline told her sister, "You're supposed to have your back to us. It isn't fair if you can see who the parcel has reached."

"She likes playing God," said Andy. "Whoops." The music had stopped and the parcel was on his lap. He ripped it open; no finer feelings. "Too bad. Give it another whirl, Gem."

Geoff was the next to remove a layer. He did it in silence as usual.

"More music?" said Gemma.

"You got it," said Andy.

Three more wrappings came off before Pauline got a turn. The parcel was appreciably smaller.

"This could be it," said Andy. "You can see the shape."

"But of what?" said Pauline "It looks like a box to me." She was pink in the face as she peeled back the paper, but it was clear that another burst of music would be necessary.

When Andy received the parcel he held it to his ear and gave it a shake. Nothing rattled.

"Come on, pass it," said Pauline, drumming her shoes on the carpet.

Geoff fumbled and dropped the parcel as the music stopped. Pauline snatched it up.

"Not so fast," said Andy. "Geoff hadn't passed it to you."

But she had already unfolded the tissue paper from around a matchbox, one of the jumbo size capable of holding two hundred and fifty matches.

"One more round, apparently," said Gemma, and she turned up the music again. To sustain the suspense, a longer stretch of "Destiny" was wanted.

"What could it be?" said Pauline.

"Matches," said Andy.

"A silk scarf would be nice," said Pauline.

"Game on," said Andy.

The matchbox was sent on its way around the three players.

"No looking," Andy reminded his wife. "We're down to the wire now. This has to be impartial."

"Faster," said Pauline.

"She's a goer, your sister," said Andy.

The matchbox fairly raced from lap to lap.

"Do you mind? I didn't know you cared," said Andy when Pauline's impetuous hand clasped his thigh.

Even Geoff was leaning forward, absorbed in the climax of the game. The music stopped just as he was passing the box to Pauline. They both had their hands on it.

"Mine," she said.

Geoff apparently knew better than to thwart his younger sister.

"I suppose it's only justice that you get the prize, as it was left on your doorstep," said Andy. "Let's see what you've got."

Unable to contain her curiosity, Gemma came over to see.

Pauline slid the box half-open, dropped it into her lap, and said in horror, "Oh, I don't believe it!"

"It's a joke, said Gemma. "It must be a joke."

"It isn't," said Pauline in a thin, strained voice. "That's somebody's thumb. Ugh!" She hooked the box off her skirt as if it were alive and dropped it on the coffee table.

Large and pale, the offending digit lay on a bed of cotton wool.

"No it isn't," said Andy. "It's too big for a thumb. It's a big toe."

"A toe?"

"Yes, it's too fleshy for a thumb."

"It must be out of a joke shop," said Gemma. "If Reg is responsible for this, I'll strangle him."

"Typical of his humor," said Andy.

Then Geoff spoke. "I think it's real."

"It *can't* be," said Gemma.

"Open it right out," said Andy.

"I'm not touching it," said Pauline.

Andy lifted the box and opened it, separating the drawer from its casing.

"I can't bear to look," said Pauline. "Keep it away from me."

"It's the real thing," said Andy. "You can see where it was—"

"God in Heaven—we don't wish to see," said Gemma. "Put it somewhere out of sight and give Pauline some of that brandy we brought."

"What a vile trick," said Pauline.

Andy reunited the two sections of the matchbox and placed it on a bookshelf before going to the brandy bottle. "Anybody else want some Dutch courage?"

Geoff gave a nod.

Andy's hand shook as he poured. Everyone was in a state of shock.

"He's gone too far this time," said Gemma. "He's ruined Christmas for all of us. I shall tell him. Are you all right, love?"

Pauline took a gulp of brandy and gave a nod.

"It's ghoulish," said Gemma.

"Sick," said Andy. "You all right, Geoff? You've gone very pale."

"I'm okay," Geoff managed to say.

"Drink some brandy, mate."

Gemma said, "Andy, would you take it right out of the room and get rid of it? It's upsetting us all."

Andy picked the matchbox off the bookshelf and left the room. Gemma collected the discarded sheets of wrapping paper and joined him in the kitchen. "Where would Reg have got such a ghoulish thing?" she whispered.

Andy shrugged. "Who knows? I don't imagine a branch manager at the Midland Bank comes across many severed toes."

"What are we going to do? Pauline's nerves are shattered and Geoff looks ready to faint."

"A fresh cup of tea is supposed to be good for shock. What am I going to do with this?"

"I don't know. Bury it in the garden."

"Pauline is sure to ask where it went."

"Then we'd better take it with us when we go. We can dump it somewhere on the way home."

"Why should we have to deal with it?" said Andy. "I'll give it back to bloody Reg. He can get rid of it."

"If he has the gall to show his face here. Just keep it out of everyone's sight in the meantime."

To satisfy himself that the toe really was of human origin, Andy slid open the matchbox again. This time he noticed a folded piece of paper tucked into one end. "Hey, there's something inside. I think it's a note." After reading the typed message, he handed it to Gemma. "What do you make of that?"

She stared at the paper. "It can't be true. It's got to be a hoax."

They joined Pauline and Geoff in the living room. "We thought you might appreciate some tea," said Gemma.

"You're marvellous," said Pauline. "I should have thought of that."

"Getting over the shock?"

"I think so."

"You too, Geoff?"

Geoff gave a nod.

Andy cleared his throat. "I found this note in the matchbox."

"A note?" said Pauline. "From Reg?"

"Apparently not. It says, 'If you want the rest of your brother—' "

"Oh, no!" said Pauline.

" 'If you want the rest of your brother, bring ten thousand pounds or equivalent to the telephone box at Chilton Leys at five-thirty. Just one of you.

If you don't, or if you call the police, you can find the bits all over Suffolk.' "

"Andy, I think she's going to faint."

"I'm all right," said Pauline. "If this is true, that toe . . ."

"But it isn't true," said Andy, spacing the words. "It's Reg having us on, as he does every year."

"Are you sure?"

"He'll turn up presently grinning all over his fat face. The best thing we can do is get on with the party."

There was little enthusiasm for unwrapping presents or eating over-cooked sausage, so they turned on the television and watched for a while.

"How could we possibly put our hands on ten thousand pounds on Christmas Day?" said Pauline during the commercial break.

"That's the giveaway," said Andy. "A professional kidnapper would know better."

"You've got three hundred in notes in your back pocket," said Gemma. "You know you have. You said we needed it over the holiday in case of emer-gencies."

"Three hundred is peanuts compared to ten grand."

"I've got about a hundred and twenty in my bag," said Gemma.

Geoff took out his wallet and counted the edges of his bank notes.

"Doesn't look as if Geoff can chip in much," said Andy.

Gemma said on a note of reproach, "Andy."

Andy said, "No offence, mate."

Geoff put his wallet away.

"Well, that's it. We couldn't afford to pay the kidnappers if they existed," Andy summed up. "How much do you have in the house, Pauline?"

"In cash? About two hundred."

"Less than eight hundred between us."

"But I've got a thousand in travellers' cheques for my holiday in Florida."

"Still a long way short," said Andy.

"Good thing it's only a hoax," said Gemma.

"There are my pearls," said Pauline, fingering them. "They cost over a thousand. And I have some valuable rings upstairs."

"If we're talking jewellery, Gemma's ruby necklace is the real thing," said Andy.

"So is your Rolex watch," Gemma countered. "And the gold ingot you wear under your shirt."

"I notice you haven't offered your earrings. They cost a bomb, if I remember right."

"Oh, shut up."

"Where the hell is Chilton Leys anyway?"

"Not far," said Pauline.

"I passed it on my way here," said Geoff.

They were silent for an interval. Then Andy said, "Well, has anyone spoken to Reg on the phone in the past twenty-four hours?"

"It must be a week since we spoke," said Pauline.

"What time is it?" said Gemma.

"Five past five."

"He would have been here by now," said Pauline. "Or if he had trouble with the car he would have phoned."

"Anyone care for another drink?" asked Andy.

"How many is that you've had already?" said Gemma.

"I want to say something," said Pauline.

"Feel free," said Andy, with the bottle in his hand.

She smoothed her skirt. "I'm not saying you're wrong, but if it wasn't a hoax and Reg really had been kidnapped, we could never forgive ourselves if these people murdered him because we did nothing about it."

"Come off it," said Andy.

"I mean, why are we refusing to respond to the note? Is it because we're afraid of making fools of ourselves? Is that all it is?"

"We don't believe it, that's why," said Gemma.

"You mean you don't want to run the risk of Reg having the last laugh? It's all about self-esteem, isn't it? How typical of our family—all inflated egos. We'd rather run the risk of Reg being murdered than lay ourselves open to ridicule."

"That isn't the point," said Andy. "We're calling his bluff."

"So you say. And if by some freak of circumstances you're mistaken, how will any of us live with it for the rest of our lives? I'm telling you, Andy, I'm frightened. I know what you're thinking. I can see it in your eyes. I'm gullible, a stupid, immature female. Well I don't mind admitting I'm bloody frightened. If none of you wants to take this seriously that's up to you. I do. I'm going to put all the money I have into a bag and take it to that phone box. If nobody comes, what have I lost? Some dignity, that's all. You can laugh at me every Christmas from now on. But I mean it." She stood up.

"Hold on," said Andy. "We've heard what you think. What about the rest of us?"

"It isn't quite the same for you, is it?" said Pauline. "He's my brother."

"He's Gemma's brother, too. And Geoff's."

Andy switched to his wife. "What do *you* want to do about it?"

Gemma hesitated.

"Or Geoff," said Andy. "Do you have an opinion, Geoff?"

Geoff's hand went to his collar as if it had tightened suddenly.

Gemma said, "Pauline is right. Ten to one it's Reg having us on, but we can't take the risk. We've got to do something."

Geoff nodded. He backed his sisters.

Pauline said, "I'm going upstairs to collect my jewellery, such as it is. We pool everything we have, right?"

"Right," said Gemma, unfixing her gold earrings and turning to Andy. "Do you want to be part of this, or not?"

Andy slapped his wad of bank notes on the table. "I don't believe in these kidnappers anyway."

"Let's have your watch, then," said Gemma. "And the ingot."

Geoff took out his wallet and emptied it.

The heap of money and valuables markedly increased when Pauline returned. She'd found some family heirlooms, including their grandmother's diamond-studded choker, worth several thousand alone. With her own pieces and the travellers' cheques, the collection must have come close to the value demanded in the note. She scooped everything into a denim bag with bamboo handles and said, "I'll get my coat."

Gemma told her, "Not you, sweetie. That's a job for one of the men."

Andy said, "Give the bag to me."

"You're not going anywhere," said Gemma. "You're way over the limit with all the brandy you've had. Besides, you don't know the way."

They turned to look at Geoff. He knew the way. He had said so.

"I'll go," he said, rising quite positively from the armchair. He looked a trifle unsteady in the upright position, but he'd been seated a long time. Maybe the brandy hadn't gone to his head. He had certainly drunk less than Andy.

Gemma still felt it necessary to ask, "Will you be all right?"

Geoff nodded. He had spoken. There was no need for more words.

Pauline asked, "Would you like me to come?"

Andy said, "The instruction was clear. If you believe it, Geoff's got to go alone."

In the hall, Pauline helped Geoff on with his padded jacket. "If you see anyone, don't take them on, will you? We just want you and Reg safely back."

Geoff looked incapable of taking anyone on as he shuffled across the gravel to his old Cortina, watched from the door by the others. He placed the bag on the passenger seat and got in.

"Is he sober?" Gemma asked.

"He only had a couple," said Andy.

"He looked just the same when he arrived," said Pauline. "He's had a hard time lately. So many businesses going bust. They don't need accountants."

Gemma said, "If anything happened to him just because Reg is acting the fool, I'd commit murder, I don't mind saying."

They heard the car start up and watched it trundle up the drive.

When the front door closed again, Gemma asked, "What time is it?"

"Twenty past," said Pauline. "He should just about make it."

Andy said, "I don't know why you two are taking this seriously. If I believed for a moment it was a genuine ransom demand I wouldn't have parted with three hundred pounds and a Rolex, I assure you."

"So what would you have done, cleverclogs?" said Gemma.

This wrongfooted Andy. He spread his hands wide as if the answer were too obvious to go into.

"Let's hear it," said Gemma. "Would you have called the police and put my brother's life at risk?"

"Certainly I'd have called them," said Andy, recovering his poise. "They have procedures for this sort of emergency. They'd know how to handle it without putting anyone's life at risk."

"For example?"

"Well, they'd observe the pickup from a distance. Probably they'd attach some tiny bugging device to the goods being handed over. They might coat some of the banknotes with a dye that responds to ultraviolet light."

Gemma turned to Pauline. "I'm wondering if we should call them."

Andy said, "It's too late. The police would have no option but to come down like a ton of bricks. Someone would get hurt."

Pauline said, "Oh God, no. Let's wait and see what happens."

"We won't have long to wait. That's one thing," said Andy. "You don't mind if I switch on the telly, Pauline?"

They sat in silence watching a cartoon film about a snowman.

Before it finished, Pauline went to the window and pulled back the curtain to look along the drive.

"See anything?" asked Gemma.

"No."

"How long has he been gone?"

"Twenty-five minutes. Chilton Leys is only ten minutes from here, if that. He ought to be back by now."

"Stop fussing, you two," said Andy. "You give me the creeps."

Just after six, Pauline announced, "A car's coming. I can see the headlights."

"Okay," said Andy from his armchair. "What are we going to do about Reg when he pisses himself laughing and says it was a hoax?"

Pauline ran to the front door and opened it. Gemma was at her side.

"That isn't Geoff's Cortina," said Gemma. "It's a bigger car."

Without appearing to hurry, Andy joined them at the door. "That's Reg's

Volvo. Didn't I tell you he was all right?"

The car drew up beside Andy's and Reg got out, smiling. He was alone. "Where's the red carpet, then?" he called out. "Merry Christmas, everyone. Wait a mo. I've got some prezzies in the back." He dipped into his car again.

"You'd think nothing had happened," muttered Gemma.

Laden with presents, Reg strutted towards them. "Who gets to kiss me first, then?" He appeared unfazed, his well-known ebullient self.

Andy remarked. "He's walking normally. We've been suckered."

Gemma said, "You bastard, Reg. Don't come near me, you sadist."

Pauline shouted, "Dickhead."

Reg's face was a study in bewilderment.

Andy said, "Where's Geoff?"

"How would I know?" answered Reg. "Hey, what is this? What am I supposed to have done?"

"Pull the other one, matey," said Andy.

"You've ruined Christmas for all of us," said Pauline, succumbing to tears.

"I wish I knew what you were on about," said Reg. "Shall we go inside and find out?"

"You're not welcome," Pauline whimpered.

"Okay, okay," said Reg. "It's a fair cop and I deserve it after all the stunts I pulled. Who thought of unloading all this on me? Andy, I bet."

Suddenly Gemma said in a hollow voice, "Andy, I don't think he knows what this is about."

"What?"

"I know my own brother. He isn't bluffing. He didn't expect this. Listen, Reg did anyone kidnap you?"

"Kidnap me?"

"We'd better go inside, all of us," said Gemma.

"Kidnap me?" repeated Reg, when they were in Pauline's living room. "I'm gobsmacked."

Pauline said, "Andy found this parcel on my doorstep and—"

"Shut up a minute," said Andy. "You're playing into his hands. Let's hear his story before we tell him what happened here. You've got some answering to do, Reg. For a start, you're a couple of hours late."

Reg frowned. "You haven't been here all afternoon?"

"Of course we have. We were here by four o'clock."

"You didn't get the message, then?"

"What message?"

"I've been had then. Geoff phoned at lunchtime to say that Pauline's heating was off. A problem with the boiler. He said the party had been relocated to his place at five."

Pauline said, "There's nothing wrong with my boiler."

"Shut up and listen," said Gemma.

Reg continued, "I turned up at Geoff's house and there was a note for me attached to the door. Hold on—I should have it here." He felt in his pocket. "Yes, here it is." He handed Gemma an envelope with his name written on it.

She took out the note and read to the others, " 'Caught YOU this year. Now go to Pauline's and see what reception you get.' It's Geoff's handwriting."

"He's a slyboots," said Reg, "but I deserve it. He was pretty annoyed by the turkey episode last year."

"You're not the only victim," said Gemma.

"Were you sent on a wild-goose chase?"

"No. But I think he may have tricked us. He *must* have. He led us to believe you were kidnapped. That's why he went to this trouble to keep you away."

"Crafty old devil."

"He took ten grand off us," said Andy.

"What?"

"He persuaded us to put up a ransom for you."

"Now who are you kidding?"

"It's true," said Gemma. "We put together everything we had, cash, jewellery, family heirlooms, and Geoff went off to deliver it to the kidnappers."

"Strike me pink!"

"And he isn't back yet," said Andy.

Pauline said, "Geoff wouldn't rob his own family."

"Don't count on it," said Reg. "He doesn't give a toss for any of us."

"Geoff?"

"Did you know he's emigrating?"

"No."

"It's true," said Reg. "He's off to Australia any day now. I picked this up on the grapevine through a colleague in the bank. I think the accident made him reconsider his plan, so to speak."

"What accident?"

"There you are, you see. I only heard about that from the same source. Old Geoff was in hospital for over a week at the end of September and the last thing he wanted was a visit from any of us."

"A road accident?"

"No, he did it himself. You know how keen he is on the garden. He's got this turfed area sloping down to the pond. He ran the mower over his foot and severed his big toe."

Edward D. Hoch

THE THEFT OF SANTA'S BEARD

The New York stores had closed at nine that evening, disgorging gift-laden Christmas shoppers by the hundreds. Most were too busy shifting the weight of their parcels and shopping bags to bother digging for coins as they passed the bell-ringing Santa on the corner. He was a bit thin and scraggly compared to the overstuffed Santas who worked the department stores and bounced tiny children on their knees while asking for their Christmas lists. His job was only to ring a little hand-held bell and accept donations in a chimney-shaped container.

This Santa's name was Russell Bajon and he'd come to the city expecting better things. After working at a variety of minimum-wage jobs and landing a couple of short-lived acting roles off Broadway, he'd taken the Santa Claus job for the holidays. There was no pay, but they supplied his meals and a place to sleep at night. And there were good fringe benefits, enough to keep him going till he was back on his feet with a part in a decent play.

After another fifteen minutes the crowd from the stores had pretty well scattered. There were still people on the dark streets, as there would be for most of the night, but those remaining hurried by his chimney without even a glance. He waited a few more minutes and then decided to pack up. The truck would be coming by shortly to collect the chimney and give him a ride back to the men's dorm where he slept.

He was bending over the chimney with its collection basket when someone bumped him from behind. He straightened and tried to turn, but by that time the thin copper wire was cutting into his throat.

By the time the second Santa Claus had been strangled to death, the tabloids had the story on page one. No Clues to Claus Killer, one of them trumpeted, while another proclaimed, Santa Strangler Strikes Again. Nick Velvet glanced over the articles with passing interest, but at that point they were nothing to directly affect him.

"Where was the latest killing?" Gloria asked as she prepared breakfast.

"In the subway. An elderly Santa on his way to work."

She shook her head. "What's this world coming to when somebody starts strangling Santa Clauses?"

The next morning Nick found out. He was seated in the office of the Intercontinental Protection Service, across the desk from a man named Grady Culhane. The office was small and somewhat plain, not what Nick had expected from the pretentious name. Culhane himself was young, barely past thirty, with black hair, thick eyebrows, and an Irish smile. He spread his hands flat on the uncluttered desktop and said, "I understand you steal things of little or no value."

"That's correct," Nick replied. "My standard fee is twenty-five thousand dollars, unless it's something especially hazardous."

"This should be simple enough. I want you to steal the beard from a department store Santa Claus. It's the Santa at Kliman's main store, and it must be done tomorrow before noon. Santa's hours there are noon to four and five to eight."

"What makes it so valuable to you?"

"Nothing. It's worth no more than any other false white beard. I just need it tomorrow."

"I usually get half the money down and the other half after the job," Nick said. "Is that agreeable?"

"Sure. It'll have to be a check. I don't have that much cash on hand."

"So long as I can cash it at your bank."

He made out the check and handed it over. "Here's a sketch map I drew of Kliman's fourth floor. This is the dressing room Santa uses."

"So the beard is probably there before noon. Why don't you just walk in and steal it?" Nick wondered. "Why do you need me?"

"You ever been in Kliman's? They've got security cameras all over the store, including hidden ones in the dressing rooms. This is only Santa's room during the Christmas season. The rest of the year it's used by the public, and the camera is probably still operational. I can't afford to be seen stealing the beard or anything else."

"What about me?"

"That's your job. That's what I'm paying you for."

"Fair enough," Nick agreed, folding the check once and slipping it into his pocket. "I'll be back here tomorrow with the beard."

Nothing had been said about the two Santa Claus killings, but somehow, as Nick Velvet left the building, he had the feeling he was becoming involved in something a lot more complex than a simple robbery.

The Santa Claus killings were still big news the following morning, and

Nick read the speculations about possible motives as he traveled into midtown on the subway. The second man to die, Larry Averly, was a retired plumber who'd been earning some spare cash as a holiday Santa Claus. The first victim, Bajon, had died on Monday evening, the fourteenth, while the second death came the following morning. Nick had the feeling the press was almost disappointed that another killing had not followed on Wednesday. Now it was Thursday, eight days before Christmas, and the street before Kliman's block-long department store was crowded with shoppers.

He entered the store with the first wave of customers when the doors opened at ten, making his way up the escalator to the fourth floor. After a half-hour of lingering in the furniture department, he wandered over to the dressing-room door that Grady Culhane had indicated on his map. When no one was looking, he slipped inside.

His first task was to locate the closed-circuit television camera. He found it without difficulty—a circular lens embedded in the very center of a round wall clock. Not wanting to blot out the view entirely and arouse the suspicion of possible observers, Nick moved a coat rack in front of the clock, blocking most of the little room. Then he quickly opened a pair of lockers. But there was no Santa Claus costume, no beard, in either one. He'd been hoping that the store's Santa changed into his costume on the premises, but it looked as if he might come to work already dressed, like the street Santa who'd been strangled in the subway.

If that was the case, however, Culhane wouldn't have told him to come to this room. It was already nearly eleven and Nick decided to wait till noon to see what happened. He positioned himself behind the clothes rack, but at the far end, away from the television camera. Exactly at eleven-thirty, the door opened and someone came in. He could see a tall, fairly broad-shouldered person carrying a large canvas tote bag. There was a flash of red as a Santa Claus suit came into view.

Nick Velvet breathed a sigh of relief. The white beard came out of the bag and he saw the prize within his grasp. He stepped from his hiding place, ready to deliver a knockout blow if necessary. "Keep quiet and give me the beard," he said.

The figure turned and Nick froze in his tracks. Santa was a woman.

She was probably in her late thirties, large boned but not unattractive, with dark brown hair that was already partly covered by the Santa Claus wig and cap. Nick's sudden appearance seemed not to have frightened her but only angered her as any unexpected interruption might. "You just made the mistake of your life, mister," she told him in a flat tone of voice.

"I don't want to hurt you. Give me that beard."

"I have a transmitter in my pocket. I've already called for help."

He realized suddenly that she thought he was the Santa strangler. "I'm not here to hurt you," he tried to assure her.

But it was too late for assurances. The dressing-room door burst open and Nick faced two men with drawn revolvers. "Freeze!" the first man ordered, crouching in a shooter's stance. "Police!"

"Look, this is all a mistake."

"And you made it, mister!" The second man moved behind Nick to frisk him.

Nick decided it was time for a bit of his own electronic technology. He brought his left arm down enough to hit the small transmitter in his breast pocket. Immediately there was a sharp crack from the direction of the furniture department, and billowing smoke could be seen through the open dressing-room door. The first man turned his head and Nick kicked the gun from his hand, poking his elbow back simultaneously to catch the second detective in the ribs. As he went out the door he made a grab for the white beard the lady Santa was holding in her hand, but he missed by several inches.

"Stop or I'll shoot!" one of the detectives yelled, but Nick knew he wouldn't. The floor was crowded with shoppers, and the cloud from Nick's well-placed smoke bomb was already enveloping everyone.

Five minutes later he was out of the store and safely away, but without the beard he'd been hired to steal.

Later that afternoon Nick returned to the office of the Intercontinental Protection Service. Grady Culhane was not in a pleasant mood. "That was you at the store this morning, wasn't it?" he asked pointedly. "The radio says someone set off a smoke bomb and two shoppers were slightly injured in the panic."

"I'm sorry if anyone was hurt. You didn't tell me Santa Claus was a woman. That threw off my timing and enabled a couple of detectives to get the drop on me."

"What about the beard?"

"I didn't get it."

Culhane cursed. "That means Santa will be back in place as soon as they get the smoke cleared out and things back to normal."

Nick was beginning to see at least a portion of the scheme. "You wanted the beard stolen so Santa couldn't appear."

"Sure. It was easier than stealing the whole costume, except that you bungled it."

"They could have found another beard quickly enough," Nick argued.

Grady Culhane shook his head. "They don't sell them in the store. I checked. The delay would have been an hour or two, and that was all I needed."

"For what?"

He eyed Nick uncertainly for a moment before deciding to yield. "All right, I'll tell you about it. But I want something in return. I want that beard tomorrow, and no slip-ups this time!"

"You'll have it, so long as you play square with me. What's this all about? Does it involve the Santa Claus killings?"

The dark-haired young man reached into a desk drawer and extracted a sheet of paper which he passed across the desk to Nick. It was a copy of a crudely printed extortion letter addressed to the president of Kliman's department store: "Tuesday, December 15—I have just come from killing my second Santa Claus of the Christmas season. The deaths of Bajon and Averly were meant as a demonstration. A third Santa Claus will die in your store, in full view of the children, unless you are prepared to pay me one million dollars in cash within forty-eight hours, by noon Thursday." There was no signature.

"Sounds like a crackpot," Nick decided, returning the letter. "He doesn't even give directions for paying the money."

"This letter was hand-delivered by a messenger service Tuesday afternoon. A second letter came yesterday, with instructions. They haven't shown me that one."

"You've been hired by Kliman's store?"

Culhane nodded. "Frankly, it's the first major client I've had. Even though the police have been called in, the store is paying me as a personal bodyguard for Santa."

"Or Mrs. Santa."

He smiled. "She's an unemployed actress named Vivian Delmos. I just met her yesterday after I talked with you. There are some female Santas around. They're good with children. If their voices are deep enough and the suit is padded enough, no one knows the difference. I didn't know the cops would be guarding her too."

"How much are they paying you?" Nick asked.

"That's proprietary information," the young man answered stiffly.

"I figure fifty thousand, at least, if you can afford to pay me twenty-five."

"I don't get a thing if the Santa strangler kills her."

"You thought he'd strike right at noon, so you needed me to keep her from going out there then. That means they decided not to pay."

"It's not just them. There are other stores involved. The killer is trying to shake down the largest stores in New York."

"The police must have a description from the messenger company that delivered this note."

Grady Culhane shook his head. "They deny any knowledge of it. One of their messengers was probably stopped in the street and paid to deliver it.

Naturally he won't admit it now and risk losing his job."

"What happens after the smoke is cleared out?"

"The Delmos woman puts on her beard and goes back out there. I'll probably have to be standing next to her, and I'm too big for those elves' costumes."

"Don't worry," Nick promised. "This time I'll get the beard."

On his second visit to the store Nick Velvet wore a grey wig and a matching false moustache. He was taking no chances on coming face-to-face with one of those detectives again. In the atrium at the center of the main floor where Santa's throne was in place, a sign announced that he would not return until noon the following day due to the illness of one of his reindeer. Nick found a pay telephone and called Culhane at his office.

"You're off the hook until tomorrow," he said.

"I just heard from the store."

"Do you still want the beard?"

"Of course—unless the police come up with the extortionist by then."

Nick hung up and decided he should know more than he did about the Santa Claus killings. He went down to the subway newsstand and bought all the local papers. It wasn't the lead item anymore but the unsolved killings still filled several columns inside each paper. The first victim, Russell Bajon, was a young homeless man—a would-be actor—who'd been staying at the men's dorm maintained by a charitable organization. He'd been collecting money for the charity at one of their Christmas chimneys when he'd been strangled. One of the other Santas, a man named Chris Stover, had come by in a van a few minutes later to find a crowd gathering around the fallen man. No one admitted to having seen the actual killing.

The second victim had followed less than twelve hours later, on Tuesday morning. Larry Averly lived in a rundown hotel on the fringes of Greenwich Village, a place where Nick had grown up. His Christmas job as a Santa Claus for a local radio station's holiday promotion involved coming to work in costume that day, since they were doing a remote broadcast from the Central Park skating rink. He'd been heading for a subway exit near the park when the killer struck. This time two people saw the attack and scared him off, but not in time to save the victim. The killer was described as a white man of uncertain age wearing a bulky coat. Averly hadn't been carrying any identification in his shabby wallet and it had taken police most of the day to trace his room key to the hotel where he'd been staying. The radio station had hired him through an employment agency and didn't even know his name. They'd finally learned it just in time for the six o'clock news.

The papers, of course, carried nothing about the extortion plot. That would have been enough to get the story back on page one. Nick read them all and then tossed them aside. He had his own problem to consider. Stealing Santa's beard the following day would be next to impossible in Kliman's store, but the alternatives were equally impossible. He knew Vivian Delmos carried her costume to work in a large canvas bag, but he wasn't about to mug her on the way to work. Still . . .

Culhane had mentioned that the lady Santa Claus was an unemployed actress. Nick phoned Actors' Equity and had her address within minutes. Vivian Delmos resided on East Forty-ninth Street. He called her number and got the expected answering machine. Next he phoned Gloria to say that he wouldn't be home till late.

The address on Forty-ninth was past Third Avenue, in an apartment building across the street from the Turtle Bay block. The Delmos woman must have been successful at some stage of her career to afford the moderately high rents in the neighborhood. There was no answer to Nick's ring so he took up a position down the block on the other side of the street. Within twenty minutes he saw Vivian Delmos appear, walking briskly and carrying her canvas bag. He crossed the street to intercept her at her door, but she was a bit faster than he'd realized. She was halfway through the door by the time he reached it.

Blocking its closing with his hand, he began, "Miss Delmos—"

She turned, recognized him instantly, and acted without a word, yanking on his wrist and pulling him inside but off balance. He felt himself falling forward as she twisted his arm behind him. Then he was on the floor, his cheek pressed against the hall carpeting, while she pulled painfully on the arm. Her foot was on his neck.

"Mister, you just made your second big mistake. I hope you don't mind a broken arm."

"Wait a minute! I just want to talk!"

"How'd you find me? Did you follow me home?"

"Through Equity."

"Got a job for me?" She gave his arm a painful wrench. "I'm real good in action parts."

"I don't doubt it! Please let me up."

"Nice and slow," she warned, relaxing the pressure on his arm. "We're going upstairs while I call the police."

"All right."

She led him ahead of her up the stairs, keeping a grip on his arm. They paused outside a door at the top while she put down the canvas bag and got out her key. "Inside!"

The apartment was large but plainly furnished, as if in some sort of limbo while awaiting its permanent decor. "I'm not trying to kill you," Nick assured her. "When you saw me earlier I was only trying to steal your beard."

"My what?"

"The beard from your Santa Claus outfit."

She released his arm and gave him a shove toward the sofa. "What's your name?"

"Nick Velvet. I steal things." He decided to stay on the sofa for the moment. Facing her now, he had a chance to confirm his earlier impressions. She was into early middle age but still had a good figure. By the strength she'd shown in overpowering him, he guessed that she worked out regularly. It had been an unlucky day from the start.

"I'm Vivian Delmos, but I guess you know that. You called me by name." She walked to the phone without taking her eyes off him.

"I was hired to steal your beard," he told her. "You have nothing to fear from me."

"The people at Kliman's weren't too happy when you set off that smoke bomb."

"I only did it to escape. If I hadn't needed it I'd have returned later and removed it."

"What does all this have to do with the Santa strangler?"

"The killings are part of an extortion plot against the big department stores. My job was to keep you from being the next victim."

"By stealing my beard?" She gave a snort of disbelief. "Kliman's wanted to replace me with a cop but I wouldn't let them. I finally convinced everyone I could take care of myself, but they still made me carry that beeper. And this noon after you tried to attack me—"

"Steal your beard," Nick corrected.

"—steal my beard, they canceled Santa's appearances for the rest of the day. I lost a day's pay because of you!"

"Give me the beard and stay home tomorrow, too. I'll pay you a thousand dollars for it."

"Are you whacky or something?"

"Just a good businessman. I'm getting too old to be tossed around by a woman who works out at the gym every day."

"Three times a week," she corrected. "I'm an actress and I find it a good way to keep fit."

Nick worked his shoulder a bit, getting the kinks out. "It sure doesn't keep me fit. How about it? A thousand dollars?"

"They'll find another beard for me, or use the cop after all." She'd moved away from the phone at least, and Nick was thankful for that.

"It's the easiest money you'll ever make. Far easier than doing some off-Broadway play eight times a week."

"How'd you know I was off-Broadway?" she asked, immediately suspicious.

"I guessed. What difference does it make?"

"You didn't—" she began and then cut herself short. "Look, I'll agree to your condition if you do one thing for me."

"What's that?"

"I want you to go down to the men's dorm at the Outreach Center and pick up Russell Bajon's belongings."

"Bajon? The first victim?"

"That's right."

"Did you know him?"

"Slightly. We appeared in a play together."

Nick shook his head. "I don't understand any of this. What right do you have to his belongings?"

"As much right as anyone. The paper says he left no family."

"But why would you want his things?"

"Just to remember him by. He was a nice guy."

"Why can't you get them yourself?"

"I don't want people to see me there."

It was a weak reason, and her whole story was weak, but Nick was into it now. Unless he wanted to risk seriously injuring her, it seemed the only way to get the beard. "All right. I'll go down there now and then I'll be back for the beard."

Outside it had started to snow a little, but somehow it didn't seem much like the week before Christmas.

The Outreach Center was a sort of nondenominational mission located on the West Side near the river. Some of their operating expenses came from the city, but much of the money was from private donors. The Center gave homeless people a safe place to sleep if they were afraid of the city shelters, but certain rules applied. Drugs, alcohol, and weapons were forbidden, and guests of the Center were expected to earn their keep. In December that often meant dressing up in a Santa Claus suit and manning one of the Center's plywood chimneys with a donation bag inside.

The first person Nick saw as he entered the front door of the Outreach Center was a young man in sweater and jeans seated at an unpretentious card table. "I've come to pick up Russell Bajon's belongings," Nick told him. "The family sent me."

The young man seemed indifferent to the request. Apparently people who stayed at the men's dorm weren't expected to have anything worth stealing. "I'll get Chris."

Nick waited in the bare hallway until the young man returned with an older worker with thinning hair, wearing a faded Giants sweatshirt. "I'm Chris Stover. What can I do for you?"

"Russell Bajon's family sent me for his belongings."

The man frowned. "Didn't know he had a family. There sure wasn't much in the way of belongings. We were going to throw them out."

"Could I see them?"

Stover hesitated and then led him down the corridor to a storage room. For all its drabness, the dormitory building seemed to be well fitted for its clients, with a metal railing along the wall and smoke alarms in the ceiling. Nick stood by the door as Stover pulled out some boxes from one shelf in the storage room. "If I'd been five minutes earlier, Russ might be alive today," he said.

"I think I saw your name in the paper—"

"Sure! I placed him there and I was picking him up. When I rounded the corner I saw a crowd of people gathering. He was dead by the time I got to him."

"Nobody saw anything?"

"I guess not. Who pays attention in New York? I swear once I was driving by Radio City Music Hall about six in the morning, when they were having their Christmas show. Some guy was walking two camels around the block for their morning exercise and hardly anyone even noticed." He slit open the tape on one of the boxes and peered inside. "Nothing but clothing in here."

"I'll just take it along anyway."

When he opened the second box he frowned a bit. "Well, there are some letters in this one, and a couple of books." He looked up at Nick. "Maybe I should have some sort of authorization to release these."

"I can give you his sister's phone number." He'd worked that out with Vivian in advance. "You can check with her."

"Never heard about a sister," the man muttered. Then, "Our director is away today. I better wait till he gets back. Come back tomorrow."

"Sure thing." Nick turned to leave, his hand unobtrusively on the door's latchbolt. Stover shut the door and they walked back down the corridor together.

"See you later," the man told him and disappeared into a little office.

Immediately Nick turned and vaulted onto the handrail that ran along the wall, steadying himself with one hand against the ceiling, With his other hand he reached toward one of the smoke alarms. This model had a plastic button in the center of the unit for testing the battery, and he shoved a thin dime between the button and the casing, keeping it depressed. Immediately a loud blaring noise filled the hall. He jumped down to the floor as people began to look out of the rooms.

Some headed immediately for the exits while others stood around looking for some sign of smoke. Nick slipped into the storeroom just as Chris Stover emerged from his office to join the others. There was little chance of getting out with two boxes so Nick settled for the one containing the letters and books. He peeked down the hall and saw that Stover had gotten a ladder from somewhere to examine the blaring alarm. Perhaps he had noticed the edge of the dime holding the button in.

Nick went out the storeroom window as the smoke alarm was suddenly silenced.

Vivian Delmos seemed just a bit surprised to see him back so soon. "I thought you were going to get me Russell Bajon's things."

"I did. They're in this box. There was another box with a few pants and shirts, but I figured this was what you wanted."

"I'll know soon enough."

She opened the box and began looking through the objects, setting aside a worn pair of shoes and some socks and handkerchiefs. When she came to the books she examined them more carefully. One was a paperback edition of some of Shakespeare's tragedies, the others were a small dictionary and a book on acting. But she soon tossed these aside too, and turned only briefly to the letters, shaking the envelopes to make certain nothing small was hidden in them.

"You got the wrong box," she grumbled.

"I'm sorry."

She seemed to relent then. "No, what I'm looking for probably wasn't in the other box either. Somebody told me Bajon was involved with a shoplifting ring, stealing watches and jewelry from fancy stores during the Christmas season. I thought if he had anything in his belongings—"

"—that you'd take it?"

She flushed a bit at Nick's words. "I'm no thief. When Russell and I were in the play together I loaned him a few hundred dollars. I could use that money now. I figured anything I found among his belongings would pay the debt."

"Any jewelry or valuables he had were probably removed by whoever went through his clothes." As he spoke he was looking down at one of the envelopes that had been in the box. It was addressed to Russell Bajon at the Outreach Center. The return address bore only the surname of the sender: *Averly*.

It took him a few seconds to realize the significance of the name. The Santa strangler's second victim had been named Larry Averly. Nick slipped the letter out of the envelope and read the few lines quickly: "Russ—I was happy to do you the favor. No need to send me any more money. Keep some of the pie for yourself. Merry Christmas! Larry." The note was undated, but the envelope had been postmarked December second.

Nick returned the letter to its envelope and slipped it into his pocket. It told him nothing, except that the two victims might have known each other.

Maybe Bajon had replaced Averly as one of the Santas.

"Thanks for your efforts anyway," Vivian Delmos said.

"I did what I could."

When he didn't move, she asked, "Are you waiting for something more?"

"Yes."

"What's that?"

"Your beard."

That evening Nick returned to Grady Culhane's little office off Times Square. The young security man seemed uneasy as soon as he walked in the door. "I was hoping you wouldn't come here," he said.

Nick opened the paper bag he was carrying. "Why's that? I've brought you the beard."

"The beard was yesterday. Things have moved beyond that now. The cops are all over the place."

"What do you mean?"

"The extortion payoff. The money was left exactly as instructed, on the upper deck of the ferry that left Staten Island at three o'clock, before the evening rush hour. The police had it covered from every angle, even if he'd tossed the package overboard to a waiting boat."

"What happened?"

"Nothing. When the ferry docked in Manhattan some little old lady picked up the package and turned it in to lost and found."

"She got to it before the extortionist."

"Maybe," Culhane answered gloomily.

"What's the matter?"

"The Outreach Center reported that someone was snooping around the first victim's things this afternoon, and stole a box."

"That was me."

"I was afraid it might be. That means the cops are after you."

"How come?"

"They figure the killer was at the Outreach Center and that's why he couldn't pick up the extortion money from the three o'clock ferry."

"I certainly don't go around strangling Santas!" Nick objected. "You didn't even hire me till after the killings."

"I know, but try to tell them that! They need a fall guy, right away, or the city could lose millions in Christmas sales this final week. Who wants to bring the kids to see Santa Claus if he might be dead?"

A thought suddenly struck Nick. "You seemed nervous when I came in. Are they watching this office?"

"I had to tell them you were the one who set off the smoke bomb in the store yesterday. They were spending too much time on that angle and I tried to show them it was a dead end by admitting my part in it. Instead they got to thinking you were involved somehow."

"Just give me the rest of my money and I'm out of here."

"I don't have it right now."

Nick decided he'd overstayed his welcome. "I'll be in touch," he promised as he headed for the door.

They were waiting in the hall. A tall black man with a badge in one hand and a gun in the other barked, "Police! Up against the wall!"

His name was Sergeant Rynor and he was no more friendly within the confines of the precinct station. "You deny you were at the Outreach Center between three and four this afternoon, Mr. Velvet?"

"I told you I want a lawyer," Nick answered.

"He'll be here soon enough. And when he arrives we're going to run a line-up. Then we'll talk about the Santa Claus killings."

Ralph Aarons was a dapper Manhattan attorney whom Nick had used on rare occasions. He wasn't in the habit of getting in legal jams, especially in the New York area. Aarons made a good appearance, but he was hardly the sort to defend an accused serial Santa strangler.

"They've got a witness named Stover," the lawyer told him. "If he can place you at the Outreach Center, it may be trouble."

"We'll see," Nick said. He'd been thinking hard while he waited for Aarons to arrive.

Sergeant Rynor appeared in the doorway. "We're ready for you, Velvet. Up here on stage, please."

There were five other men, and Nick took the third position. The others were about his age and size but with different coloring and appearance. He guessed at least two of them were probably detectives. Chris Stover was brought in and escorted into a booth with a one-way glass. Over a loudspeaker, each of them was asked to step forward in turn. Then it was over. Apparently it had taken only a moment for Stover to identify him.

As Nick was being led away, Chris Stover and the other detectives came out of the booth. Nick paused ten feet from him and pointed dramatically. "That's the man!" his voice thundered like the wrath of God. "He's the one who killed the Santas and I can prove it!"

Nick couldn't prove it, and Chris Stover should have snorted and kept on walking. But he was taken off guard, startled into a foolish action. Perhaps in that unthinking instant he imagined the whole lineup had been merely a trick to unmask him. He gave one terrified glance at Nick and then tried to run, shoving two detectives out of the way in his dash for freedom.

It was Sergeant Rynor who finally grabbed him, before he even got close to the door.

"We're holding him," the black detective told Nick Velvet ten minutes later in the interrogation room, "but you'd better have a good story. Are you trying to tell us that Chris Stover is the extortionist who's been threatening the city's department stores for the past several days?"

"I don't think there was ever a real extortion plot. It was a matter of a big threat being used as a smokescreen to hide a smaller but no less deadly crime— the murders of Russell Bajon and Larry Averly."

"You'd better explain that."

Nick leaned back in the chair and collected his thoughts. "Grady Culhane told me about the extortion threats and even showed me a copy of the first letter. It was delivered to Kliman's president on Tuesday afternoon, shortly after the second strangling of a Santa Claus. Those two killings were meant to appear to be random acts against two random Santas, committed as a demonstration that the extortionist meant business. But the note mentioned the names of the two victims—Bajon and Averly. You didn't identify the second victim until later that day, and the killer had no chance to steal identification from his victim. The strangler knew the names of Bajon and Averly because these killings weren't random at all. He deliberately selected these victims, not as part of an extortion plot but for another motive altogether."

Rynor was making notes now, along with taping Nick's interrogation. Ralph Aarons, perhaps sensing things were going well for Nick, made no attempt to interrupt. "What other motive?" the detective asked.

"I learned earlier today that Bajon might have been involved in a shoplifting ring. And I also have a letter here that the second victim sent to Bajon two weeks ago. Not only did they know each other, but Averly had arranged for Bajon to take over some money-making enterprise from him. I think you'll find that Averly used to act as a Santa Claus for the Outreach Center. This year he passed the job on to Bajon, who became involved with the shoplifting."

"You're telling me that a man dressed in a bulky and highly visible Santa Claus costume was shoplifting?"

"No, I'm telling you that Santa stood on the corner with his collection chimney and the shoplifters came out of the stores with watches, rings, and other jewelry, and dropped them in the chimney. If the man was caught, there was no evidence on him, and the store detectives never considered Santa as an accessory."

"It's just wild enough to be true. But why would Stover kill them?"

"Bajon must have been skimming off the loot, or threatening to blackmail Stover. Once he decided to kill Bajon, he knew he had to kill Averly too, because the older man knew what was going on. When I guessed about Santa's chimney being used for shoplifting loot, Chris Stover became the most likely brains behind the operation. After all, he was the one who picked up the Santas and chimneys each night. He was the one who told them where to stand. Only Monday night he parked the van in the next block and walked up and strangled Bajon, then hurried back to the van and acted like he was just driving up."

"Maybe," Sergeant Rynor said thoughtfully. "It could have been like that. The extortion letter was just a red herring to cover the real motive. He never had any intention of going after that money on the Staten Island ferry."

"Can you prove all this?" Aarons asked, his legal mind in gear.

"We'll get a search warrant for Stover's office and room at the Center. If we find any shoplifted items there, I think he'll be ready to talk, and name the rest of the gang."

Nick knew he wasn't off the hook unless they found what they were looking for, but he came up lucky. The police uncovered dozens of jewelry items, along with a spool of wire that matched the wire used to kill the two Santas. After that, Chris Stover ceased his denials.

The way things turned out, Nick never did collect the balance of his fee from Grady Culhane. Some people just didn't have any Christmas spirit.

Georges Simenon

A MATTER OF LIFE
AND DEATH

"At home we always used to go to Midnight Mass. I can't remember a Christmas when we missed it, though it meant a good half hour's drive from the farm to the village."

The speaker, Sommer, was making some coffee on a little electric stove.

"There were five of us," he went on. "Five boys, that is. The winters were colder in those days. Sometimes we had to go by sledge."

Lecœur, on the switchboard, had taken off his earphones to listen. "In what part of the country was that?"

"Lorraine."

"The winters in Lorraine were no colder thirty or forty years ago than they are now—only, of course, in those days the peasant had no cars. How many times did you go to Midnight Mass by sledge?"

"Couldn't say, exactly."

"Three times? Twice? Perhaps no more than once. Only it made a great impression on you, as you were a child."

"Anyhow, when we got back, we'd all have black pudding, and I'm not exaggerating when I tell you I've never had anything like it since. I don't know what my mother used to put in them, but her *boudins* were quite different from anyone else's. My wife's tried, but it wasn't the same thing, though she had the exact recipe from my eldest sister—at least, my sister swore it was."

He walked over to one of the huge, uncurtained windows, through which was nothing but blackness, and scratched the pane with a fingernail.

"Hallo, there's frost forming. That again reminds me of when I was little. The water used to freeze in our rooms and we'd have to break the ice in the morning when we wanted to wash."

"People didn't have central heating in those days," answered Lecœur coolly.

There were three of them on night duty. *Les nuiteux*, they were called. They had been in that vast room since eleven o'clock, and now, at six on that

309

Christmas morning, all three were looking a bit jaded. Three or four empty bottles were lying about, with the remains of the sandwiches they had brought with them.

A lamp no bigger than an aspirin tablet lit up on one of the walls. Its position told Lecœur at once where the call came from.

"Thirteenth Arrondissement, Croulebarbe," he murmured, replacing his earphones. He seized a plug and pushed it into a hole.

"Croulebarbe? Your car's been called out—what for?"

"A call from the Boulevard Masséna. Two drunks fighting."

Lecœur carefully made a little cross in one of the columns of his notebook.

"How are you getting on down your way?"

"There are only four of us here. Two are playing dominoes."

"Had any *boudin* tonight?"

"No. Why?"

"Never mind. I must ring off now. There's a call from the Sixteenth."

A gigantic map of Paris was drawn on the wall in front of him and on it each police station was represented by a little lamp. As soon as anything happened anywhere, a lamp would light up and Lecœur would plug into the appropriate socket.

"Chaillot? Hallo! Your car's out?"

In front of each police station throughout the twenty arrondissements of Paris, one or more cars stood waiting, ready to dash off the moment an alarm was raised.

"What with?"

"Veronal."

That would be a woman. It was the third suicide that night, the second in the smart district of Passy.

Another little cross was entered in the appropriate column of Lecœur's notebook. Mambret, the third member of the watch, was sitting at a desk filling out forms.

"Hallo! Odéon? What's going on? Oh, a car stolen."

That was for Mambret, who took down the particulars, then phoned them through to Piedbœuf in the room above. Piedbœuf, the teleprinter operator, had such a resounding voice that the others could hear it through the ceiling. This was the forty-eighth car whose details he had circulated that night.

An ordinary night, in fact—for them. Not so for the world outside. For this was the great night, *la nuit de Noël*. Not only was there the Midnight Mass, but all the theaters and cinemas were crammed, and at the big stores, which stayed open till twelve, a crowd of people jostled each other in a last-minute scramble to finish off their Christmas shopping.

Indoors were family gatherings feasting on roast turkey and perhaps also on *boudins* made, like the ones Sommer had been talking about, from a secret recipe handed down from mother to daughter.

There were children sleeping restlessly while their parents crept about playing the part of Santa Claus, arranging the presents they would find on waking.

At the restaurants and cabarets every table had been booked at least a week in advance. In the Salvation Army barge on the Seine, tramps and paupers queued up for an extra special.

Sommer had a wife and five children. Piedbœuf, the teleprinter operator upstairs, was a father of one week's standing. Without the frost on the windowpanes, they wouldn't have known it was freezing outside. In that vast, dingy room they were in a world apart, surrounded on all sides by the empty offices of the Préfecture de Police, which stood facing the Palais de Justice. It wasn't till the following day that those offices would once again be teeming with people in search of passport visas, driving licenses, and permits of every description.

In the courtyard below, cars stood waiting for emergency calls, the men of the flying squad dozing on the seats. Nothing, however, had happened that night of sufficient importance to justify their being called out. You could see that from the little crosses in Lecœur's notebook. He didn't bother to count them, but he could tell at a glance that there were something like two hundred in the drunks' column.

No doubt there'd have been a lot more if it hadn't been that this was a night for indulgence. In most cases the police were able to persuade those who had had too much to go home and keep out of trouble. Those arrested were the ones in whom drink raised the devil, those who smashed windows or molested other people.

Two hundred of that sort—a handful of women among them—were now out of harm's way, sleeping heavily on the wooden benches in the lock-ups.

There'd been five knifings. Two near the Porte d'Italie. Three in the remoter part of Montmartre, not in the Montmartre of the Moulin Rouge and the Lapin Agile but in the Zone, beyond where the Fortifs used to be, whose population included over 100,000 Arabs living in huts made of old packing cases and roofing-felt.

A few children had been lost in the exodus from the churches, but they were soon returned to their anxious parents.

"Hallo! Chaillot? How's your veronal case getting on?"

She wasn't dead. Of course not! Few went as far as that. Suicide is all very well as a gesture—indeed, it can be a very effective one. But there's no need to go and kill yourself!

"Talking of *boudin*," said Mambret, who was smoking an enormous meerschaum pipe, "that reminds me of—"

They were never to know what he was reminded of. There were steps in the corridor, then the handle of the door was turned. All three looked round at once, wondering who could be coming to see them at ten past six in the morning.

"Salut!" said the man who entered, throwing his hat down on a chair.

"Whatever brings you here, Janvier?"

It was a detective of the Brigade des Homicides, who walked straight to the stove to warm his hands.

"I got pretty bored sitting all by myself and I thought I might as well come over here. After all, if the killer's going to do his stuff I'd hear about it quicker here than anywhere."

He, too, had been on duty all night, but round the corner, in the Police Judiciaire.

"You don't mind, do you?" he asked, picking up the coffeepot. "There's a bitter wind blowing."

It had made his ears red.

"I don't suppose we'll hear till eight, probably later," said Lecœur.

For the last fifteen years, he had spent his nights in that room, sitting at the switchboard, keeping an eye on the big map with the little lamps. He knew half the police in Paris by name, or, at any rate, those who did night duty. Of many he knew even their private affairs, as, when things were quiet, he would have long chats with them over the telephone to pass the time away. "Oh, it's you, Dumas. How are things at home?"

But though there were many whose voices were familiar, there were hardly any of them he knew by sight.

Nor was his acquaintance confined to the police. He was on equally familiar terms with many of the hospitals.

"Hallo! Bichat? What about the chap who was brought in half an hour ago? Is he dead yet?"

He was dead, and another little cross went into the notebook. The latter was, in its unpretentious way, quite a mine of information. If you asked Lecœur how many murders in the last twelve months had been done for the sake of money, he'd give the answer in a moment—sixty-seven.

"How many murders committed by foreigners?"

"Forty-two. "

You could go on like that for hours without being able to trip him up. And yet he trotted out his figures without a trace of swank. It was his hobby, that was all.

For he wasn't obliged to make those crosses. It was his own idea. Like the chats over the telephone lines, they helped to pass the time away, and the result gave him much the same satisfaction that others derive from a collection of stamps.

He was unmarried. Few knew where he lived or what sort of a life he led outside that room. It was difficult to picture him anywhere else, even to think of him walking along the street like an ordinary person. He turned to Janvier to say: "For your cases, we generally have to wait till people are up and about. It's when a concierge goes up with the post or when a maid takes her mistress's breakfast into the bedroom that things like that come to light."

He claimed no special merit in knowing a thing like that. It was just a fact. A bit earlier in summer, of course, and later in winter. On Christmas Day probably later still, as a considerable part of the population hadn't gotten to bed until two or even later, to say nothing of their having to sleep off a good many glasses of champagne.

Before then, still more water would have gone under the bridge—a few more stolen cars, a few belated drunks.

"Hallo! Saint-Gervais?"

His Paris was not the one known to the rest of us—the Eiffel Tower, the Louvre, the Opéra—but one of somber, massive buildings with a police car waiting under the blue lamp and the bicycles of the *agents cyclistes* leaning against the wall.

"The chief is convinced the chap'll have another go tonight," said Janvier. "It's just the night for people of that sort. Seems to excite them."

No name was mentioned, for none was known. Nor could he be described as the man in the fawn raincoat or the man in the grey hat, since no one had ever seen him. For a while the papers had referred to him as Monsieur Dimanche, as his first three murders had been on Sunday, but since then five others had been on weekdays, at the rate of about one a week, though not quite regularly.

"It's because of him you've been on all night, is it?" asked Mambret.

Janvier wasn't the only one. All over Paris extra men were on duty, watching or waiting.

"You'll see," put in Sommer, "when you do get him you'll find he's only a loony."

"Loony or not, he's killed eight people," sighed Janvier, sipping his coffee. "Look, Lecœur—there's one of your lamps burning."

"Hallo! Your car's out? What's that? Just a moment."

They could see Lecœur hesitate, not knowing in which column to put a cross. There was one for hangings, one for those who jumped out of the window, another for—

"Here, listen to this. On the Pont d'Austerlitz, a chap climbed up onto the parapet. He had his legs tied together and a cord round his neck with the end made fast to a lamppost, and as he threw himself over he fired a shot into his head!"

"Taking no risks, what? And which column does that one go into?"

"There's one for neurasthenics. We may as well call it that."

Those who hadn't been to Midnight Mass were now on their way to early service. With hands thrust deep in their pockets and drops on the ends of their noses, they walked bent forward into the cutting wind, which seemed to blow up a fine, icy dust from the pavements. It would soon be time for the children to be waking up, jumping out of bed, and gathering barefoot around lighted Christmas trees.

"But it's not at all sure the fellow's mad. In fact, the experts say that if he was he'd always do it the same way. If it was a knife, then it would always be a knife."

"What did he use this time?"

"A hammer."

"And the time before?"

"A dagger."

"What makes you think it's the same chap?"

"First of all, the fact that there've been eight murders in quick succession. You don't get eight new murderers cropping up in Paris all at once." Belonging to the Police Judiciaire, Janvier had, of course, heard the subject discussed at length. "Besides, there's a sort of family likeness between them all. The victims are invariably solitary people, people who live alone, without any family or friends."

Sommer looked at Lecœur, whom he could never forgive for not being a family man. Not only had he five children himself, but a sixth was already on the way. "You'd better look out, Lecœur—you see the kind of thing it leads to!"

"Then, not one of the crimes has been committed in one of the wealthier districts."

"Yet he steals, doesn't he?"

"He does, but not much. The little hoards hidden under the mattress—that's his mark. He doesn't break in. In fact, apart from the murder and the money missing, he leaves no trace at all."

Another lamp burning. A stolen car found abandoned in a little side street near the Place des Ternes.

"All the same, I can't help laughing over the people who had to walk home."

Another hour or more and they would be relieved, except Lecœur, who had promised to do the first day shift as well so that his opposite number could join in a family Christmas party somewhere near Rouen.

It was a thing he often did, so much so that he had come to be regarded as an ever-ready substitute for anybody who wanted a day off.

"I say, Lecœur, do you think you could look out for me on Friday?"

At first the request was proffered with a suitable excuse—a sick mother, a funeral, or a First Communion, and he was generally rewarded with a bottle of wine. But now it was taken for granted and treated quite casually.

To tell the truth, had it been possible, Lecœur would have been only too glad to spend his whole life in that room, snatching a few hours' sleep on a camp bed and picnicking as best he could with the aid of the little electric stove. It was a funny thing—although he was as careful as any of the others about his personal appearance, and much more so than Sommer, who always looked a bit tousled, there was something a bit drab about him which betrayed the bachelor.

He wore strong glasses, which gave him big, globular eyes, and it came as a surprise to everyone when he took them off to wipe them with the bit of chamois leather he always carried about to see the transformation. Without them, his eyes were gentle, rather shy, and inclined to look away quickly when anyone looked his way.

"Hallo! Javel?"

Another lamp. One near the Quai de Javel in the 15th Arrondissement, a district full of factories.

"Votre car est sorti?"

"We don't know yet what it is. Someone's broken the glass of the alarm in the Rue Leblanc."

"Wasn't there a message?"

"No. We've sent our car to investigate. I'll ring you again later."

Scattered here and there all over Paris are red-painted telephone pillars standing by the curb, and you have only to break the glass to be in direct telephone communication with the nearest police station. Had a passerby broken the glass accidentally? It looked like it, for a couple of minutes later Javel rang up again.

"Hallo! Central? Our car's just got back. Nobody about. The whole district seems quiet as the grave. All the same, we've sent out a patrol."

How was Lecœur to classify that one? Unwilling to admit defeat, he put a little cross in the column on the extreme right headed "Miscellaneous."

"Is there any coffee left?" he asked.

"I'll make some more."

The same lamp lit up again, barely ten minutes after the first call.

"Javel? What's it this time?"

"Same again. Another glass broken."

"Nothing said?"

"Not a word. Must be some practical joker. Thinks it funny to keep us on the hop. When we catch him he'll find out whether it's funny or not!"

"Which one was it?"

"The one on the Pont Mirabeau."

"Seems to walk pretty quickly, your practical joker!"

There was indeed quite a good stretch between the two pillars.

So far, nobody was taking it very seriously. False alarms were not uncommon. Some people took advantage of these handy instruments to express their feelings about the police. *"Mort aux flics!"* was the favorite phrase.

With his feet on a radiator, Janvier was just dozing off when he heard Lecœur telephoning again. He half opened his eyes, saw which lamp was on, and muttered sleepily, "There he is again."

He was right. A glass broken at the top of the Avenue de Versailles.

"Silly ass," he grunted, settling down again.

It wouldn't be really light until half past seven or even eight. Sometimes they could hear a vague sound of church bells, but that was in another world. The wretched men of the flying squad waiting in the cars below must be half frozen.

"Talking of *boudin*—"

"What *boudin?*" murmured Janvier, whose cheeks were flushed with sleep.

"The one my mother used to—"

"Hallo! What? You're not going to tell me someone's smashed the glass of one of your telephone pillars? Really? It must be the same chap. We've already had two reported from the Fifteenth. Yes, they tried to nab him but couldn't find a soul about. Gets about pretty fast, doesn't he? He crossed the river by the Pont Mirabeau. Seems to be heading in this direction. Yes, you may as well have a try."

Another little cross. By half past seven, with only half an hour of the night watch to go, there were five crosses in the Miscellaneous column.

Mad or sane, the person was a good walker. Perhaps the cold wind had something to do with it. It wasn't the weather for sauntering along.

For a time it had looked as though he was keeping to the right bank of the Seine, then he had sheered off into the wealthy Auteuil district, breaking a glass in the Rue la Fontaine.

"He's only five minutes' walk from the Bois de Boulogne," Lecœur had said. "If he once gets there, they'll never pick him up."

But the fellow had turned round and made for the quays again, breaking a glass in the Rue Berton, just around the corner from the Quai de Passy.

316

The first calls had come from the poorer quarters of Grenelle, but the man had only to cross the river to find himself in entirely different surroundings—quiet, spacious, and deserted streets, where his footfalls must have rung out clearly on the frosty pavements.

Sixth call. Skirting the Place du Trocadéro, he was in the Rue de Longchamp.

"The chap seems to think he's on a paper chase," remarked Mambret. "Only he uses broken glass instead of paper."

Other calls came in in quick succession. Another stolen car, a revolver-shot in the Rue de Flandres, whose victim swore he didn't know who fired it, though he'd been seen all through the night drinking in company with another man.

"Hallo! Here's Javel again. Hallo! Javel? It can't be your practical joker this time: he must be somewhere near the Champs Elysées by now. Oh, yes. He's still at it. Well, what's your trouble? What? Spell it, will you? Rue Michat. Yes, I've got it. Between the Rue Lecourbe and the Boulevard Felix Faure. By the viaduct—yes, I know. Number 17. Who reported it? The concierge? She's just been up, I suppose. Oh, shut up, will you! No, I wasn't speaking to you. It's Sommer here, who can't stop talking about a *boudin* he ate thirty years ago!"

Sommer broke off and listened to the man on the switchboard.

"What were you saying? A shabby seven-story block of flats. Yes—"

There were plenty of buildings like that in the district, buildings that weren't really old, but of such poor construction that they were already dilapidated. Buildings that as often as not thrust themselves up bleakly in the middle of a bit of wasteland, towering over the little shacks and hovels around them, their blind walls plastered with advertisements.

"You say she heard someone running downstairs and then a door slam. The door of the house, I suppose. On which floor is the flat? The *entresol.* Which way does it face? Onto an inner courtyard— Just a moment, there's a call coming in from the Eighth. That must be our friend of the telephone pillars."

Lecœur asked the new caller to wait, then came back to Javel.

"An old woman, you say. Madame Fayet. Worked as charwoman. Dead? A blunt instrument. Is the doctor there? You're sure she's dead? What about her money? I suppose she had some tucked away somewhere. Right. Call me back. Or I'll ring you."

He turned to the detective, who was now sleeping soundly.

"Janvier! Hey, Janvier! This is for you."

"What? What is it?"

"The killer."

"Where?"

"Near the Rue Lecourbe. Here's the address. This time he's done in an old charwoman, a Madame Fayet."

Janvier put on his overcoat, looked round for his hat, and gulped down the remains of the coffee in his cup.

"Who's dealing with it?"

"Gonesse, of the Fifteenth."

"Ring up the P.J., will you, and tell them I've gone there."

A minute or two later, Lecœur was able to add another little cross to the six that were already in the column. Someone had smashed the glass of the pillar in the Avenue d'Iéna only one hundred and fifty yards from the Arc de Triomphe.

"Among the broken glass they found a handkerchief flecked with blood. It was a child's handkerchief."

"Has it got initials?"

"No. It's a blue-check handkerchief, rather dirty. The chap must have wrapped it round his knuckles for breaking the glass."

There were steps in the corridor. The day shift coming to take over. They looked very clean and close-shaven and the cold wind had whipped the blood into their cheeks.

"Happy Christmas!"

Sommer closed the tin in which he brought his sandwiches. Mambret knocked out his pipe. Only Lecœur remained in his seat, since there was no relief for him.

The fat Godin had been the first to arrive, promptly changing his jacket for the grey-linen coat in which he always worked, then putting some water on to boil for his grog. All through the winter he suffered from one never-ending cold which he combated, or perhaps nourished, by one hot grog after another.

"Hallo! Yes, I'm still here. I'm doing a shift for Potier, who's gone down to his family in Normandy. Yes. I want to hear all about it. Most particularly. Janvier's gone, but I'll pass it on to the P.J. An invalid, you say? What invalid?"

One had to be patient on that job, as people always talked about their cases as though everyone else was in the picture.

"A low building behind, right. Not in the Rue Michat, then? Rue Vasco de Gamma. Yes, yes. I know. The little house with a garden behind some railings. Only I didn't know he was an invalid. Right. He doesn't sleep much. Saw a young boy climbing up a drainpipe? How old? He couldn't say? Of course not, in the dark. How did he know it was a boy, then? Listen, ring me up again, will you? Oh, you're going off. Who's relieving you? Jules? Right. Well, ask him to keep me informed."

"What's going on?" asked Godin.

"An old woman who's been done in. Down by the Rue Lecourbe."

"Who did it?"

"There's an invalid opposite who says he saw a small boy climbing up a drainpipe and along the top of a wall."

"You mean to say it was a boy who killed the old woman?"

"We don't know yet."

No one was very interested. After all, murders were an everyday matter to these people. The lights were still on in the room, as it was still only a bleak, dull daylight that found its way through the frosty window panes. One of the new watch went and scratched a bit of the frost away. It was instinctive. A childish memory perhaps, like Sommer's *boudin*.

The latter had gone home. So had Mambret. The newcomers settled down to their work, turning over the papers on their desks.

A car stolen from the Square la Bruyère.

Lecœur looked pensively at his seven crosses. Then, with a sigh, he got up and stood gazing at the immense street plan on the wall.

"Brushing up on your Paris?"

"I think I know it pretty well already. Something's just struck me. There's a chap wandering about smashing the glass of telephone pillars. Seven in the last hour and a half. He hasn't been going in a straight line but zigzagging—first this way, then that."

"Perhaps he doesn't know Paris."

"Or knows it only too well! Not once has he ventured within sight of a police station. If he'd gone straight, he'd have passed two or three. What's more, he's skirted all the main crossroads where there'd be likely to be a man on duty." Lecœur pointed them out. "The only risk he took was in crossing the Pont Mirabeau, but if he wanted to cross the river he'd have run that risk at any of the bridges."

"I expect he's drunk," said Godin, sipping his rum.

"What I want to know is why he's stopped."

"Perhaps he's got home."

"A man who's down by the Quai de Javel at half past six in the morning isn't likely to live near the Etoile."

"Seems to interest you a lot."

"It's got me scared!"

"Go on."

It was strange to see the worried expression on Lecœur's face. He was notorious for his calmness and his most dramatic nights were coolly summarized by the little crosses in his notebook.

"Hallo! Javel? Is that Jules? Lecœur speaking. Look here, Jules, behind the flats in the Rue Michat is the little house where the invalid lives. Well, now, on one side of it is an apartment house, a red-brick building with a grocer's shop on the ground floor. You know it?

"Good. Has anything happened there? Nothing reported. No, we've heard nothing here. All the same, I can't explain why, but I think you ought to inquire."

He was hot all at once. He stubbed out a half finished cigarette.

"Hallo! Ternes? Any alarms gone off in your neighborhood? Nothing? Only drunks? Is the *patrouille cycliste* out? Just leaving? Ask them to keep their eyes open for a young boy looking tired and very likely bleeding from the right hand. Lost? Not exactly that. I can't explain now."

His eyes went back to the street plan on the wall, in which no light went on for a good ten minutes, and then only for an accidental death in the Eighteenth Arrondissement, right up at the top of Montmartre, caused by an escape of gas.

Outside, in the cold streets of Paris, dark figures were hurrying home from the churches . . .

One of the sharpest impressions Andre Lecœur retained of his infancy was one of immobility. His world at that period was a large kitchen in Orleans, on the outskirts of the town. He must have spent his winters there, too, but he remembered it best flooded with sunlight, with the door wide open onto a little garden where hens clucked incessantly and rabbits nibbled lettuce leaves behind the wire netting of their hutches. But, if the door was open, its passage was barred to him by a little gate which his father had made one Sunday for that express purpose.

On weekdays, at half past eight, his father went off on his bicycle to the gas works at the other end of the town. His mother did the housework, doing the same things in the same order every day. Before making the beds, she put the bedclothes over the windowsill for an hour to air.

At ten o'clock, a little bell would ring in the street. That was the green-grocer, with his barrow, passing on his daily round. Twice a week at eleven, a bearded doctor came to see his little brother, who was constantly ill. Andre hardly ever saw the latter, as he wasn't allowed into his room.

That was all, or so it seemed in retrospect. He had just time to play a bit and drink his milk, and there was his father home again for the midday meal.

If nothing had happened at home, lots had happened to him. He had been to read the meters in any number of houses and chatted with all sorts of people, about whom he would talk during dinner.

As for the afternoon, it slipped away quicker still, perhaps because he was made to sleep during the first part of it.

For his mother, apparently, the time passed just as quickly. Often had he heard her say with a sigh: "There, I've no sooner washed up after one meal than it's time to start making another!"

Perhaps it wasn't so very different now. Here in the Préfecture de Police the nights seemed long enough at the time, but at the end they seemed to have slipped by in no time, with nothing to show for them except for these columns of the little crosses in his notebook.

A few more lamps lit up. A few more incidents reported, including a collision between a car and a bus in the Rue de Clignancourt, and then once again it was Javel on the line.

It wasn't Jules, however, but Gonesse, the detective who'd been to the scene of the crime. While there he had received Lecœur's message suggesting something might have happened in the other house in the Rue Vasco de Gama. He had been to see.

"Is that you, Lecœur?" There was a queer note in his voice. Either irritation or suspicion.

"Look here, what made you think of that house? Do you know the old woman, Madame Fayet?"

"I've never seen her, but I know all about her."

What had finally come to pass that Christmas morning was something that Andre Lecœur had foreseen and perhaps dreaded for more than ten years. Again and again, as he stared at the huge plan of Paris, with its little lamps, he had said to himself, "It's only a question of time. Sooner or later, it'll be something that's happened to someone I know."

There'd been many a near miss, an accident in his own street or a crime in a house nearby. But, like thunder, it had approached only to recede once again into the distance.

This time it was a direct hit.

"Have you seen the concierge?" he asked. He could imagine the puzzled look on the detective's face as he went on: "Is the boy at home?"

And Gonesse muttered, "Oh? So you know him, too?"

"He's my nephew. Weren't you told his name was Lecœur?"

"Yes, but—"

"Never mind about that. Tell me what's happened."

"The boy's not there."

"What about his father?"

"He got home just after seven."

"As usual. He does night work, too."

"The concierge heard him go up to his flat—on the third floor at the back of the house."

"I know it."

"He came running down a minute or two later in a great state. To use her expression, he seemed out of his wits."

"The boy had disappeared?"

"Yes. His father wanted to know if she'd seen him leave the house. She hadn't. Then he asked if a telegram had been delivered."

"Was there a telegram?"

"No. Can you make head or tail of it? Since you're one of the family, you might be able to help us. Could you get someone to relieve you and come round here?"

"It wouldn't do any good. Where's Janvier?"

"In the old woman's room. The men of the Identité Judiciaire have already got to work. The first thing they found were some child's fingerprints on the handle of the door. Come on—jump into a taxi and come round."

"No. In any case, there's no one to take my place."

That was true enough up to a point. All the same, if he'd really got to work on the telephone he'd have found someone all right. The truth was he didn't want to go and didn't think it would do any good if he did.

"Listen, Gonesse, I've got to find that boy, and I can do it better from here than anywhere. You understand, don't you? Tell Janvier I'm staying here. And tell him old Madame Fayet had plenty of money, probably hidden away somewhere in the room."

A little feverish, Lecœur stuck his plug into one socket after another, calling up the various police stations of the Eighth Arrondissement.

"Keep a lookout for a boy of ten, rather poorly dressed. Keep all telephone pillars under observation."

His two fellow-watchkeepers looked at him with curiosity.

"Do you think it was the boy who did the job?"

Lecœur didn't bother to answer. The next moment he was through to the teleprinter room, where they also dealt with radio messages.

"Justin? Oh, you're on, are you? Here's something special. Will you send out a call to all cars on patrol anywhere near the Etoile to keep a lookout for—"

Once again the description of the boy, Francois Lecœur.

"No. I've no idea in which direction he'll be making. All I can tell you is that he seems to keep well clear of police stations, and as far as possible from any place where there's likely to be anyone on traffic duty."

He knew his brother's flat in the Rue Vasco de Gama. Two rather dark rooms and a tiny kitchen. The boy slept there alone while his father was at work. From the windows you could see the back of the house in the Rue Michat, across a courtyard generally hung with washing. On some of the windowsills were pots of geraniums, and through the windows, many of which were uncurtained, you could catch glimpses of a miscellaneous assortment of humanity.

As a matter of fact, there, too, the windowpanes ought to be covered with frost. He stored that idea up in a corner of his mind. It might be important.

"You think it's a boy who's been smashing the alarm glasses?"

"It was a child's handkerchief they found," said Lecœur curtly. He didn't want to be drawn into a discussion. He sat mutely at the switchboard, wondering what to do next.

In the Rue Michat, things seemed to be moving fast. The next time he got through it was to learn that a doctor was there as well as an examining magistrate who had most likely been dragged from his bed.

What help could Lecœur have given them? But if he wasn't there, he could see the place almost as clearly as those that were, the dismal houses and the grimy viaduct of the Métro which cut right across the landscape.

Nothing but poor people in that neighborhood. The younger generation's one hope was to escape from it. The middle-aged already doubted whether they ever would, while the old ones had already accepted their fate and tried to make the best of it.

He rang Javel once again.

"Is Gonesse still there?"

"He's writing up his report. Shall I call him?"

"Yes, please. Hallo, Gonesse, Lecœur speaking. Sorry to bother you, but did you go up to my brother's flat? Had the boy's bed been slept in? It had? Good. That makes it look a bit better. Another thing: were there any parcels there? Yes, parcels, Christmas presents. What? A small square radio. Hadn't been unpacked. Naturally. Anything else? A chicken, a *boudin*, a Saint-Honoré. I suppose Janvier's not with you? Still on the spot. Right. Has he rung-up the P.J.? Good."

He was surprised to see it was already half past nine. It was no use now expecting anything from the neighborhood of the Etoile. If the boy had gone on walking as he had been earlier, he could be pretty well anywhere by this time.

"Hallo! Police Judiciaire? Is Inspector Saillard there?"

He was another whom the murder had dragged from his fireside. How many people were there whose Christmas was going to be spoiled by it?

"Excuse my troubling you, Monsieur le Commissaire. It's about that young boy, Francois Lecœur."

"Do you know anything? Is he a relation of yours?"

"He's my brother's son. And it looks as if he may well be the person who's been smashing the glasses of the telephone pillars. Seven of them. I don't know whether they've had time to tell you about that. What I wanted to ask was whether I might put out a general call?"

"Could you nip over to see me?"

"There's no one here to take my place."

"Right. I'll come over myself. Meanwhile you can send out the call."

Lecœur kept calm, though his hand shook slightly as he plugged in once again to the room above.

"Justin? Lecœur again. Appel General. Yes. It's the same boy. Francois Lecœur. Ten and a half, rather tall for his age, thin. I don't know what he's wearing, probably a khaki jumper made from American battle-dress. No, no cap. He's always bare-headed, with plenty of hair flopping over his forehead. Perhaps it would be as well to send out a description of his father, too. That's not so easy. You know me, don't you? Well, Olivier Lecœur is rather like a paler version of me. He has a timid look about him and physically he's not robust. The sort that's never in the middle of the pavement but always dodging out of other people's way. He walks a bit queerly, owing to a wound he got in the first war. No, I haven't the least idea where they might be going, only I don't think they're together. To my mind, the boy is probably in danger. I can't explain why—it would take too long. Get the descriptions out as quickly as possible, will you? And let me know if there's any response."

By the time Lecœur had finished telephoning, Inspector Saillard was there, having only had to come round the corner from the Quai des Orfèvres. He was an imposing figure of a man, particularly in his bulky overcoat. With a comprehensive wave of the hand, he greeted the three men on watch, then, seizing a chair as though it were a wisp of straw, he swung it round towards him and sat down heavily. "The boy?" he inquired, looking keenly at Lecœur.

"I can't understand why he's stopped calling us up."

"Calling us up?"

"Attracting our attention, anyway."

"But why should he attract our attention and then not say anything?"

"Supposing he was followed. Or was following someone."

"I see what you mean. Look here, Lecœur, is your brother in financial straits?"

"He's a poor man, yes."

"Is that all?"

"He lost his job three months ago."

"What job?"

"He was linotype operator at *La Presse* in the Rue du Croissant. He was on the night shift. He always did night work. Runs in the family."

"How did he come to lose his job?"

"I suppose he fell out with somebody."

"Is that a failing of his?"

They were interrupted by an incoming call from the Eighteenth to say that a boy selling branches of holly had been picked up in the Rue Lepic. It turned out, however, to be a little Pole who couldn't speak any French.

"You were asking if my brother was in the habit of quarreling with people. I hardly know what to answer. He was never strong. Pretty well all his childhood he was ill on and off. He hardly ever went to school. But he read a great deal alone in his room."

"Is he married?"

"His wife died two years after they were married, leaving him with a baby ten months old."

"Did he bring it up himself?"

"Entirely. I can see him now bathing the little chap, changing his diapers, and warming the milk for his bottle."

"That doesn't explain why he quarrels with people."

Admittedly. But it was difficult to put it into words.

"Soured?"

"Not exactly. The thing is—"

"What?"

"That he's never lived like other people. Perhaps Olivier isn't really very intelligent. Perhaps, from reading so much, he knows too much about some things and too little about others."

"Do you think him capable of killing the old woman?"

The Inspector puffed at his pipe. They could hear the people in the room above walking about. The two other men fiddled with their papers, pretending not to listen.

"She was his mother-in-law," sighed Lecœur. "You'd have found it out anyhow, sooner or later."

"They didn't hit it off?"

"She hated him."

"Why?"

"She considered him responsible for her daughter's death. It seems she could have been saved if the operation had been done in time. It wasn't my brother's fault. The people at the hospital refused to take her in. Some silly question of her papers not being in order. All the same, Madame Fayet held to it that Olivier was to blame."

"Did they see each other?"

"Not unless they passed each other in the street, and then they never spoke."

"Did the boy know?"

"That she was his grandmother? I don't think so."

"You think his father never told him?"

*　　*　　*

Never for more than a second or two did Lecœur's eyes leave the plan of Paris, but, besides being Christmas, it was the quiet time of the day, and the little lamps lit up rarely. Two or three street accidents, a lady's handbag snatched in the Métro, a suitcase pinched at the Gare de l'Est.

No sign of the boy. It was surprising considering how few people were about. In the poor quarters a few little children played on the pavements with their new toys, but on the whole the day was lived indoors. Nearly all the shops were shuttered and the cafes and the little bars were almost empty.

For a moment, the town came to life a bit when the church bells started pealing and families in their Sunday best hurried to High Mass. But soon the streets were quiet again, though haunted here and there by the vague rumble of an organ or a sudden gust of singing.

The thought of churches gave Lecœur an idea. Might not the boy have tucked himself away in one of them? Would the police think of looking there? He spoke to Inspector Saillard about it and then got through to Justin for the third time.

"The churches. Ask them to have a look at the congregations. They'll be doing the stations, of course—that's most important."

He took off his glasses for a moment, showing eyelids that were red, probably from lack of sleep.

"Hallo! Yes. The Inspector's here. Hold on."

He held the receiver to Saillard. "It's Janvier."

The bitter wind was still driving through the streets. The light was harsh and bleak, though here and there among the closely packed clouds was a yellowy streak which could be taken as a faint promise of sunshine to come.

When the Inspector put down the receiver, he muttered, "Dr. Paul says the crime was committed between five and half past six this morning. The old woman wasn't killed by the first blow. Apparently she was in bed when she heard a noise and got up and faced the intruder. Indeed, it looks as though she tried to defend herself with the only weapon that came to hand—a shoe."

"Have they found the weapon she was killed with?"

"No. It might have been a hammer. More likely a bit of lead piping or something of that sort."

"Have they found her money?"

"Only her purse, with some small change in it and her identity card. Tell me, Lecœur, did you know she was a money-lender?"

"Yes. I knew."

"And didn't you tell me your brother's been out of work for three months?"

"He has."

"The concierge didn't know. "

"Neither did the boy. It was for his sake he kept it dark."

The Inspector crossed and uncrossed his legs. He was uncomfortable. He glanced at the other two men who couldn't help hearing everything, then turned with a puzzled look to stare at Lecœur.

"Do you realize what all this is pointing to?"

"I do."

"You've thought of it yourself?"

"No."

"Because he's your brother?"

"No."

"How long is it that this killer's been at work? Nine weeks, isn't it?"

Without haste, Lecœur studied the columns of his notebook.

"Yes. Just over nine weeks. The first was on the twentieth of October, in the Epinettes district."

"You say your brother didn't tell his son he was out of a job. Do you mean to say he went on leaving home in the evening just as though he was going to work?"

"Yes. He couldn't face the idea of telling him. You see—it's difficult to explain. He was completely wrapped up in the boy. He was all he had to live for. He cooked and scrubbed for him, tucked him up in bed before going off, and woke him up in the morning."

"That doesn't explain why he couldn't tell him."

"He couldn't bear the thought of appearing to the kid as a failure, a man nobody wanted and who had doors slammed in his face."

"But what did he do with himself all night?"

"Odd jobs. When he could get them. For a fortnight, he was employed as night watchman in a factory in Billancourt, but that was only while the regular man was ill. Often he got a few hours' work washing down cars in one of the big garages. When that failed, he'd sometimes lend a hand at the market unloading vegetables. When he had one of his bouts—"

"Bouts of what?"

"Asthma. He had them from time to time. Then he'd lie down in a station waiting room. Once he spent a whole night here, chatting with me."

"Suppose the boy woke up early this morning and saw his father at Madame Fayet's?"

"There was frost on the windows."

"There wouldn't be if the window was open. Lots of people sleep with their windows open even in the coldest weather."

"It wasn't the case with my brother. He was always a chilly person. And he was much too poor to waste warmth."

"As far as his window was concerned, the boy had only to scratch away the frost with his fingernail. When I was a boy—

"Yes. So did I. The thing is to find out whether the old woman's window was open."

"It was, and the light was switched on."

"I wonder where Francois can have got to."

"The boy?"

It was surprising and a little disconcerting the way he kept all the time reverting to him. The situation was certainly embarrassing, and somehow made all the more so by the calm way in which Andre Lecœur gave the Inspector the most damaging details about his brother.

"When he came in this morning," began Saillard again, "he was carrying a number of parcels. You realize—"

"It's Christmas."

"Yes. But he'd have needed quite a bit of money to buy a chicken, a cake, and that new radio. Has he borrowed any from you lately?"

"Not for a month. I haven't seen him for a month. I wish I had. I'd have told him that I was getting a radio for Francois myself. I've got it here. Downstairs, that is, in the cloakroom. I was going to take it straight round as soon as I was relieved."

"Would Madame Fayet have consented to lend him money?"

"It's unlikely. She was a queer lot. She must have had quite enough money to live on, yet she still went out to work, charring from morning to evening. Often she lent money to the people she worked for. At exorbitant interest, of course. All the neighborhood knew about it, and people always came to her when they needed something to tide them over till the end of the month."

Still embarrassed, the Inspector rose to his feet. "I'm going to have a look," he said.

"At Madame Fayet's?"

"There and in the Rue Vasco de Gama. If you get any news, let me know, will you?"

"You won't find any telephone there, but I can get a message to you through the Javel police station."

The Inspector's footsteps had hardly died away before the telephone bell rang. No lamp had lit up on the wall. This was an outside call, coming from the Gare d'Austerlitz.

"Lecœur? Station police speaking. We've got him."

"Who?"

"The man whose description was circulated. Lecœur. Same as you. Olivier

Lecœur. No doubt about it, I've seen his identity card."

"Hold on, will you?"

Lecœur dashed out of the room and down the stairs just in time to catch the Inspector as he was getting into one of the cars belonging to the Préfecture.

"Inspector! The Gare d'Austerlitz is on the phone. They've found my brother."

Saillard was a stout man and he went up the stairs puffing and blowing. He took the receiver himself.

"Hallo! Yes. Where was he? What was he doing? What? No, there's no point in your questioning him now. You're sure he didn't know? Right. Go on looking out. It's quite possible. As for him, send him here straightaway. At the Préfecture, yes."

He hesitated for a second and glanced at Lecœur before saying finally, "Yes. Send someone with him. We can't take any risks."

The Inspector filled his pipe and lit it before explaining, and when he spoke he looked at nobody in particular.

"He was picked up after he'd been wandering about the station for over an hour. He seemed very jumpy. Said he was waiting there to meet his son, from whom he'd received a message."

"Did they tell him about the murder?"

"Yes. He appeared to be staggered by the news and terrified. I asked them to bring him along." Rather diffidently he added: "I asked them to bring him here. Considering your relationship, I didn't want you to think—"

Lecœur had been in that room since eleven o'clock the night before. It was rather like his early years when he spent his days in his mother's kitchen. Around him was an unchanging world. There were the little lamps, of course, that kept going on and off, but that's what they always did. They were part and parcel of the immutability of the place. Time flowed by without anyone noticing it.

Yet, outside, Paris was celebrating Christmas. Thousands of people had been to Midnight Mass, thousands more had spent the night roistering, and those who hadn't known where to draw the line had sobered down in the police station and were now being called upon to explain things they couldn't remember doing.

What had his brother Olivier been doing all through the night? An old woman had been found dead. A boy had started before dawn on a breathless race through the streets, breaking the glass of the telephone pillars as he passed them, having wrapped his handkerchief round his fist.

And what was Olivier waiting for at the Gare d'Austerlitz, sometimes in the overheated waiting rooms, sometimes on the windswept platforms, too nervous to settle down in any one place for long?

Less than ten minutes elapsed, just time enough for Godin, whose nose really was running, to make himself another glass of hot grog.

"Can I offer you one, Monsieur le Commissaire?"

"No, thanks."

Looking more embarrassed than ever, Saillard leaned over towards Lecœur to say in an undertone, "Would you like us to question him in another room?"

No. Lecœur wasn't going to leave his post for anything. He wanted to stay there, with his little lamps and his switchboard. Was it that he was thinking more of the boy than of his brother?

Olivier came in with a detective on either side, but they had spared him the handcuffs. He looked dreadful, like a bad photograph faded with age. At once he turned to Andre. "Where's Francois?"

"We don't know. We're hunting for him."

"Where?"

Andre Lecœur pointed to his plan of Paris and his switchboard of a thousand lines. "Everywhere."

The two detectives had already been sent away.

"Sit down," said the Inspector. "I believe you've been told of Madame Fayet's death."

Olivier didn't wear spectacles, but he had the same pale and rather fugitive eyes as his brother had when he took his glasses off. He glanced at the Inspector, by whom he didn't seem the least overawed, then turned back to Andre. "He left a note for me," he said, delving into one of the pockets of his grubby mackintosh. "Here. See if you can understand."

He held out a bit of paper torn out of a schoolboy's exercise book. The writing wasn't any too good. It didn't look as though Francois was the best of pupils. He had used an indelible pencil, wetting the end in his mouth, so that his lips were very likely stained with it.

"Uncle Gedeon arrives this morning Gare d'Austerlitz. Come as soon as you can and meet us there. Love. Bib."

Without a word, Andre Lecœur passed it on to the Inspector, who turned it over and over with his thick fingers. "What's Bib stand for?"

"It's his nickname. A baby name. I never use it when other people are about. It comes from *biberon*. When I used to give him his bottle—" He spoke in a toneless voice. He seemed to be in a fog and was probably only dimly conscious of where he was.

"Who's Uncle Gedeon?"

"There isn't any such person."

Did he realize he was talking to the head of the Brigade des Homicides, who was at the moment investigating a murder?

It was his brother who came to the rescue, explaining, "As a matter of fact, we had an Uncle Gedeon but he's been dead for some years. He was one of my mother's brothers who emigrated to America as a young man."

Olivier looked at his brother as much as to say: What's the point of going into that?

"We got into the habit, in the family, of speaking—jocularly, of course—of our rich American uncle and of the fortune he'd leave us one day."

"Was he rich?"

"We didn't know. We never heard from him except for a postcard once a year, signed Gedeon. Wishing us a happy New Year."

"He died?"

"When Francois was four."

"Really, Andre, do you think it's any use—"

"Let me go on. The Inspector wants to know everything. My brother carried on the family tradition, talking to his son about our Uncle Gedeon, who had become by now quite a legendary figure. He provided a theme for bedtime stories, and all sorts of adventures were attributed to him. Naturally he was fabulously rich, and when one day he came back to France—"

"I understand. He died out there?"

"In a hospital in Cleveland. It was then we found out he had been really a porter in a restaurant. It would have been too cruel to tell the boy that, so the legend went on."

"Did he believe in it?"

It was Olivier who answered. "My brother thought he didn't, that he'd guessed the truth but wasn't going to spoil the game. But I always maintained the contrary and I'm still practically certain he took it all in. He was like that. Long after his schoolfellows had stopped believing in Father Christmas, he still went on."

Talking about his son brought him back to life, transfigured him.

"But as for this note he left, I don't know what to make of it. I asked the concierge if a telegram had come. For a moment I thought Andre might have played us a practical joke, but I soon dismissed the idea. It isn't much of a joke to get a boy dashing off to a station on a freezing night. Naturally I dashed off to the Gare d'Austerlitz as fast as I could. There I hunted high and low, then wandered about, waiting anxiously for him to turn up. Andre, you're sure he hasn't been—"

He looked at the street plan on the wall and at the switchboard. He knew very well that every accident was reported.

"He hasn't been run over," said Andre. "At about eight o'clock he was near the Etoile, but we've completely lost track of him since then."

331

"Near the Etoile? How do you know?"

"It's rather a long story, but it boils down to this—that a whole series of alarms were set off by someone smashing the glass. They followed a circuitous route from your place to the Arc de Triomphe. At the foot of the last one, they found a blue-check handerchief, a boy's handkerchief, among the broken glass."

"He has handkerchiefs like that."

"From eight o'clock onward, not a sign of him."

"Then I'd better get back to the station. He's certain to go there, if he told me to meet him there."

He was surprised at the sudden silence with which his last words were greeted. He looked from one to the other, perplexed, then anxious.

"What is it?"

His brother looked down at the floor. Inspector Saillard cleared his throat, hesitated, then asked, "Did you go to see your mother-in-law last night?"

Perhaps, as his brother had suggested, Olivier was rather lacking in intelligence. It took a long time for the words to sink in. You could follow their progress in his features.

He had been gazing rather blankly at the Inspector. Suddenly he swung around on his brother, his cheeks red, his eyes flashing. "Andre, you dare to suggest that I—"

Without the slightest transition, his indignation faded away. He leaned forward in his chair, took his head in his two hands, and burst into a fit of raucous weeping.

Ill at ease, Inspector Saillard looked at Andre Lecœur, surprised at the latter's calmness, and a little shocked, perhaps, by what he may well have taken for heartlessness. Perhaps Saillard had never had a brother of his own. Andre had known his since childhood. It wasn't the first time he had seen Olivier break down. Not by any means. And this time he was almost pleased, as it might have been a great deal worse. What he had dreaded was the moment of indignation, and he was relieved that it had passed so quickly. Had he continued on that tack, he'd have ended by putting everyone's back up, which would have done him no good at all.

Wasn't that how he'd lost one job after another? For weeks, for months, he would go meekly about his work, toeing the line and swallowing what he felt to be humiliations, till all at once he could hold no more, and for some trifle—a chance word, a smile, a harmless contradiction—he would flare up unexpectedly and make a nuisance of himself to everybody.

What do we do now? The Inspector's eyes were asking.

Andre Lecœur's eyes answered, Wait.

*   *   *

It didn't last very long. The emotional crisis waned, started again, then petered out altogether. Olivier shot a sulky look at the Inspector, then hid his face again.

Finally, with an air of bitter resignation, he sat up, and with even a touch of pride said: "Fire away. I'll answer."

"At what time last night did you go to Madame Fayet's? Wait a moment. First of all, when did you leave your flat?"

"At eight o'clock, as usual, after Francois was in bed."

"Nothing exceptional happened?"

"No. We'd had supper together. Then he'd helped me to wash up."

"Did you talk about Christmas?"

"Yes. I told him he'd be getting a surprise."

"The table radio. Was he expecting one?"

"He'd been longing for one for some time. You see, he doesn't play with the other boys in the street. Practically all his free time he spends at home."

"Did it ever occur to you that the boy might know you'd lost your job at the *Presse*? Did he ever ring you up there?"

"Never. When I'm at work, he's asleep."

"Could anyone have told him?"

"No one knew. Not in the neighborhood, that is."

"Is he observant?"

"Very. He notices everything."

"You saw him safely in bed and then you went off. Do you take anything with you—anything to eat, I mean?"

The Inspector suddenly thought of that, seeing Godin produce a ham sandwich. Olivier looked blankly at his empty hands.

"My tin."

"The tin in which you took your sandwiches?"

"Yes. I had it with me when I left. I'm sure of that. I can't think where I could have left it, unless it was at—"

"At Madame Fayet's?"

"Yes."

"Just a moment. Lecoeur, get me Javel on the phone, will you? Hallo! Who's speaking? Is Janvier there? Good, ask him to speak to me. Hallo! Is that you, Janvier? Have you come across a tin box containing some sandwiches? Nothing of the sort. Really? All the same, I'd like you to make sure. Ring me back. It's important."

And, turning again to Olivier: "Was Francois actually sleeping when you left?"

"No. But he'd snuggled down in bed and soon would be. Outside, I wandered about for a bit. I walked down to the Seine and waited on the embankment."

"Waited? What for?"

"For Francois to be fast asleep. From his room you can see Madame Fayet's windows."

"So you'd made up your mind to go and see her."

"It was the only way. I hadn't a bean left."

"What about your brother?"

Olivier and Andre looked at each other.

"He'd already given me so much. I felt I couldn't ask him again."

"You rang at the house door, I suppose. At what time?"

"A little after nine. The concierge saw me. I made no attempt to hide—except from Francois."

"Had your mother-in-law gone to bed?"

"No. She was fully dressed when she opened her door. She said, 'Oh, it's you, you wretch!' "

"After that beginning, did you still think she'd lend you money?"

"I was sure of it."

"Why?"

"It was her business. Perhaps also for the pleasure of squeezing me if I didn't pay her back. She lent me ten thousand francs, but made me sign an I.O.U. for twenty thousand."

"How soon had you to pay her back?"

"In a fortnight's time."

"How could you hope to?"

"I don't know. Somehow. The thing that mattered was for the boy to have a good Christmas."

Andre Lecœur was tempted to butt in to explain to the puzzled Inspector, "You see! He's always been like that!"

"Did you get the money easily?"

"Oh, no. We were at it for a long time."

"How long?"

"Half an hour, I daresay, and during most of that time she was calling me names, telling me I was no good to anyone and had ruined her daughter's life before I finally killed her. I didn't answer her back. I wanted the money too badly."

"You didn't threaten her?"

Olivier reddened. "Not exactly. I said if she didn't let me have it I'd kill myself."

"Would you have done it?"

"I don't think so. At least, I don't know. I was fed up, worn out."

"And when you got the money?"

"I walked to the nearest Métro station, Lourmel, and took the underground to Palais Royal. There I went into the Grands Magasins du Louvre. The place was crowded, with queues at many of the counters."

"What time was it?"

"It was after eleven before I left the place. I was in no hurry. I had a good look around. I stood a long time watching a toy electric train."

Andre couldn't help smiling at the Inspector. "You didn't miss your sandwich tin?"

"No. I was thinking about Francois and his present."

"And with money in your pocket you banished all your cares!"

The Inspector hadn't known Olivier Lecœur since childhood, but he had sized him up all right. He had hit the nail on the head. When things were black, Olivier would go about with drooping shoulders and a hangdog air, but no sooner had he a thousand-franc note in his pocket than he'd feel on top of the world.

"To come back to Madame Fayet, you say you gave her a receipt. What did she do with it?"

"She slipped it into an old wallet she always carried about with her in a pocket somewhere under her skirt."

"So you knew about the wallet?"

"Yes. Everybody did. "

The Inspector turned towards Andre.

"It hasn't been found!"

Then to Olivier: "You bought some things. In the Louvre?"

"No. I bought the little radio in the Rue Montmartre."

"In which shop?"

"I don't know the name. It's next door to a shoe shop."

"And the other things?"

"A little farther on. "

"What time was it when you'd finished shopping?"

"Close on midnight. People were coming out of the theaters and movies and crowding into the restaurants. Some of them were rather noisy."

His brother at that time was already here at his switchboard.

"What did you do during the rest of the night?"

"At the corner of the Boulevard des Italiens, there's a movie that stays open all night."

"You'd been there before?"

Avoiding his brother's eye, Olivier answered rather sheepishly: "Two or three times. After all, it costs no more than going into a cafe and you can stay there as long as you like. It's nice and warm. Some people go there regularly to sleep."

"When was it you decided to go to the movies?"

"As soon as I left Madame Fayet's."

Andre Lecœur was tempted to intervene once again to say to the Inspector: "You see, these people who are down and out are not so utterly miserable after all. If they were, they'd never stick it out. They've got a world of their own, in odd corners of which they can take refuge and even amuse themselves."

It was all so like Olivier! With a few notes in his pocket—and Heaven only knew how he was ever going to pay them back—with a few notes in his pocket, his trials were forgotten. He had only one thought: to give his boy a good Christmas. With that secured, he was ready to stand himself a little treat.

So while other families were gathered at table or knelt at Midnight Mass, Olivier went to the movies all by himself. It was the best he could do.

"When did you leave the movie?"

"A little before six."

"What was the film?"

"*Cœurs Ardents*. With a documentary on Eskimos."

"How many times did you see the program?"

"Twice right through, except for the news, which was just coming on again when I left."

Andre Lecœur knew that all this was going to be verified, if only as a matter of routine. It wasn't necessary, however. Diving into his pockets, Olivier produced the torn-off half of a movie ticket, then another ticket—a pink one. "Look at that. It's the Métro ticket I had coming home."

It bore the name of the station—Opéra—together with the date and the time.

Olivier had been telling the truth. He couldn't have been in Madame Fayet's flat any time between five and six-thirty.

There was a little spark of triumph in his eye, mixed with a touch of disdain. He seemed to be saying to them all, including his brother Andre: "Because I'm poor and unlucky I come under suspicion. I know—that's the way things are. I don't blame you."

And, funnily enough, it seemed as though all at once the room had grown colder. That was probably because, with Olivier Lecœur cleared of suspicion, everyone's thoughts reverted to the child. As though moved by one impulse, all eyes turned instinctively toward the huge plan on the wall.

Some time had elapsed since any of the lamps had lit up. Certainly it was a quiet morning. On any ordinary day there would be a street accident coming in every few minutes, particularly old women knocked down in the crowded thoroughfares of Montmartre and other overpopulated quarters.

Today the streets were almost empty—emptier than in August, when half Paris is away on holiday.

Half past eleven. For three and a half hours there'd been no sign of Francois Lecœur.

"Hallo! Yes, Saillard speaking. Is that Janvier? You say you couldn't find a tin anywhere? Except in her kitchen, of course. Now, look here, was it you who went through the old girl's clothes? Oh, Gonesse had already done it. There should have been an old wallet in a pocket under her skirt. You're sure there wasn't anything of that sort? That's what Gonesse told you, is it? What's that about the concierge? She saw someone go up a little after nine last night. I know. I know who it was. There were people coming in and out the best part of the night? Of course. I'd like you to go back to the house in the Rue Vasco de Gama. See what you can find out about the comings and goings there, particularly on the third floor. Yes. I'll still be here."

He turned back to the boy's father, who was now sitting humbly in his chair, looking as intimidated as a patient in a doctor's waiting room.

"You understand why I asked that, don't you? Does Francois often wake up in the course of the night?"

"He's been known to get up in his sleep."

"Does he walk about?"

"No. Generally he doesn't even get right out of bed—just sits up and calls out. It's always the same thing. He thinks the house is on fire. His eyes are open, but I don't think he sees anything. Then, little by little, he calms down and with a deep sigh lies down again. The next day he doesn't remember a thing."

"Is he always asleep when you get back in the morning?"

"Not always. But if he isn't, he always pretends to be so that I can wake him up as usual with a hug."

"The people in the house were probably making more noise than usual last night. Who have you got in the next flat?"

"A Czech who works at Renault's."

"Is he married?"

"I really don't know. There are so many people in the house and they change so often we don't know much about them. All I can tell you is that on Sundays other Czechs come there and they sing a lot of their own songs."

"Janvier will tell us whether there was a party there last night. If there was, they may well have awakened the boy. Besides, children are apt to sleep more lightly when they're excited about a present they're expecting. If he got out of bed, he might easily have looked out of the window, in which case he might have seen you at Madame Fayet's. He didn't know she was his grandmother, did he?"

"No. He didn't like her. He sometimes passed her in the street and he used to say she smelled like a squashed bug."

The boy would probably know what he was talking about. A house like his was no doubt infested with vermin.

"He'd have been surprised to see you with her?"

"Certainly."

"Did he know she lent money?"

"Everyone knew."

"Would there be anybody working at the *Presse* on a day like this?"

"There's always somebody there."

The Inspector asked Andre to ring them up.

"See if anyone's ever been round to ask for your brother."

Olivier looked uncomfortable, but when his brother reached for the telephone directory, he gave him the number. Both he and the Inspector stared at Andre while he got through.

"It's very important, Mademoiselle. It may even be a matter of life and death. Yes, please. See if you can find out. Ask everybody who's in the building now. What? Yes, I know it's Christmas Day. It's Christmas Day here, too, but we have to carry on just the same."

Between his teeth he muttered, "Silly little bitch!"

He could hear the linotypes clicking as he held the line, waiting for her answer.

"Yes. What? Three weeks ago. A young boy—"

Olivier went pale in the face. His eyes dropped, and during the rest of the conversation he stared obstinately at his hands.

"He didn't telephone? Came round himself. At what time? On a Thursday, you say. What did he want? Asked if Olivier Lecœur worked there? What? What was he told?"

Looking up, Olivier saw a flush spread over his brother's face before he banged down the receiver.

"Francois went there one Thursday afternoon. He must have suspected something. They told him you hadn't been working there for some time."

There was no point in repeating what he had heard. What they'd said to the boy was: "We chucked the old fool out weeks ago."

Perhaps not out of cruelty. They may not have thought it was the man's son they were speaking to.

"Do you begin to understand, Olivier?"

Did he realize that the situation was the reverse of what he had imagined? He had been going off at night, armed with his little box of sandwiches, keeping up an elaborate pretense. And in the end he had been the one to be taken in!

338

The boy had found him out. And wasn't it only fair to suppose that he had seen through the Uncle Gedeon story, too?

He hadn't said a word. He had simply fallen in with the game.

No one dared say anything for fear of saying too much, for fear of evoking images that would be heartrending.

A father and a son each lying to avoid hurting the other.

They had to look at it through the eyes of the child, with all childhood's tragic earnestness. His father kisses him good night and goes off to the job that doesn't really exist, saying: "Sleep well. There'll be a surprise for you in the morning."

A radio. It could only be that. And didn't he know that his father's pockets were empty? Did he try to go to sleep? Or did he get up as soon as his father had gone, to sit miserably staring out of the window obsessed by one thought? *His father had no money—yet he was going to buy him a radio!*

To the accompaniment, in all probability, of a full-throated Czech choir singing their national songs on the other side of the thin wall!

The Inspector sighed and knocked out his pipe on his heel.

"It looks as though he saw you at Madame Fayet's."

Olivier nodded.

"We'll check up on this, but it seems likely that, looking down from his window, he wouldn't see very far into the room."

"That's quite right."

"Could he have seen you leave the room?"

"No. The door's on the opposite side from the window."

"Do you remember going near the window?"

"At one time I was sitting on the windowsill."

"Was the window open then? We know it was later."

"It was open a few inches. I'm sure of that, because I moved away from it, as I felt an icy draught on my back. She lived with us for a while, just after our marriage, and I know she couldn't bear not to have her window open all the year round. You see, she'd been brought up in the country."

"So there'd be no frost on the panes. He'd certainly have seen you if he was looking."

A call. Lecœur thrust his contact plug into one of the sockets.

"Yes. What's that? A boy?"

The other two held their breath.

"Yes. Yes. What? Yes. Send out the *agents cyclistes*. Comb the whole neighborhood. I'll see about the station. How long ago was it? Half an hour? Couldn't he have let us know sooner?"

Without losing time over explanations, Lecœur plugged in to the Gare du

Nord.

"Hallo! Gare du Nord! Who's speaking? Ah, Lambert. Listen, this is urgent. Have the station searched from end to end. Ask everybody if they've seen a boy of ten wandering about. What? Alone? He may be. Or he may be accompanied. We don't know. Let me know what you find out. Yes, of course. Grab him at once if you set eyes on him."

"Did you say accompanied?" asked Olivier anxiously.

"Why not? It's possible. Anything's possible. Of course, it may not be him. If it is, we're half an hour late. It was a small grocer in the Rue de Maubeuge whose shopfront is open onto the street. He saw a boy snatch a couple of oranges and make off. He didn't run after him. Only later, when a policeman passed, he thought he might as well mention it."

"Had your son any money?" asked the Inspector.

"Not a sou."

"Hasn't he got a money-box?"

"Yes. But I borrowed what was in it two days ago, saying that I didn't want to change a banknote."

A pathetic little confession, but what did things like that matter now?

"Don't you think it would be better if I went to the Gare du Nord myself?"

"I doubt if it would help, and we may need you here."

They were almost prisoners in that room. With its direct links with every nerve center of Paris, that was the place where any news would first arrive. Even in his room in the Police Judiciaire, the Inspector would be less well placed. He had thought of going back there, but now at last took off his overcoat, deciding to see the job through where he was.

"If he had no money, he couldn't take a bus or the Métro. Nor could he go into a cafe or use a public telephone. He probably hasn't had anything to eat since his supper last night."

"But what can he be doing?" exclaimed Olivier, becoming more and more nervous. "And why should he have sent me to the Gare d'Austerlitz?"

"Perhaps to help you get away," grunted Saillard.

"Get away? Me?"

"Listen. The boy knows you're down and out. Yet you're going to buy him a little radio. I'm not reproaching you. I'm just looking at the facts. He leans on the windowsill and sees you with the old woman he knows to be a money-lender. What does he conclude?"

"I see."

"That you've gone to her to borrow money. He may be touched by it, he may be saddened—we don't know. He goes back to bed and to sleep."

"You think so?"

"I'm pretty sure of it. Anyhow, we've no reason to think he left the house then."

"No. Of course not."

"Let's say he goes back to sleep, then. But he wakes up early, as children mostly do on Christmas Day. And the first thing he notices is the frost on the window. The first frost this winter, don't forget that. He wants to look at it, to touch it."

A faint smile flickered across Andre Lecœur's face. This massive Inspector hadn't forgotten what it was like to be a boy.

"He scratches a bit of it away with his nails. It won't be difficult to get confirmation, for once the frost is tampered with it can't form again in quite the same pattern. What does he notice then? That in the buildings opposite one window is lit up, and one only—the window of the room in which a few hours before he had seen his father. It's guesswork, of course, but I don't mind betting he saw the body, or part of it. If he'd merely seen a foot it would have been enough to startle him."

"You mean to say—" began Olivier, wide-eyed.

"That he thought you'd killed her. As I did myself—for a moment. And very likely not her only. Just think for a minute. The man who's been committing all these murders is a man, like you, who wanders about at night. His victims live in the poorer quarters of Paris, like Madame Fayet in the Rue Michat. Does the boy know anything of how you've been spending your nights since you lost your job? No. All that he has to go on is that he has seen you in the murdered woman's room. Would it be surprising if his imagination got to work?

"You said just now that you sat on the windowsill. Might it be there that you put down your box of sandwiches?"

"Now I come to think of it, yes. I'm practically sure."

"Then he saw it. And he's quite old enough to know what the police would think when they saw it lying there. Is your name on it?"

"Yes. Scratched on the lid."

"You see! He thought you'd be coming home as usual between seven and eight. The thing was to get you as quickly as possible out of the danger zone."

"You mean—by writing me that note?"

"Yes. He didn't know what to say. He couldn't refer to the murder without compromising you. Then he thought of Uncle Gedeon. Whether he believed in his existence or not doesn't matter. He knew you'd go to the Gare d'Austerlitz."

"But he's not yet eleven!"

"Boys of that age know a lot more than you think. Doesn't he read detective stories?"

"Yes."

"Of course he does. They all do. If they don't read them, they get them on the radio. Perhaps that's why he wanted a set of his own so badly."

"It's true."

"He couldn't stay in the flat to wait for you, for he had something more important to do. He had to get hold of that box. I suppose he knew the court-yard well. He'd played there, hadn't he?"

"At one time, yes. With the concierge's little girl."

"So he'd know about the rainwater pipes, may even have climbed up them for sport."

"Very well," said Olivier, suddenly calm, "let's say he gets into the room and takes the box. He wouldn't need to climb down the way he'd come. He could simply walk out of the flat and out of the house. You can open the house door from inside without knocking up the concierge. You say it was at about six o'clock, don't you?"

"I see what you're driving at," grunted the Inspector. "Even at a leisurely pace, it would hardly have taken him two hours to walk to the Gare d'Austerlitz. Yet he wasn't there."

Leaving them to thrash it out, Lecœur was busy telephoning.

"No news yet?"

And the man at the Gare du Nord answered, "Nothing so far. We've pounced on any number of boys, but none of them was Francois Lecœur."

Admittedly, any street boy could have pinched a couple of oranges and taken to his heels. The same couldn't be said for the broken glass of the tele-phone pillars, however. Andre Lecœur looked once again at the column with the seven crosses, as though some clue might suddenly emerge from them. He had never thought himself much cleverer than his brother. Where he scored was in patience and perseverance.

"If the box of sandwiches is ever found, it'll be at the bottom of the Seine near the Pont Mirabeau," he said.

Steps in the corridor. On an ordinary day they would not have been noticed, but in the stillness of a Christmas morning everyone listened.

It was an *agent cycliste*, who produced a bloodstained blue-check hand-kerchief, the one that had been found among the glass splinters at the seventh telephone pillar.

"That's his, all right," said the boy's father.

"He must have been followed," said the Inspector. "If he'd had time, he wouldn't merely have broken the glass. He'd have said something."

"Who by?" asked Olivier, who was the only one not to understand. "Who'd want to follow him?" he asked. "And why should he call the police?"

They hesitated to put him wise. In the end it was his brother who explained:

"When he went to the old woman's he thought you were the murderer. When he came away, he knew you weren't. He knew—"

"Knew what?"

"He knew who was. Do you understand now? He found out something, though we don't know what. He wants to tell us about it, but someone's stopping him."

"You mean?"

"I mean that Francois is after the murderer or the murderer is after him. One is following, one is followed—we don't know which. By the way, Inspector, is there a reward offered?"

"A handsome reward was offered after the third murder and it was doubled last week. It's been in all the papers."

"Then my guess," said Andre Lecœur, "is that it's the kid who's doing the following. Only in that case—"

It was twelve o'clock, four hours since they'd lost track of him. Unless, of course, it was he who had snaffled the oranges in the Rue Maubeuge.

Might not this be his great moment? Andre Lecœur had read somewhere that even to the dullest and most uneventful lives such a moment comes sooner or later.

He had never had a particularly high opinion of himself or of his abilities. When people asked him why he'd chosen so dreary and monotonous a job rather than one in, say, the Brigade des Homicides, he would answer: "I suppose I'm lazy."

Sometimes he would add:

"I'm scared of being knocked about."

As a matter of fact, he was neither lazy nor a coward. If he lacked anything it was brains.

He knew it. All he had learned at school had cost him a great effort. The police exams that others took so easily in their stride, he had only passed by dint of perseverance.

Was it a consciousness of his own shortcomings that had kept him single? Possibly. It seemed to him that the sort of woman he would want to marry would be his superior, and he didn't relish the idea of playing second fiddle in the home.

But he wasn't thinking of all this now. Indeed, if this was his moment of greatness, it was stealing upon him unawares.

Another team arrived, those of the second day shift looking very fresh and well groomed in their Sunday clothes. They had been celebrating Christmas with their families, and they brought in with them, as it were, a whiff of good viands and liqueurs.

Old Bedeau had taken his place at the switchboard, but Lecœur made no move to go.

"I'll stay on a bit," he said simply.

Inspector Saillard had gone for a quick lunch at the Brasserie Dauphine just around the corner, leaving strict injunctions that he was to be fetched at once if anything happened. Janvier was back at the Quai des Orfèvres, writing up his report.

If Lecœur was tired, he didn't notice it. He certainly wasn't sleepy and couldn't bear the thought of going home to bed. He had plenty of stamina. Once, when there were riots in the Place de la Concorde, he had done thirty-six hours nonstop, and on another occasion, during a general strike, they had all camped in the room for four days and nights.

His brother showed the strain more. He was getting jumpy again.

"I'm going," he announced suddenly.

"Where to?"

"To find Bib."

"Where?"

"I don't know exactly. I'll start round the Gare du Nord."

"How do you know it was Bib who stole the oranges? He may be at the other end of Paris. We might get news at any minute. You'd better stay."

"I can't stand this waiting."

He was nevertheless persuaded to. He was given a chair in a corner. He refused to lie down. His eyes were red with anxiety and fatigue. He sat fidgeting, looking rather as, when a boy, he had been put in the corner.

With more self-control, Andre forced himself to take some rest. Next to the big room was a little one with a wash-basin, where they hung their coats and which was provided with a couple of camp beds on which the *nuiteux* could lie down during a quiet hour.

He shut his eyes, but only for a moment. Then his hand felt for the little notebook with never left him, and lying on his back he began to turn over the pages.

There were nothing but crosses, columns and columns of tiny little crosses which, month after month, year after year, he had accumulated, Heaven knows why. Just to satisfy something inside him. After all, other people keep a diary—or the most meticulous household accounts, even when they don't need to economize at all.

Those crosses told the story of the night life of Paris.

"Some coffee, Lecœur?"

"Thanks."

Feeling rather out of touch where he was, he dragged his camp bed into the big room, placing it in a position from which he could see the wall-plan. There he sipped his coffee, after which he stretched himself out again, sometimes studying his notebook, sometimes lying with his eyes shut. Now and again he stole a glance at his brother, who sat hunched in his chair with drooping shoulders, the twitching of his long white fingers being the only sign of the torture he was enduring.

There were hundreds of men now, not only in Paris but in the suburbs, keeping their eyes skinned for the boy whose description had been circulated. Sometimes false hopes were raised, only to be dashed when the exact particulars were given.

Lecœur shut his eyes again, but opened them suddenly next moment, as though he had actually dozed off. He glanced at the clock, then looked round for the Inspector.

"Hasn't Saillard got back yet?" he asked, getting to his feet.

"I expect he's looked in at the Quai des Orfèvres."

Olivier stared at his brother, surprised to see him pacing up and down the room. The latter was so absorbed in his thoughts that he hardly noticed that the sun had broken through the clouds, bathing Paris on that Christmas afternoon in a glow of light more like that of spring.

While thinking, he listened, and it wasn't long before he heard Inspector Saillard's heavy tread outside.

"You'd better go and get some sandwiches," he said to his brother. "Get some for me, too."

"What kind?"

"Ham. Anything. Whatever you find."

Olivier went out, after a parting glance at the map, relieved, in spite of his anxiety, to be doing something.

The men of the afternoon shift knew little of what was afoot, except that the killer had done another job the previous night and that there was a general hunt for a small boy. For them, the case couldn't have the flavor it had for those who were involved. At the switchboard, Bedeau was doing a crossword with his earphones on his head, breaking off from time to time for the classic: "Hallo! Austerlitz. Your car's out."

A body fished out of the Seine. You couldn't have a Christmas without that!

"Could I have a word with you, Inspector?"

The camp bed was back in the cloakroom. It was there that Lecœur led the chief of the homicide squad.

"I hope you won't mind my butting in. I know it isn't for me to make suggestions. But, about the killer—"

He had his little notebook in his hand. He must have known its contents almost by heart.

"I've been doing a lot of thinking since this morning and—"

A little while ago, while he was lying down, it had seemed so clear, but now that he had to explain things, it was difficult to put them in logical order.

"It's like this. First of all, I noticed that all the murders were committed after two in the morning, most of them after three."

He could see by the look on the Inspector's face that he hadn't exactly scored a hit, and he hurried on:

"I've been looking up the time of other murders over the past three years. They were nearly always between ten in the evening and two in the morning."

Neither did that observation seem to make much impression. Why not take the bull by the horns and say straight out what was on his mind?

"Just now, looking at my brother, it occurred to me that the man you're looking for might be a man like him. As a matter of fact, I, too, for a moment wondered whether it wasn't him. Wait a moment—"

That was better. The look of polite boredom had gone from Saillard's face.

"If I'd had more experience in this sort of work I'd be able to explain myself better. But you'll see in a moment. A man who's killed eight people one after the other is, if not a madman, at any rate a man who's been thrown off his balance. He might have had a sudden shock. Take my brother, for instance. When he lost his job it upset him so much that he preferred to live in a tissue of lies rather than let his son—"

No. Put into words, it all sounded very clumsy.

"When a man suddenly loses everything he has in life—"

"He doesn't necessarily go mad."

"I'm not saying he's actually mad. But imagine a person so full of resentment that he considers himself justified in revenging himself on his fellow-men. I don't need to point out to you, Inspector, that other murderers always kill in much the same way. This one has used a hammer, a knife, a spanner, and one woman he strangled. And he's never been seen, never left a clue. Wherever he lives in Paris, he must have walked miles and miles at night when there was no transport available, sometimes, when the alarm had been given, with the police on the lookout, questioning everybody they found in the streets. How is it he avoided them?"

He was certain he was on the right track. If only Saillard would hear him out.

The Inspector sat on one of the camp beds. The cloakroom was small, and as Lecœur paced up and down in front of him he could do no more than three paces each way.

"This morning, for instance, assuming he was with the boy, he went halfway across Paris, keeping out of sight of every police station and every traffic point where there'd be a man on duty."

"You mean he knows the Fifteenth and Sixteenth Arrondissements by heart?"

"And not those only. At least two there, the Twelfth and the Twentieth, as he showed on previous occasions. He didn't choose his victims haphazardly. He knew they lived alone and could be done in without any great risk."

What a nuisance! There was his brother, saying: "Here are the sandwiches, Andre."

"Thanks. Go ahead, will you? Don't wait for me. I'll be with you in a moment."

He bundled Olivier back into his corner and returned to the cloakroom. He didn't want him to hear.

"If he's used a different weapon each time, it's because he knows it will puzzle us. He knows that murderers generally have their own way and stick to it."

The Inspector had risen to his feet and was staring at Andre with a far-away look, as though he was following a train of thought of his own.

"You mean that he's—"

"That he's one of us—or has been. I can't get the idea out of my head." He lowered his voice.

"Someone who's been up against it in the same sort of way as my brother. A discharged fireman might take to arson. It's happened two or three times. A policeman—"

"But why should he steal?"

"Wasn't my brother in need of money? This other chap may be like him in more ways than one. Supposing he, too, was a night worker and goes on pretending he's still in a job. That would explain why the crimes are committed so late. He has to be out all night. The first part of it is easy enough—the cafes and bars are open. Afterward, he's all alone with himself."

As though to himself, Saillard muttered: "There wouldn't be anybody in the personnel department on a day like this."

"Perhaps you could ring up the director at his home. He might remember . . ."

"Hallo! Can I speak to Monsieur Guillaume, please? He's not in? Where could I reach him? At his daughter's in Ateuil? Have you got the number?"

"Hallo! Monsieur Guillaume? Saillard speaking. I hope I'm not disturbing you too much. Oh, you'd finished, had you? Good. It's about the killer. Yes, there's been another one. No. Nothing definite. Only we have an idea that needs checking, and it's urgent. Don't be too surprised at my question.

"Has any member of the Paris police been sacked recently—say two or three months ago? I beg your pardon? Not a single one this year? I see."

Lecœur felt a sudden constriction around his heart, as though overwhelmed by a catastrophe, and threw a pathetic, despairing look at the wall-map. He had already given up and was surprised to hear his chief go on:

"As a matter of fact, it doesn't need to be as recent as all that. It would be someone who had worked in various parts of Paris, including the Fifteenth and Sixteenth. Probably also the Twelfth and Twentieth. Seems to have done a good deal of night work. Also to have been embittered by his dismissal. What?"

The way Saillard pronounced that last word gave Lecœur renewed hope.

"Sergeant Loubet? Yes, I remember the name, though I never actually came across him. Three years ago! You wouldn't know where he lived, I suppose? Somewhere near Les Halles?"

Three years ago. No, it wouldn't do, and Lecœur's heart sank again. You could hardly expect a man to bottle up his resentments for three years and then suddenly start hitting back.

"Have you any idea what became of him? No, of course not. And it's not a good day for finding out."

He hung up and looked thoughtfully at Lecœur. When he spoke, it was as though he was addressing an equal.

"Did you hear? Sergeant Loubet. He was constantly getting into trouble and was shifted three or four times before being finally dismissed. Drink. That was his trouble. He took his dismissal very hard. Guillaume can't say for certain what has become of him, but he thinks he joined a private detective agency. If you'd like to have a try—"

Lecœur set to work. He had little hope of succeeding, but it was better to do something than sit watching for the little lamps in the street-plan. He began with the agencies of the most doubtful reputation, refusing to believe that a person such as Loubet would readily find a job with a reputable firm. Most of the offices were shut, and he had to ring up their proprietors at home.

"Don't know him. You'd better try Tisserand in the Boulevard Saint-Martin. He's the one who takes all the riffraff."

But Tisserand, a firm that specialized in shadowings, was no good, either.

"Don't speak to me of that good-for-nothing. It's a good two months or more since I chucked him out, in spite of his threatening to blackmail me. If he ever shows up at my office again, I'll throw him down the stairs."

"What sort of job did he have?"

"Night work. Watching blocks of flats."

"Did he drink much?"

"He wasn't often sober. I don't know how he managed it, but he always

348

knew where to get free drinks. Blackmail again, I suppose."

"Can you give me his address?"

"Twenty-seven bis, Rue du Pas-de-la-Mule."

"Does he have a telephone?"

"Maybe. I don't know. I've never had the slightest desire to ring him up. Is that all? Can I go back to my game of bridge?"

The Inspector had already snatched up the telephone directory and was looking for Loubet's number. He rang up himself. There was now a tacit understanding between him and Lecœur. They shared the same hope, the same trembling eagerness, while Olivier, realizing that something important was going on, came and stood near them.

Without being invited, Andre did something he wouldn't have dreamed of doing that morning. He picked up the second earphone to listen in. The bell rang in the flat in the Rue du Pas-de-la-Mule. It rang for a long time, as though the place was deserted, and his anxiety was becoming acute when at last it stopped and a voice answered.

Thank Heaven! It was a woman's voice, an elderly one. "Is that you at last? Where are you?"

"Hallo! This isn't your husband here, Madame."

"Has he met with an accident?"

From the hopefulness of her tone, it sounded as though she had long been expecting one and wouldn't be sorry when it happened.

"It is Madame Loubet I'm speaking to, isn't it?"

"Who else would it be?"

"Your husband's not at home?"

"First of all, who are you?"

"Inspector Saillard."

"What do you want him for?"

The Inspector put his hand over the mouthpiece to say to Lecœur: "Get through to Janvier. Tell him to dash round there as quick as he can."

"Didn't your husband come home this morning?"

"You ought to know! I thought the police knew everything!"

"Does it often happen?"

"That's his business, isn't it?"

No doubt she hated her drunkard of a husband, but now that he was threatened she was ready to stand up for him.

"I suppose you know he no longer belongs to the police force."

"Perhaps he found a cleaner job."

"When did he stop working for the Agence Argus?"

"What's that? What are you getting at?"

"I assure you, Madame, your husband was dismissed from the Agence

Argus over two months ago."

"You're lying."

"Which means that for these last two months he's been going off to work every evening."

"Where else would he be going? To the Folies Bergère?"

"Have you any idea why he hasn't come back today? He hasn't telephoned, has he?"

She must have been afraid of saying the wrong thing, for she rang off without another word.

When the Inspector put his receiver down, he turned round to see Lecœur standing behind him, looking away. In a shaky voice, the latter said:

"Janvier's on his way now."

He was treated as an equal. He knew it wouldn't last, that tomorrow, sitting at his switchboard, he would be once more but a small cog in the huge wheel.

The others simply didn't count—not even his brother, whose timid eyes darted from one to the other uncomprehendingly, wondering why, if his boy's life was in danger, they talked so much instead of doing something.

Twice he had to pluck at Andre's sleeve to get a word in edgewise.

"Let me go and look for him myself," he begged.

What could he do? The hunt had widened now. A description of ex-Sergeant Loubet had been passed to all police stations and patrols.

It was no longer only a boy of ten who was being looked for, but also a man of fifty-eight, probably the worse for drink, dressed in a black overcoat with a velvet collar and an old grey-felt hat, a man who knew his Paris like the palm of his hand, and who was acquainted with the police.

Janvier had returned, looking fresher than the men there in spite of his night's vigil.

"She tried to slam the door in my face, but I'd taken the precaution of sticking my foot in. She doesn't know anything. She says he's been handing over his pay every month."

"That's why he had to steal. He didn't need big sums. In fact, he wouldn't have known what to do with them. What's she like?"

"Small and dark, with piercing eyes. Her hair's dyed a sort of blue. She must have eczema or something of the sort—she wears mittens."

"Did you get a photo of him?"

"There was one on the dining-room sideboard. She wouldn't give it to me, so I just took it."

A heavy-built, florid man, with bulging eyes, who in his youth had probably been the village beau and had conserved an air of stupid arrogance. The photograph was some years old. No doubt he looked quite different now.

"She didn't give you any idea where he was likely to be, did she?"

"As far as I could make out, except at night, when he was supposed to be at work, she kept him pretty well tied to her apron strings. I talked to the concierge, who told me he was scared stiff of his wife. Often she's seen him stagger home in the morning, then suddenly pull himself together when he went upstairs. He goes out shopping with his wife. In fact, he never goes out alone in the daytime. If she goes out when he's in bed, she locks him in."

"What do you think, Lecœur?"

"I'm wondering whether my nephew and he aren't together."

"What do you mean?"

"They weren't together at the beginning, or Loubet would have stopped the boy giving the alarm. There must have been some distance between them. One was following the other."

"Which way round?"

"When the kid climbed up the drainpipe, he thought his father was guilty. Otherwise, why should he have sent him off to the Gare d'Austerlitz, where no doubt he intended to join him after getting rid of the sandwich tin?"

"It looks like it."

"No, Andre. Francois could never have thought—"

"Leave this alone. You don't understand. At that time the crime had certainly been committed. Francois wouldn't have dreamed of burgling someone's flat for a tin box if it hadn't been that he'd seen the body."

"From his window," put in Janvier, "he could see most of the legs."

"What we don't know is whether the murderer was still there."

"I can't believe he was," said Saillard. "If he had been, he'd have kept out of sight, let the boy get into the room, and then done the same to him as he'd done to the old woman."

"Look here, Olivier. When you got home this morning, was the light on?"

"Yes."

"In the boy's room?"

"Yes. It was the first thing I noticed. It gave me a shock. I thought perhaps he was ill."

"So the murderer very likely saw it and feared his crime had had a witness. He certainly wouldn't have expected anyone to climb up the drainpipe. He must have rushed straight out of the house."

"And waited outside to see what would happen."

Guesswork! Yes. But that was all they could do. The important thing was to guess right. For that you had to put yourself in the other chap's place and think as he had thought. The rest was a matter of patrols, of the hundreds of policemen scattered all over Paris, and, lastly, of luck.

351

"Rather than go down the way he'd come, the boy must have left the house by the entrance in the Rue Michat."

"Just a moment, Inspector. By that time he probably knew that his father wasn't the murderer."

"Why?"

"Janvier said just now that Madame Fayet lost a lot of blood. If it had been his father, the blood would have had time to dry up more or less. It was some nine hours since Francois had seen him in the room. It was on leaving the house that he found out who had done it, whether it was Loubet or not. The latter wouldn't know whether the boy had seen him up in the room. Francois would have been scared and taken to his heels."

This time it was the boy's father who interrupted. "No. Not if he knew there was a big reward offered. Not if he knew I'd lost my job. Not if he'd seen me go to the old woman to borrow some money."

The Inspector and Andre Lecœur exchanged glances. They had to admit Olivier was right, and it made them afraid.

No, it had to be pictured otherwise. A dark, deserted street in an outlying quarter of Paris two hours before dawn.

On the other hand, the ex-policeman, obsessed by his sense of grievance, who had just committed his ninth murder to revenge himself on the society that had spurned him, and perhaps still more to prove to himself he was still a man by defying the whole police force—indeed, the whole world.

Was he drunk again? On a night like that, when the bars were open long after their usual closing time, he had no doubt had more than ever. And in that dark, silent street, what did he see with his bulging drink-inflamed eyes? A young boy, the first person who had found him out, and who would now—

"I'd like to know whether he's got a gun on him," sighed the Inspector.

Janvier answered at once:

"I asked his wife. It seems he always carries one about. An automatic pistol, but it's not loaded."

"How can she know that?"

"Once or twice, when he was more than usually drunk, he rounded on her, threatening her with the gun. After that, she got hold of his ammunition and locked it up, telling him an unloaded pistol was quite enough to frighten people without his having to fire it."

Had those two really stalked each other through the streets of Paris? A strange sort of duel in which the man had the strength and the boy the speed?

The boy may well have been scared, but the man stood for something precious enough to push fear into the background: a fortune and the end of his father's worries and humiliations.

*　　*　　*

Having got so far, there wasn't a lot more to be said by the little group of people waiting in the Préfecture de Police. They sat gazing at the street-plan with a picture in their minds of a boy following a man, the boy no doubt keeping his distance. Everyone else was sleeping. There was no one in the streets who could be a help to the one or a menace to the other. Had Loubet produced his gun in an attempt to frighten the boy away?

When people woke up and began coming out into the streets, what would the boy do then? Would he rush up to the first person he met and start screaming "Murder"?

"Yes. It was Loubet who walked in front," said Saillard slowly.

"And it was I," put in Andre Lecœur, "who told the boy all about the pillar telephone system."

The little crosses came to life. What had at first been mysterious was now almost simple. But it was tragic.

The child was risking his skin to save his father. Tears were slowly trickling down the latter's face. He made no attempt to hide them.

He was in a strange place, surrounded by outlandish objects, and by people who talked to him as though he wasn't there, as though he was someone else. And his brother was among these people, a brother he could hardly recognize and whom he regarded with instinctive respect.

Even when they did speak, it wasn't necessary to say much. They understood each other. A word sufficed.

"Loubet couldn't go home, of course."

Andre Lecœur smiled suddenly as a thought struck him.

"It didn't occur to him that Francois hadn't a centime in his pocket. He could have escaped by diving into the Métro."

No. That wouldn't hold water. The boy had seen him and would give his description.

Place du Trocadéro, the Etoile. The time was passing. It was practically broad daylight. People were up and about. Why hadn't Francois called for help? Anyhow, with people in the streets it was no longer possible for Loubet to kill him.

The Inspector was deep in thought.

"For one reason or another," he murmured, "I think they're going about together now."

At the same moment, a lamp lit up on the wall. As though he knew it would be for him, Lecœur answered in place of Bedeau.

"Yes. I thought as much."

"It's about the two oranges. They found an Arab boy asleep in the third-class waiting room at the Gare du Nord. He still had the oranges in his pockets. He'd run away from home because his father had beaten him."

"Do you think Bib's dead?"

"If he was dead, Loubet would have gone home, as he would no longer have anything to fear."

So the struggle was still going on somewhere in this now sunny Paris in which families were sauntering along the boulevards taking the air.

It would be the fear of losing him in the crowd that had brought Francois close to his quarry. Why didn't he call for help? No doubt because Loubet had threatened him with his gun. "One word from you, my lad, and I'll empty this into your guts."

So each was pursuing his own goal: for the one to shake off the boy somehow, for the other to watch for the moment when the murderer was off his guard and give the alarm before he had time to shoot.

It was a matter of life and death.

"Loubet isn't likely to be in the center of the town, where policemen are too plentiful for his liking, to say nothing of the fact that many of them know him by sight."

Their most likely direction from the Etoile was towards Montmartre—not to the amusement quarter, but to the remoter and quieter parts.

It was half past two. Had they had anything to eat? Had Loubet, with his mind set on escape, been able to resist the temptation to drink?

"Monsieur le Commissaire—"

Andre Lecœur couldn't speak with the assurance he would have liked. He couldn't get rid of the feeling that he was an upstart, if not a usurper.

"I know there are thousands of little bars in Paris. But if we chose the more likely districts and put plenty of men on the job—"

Not only were all the men there roped in, but Saillard got through to the Police Judiciaire, where there were six men on duty, and set every one of them to work on six different telephone lines.

"Hallo! Is that the Bar des Amis? In the course of the day have you seen a middle-aged man accompanied by a boy of ten? The man's wearing a black overcoat and a—"

Again Lecœur made little crosses, not in his notebook this time, but in the telephone directory. There were ten pages of bars, some of them with the weirdest names.

A plan of Paris was spread out on a table all ready and it was in a little alley of ill-repute behind the Place Clichy that the Inspector was able to make the first mark in red chalk.

"Yes, there was a man of that description here about twelve o'clock. He drank three glasses of Calvados and ordered a glass of white wine for the boy.

The boy didn't want to drink at first, but he did in the end and he wolfed a couple of eggs."

By the way Olivier Lecœur's face lit up, you might have thought he heard his boy's voice.

"You don't know which way they went?"

"Towards the Boulevard des Batignolles, I think. The man looked as though he'd already had one or two before he came in."

"Hallo! Zanzi-Bar? Have you at any time seen a—"

It became a refrain. As soon as one man had finished, the same words, or practically the same, were repeated by his neighbor.

Rue Damrémont. Montmartre again, only farther out this time. One-thirty. Loubet had broken a glass, his movements by this time being somewhat clumsy. The boy got up and made off in the direction of the lavatory, but when the man followed, he thought better of it and went back to his seat.

"Yes. The boy did look a bit frightened. As for the man, he was laughing and smirking as though he was enjoying a huge joke."

"Do you hear that, Olivier? Bib was still there at one-forty."

Andre Lecœur dared not say what was in his mind. The struggle was nearing its climax. Now that Loubet had really started drinking if was just a question of time. The only thing was: would the boy wait long enough?

It was all very well for Madame Loubet to say the gun wasn't loaded. The butt of an automatic was quite hard enough to crack a boy's skull.

His eyes wandered to his brother, and he had a vision of what Olivier might well have come to if his asthma hadn't prevented him drinking.

"Hallo! Yes. Where? Boulevard Ney?"

They had reached the outskirts of Paris. The ex-Sergeant seemed still to have his wits about him. Little by little, in easy stages, he was leading the boy to one of those outlying districts where there were still empty building sites and desolate spaces.

Three police cars were promptly switched to that neighborhood, as well as every available *agent cycliste* within reach. Even Janvier dashed off, taking the Inspector's little car, and it was all they could do to prevent Olivier from running after him.

"I tell you, you'd much better stay here. He may easily go off on a false trail, and then you won't know anything."

Nobody had time for making coffee. The men of the second day shift had not thoroughly warmed to the case. Everyone was strung up.

"Hallo! Yes. Orient Bar. What is it?"

It was Andre Lecœur who took the call. With the receiver to his ear, he rose to his feet, making queer signs that brought the whole room to a hush.

"What? Don't speak so close to the mouthpiece."

In the silence, the others could hear a high-pitched voice.

"It's for the police! Tell the police I've got him! The killer! Hallo? What? Is that Uncle Andre?"

The voice was lowered a tone to say shakily: "I tell you, I'll shoot, Uncle Andre."

Lecœur hardly knew to whom he handed the receiver. He dashed out of the room and up the stairs, almost breaking down the door of the room.

"Quick, all cars to the Orient Bar, Porte Clignancourt."

And without waiting to hear the message go out, he dashed back as fast as he'd come. At the door he stopped dead, struck by the calm that had suddenly descended on the room.

It was Saillard who held the receiver into which, in the thickest of Parisian dialects, a voice was saying:

"It's all right. Don't worry. I gave the chap a crack on the head with a bottle. Laid him out properly. God knows what he wanted to do to the kid. What's that? You want to speak to him? Here, little one, come here. And give me your popgun. I don't like those toys. Why, it isn't loaded."

Another voice. "Is that Uncle Andre?"

The Inspector looked round, and it was not to Andre but to Olivier that he handed the receiver.

"Uncle Andre. I got him."

"Bib! It's me."

"What are you doing there, Dad?"

"Nothing. Waiting to hear from you. It's been—"

"You can't think how bucked I am. Wait a moment, here's the police. They're just arriving."

Confused sounds. Voices, the shuffling of feet, the clink of glasses. Olivier Lecœur listened, standing there awkwardly, gazing at the wall-map which he did not see, his thoughts far away at the northern extremity of Paris, in a windswept boulevard.

"They're taking me with them."

Another voice. "Is that you, Chief? Janvier here."

One might have thought it was Olivier Lecœur who had been knocked on the head with a bottle by the way he held the receiver out, staring blankly in front of him.

"He's out, right out, Chief. They're lugging him away now. When the boy heard the telephone ringing, he decided it was his chance. He grabbed Loubet's gun from his pocket and made a dash for the phone. The proprietor here's a pretty tough nut. If it hadn't been for—"

A little lamp lit up in the plan of Paris.

"Hallo! Your car's gone out?"

"Someone's smashed the glass of the pillar telephone in the Place Clignancourt. Says there's a row going on in a bar. I'll ring up again when we know what's going on."

It wouldn't be necessary.

Nor was it necessary for Andre Lecœur to put a cross in his notebook under Miscellaneous.

—translated by Geoffrey Sainsbury

Margery Allingham

MURDER UNDER THE MISTLETOE

Murder under the mistletoe—and the man who must have done it couldn't have done it. That's my Christmas and I don't feel merry thank you very much all the same." Superintendent Stanislaus Oates favored his old friend Mr. Albert Campion with a pained smile and sat down in the chair indicated.

It was the afternoon of Christmas Day and Mr. Campion, only a trifle more owlish than usual behind his horn rims, had been fetched down from the children's party which he was attending at his brother-in-law's house in Knightsbridge to meet the Superintendent, who had moved heaven and earth to find him.

"What do you want?" Mr. Campion inquired facetiously. "A little armchair miracle?"

"I don't care if you do it swinging from a trapeze. I just want a reasonable explanation." Oates was rattled. His dyspeptic face with the perpetually sad expression was slightly flushed and not with festivity. He plunged into his story.

"About eleven last night a crook called Sampson was found shot dead in the back of a car in a garage under a small drinking club in Alcatraz Mews—the club is named The Humdinger. A large bunch of mistletoe which had been lying on the front seat ready to be driven home had been placed on top of the body partially hiding it—which was why it hadn't been found before. The gun, fitted with a silencer, but wiped of prints, was found under the front seat. The dead man was recognized at once by the owner of the car who is also the owner of the club. He was the owner's current boyfriend. She is quite a well-known West End character called 'Girlski.' What did you say?"

"I said, 'Oo-er'," murmured Mr. Campion. "One of the Eumenides, no doubt?"

"No." Oates spoke innocently. "She's not a Greek. Don't worry about her. Just keep your mind on the facts. She knows, as we do, that the only person who wanted to kill Sampson is a nasty little snake called Kroll. He has been out of circulation for the best of reasons. Sampson turned Queen's evidence against him in a matter concerning a conspiracy to rob Her Majesty's mails and when he was released last Tuesday Kroll came out breathing retribution."

"Not the Christmas spirit," said Mr. Campion inanely.

"That is exactly what *we* thought," Oates agreed. "So about five o'clock yesterday afternoon two of our chaps, hearing that Kroll was at The Humdinger, where he might have been expected to make trouble, dropped along there and brought him in for questioning and he's been in custody ever since.

"Well, now. We have at least a dozen reasonably sober witnesses to prove that Kroll did not meet Sampson at the Club. Sampson had been there earlier in the afternoon but he left about a quarter to four saying he'd got to do some Christmas shopping but promising to return. Fifteen minutes or so later Kroll came in and stayed there in full view of Girlski and the customers until our men turned up and collected him. *Now* what do you say?"

"Too easy!" Mr. Campion was suspicious. "Kroll killed Sampson just before he came in himself. The two met in the dusk outside the club. Kroll forced Sampson into the garage and possibly into the car and shot him. With the way the traffic has been lately, he'd hardly have attracted attention had he used a mortar, let alone a gun with a silencer. He wiped the weapon, chucked it in the car, threw the mistletoe over the corpse, and went up to Girlski to renew old acquaintance and establish an alibi. Your chaps, arriving when they did, must have appeared welcome."

Oates nodded. "We thought that. *That is what happened.* That is why this morning's development has set me gibbering. We now have two unimpeachable witnesses who swear that the dead man was in Chipperwood West at six last evening delivering some Christmas purchases he had made on behalf of a neighbor. That is *a whole hour* after Kroll was pulled in.

"The assumption is that Sampson returned to Alcatraz Mews sometime later in the evening and was killed by someone else—which we know is not true. Unfortunately, the Chipperwood West witnesses are not the kind of people we are going to shake. One of them is a friend of yours. She asked our Inspector if he knew you because you were 'so good at crime and all that nonsense'."

"Good Heavens!" Mr. Campion spoke piously as the explanation of the Superintendent's unlikely visitation was made plain to him. "I don't think I know Chipperwood West."

"It's a suburb which is becoming fashionable. Have you ever heard of Lady Larradine?"

"Old Lady 'ell?" Mr. Campion let the joke of his salad days escape without its being noticed by either of them. "I don't believe it. She must be dead by this time!"

"There's a type of woman who never dies before you do," said Oates with apparent sincerity. "She's quite a dragon, I understand from our Inspector. However, she isn't the actual witness. There are two of them. Brigadier Brose is one. Ever heard of *him*?"

"I don't think I have."

"My information is that you'd remember him if you'd met him. Well, we'll find out. I'm taking you with me, Campion. I hope you don't mind?"

"My sister will hate it. I'm due to be Santa Claus in about an hour."

"I can't help that." Oates was adamant. "If a bunch of silly crooks want to get spiteful at the festive season, someone must do the homework. Come and play Santa Claus with me. It's your last chance. I'm retiring this summer."

Oates continued in the same vein as he and Mr. Campion sat in the back of a police car threading their way through the deserted Christmas streets where the lamps were growing bright in the dusk.

"I've had bad luck lately," the Superintendent said seriously. "Too much. It won't help my memoirs if I go out in a blaze of no-enthusiasm."

"You're thinking of the Phaeton Robbery," Mr. Campion suggested. "What are you calling your memoirs? *Man-Eaters of the Yard?*"

Oates's mild old eyes brightened, but not greatly.

"Something of the kind," he admitted. "But no one could be blamed for not solving that blessed Phaeton business. Everyone concerned was bonkers. A silly old musical star, for thirty years the widow of an eccentric Duke, steps out into her London garden one autumn morning leaving the street door wide open and all her most valuable jewelry collected from strong-rooms all over the country lying in a brown paper parcel on her bureau in the first room off the hall. Her excuse was that she was just going to take it to the Bond Street auctioneers and was carrying it herself for safety! The thief was equally mental to lift it."

"It wasn't saleable?"

"Saleable? It couldn't even be broken up. The stuff is just about as well-known as the Crown Jewels. Great big enamels which the old Duke had collected at great expense. No fence would stay in the same room with them, yet, of course, they are worth the Earth as every newspaper has told us at length ever since they were pinched!"

"He didn't get anything else either, did he?"

"He was a madman." Oates dismissed him with contempt. "All he gained was the old lady's housekeeping money for a couple of months which was in her handbag—about a hundred and fifty quid—and the other two items which were on the same shelf, a soapstone monkey and a plated paperknife. He simply wandered in, took the first things he happened to see and wandered out again. Any sneak thief, tramp, or casual snapper-upper could have done it and who gets blamed? *Me!*"

He looked so woebegone that Mr. Campion hastily changed the subject. "Where are we going?" he inquired. "To call on her ladyship? Do I understand that at the age of one hundred and forty-six or whatever it is she is cohabiting with a Brig? Which war?"

"I can't tell you." Oates was literal as usual. "It could be the South African. They're all in a nice residential hotel—the sort of place that is very popular with the older members of the landed gentry just now."

"When you say landed, you mean as in Fish?"

"Roughly, yes. Elderly people living on capital. About forty of them. This place used to be called *The Haven* and has now been taken over by two ex-society widows and renamed *The Ccraven*—with two Cs. It's a select hotel-cum-Old Ducks' Home for Mother's Friends. You know the sort of place?"

"I can envisage it. Don't say your murdered chum from The Humdinger lived there too?"

"No, he lived in a more modest place whose garden backs on the CCraven's grounds. The Brigadier and one of the other residents, a Mr. Charlie Taunton, who has become a bosom friend of his, were in the habit of talking to Sampson over the wall. Taunton is a lazy man who seldom goes out and has little money but he very much wanted to get some gifts for his fellow guests—something in the nature of little jokes from the chain stores, I understand; but he dreaded the exertion of shopping for them and Sampson appears to have offered to get him some little items wholesale and to deliver them by six o'clock on Christmas Eve—in time for him to package them up and hand them to Lady Larradine who was dressing the tree at seven."

"And did you say Sampson actually did this?" Mr. Campion sounded bewildered.

"Both old gentlemen—the Brigadier and Taunton—swear to it. They insist they went down to the wall at six and Sampson handed the parcel over as arranged. My Inspector is an experienced man and he doesn't think we'll be able to shake either of them."

"That leaves Kroll with a complete alibi. How did these Chipperwood witnesses hear of Sampson's death?"

"Routine. The local police called at Sampson's home address this morning to report the death, only to discover the place closed. The landlady and her family are away for the holiday and Sampson himself was due to spend it with Girlski. The police stamped about a bit, making sure of all this, and in the course of their investigations they were seen and hailed by the two old boys in the adjoining garden. The two were shocked to hear that their kind acquaintance was dead and volunteered the information that he had been with them at six."

Mr. Campion looked blank. "Perhaps they don't keep the same hours as anybody else," he suggested. "Old people can be highly eccentric."

Oates shook his head. "We thought of that. My Inspector, who came down the moment the local police reported, insists that they are perfectly normal and quite positive. Moreover, they had the purchases. He saw the packages already on the tree. Lady Larradine pointed them out to him when she asked after you. She'll be delighted to see you, Campion."

"I can hardly wait!"

"You don't have to," said Oates grimly as they pulled up before a huge Edwardian villa. "It's all yours."

"My dear Boy! You haven't aged any more than I have!"

Lady Larradine's tremendous voice—one of her chief terrors, Mr. Campion recollected—echoed over the crowded first-floor room where she received them. There she stood in an outmoded but glittering evening gown looking, as always, exactly like a spray-flecked seal.

"I *knew* you'd come," she bellowed. "As soon as you got my oblique little S.O.S. How do you like our little hideout? Isn't it *fun*! Moira Spryg-Fysher and Janice Poole-Poole wanted something to do, so we all put our pennies in it and here we are!"

"Almost too marvelous," murmured Mr. Campion in all sincerity. "We really want a word with Brigadier Brose and Mr. Taunton."

"Of course you do and so you shall! We're all waiting for the Christmas tree. Everybody will be there for that in about ten minutes in the drawing room. My dear, when *we* came they were calling it the Residents' Lounge!"

Superintendent Oates remained grave. He was startled to discover that the dragon was not only fierce but also wily. The news that her apparently casual mention of Mr. Campion to the Inspector had been a ruse to get hold of him shocked the innocent Superintendent. He retaliated by insisting that he must see the witnesses at once.

Lady Larradine silenced him with a friendly roar. "My dear man, you can't! They've gone for a walk. I always turn men out of the house after Christmas luncheon. They'll soon be back. The Brigadier won't miss his Tree! Ah. Here's Fiona. This is Janice Poole-Poole's daughter, Albert. Isn't she a pretty girl?"

Mr. Campion saw Miss Poole-Poole with relief, knowing of old that Oates was susceptible to the type. The newcomer was young and lovely and even her beehive hair and the fact that she appeared to have painted herself with two black eyes failed to spoil the exquisite smile she bestowed on the helpless officer.

"Fabulous to have you really here," she said and sounded as if she meant it. While he was still recovering, Lady Larradine led Oates to the window.

"You can't see it because it's pitch-dark," she said, "but out there, down in the garden, there's a wall and it was over it that the Brigadier and Mr. Taunton spoke to Mr. Sampson at six o'clock last night. No one liked the man Sampson—

I think Mr. Taunton was almost afraid of him. Certainly he seems to have died very untidily!"

"But he *did* buy Mr. Taunton's Christmas gifts for him?"

The dragon lifted a webby eyelid. "You have already been told that. At six last night Mr. Taunton and the Brigadier went to meet him to get the box. I got them into their mufflers so I know! I had the packing paper ready, too, for Mr. Taunton to take up to his room . . . Rather a small one on the third floor."

She lowered her voice to reduce it to the volume of distant traffic. "Not many pennies, but a dear little man!"

"Did you *see* these presents, Ma'am?"

"Not before they were wrapped! That would have spoiled the surprise!"

"I shall have to see them." There was a mulish note in the Superintendent's voice which the lady was too experienced to ignore.

"I've thought how to do that without upsetting anybody," she said briskly. "The Brigadier and I will cut the presents from the Tree and Fiona will be handing them round. All Mr. Taunton's little gifts are in the very distinctive black and gold paper I bought from Millie's Boutique and so, Fiona, you must give every package in black and gold not to the person to whom it is addressed but to the Superintendent. Can you do that, dear?"

Miss Poole-Poole seemed to feel the task difficult but not impossible and the trusting smile she gave Oates cut short his objection like the sun melting frost.

"Splendid!" The dragon's roar was hearty. "Give me your arm, Superintendent. You shall take me down."

As the procession reached the hall, it ran into the Brigadier himself. He was a large, pink man, affable enough, but of a martial type and he bristled at the Superintendent. "Extraordinary time to do your business—middle of Christmas Day!" he said after acknowledging the introductions.

Oates inquired if he had enjoyed his walk.

"Talk?" said the Brigadier. "I've not been talking. I've been asleep in the card room. Where's old Taunton?"

"He went for a walk, Athole dear," bellowed the dragon gaily.

"So he did. You sent him! Poor feller."

As the old soldier led the way to the open door of the drawing room, it occurred to both the Superintendent and Mr. Campion that the secret of Lady Larradine's undoubted attraction for the Brigadier lay in the fact that he could hear *her* if no one else. The discovery cast a new light altogether on the story of the encounter with Sampson in the garden.

Meanwhile, they had entered the drawing room and the party had begun. As Mr. Campion glanced at the company, ranged in a full circle round a magnificent tree loaded with gifts and sparkling like a waterfall, he saw face after familiar face. They were elder acquaintances of the dizzy 1930s whom he had mourned as gone forever, when he thought of them at all. Yet here they all were, not only alive but released by great age from many of the restraints of convention.

He noticed that every type of headgear from night-cap to tiara was being sported with fine individualistic enthusiasm. But Lady Larradine gave him little time to look about. She proceeded with her task immediately.

Each guest had been provided with a small invalid table beside his arm-chair, and Oates, reluctant but wax in Fiona's hands, was no exception. The Superintendent found himself seated between a mountain in flannel and a wraith in mauve mink, waiting his turn with the same beady-eyed avidity.

Christmas Tree procedure at the CCraven proved to be well organized. The dragon did little work herself. Armed with a swagger stick, she merely prodded parcel after parcel hanging amid the boughs while the task of detaching them was performed by the Brigadier who handed them to Fiona. Either to add to the excitement or perhaps to muffle any unfortunate comment on gifts received by the uninhibited company, jolly Christmas music was played throughout, and under cover of the noise Mr. Campion was able to tackle his hostess.

"Where is Taunton?" he whispered.

"Such a nice little man. Most presentable, but just a little teeny-weeny bit dishonest."

Lady Larradine ignored the question in his eyes and continued to put him in the picture at great speed, while supervising the Tree at the same time. "Fifty-seven convictions, I believe, but only small ones. I only got it all out of him last week. Shattering! He'd been so *useful*, amusing the Brigadier. When he came, he looked like a lost soul with no luggage, but after no time at all he settled in perfectly."

She paused and stabbed at a ball of colored cellophane with her stick before returning to her startled guest.

"Albert, I am terribly afraid that it was poor Mr. Taunton who took that dreadful jewelry of Maisie Phaeton's. It appears to have been entirely her fault. He was merely wandering past her house, feeling in need of care and attention. The door was wide open and Mr. Taunton suddenly found himself inside, picking up a few odds and ends. When he discovered from all that fuss in the newspapers what he had got hold of—how well-known it was, I mean—he was quite horrified and had to hide. And where better place than here with us where he never had to go out?"

"Where indeed!" Mr. Campion dared not glance across the room at the Superintendent unwrapping his black and gold parcels. "Where is he now? Poor Mr. Taunton, I mean."

"Of course I hadn't the faintest idea what was worrying the man until he confessed," the dragon went on stonily. "Then I realized that something would have to be done at once to protect everybody. The wretch had hidden all that frightful stuff in our toolshed for three months, not daring to keep it in the house; and to make matters worse, the impossible person at the end of the garden, Mr. Sampson, had recognized him and *would* keep speaking. Apparently people in the—er—underworld all know each other just like those of us in—er—other closed circles do."

Mr. Campion, whose hair was standing on end, had a moment of inspiration. "This absurd rigmarole about Taunton getting Sampson to buy him some Christmas gifts wholesale was *your* idea!" he said accusingly.

The dragon stared. "It seemed the best way of getting Maisie's jewelry back to her without any *one* person being involved," she said frankly. "I knew we should all recognize the things the moment we saw them and I was certain that after a lot of argument we should decide to pack them up and send them round to her. But, if there *were* any repercussions, we should *all* be in it—quite a formidable array, dear Boy—and the blame could be traced to Mr. Sampson if absolutely necessary. You see, the Brigadier is convinced that Sampson *was* there last night. Mr. Taunton very cleverly left him on the lawn and went behind the tool shed and came back with the box."

"How completely immoral!" Mr. Campion couldn't restrain himself.

The dragon had the grace to look embarrassed.

"I don't think the Sampson angle would ever have arisen," she said. "But if it had, Sampson was quite a terrible person. Almost a blackmailer. Utterly dishonest and inconsiderate. Think how he has spoiled everything and endangered us all by getting himself killed on the *one* afternoon when we said he was here, so that the police were brought in. Just the *one* thing I was trying to avoid. When the Inspector appeared this morning I was so upset I thought of you!"

In his not unnatural alarm Mr. Campion so far forgot himself as to touch her sleeve. "Where is Taunton now?"

The dragon threshed her train. "Really, Boy! What a fidget you are! If you must know, I gave him his Christmas present—every penny I had in cash for he was broke again, he told me—and sent him for a nice long walk after lunch. Having seen the Inspector here this morning he was glad to go."

She paused and a granite gleam came into her hooded eyes. "If that Superintendent friend of yours has the stupidity to try to find him once Maisie has her monstrosities back, none of us will be able to identify him, I'm afraid. And there's another thing. If the Brigadier should be *forced* to give evidence, I am sure he will stick to his guns about Mr. Sampson being down in the garden here at six o'clock last night. That would mean that the man Kroll would have to go unpunished for his revenge murder, wouldn't it? Sampson was a terrible person—but *no one* should have killed him."

Mr. Campion was silenced. He glanced fearfully across the room.

The Superintendent was seated at his table wearing the strained yet slap-happy expression of a man with concussion. On his left was a pile of black and gold wrappings, on his right a rajah's ransom in somewhat specialized form.

From where he stood, Mr. Campion could see two examples amid the rest—a breastplate in gold, pearl, and enamel in the shape of a unicorn and an item which looked like a plover's egg in tourmaline encased in a ducal coronet. There was also a soapstone monkey and a solid-silver paperknife.

Much later that evening Mr. Campion and the Superintendent drove quietly back to headquarters. Oates had a large cardboard box on his knee. He clasped it tenderly.

He had been silent for a long time when a thought occurred to him. "Why did they take him into the house in the first place?" he said. "An elderly crook looking lost! And no luggage!"

Mr. Campion's pale eyes flickered behind his spectacles.

"Don't forget the Duchess' housekeeping money," he murmured. "I should think he offered one of the widows who really run that place the first three months' payment in cash, wouldn't you? That must be an impressive phenomenon in that sort of business, I fancy."

Oates caught his breath and fell silent once more. Presently he burst out again.

"Those people! That woman!" he exploded. "When they were younger they led me a pretty dance—losing things or getting themselves swindled. But now they're old they take the blessed biscuit! Do you see how she's tied my hands, Campion?"

Mr. Campion tried not to grin.

"Snapdragons are just permissible at Christmas," he said. "Handled with extreme caution they burn very few fingers, it seems to me."

Mr. Campion tapped the cardboard box. "And some of them provide a few plums for retiring coppers, don't they, Superintendent?"

Patricia Moyes

WHO KILLED FATHER CHRISTMAS?

"Good morning, Mr. Borrowdale. Nippy out, isn't it? You're in early, I see." Little Miss MacArthur spoke with her usual brisk brightness, which failed to conceal both envy and dislike. She was unpacking a consignment of stout Teddy bears in the stockroom behind the toy department at Barnum and Thrums, the London store. "Smart as ever, Mr. Borrowdale," she added, jealously.

I laid down my curly-brimmed bowler hat and cane and took off my British warm overcoat. I don't mind admitting that I do take pains to dress as well as I can, and for some reason it seems to infuriate the Miss MacArthurs of the world.

She prattled on. "Nice looking, these Teddies, don't you think? Very reasonable, too. Made in Hong Kong, that'll be why. I think I'll take one for my sister's youngest."

The toy department at Barnum's has little to recommend it to anyone over the age of twelve, and normally it is tranquil and little populated. However, at Christmastime it briefly becomes the bustling heart of the great shop, and also provides useful vacation jobs for chaps like me who wish to earn some money during the weeks before the university term begins in January. Gone, I fear, are the days when undergraduates were the gilded youth of England. We all have to work our passages these days, and sometimes it means selling toys.

One advantage of the job is that employees—even temporaries like me—are allowed to buy goods at a considerable discount, which helps with the Christmas gift problem. As a matter of fact, I had already decided to buy a Teddy bear for one of my nephews, and I mentioned as much.

"Well, you'd better take it right away," remarked Miss MacArthur, "because I heard Mr. Harrington say he was taking two, and I think Disaster has her eye on one." Disaster was the unfortunate but inevitable nickname of Miss Aster, who had been with the store for thirty-one years but still made mistakes with her stockbook. I felt sorry for the old girl. I had overheard a conversation

367

between Mr. Harrington, the department manager, and Mr. Andrews, the deputy store manager, and so I knew—but Disaster didn't—that she would be getting the sack as soon as the Christmas rush was over.

Meanwhile, Miss MacArthur was arranging the bears on a shelf. They sat there in grinning rows, brown and woolly, with boot-button eyes and red ribbons round their necks.

It was then that Father Christmas came in. He'd been in the cloakroom changing into his costume—white beard, red nose, and all. His name was Bert Denman. He was a cheery soul who got on well with the kids, and he'd had the Father Christmas job at Barnum's each of the three years I'd been selling there. Now he was carrying his sack, which he filled every morning from the cheap items in the stockroom. A visit to Father Christmas cost 50 pence, so naturally the gift that was fished out of the sack couldn't be worth more than 20 pence. However, to my surprise, he went straight over to the row of Teddy bears and picked one off the shelf. For some reason, he chose the only one with a blue instead of a red ribbon.

Miss MacArthur was on to him in an instant. "What d'you think you're doing, Mr. Denman? Those Teddies aren't in your line at all—much too dear. One pound ninety, they are."

Father Christmas did not answer, and suddenly I realized that it was not Bert Denman under the red robe. "Wait a minute," I said. "Who are you? You're not our Father Christmas."

He turned to face me, the Teddy bear in his hand. "That's all right," he said. "Charlie Burrows is my name. I live in the same lodging house with Bert Denman. He was taken poorly last night, and I'm standing in for him."

"*Well*," said Miss MacArthur. "How very odd. Does Mr. Harrington know?"

"Of course he does," said Father Christmas.

As if on cue, Mr. Harrington himself came hurrying into the stockroom. He always hurried everywhere, preceded by his small black mustache. He said, "Ah, there you are, Burrows. Fill up your sack, and I'll explain the job to you. Denman told you about the Teddy bear, did he?"

"Yes, Mr. Harrington."

"Father Christmas can't give away an expensive bear like that, Mr. Harrington," Miss MacArthur objected.

"Now, now, Miss MacArthur, it's all arranged," said Harrington fussily. "A customer came in yesterday and made a special request that Father Christmas should give his small daughter a Teddy bear this morning. I knew this consignment was due on the shelves, so I promised him one. It's been paid for. The important thing, Burrows, is to remember the child's name. It's . . . er . . . I have it written down somewhere."

"Annabel Whitworth," said Father Christmas. "Four years old, fair hair, will be brought in by her mother."

"I see that Denman briefed you well," said Mr. Harrington, with an icy smile. "Well, now, I'll collect two bears for myself—one for my son and one for my neighbor's boy—and then I'll show you the booth."

Miss Aster arrived just then. She and Miss MacArthur finished uncrating the bears and took one out to put on display next to a female doll that, among other endearing traits, actually wet its diaper. Mr. Harrington led our surrogate Father Christmas to his small canvas booth, and the rest of us busied and braced ourselves for the moment when the great glass doors opened and the floodtide was let in. The toy department of a big store on December 23 is no place for weaklings.

It is curious that even such an apparently random stream of humanity as Christmas shoppers displays a pattern of behavior. The earliest arrivals in the toy department are office workers on their way to their jobs. The actual toddlers, bent on an interview with Father Christmas, do not appear until their mothers have had time to wash up breakfast, have a bit of a go around the house, and catch the bus from Kensington or the tube from Uxbridge.

On that particular morning it was just twenty-eight minutes past ten when I saw Disaster, who was sitting in a decorated cash desk labeled "The Elfin Grove," take 50 pence from the first parent to usher her child into Santa's booth. For about two minutes the mother waited, chatting quietly with Disaster. Then a loudly wailing infant emerged from the booth.

The mother snatched her up, and—with that sixth sense that mothers everywhere seem to develop—interpreted the incoherent screams. "She says that Father Christmas won't talk to her. She says he's asleep."

It was clearly an emergency, even if a minor one, and Disaster was already showing signs of panic. I excused myself from my customer—a middle-aged gentleman who was playing with an electric train set—and went over to see what I could do. By then, the mother was indignant.

"Fifty pence and the old man sound asleep and drunk as like as not, and at half-past ten in the morning. Disgraceful, I call it. And here's poor little Poppy what had been looking forward to—"

I rushed into Father Christmas's booth. The man who called himself Charlie Burrows was slumped forward in his chair, looking for all the world as if he were asleep; but when I shook him, his head lolled horribly, and it was obvious that he was more than sleeping. The red robe concealed the blood until it made my hand sticky. Father Christmas had been stabbed in the back, and he was certainly dead.

I acted as fast as I could. First of all, I told Disaster to put up the CLOSED sign outside Santa's booth. Then I smoothed down Poppy's mother by leading her to a counter where I told her she could select any toy up to one pound and have it free. Under pretext of keeping records, I got her name and address. Finally I cornered Mr. Harrington in his office and told him the news.

I thought he was going to faint. "Dead? Murdered? Are you sure, Mr. Borrowdale?"

"Quite sure, I'm afraid. You'd better telephone the police, Mr. Harrington."

"The police! In Barnum's! What a terrible thing! I'll telephone the deputy store manager first and *then* the police."

As a matter of fact, the police were surprisingly quick and discreet. A plainclothes detective superintendent and his sergeant, a photographer, and the police doctor arrived, not in a posse, but as individuals, unnoticed among the crowd. They assembled in the booth, where the deputy manager—Mr. Andrews—and Mr. Harrington and I were waiting for them.

The superintendent introduced himself—his name was Armitage—and inspected the body with an expression of cold fury on his face that I couldn't quite understand, although the reason became clear later. He said very little. After some tedious formalities Armitage indicated that the body might be removed.

"What's the least conspicuous way to do it?" he asked.

"You can take him out through the back of the booth," I said. "The canvas overlaps right behind Santa's chair. The door to the staff quarters and the stockroom is just opposite, and from there you can take the service lift to the goods entrance in the mews."

The doctor and the photographer between them carried off their grim burden on a collapsible stretcher, and Superintendent Armitage began asking questions about the arrangements in the Father Christmas booth. I did the explaining, since Mr. Harrington seemed to be verging on hysteria.

Customers paid their 50 pence to Disaster in the Elfin Grove, and then the child—usually alone—was propelled through the door of the booth and into the presence of Father Christmas, who sat in his canvas-backed director's chair on a small dais facing the entrance, with his sack of toys beside him. The child climbed onto his knee, whispered its Christmas wishes, and was rewarded with a few friendly words and a small gift from Santa's sack.

What was not obvious to the clientele was the back entrance to the booth, which enabled Father Christmas to slip in and out unobserved. He usually had his coffee break at about 11:15, unless there was a very heavy rush of business. Disaster would pick a moment when custom seemed slow, put up the CLOSED notice, and inform Bert that he could take a few minutes off. When he returned, he pressed a button by his chair that rang a buzzer in the cashier's booth. Down would come the notice, and Santa was in business again.

Before Superintendent Armitage could comment on my remarks, Mr. Harrington broke into a sort of despairing wait, "It must have been one of the customers!" he cried.

"I don't think so, sir," said Armitage. "This is an inside job. He was stabbed in the back with a long thin blade of some sort. The murderer must have opened the back flap and stabbed him clean through the canvas back of his chair. That must have been someone who knew the exact arrangements. The murderer then used the back way to enter the booth—"

"I don't see how you can say that!" Harrington's voice was rising dangerously. "If the man was stabbed from outside, what makes you think anybody came into the booth?"

"I'll explain that in a minute, sir."

Ignoring Armitage, Harrington went on. "In any case, he wasn't our regular Father Christmas! None of us had ever seen him before. Why on earth would anybody kill a man that nobody knew?"

Armitage and the deputy manager exchanged glances. Then Armitage said, "*I* knew him, sir. Very well. Charlie Burrows was one of our finest plainclothes narcotics officers."

Mr. Harrington had gone green. "You mean—he was a policeman?"

"Exactly, sir. I'd better explain. A little time ago we got a tipoff from an informer that an important consignment of high-grade heroin was to be smuggled in from Hong Kong in a consignment of Christmas toys. Teddy bears, in fact. The drug was to be in the Barnum and Thrums carton, hidden inside a particular Teddy bear, which would be distinguished by having a blue ribbon around its neck instead of a red one."

"Surely," I said, "you couldn't get what you call an important consignment inside one Teddy bear, even a big one."

Armitage sighed. "Shows you aren't familiar with the drug scene, sir," he said. "Why, half a pound of pure high-grade heroin is worth a fortune on the streets."

With a show of bluster Harrington said, "If you knew this, Superintendent, why didn't you simply intercept the consignment and confiscate the drug? Look at the trouble that's been—"

Armitage interrupted him. "If you'd just hear me out, sir. What I've told you was the sum total of our information. We didn't know who in Barnum's was going to pick up the heroin, or how or where it was to be disposed of. We're more interested in getting the people—the pushers—than confiscating the cargo. So I had a word with Mr. Andrews here, and he kindly agreed to let Charlie take on the Father Christmas job. And Charlie set a little trap. Unfortunately, he paid for it with his life." There was an awkward silence.

He went on. "Mr. Andrews told us that the consignment had arrived and was to be unpacked today. We know that staff get first pick, as it were, at new stock, and we were naturally interested to see who would select the bear with the blue ribbon. It was Charlie's own idea to concoct a story about a special present for a little girl—"

"You mean, that wasn't true?" Harrington was outraged. "But I spoke to the customer myself!"

"Yes, sir. That's to say, you spoke to another of our people, who was posing as the little girl's father."

"You're very thorough," Harrington said.

"Yes, sir. Thank you, sir. Well, as I was saying, Charlie made a point of selecting the bear with the blue ribbon and taking it off in his sack. He knew that whoever was picking up the drop would have to come and get it—or try to. You see, if we'd just allowed one of the staff to select it, that person could simply have said that it was pure coincidence—blue was such a pretty color. Difficult to prove criminal knowledge. You understand?"

Nobody said anything. With quite a sense of dramatic effect Armitage reached down into Santa's sack and pulled out a Teddy bear. It had a blue ribbon round its neck.

In a voice tense with strain Mr. Andrews said, "So the murderer didn't get away with the heroin. I thought you said—"

Superintendent Armitage produced a knife from his pocket. "We'll see," he said. "With your permission, I'm going to open this bear."

"Of course."

The knife ripped through the nobbly brown fabric, and a lot of stuffing fell out. Nothing else. Armitage made a good job of it. By the time he had finished, the bear was in shreds: and nothing had emerged from its interior except kapok.

Armitage surveyed the wreckage with a sort of bleak satisfaction. Suddenly brisk, he said, "Now. Which staff members took bears from the stockroom this morning?"

"I did," I said at once.

"Anybody else?"

There was a silence. I said, "I believe you took two, didn't you, Mr. Harrington?"

"I . . . em . . . yes, now that you mention it."

"Miss MacArthur took one," I said. "It was she who unpacked the carton. She said that Dis—Miss Aster—was going to take one."

"I see." Armitage was making notes. "I presume you each signed for your purchases, and that the bears are now with your things in the staff cloakroom." Without waiting for an answer he turned to me. "How many of these people saw Burrows select the bear with the blue ribbon?"

"All of us," I said. "Isn't that so, Mr. Harrington?"

Harrington just nodded. He looked sick.

"Well, then," said Armitage, "I shall have to inspect all the bears that you people removed from the stockroom."

There was an element of black humor in the parade of the Teddies, with their inane grins and knowing, beady eyes: but as one after the other was dis-membered, nothing more sensational was revealed than a growing pile of kapok. The next step was to check the stockbook numbers—and sure enough, one bear was missing.

It was actually Armitage's Sergeant who found it. It had been ripped open and shoved behind a pile of boxes in the stockroom in a hasty attempt at con-cealment. There was no ribbon round its neck, and it was constructed very dif-ferently from the others. The kapok merely served as a thin layer of stuffing between the fabric skin and a spherical womb of pink plastic in the toy's cen-ter. This plastic had been cut open and was empty. It was abundantly clear what it must have contained.

"Well," said the Superintendent, "it's obvious what happened. The mur-derer stabbed Burrows, slipped into the booth, and substituted an innocent Teddy bear for the loaded one, at the same time changing the neck ribbon, But he—or she—didn't dare try walking out of the store with the bear, not after a murder. So, before Charlie's body was found, the murderer dismembered the bear, took out the heroin, and hid it." He sighed again. "I'm afraid this means a body search. I'll call the Yard for a police matron for the ladies."

It was all highly undignified and tedious, and poor old Disaster nearly had a seizure, despite the fact that the police matron seemed a thoroughly nice and kind woman. When it was all over, however, and our persons and clothing had been practically turned inside out, still nothing had been found. The four of us were required to wait in the staff restroom while exhaustive searches were made for both the heroin and the weapon.

Disaster was in tears, Miss MacArthur was loudly indignant and threatened to sue the police for false arrest, and Mr. Harrington developed what he called a nervous stomach, on account, he said, of the way the toy department was being left understaffed and unsupervised on one of the busiest days of the year.

At long last Superintendent Armitage came in. He said, "Nothing. Abso-bloody-lutely nothing. Well, I can't keep you people here indefinitely. I suggest you all go out and get yourselves some lunch." He sounded very tired and cross and almost human.

With considerable relief we prepared to leave the staffroom. Only Mr. Harrington announced that he felt too ill to eat anything, and that he would remain in the department. The Misses MacArthur and Aster left together. I put on my coat and took the escalator down to the ground floor, among the bur-dened, chattering crowd.

I was out in the brisk air of the street when I heard Armitage's voice behind me.

"Just one moment, if you please, Mr. Borrowdale."

I turned. "Yes, Superintendent. Can I help you?"

"You're up at the university, aren't you, sir? Just taken a temporary job at Barnum's for the vacation?"

"That's right."

"Do quite a bit of fencing, don't you?"

He had my cane out of my hand before I knew what was happening. The sergeant, an extraordinarily tough and unattractive character, showed surprising dexterity and speed in getting an arm grip on me. Armitage had unscrewed the top of the cane, and was whistling in a quiet, appreciative manner. "Very nice. Very nice little sword stick. Something like a stilletto. I don't suppose Charlie felt a thing."

"Now, look here," I said. "You can't make insinuations like that. Just because I'm known as a bit of dandy, and carry a sword stick, that's no reason—"

"A dandy, eh?" said Armitage thoughtfully. He looked me up and down in a curious manner, as if he thought something was missing.

It was at that moment that Miss MacArthur suddenly appeared round the corner of the building.

"Oh, Mr. Borrowdale, look what I found! Lying down in the mews by the goods entrance! It must have fallen out of the staffroom window! Lucky I've got sharp eyes—it was behind a rubbish bin, I might easily have missed it!" And she handed me my bowler hat.

That is to say, she would have done if Armitage hadn't intercepted it. It didn't take him more than five seconds to find the packages of white powder hidden between the hard shell of the hat and the oiled-silk lining.

Armitage said, "So you were going to peddle this stuff to young men and women at the university, were you? Charming, I must say. Now you can come back to the Yard and tell us all about your employers—if you want a chance at saving your own neck, that is."

Miss MacArthur was goggling at me. "Oh, Mr. Borrowdale!" she squeaked. "Have I gone and done something wrong?"

I never did like Miss MacArthur.